UNNATURAL
CAUSES

UNNATURAL CAUSES

Based on the
Central television series

JAVELIN BOOKS

Poole · New York · Sydney

First published in the UK 1986 by Javelin Books,
Link House, West Street, Poole, Dorset, BH15 1LL

This publication is based on the television series UNNATURAL CAUSES
produced by Central Independent Television plc

HOME COOKING: This novelisation © Central Independent Television plc 1986,
based on television script © Paula Milne 1986
LOST PROPERTY: This novelisation © Central Independent Television plc 1986,
based on television script © Peter J. Hammond 1986
LADIES' NIGHT: This novelisation © Kerr-Neale Productions Ltd 1986,
based on television script © Kerr-Neale Productions Ltd 1986
WINDOW, SIR?: This novelisation © Caroline Hunt 1986,
based on television script © Ron Hutchinson 1986
HIDDEN TALENTS: This novelisation © Lynda La Plante 1986,
based on television script © Lynda La Plante 1986
EVENSONG: This novelisation © Beryl Bainbridge 1986,
based on television script © Beryl Bainbridge 1986
PARTNERS: This novelisation © Nicholas Palmer 1986,
based on television script © Nicholas Palmer 1986

Central logo copyright © Central Independent Television plc 1982

Distributed in Australia by Capricorn Link (Australia) Pty Ltd,
PO Box 665, Lane Cove, NSW 2066

British Library Cataloguing in Publication Data

Unnatural Causes.
  1. Short stories, English   2. English
  fiction — 20th century
  823′. 01′08 [FS]   PR1309. S5

ISBN 0 7137 1921 4

Typeset by Nene Phototypesetters Ltd, Northampton
Printed in Great Britain by
Cox & Wyman Ltd, London and Reading

CONTENTS

INTRODUCTION

Beryl Bainbridge

My mother once told me that when she was a young girl in Liverpool she had gone to tea at the house of a Mr Wallace; that chess player and agent for the Prudential Assurance company who was later to be brought to trial for the murder of his wife and acquitted for lack of evidence. My mother described that room in which she had sat, the colour of the rug at the hearth, the shape of the cheap clock on the mantelpiece.

At the trial much was made of a mysterious phone call received by Wallace, asking him to go to a house in Menlove Gardens East. There is no such address, though there is a Menlove Gardens and a Menlove Avenue, in which street I was born.

Wallace and his wife were musical, she playing the piano and he the violin, and when no bloodstains were found on his clothing – save for a mackintosh hanging up in the hall – the ingenious theory was put forward that Mr Wallace, stark naked under his raincoat, had exchanged one instrument for another less musical and battered his wife to death. It is a powerful image and yet, it is my mother's description of the dutch clock on the mantelshelf and the rag rug before the fender that remains fixed in my mind.

To this day I consider the most important ingredient of a murder story, far beyond means or motives, to be a sense of place; that geographical location or domestic setting which has the power to haunt the imagination long after the details of the ghastly deed itself have been forgotten.

It is not the abnormality of murder that is compelling, but the normality of the surroundings in which most of it is perpetrated. For me, fascination lies in that common bond of houses and possessions which connect us to those who do murder, rather than in the subtle insanity that separates us.

George Joseph Smith drowned his victims in the bath tubs of small lodging houses up and down the country. Sometimes there was a bathroom and sometimes the tub was carried through into the bedroom; below in the parlours those tell-tale stains of water appeared upon the ceilings.

In the Villa Madeira in Bournemouth, to the beat of a dance band record on the wind-up gramophone, Mrs Rattenbury was foxtrotting by herself between the occasional tables in her lounge when the police arrived to find her husband dying from blows to the head.

Patrick Mahon rented the 'Officer's House', a somewhat grandiose name for the seaside bungalow in Sussex where he killed his young lady during a thunderstorm. He tried to dispose of her head by burning it on the fire. Above him, on the wall beside the hearth, hung a china plate painted with columbine.

Nobody knows for sure in what room in the house in Hilldrop Crescent Dr Crippen murdered his flamboyant wife, but he put poison in her coffee and it was probably in her bed that she died. A photograph on the dressing table showed her done up to the nines, rouge on her cheeks and feathers in her hair.

These, of course, were real murders done by real people, while the stories in this collection concern fictional acts of savagery, either premeditated or committed accidentally, on purpose. Here, the causes of death are as various as the backgrounds of the characters; the victims die from induced heart attacks, electrocution, the wielding of cricket bats, of bill-hooks and candlesticks, the effects of steam heat.

Consider the dilemma of a woman who runs a small seedy hotel and whose only love is cooking; she has both an admirer and a philandering husband whom she detests. Worse, she suspects him of being wanted as a rapist and murderer. The lock of the new Sauna Room is 'faulty', upstairs in a suitcase lies a red plaid scarf. . . .

Or what of the situation of the yeast manufacturer, his

7

wife and his secretary who are entangled in a tired *ménage à trois*? It is customary for the husband and his mistress every lunchtime to cross the yard from office to house, where the wife has a meal waiting for them on the table. Under the cushion on her chair lies a murderous weapon, but before it can be used the would-be murderer is struck down by a far more deadly force. . . .

And what of Colonel Waley, the Hon. Secretary of the Hunters Club, who has been persuaded, by penury and against his better judgment, to allow women on the club premises every Monday night? When the dreadful Mrs Tripp arrives, pronouncing the foot uneatable, the traditions of the club laughable and the trophies on the hallowed walls moth-eaten, if not disgusting, it is unthinkable that a woman should be allowed to criticise let alone jeopardise the future of the Colonel's beloved establishment. Faced by a modern man-eater, the members close ranks. Taking the ancient guns down from the racks they gather for the kill. . . .

A chilling selection of stories, concerning brutal acts compounded by being conducted in the ordinary and familiar surroundings of sitting room and school-house and vicarage garden.

But then, as Dorothy Parker said, *Why shouldn't readers be harrowed? Surely there is enough happiness in life without having to go to books for it.*

HOME COOKING

The blade of the axe rose and fell relentlessly, slicing through flesh, sinew and muscle. The liquid trickle of blood permeated the meat, running over the scrubbed pine surface and collecting in shallow, widening pools.

The kitchen was large, rather shabby and Victorian in character with a high ceiling and massive banks of shelf space. Scattered on these shelves and around the many surfaces were a number of gadgets – food processor, dish-washer, sandwich toaster and a barbecue roasting spit. Towards the back of the kitchen, resting in a recess, stood an Aga cooker and a large double gas stove. Saucepans were frothing and simmering as the axe continued to fall, slicing into the bloodied meat again and again. A blanket of steam hung hazily over the room like a limp mist. Through it the sharp knives on the rack gleamed and a small television set, on a high shelf in the corner of the kitchen, constantly flickered. A low-pitched conversational sound came from the newscaster, but the news was drowned out as the axe thudded down and down again.

Wielding her meat cleaver, Judith stood at the solid wooden table, which occupied the centre of the room. It was covered with neatly-arranged bowls and plates of food. Around it were cash-and-carry sized bags of flour, sugar and coffee, vegetables in assorted heaps, raw meat and fish – all purposefully put in order.

Middle-aged, not exactly pretty but distinctive, Judith was wholly absorbed in her gory task. She was preparing food on a large scale, with the professionalism born of many years standing at her scrubbed wooden table. Yet although she was obviously enjoying every moment of it, there was

9

something wrung-out and exhausted about her attitude, as if she had learnt that her best form of defence was not attack, but acquiescence.

Judith had her back to the television and, as it babbled on, she was quite unaware of it; it had become a familiar background noise now.

A little girl sat near her on a high stool, legs swinging, watching the murmuring screen. She was six years old and had a strange, almost vacant look about her. Quite suddenly, as Judith's cleaver finished its grisly job, the drowned words from the television began to seep into the misty kitchen.

'. . . the fourth victim, a local housewife, was found dazed and bloodied, wandering in an alley . . .' announced the male newscaster, and the smiling photograph of a woman's face replaced his own. The little girl stared silently at the image on the screen without the slightest reaction or expression passing her impassive features. Another woman's face flashed up, looking strangely puzzled.

'. . . victim number five, a local infant school teacher, was attacked and raped while returning home from a party. . . .' The voice of the newscaster continued as Judith raised her cleaver once again and began swiftly cutting the meat into even smaller portions.

. The child kept her eyes unflinchingly on the screen as the sequence of photographs faded away to a news film. Then another woman's face appeared, animate, pitifully bruised and swollen. She was lying in a hospital bed.

'. . . then, last night, victim number six. Karen Wilkes, a hairdresser, was attacked as she walked home from the bus station. . . .' The newscaster read from his script, his voice punctuated by the thud of Judith's cleaver.

A girl in her late twenties and dressed as a chamber maid walked into the kitchen. She looked unkempt: her tights were laddered, her hair was coming adrift from a hair comb and there was a kind of indolent sexuality about her as she carried in some glasses on a tray. She paused to snatch a glance at the television as an identikit picture of a man's face was shown. The fixed and dead lines of the drawing gave him a strange, anonymous intensity.

The newscaster continued reading: '. . . are looking for a thick-set man in his mid to late forties. Brown hair, receding. Last seen wearing a beige, belted mackintosh. . . .'

'Looks a bit like Mr Vic,' said the maid Nancy. Her voice was light, and uninterested.

The cleaver hovered as Judith cast a quick glance at the screen for the first time. Her glance settled on the child. 'Should she be watching that?'

Nancy shrugged indifferently. 'Life, isn't it? Can't protect 'em from it.' She put the tray down and disappeared as the newscaster's voice spoke over the identikit picture.

'. . . a police statement said it was not only the rapes which were of concern, but the inhuman and sadistic nature of the attacks which accompanied them. . . .'

The identikit face evaporated as Judith reached up and abruptly changed channels.

'The King was in his Counting house, Counting out his money . . .' announced the *Play School* host, beaming.

In the lounge next door Vic, a middle-aged, heavily built man, was going through the till. There was something slightly coarse about him as if the passing years had somehow brutalised him.

The till was positioned behind a small, semi-circular optics bar. On the wall next to it hung a darts board, and grouped in the centre of the room, as if stranded there, were a few shabby armchairs. In one corner was a very large colour television and underneath it a dusty, slightly stained video recorder. A dank atmosphere of stale nicotine hung over the room; almost as a pall, certainly as a sour after-taste.

The tattiness was heightened by a bead curtain through which several dining tables could be seen set for supper, sauce bottles in predominance.

Vic slowly pocketed some of the money from the cash register, whilst from the kitchen came the muffled strains of the television:

11

'. . . Wasn't that a dainty dish to set before a king?' chanted the *Play School* presenter.

Vic unscrewed one of the optic bottles and went out. Beyond him a small neon sign flashed in the window. It read 'Vacancies'.

'How's progress, lads?' asked Vic, now standing over some workmen in the cellar, surrounded by a half-made sauna.

'Oh, slow and steady, Mr Hatton,' replied one of them cautiously.

'Not too slow, eh? Don't want to get behind schedule, do we?' His eyes rested on a tray laden with cups of tea. 'Send someone up with those cups,' he added briskly.

As Vic clambered back up the cellar steps Jim touched a forelock in mock-subservience and a muffled gust of laughter escaped from his workmates.

In the kitchen, Judith was putting the now miniature portions of meat into a tray as Vic ambled in, the optic bottle in one hand.

'Did you take that tea down to the builders?'

'Yes.'

'Don't. They spend half the time sitting around on their backsides as it is.'

They had a strange, almost formal way of addressing each other which barely masked an unspoken hostility.

He paused by the meat. 'Tonight's?'

She nodded dumbly and Vic moved towards a small blackboard, propped up on a work surface; a menu was chalked on it.

'Beef in – what's this?'

'Aspic.'

'What?'

'Jelly, made from meat juices.' Her voice was flat.

Vic said nothing, removing a lid from a silver platter which contained the beef in aspic. It was delicately and ornately arranged, with sprigs of parsley and anchovies. He groaned.

12

'It's like steak tartar. You eat it raw,' said Judith in the same flat voice.

'Looks like congealed sheeps' doings,' he commented, knowing that it would provoke her – and enjoying the provocation.

But Judith was looking at the little girl still watching television.

'Best-quality beef?' continued Vic unpleasantly.

'Yes.'

'God.' He went to the sink to top up the alcohol in the optic bottle with water. 'What they want is good, whole-some home cooking. Not that fancy *cordon bleu* muck.' His voice was slow, the insult studied.

'The point of a mixed menu is to cater for mixed palates, isn't it?' She spoke without looking at him, her body rigid and her voice, for once, defensive.

'Next time, stick a bit of scrag end in the tenderiser. They'll never know the difference. Or better still, strain that bloody jelly off and make it into a stew.' Vic went out.

For a moment Judith stood quite motionless at the table. Then, abruptly, she walked over to the plate of beef, picked it up, carried it to the sink and switched on the waste disposal. Sinking her hands deep into the jelly she shovelled it violently down the shute, her movements quick and angry but her face, like the child's, registering no emotion whatever. . . .

After a few seconds, Judith switched off the noisily gobbling waste unit and stood motionless again, her anger spent.

Another sound drifted into the kitchen – a girlish giggle. Judith turned to catch a glimpse of Nancy, playfully slapping at Vic's hand in the hall beyond the kitchen. Judith's face was still expressionless as she stood there by the waste unit, her hands moist with the dripping jelly.

Vic had taken himself off to the Reception desk of their small hotel. Once behind it, his personality underwent a drastic, although superficial change: standing the other side was a woman in her early thirties. She was immaculately

13

and expensively dressed, strikingly attractive, and confident in the knowledge of her attractiveness. She had an air of intelligence and Vic felt a little disconcerted by her presence as he signed her in.

As she waited, Helen studied the signs about the Reception desk: 'Sauna available on request.' 'Home cooking is our speciality.' On the right-hand side was a provocative girlie calendar, advertising a local cash & carry. Helen frowned.

Vic handed the pen to her deferentially.

'Thank you,' said Helen, leaning over to write. She was only inches from Vic's face and he watched her, curiously.

'Would that be *Miss* Cassady, or . . . ?'

'Ms.'

It was the answer Vic had expected. He continued to watch her as she wrote. 'How many nights, Ms Cassady?' He gave the very slightest emphasis to the 'Ms'.

'Until Thursday. . . . Everywhere I tried was full,' she said pointedly. 'I'm on one of these tedious sales conferences. It shouldn't go on longer than two days.' She passed the pen back to him and their fingers met.

Vic hung on just a shade too long. 'You'll have something in common with our other guests then.'

Helen gave him a look of purely polite interest.

'Most of them are in the selling line, one way or another,' he added by way of explanation.

'What time is dinner?' asked Helen, ignoring his comment.

'Six-thirty to eight,' said Vic, a little sharply.

'I might have a sauna, while I'm waiting.'

'No can do.'

She glanced at him rather irritably.

'We've got a bit ahead of ourselves. Builders' promises, promises.'

Helen made no response. Instead she held out her car keys. 'My bags are in the car. Perhaps someone could fetch them in for me?'

'My pleasure.' He took the car keys and moved his other hand up to Helen's. Slowly and deliberately he put her room key into her hands, then folded her fingers over the key with his eyes on her face.

But Helen simply regarded him with a kind of detached amusement.

'Room number eight. Our best,' said Vic, conscious that his well-practised technique was not working.

With great efficiency, Helen disengaged her hand and moved towards the stairs. Her legs were slender, her movements supple and Vic's eyes rested upon her a little too long as she mounted the stairs.

On the other side of the beaded curtains, in the dining room, Judith was fiddling with the cutlery on a table. She was watching him.

Half-an-hour later supper was in progress and several men in suits – obviously reps – were eating at their separate tables. Judith, threading her way between them, was serving. One of her regular hotel guests watched her over his paper. Gordon was like Vic, well-built, but more gauche, more hesitant, more sensitive. His suit was shiny with use and his cuffs were frayed. But there was a neatness about him that was attractive.

'Anything to follow?' asked Judith, pausing by Helen's table.

'The fresh fruit salad? No cream. And coffee, black.'

'Coffee will be served in the lounge,' Judith said flatly, picking her way out of the room with her tray.

Gordon picked up his paper. On the back, Helen read, 'Rapist claims victim number six'.

Nancy appeared. 'The heater in number eleven is on the blink again. I've told Mr Vic,' she said, carelessly chucking an anorak at the child who was still seated on the stool, numbly watching yet more news footage about the rape. The girl with the swollen face was being interviewed from her hospital bed. Nancy tugged on her coat as Judith, outwardly oblivious, worked on the fruit salads. 'I'll have it seen to,' Judith said.

There was the slightest hesitation before Nancy spoke again. 'He . . . offered us a lift home. Me and the kid.'

'. . . Fine.'

'Say night-night, Laura.'

'Night-night,' said Laura.

Nancy took the child by the hand and hesitated again. 'Oh and er . . . ta ever-so for letting me bring her in again, Mrs Hatton.'

'Can't her father help you out, Nancy?'

'If we knew where he was, he might. . . .' She had her coat buttoned by now. 'Cheery-bye then.'

'Goodnight,' said Judith, still busy with the food.

Vic appeared in the hall with Nancy and her little girl. He swept the child into his arms, while Nancy indulgently watched him. Then putting Laura down, he shrugged himself into a belted raincoat, threw a plaid scarf round his neck, and said in mock complaint to the child, 'How's my best girl then? Eh? Not even a kiss for your old Vic. Dearie me. . . .'

Judith stood in the kitchen watching him. A trace of emotion flickered in her face now but it would have been hard to define. She turned back to the television. Once again the identikit picture filled the screen and the newscaster was saying urgently '. . . a heavy-set man in his mid-forties. Brown hair receding. Last seen wearing a scarf, belted raincoat, grey trousers. . . .'

On a sudden impulse, Judith spun around to look again at the hall. But it was empty.

It was gone nine, supper was finished and Judith was hauling a carcass from the deep freeze in the cellar. She struggled, prising a frozen slab from a large plastic bag. Eventually it emerged, forced out with the aid of a large kitchen knife. As she began to re-seal the bag, she became aware of sounds behind her and she turned towards the half-finished sauna which now possessed a door. Inside, she could see a beam of light. Standing motionless, the knife in her hand, Judith listened intently, trying to identify the sound she thought she heard. Yes – it was there – someone breathing.

Slowly, Judith moved towards the sauna and as she did

so, the breathing seemed to increase in intensity. Using the blade of her knife, she cautiously prised open the sauna door. Crouched in one corner was the figure of a man. Judith felt a scream rising in her throat. Then, almost instantly, she recognised the figure. It was one of the workman who, with a wrench in his hand and a small paraffin lamp beside him, was struggling to fix a pipe. For an instant he did not notice her – he only saw the knife, gleaming viciously in the wan light of the paraffin lamp. Then, his eyes travelled up to her face and they stared at each other without speaking.

'I . . . thought you'd all gone,' said Judith finally, feeling rather foolish.

'Trying to get some of these pipes sorted . . . gotta get the floor down tomorrow.'

Judith stood there without saying a word, frozen between her original fear and the embarrassment creeping over her. Then with a muttered apology she turned away and made her way out of the sauna and up the cellar steps. Jim watched her go curiously.

In the lounge the male guests were grouped apathetically around the optic bar while a couple of them lobbed darts at the battered board. The television droned on as always, unwatched and unnoticed.

Gordon, seated in one of the shabby armchairs, was watching Judith through the gently swaying bead curtains as she set the tables for breakfast. His newspaper lay unheeded in his lap.

The men lounging around the bar laughed throatily at the latest dirty joke. They exuded a coarse camaraderie. Clearing his throat impatiently Gordon put down his paper. He had seen Judith leave the dining room with a tray of dirty supper plates and he knew that an opportunity might, at last, have come.

Rising to his feet, he walked into the dining room, picked up a couple of plates and followed Judith through to the kitchen. There he found her silently loading the dishwasher and a sudden shyness overcame him. For a moment, he lost his nerve and almost walked out. Then he said abruptly, 'How do you do it?'

She glanced up at him, startled by his intrusion.

'Just on your own, like this,' Gordon nervously continued.

'Practice,' replied Judith.

He stood in front of her, plates in hands, looking rather helpless. 'Where do you want these?' he asked.

She put out her hands to receive them, as if in some religious rite, and Gordon began to lose his confidence again. 'Need a dryer-upper?' he offered. 'I promise I won't break anything.'

'It's virtually done,' she said, adding as an afterthought, 'Thank you. I'll bring the coffee through.'

'No hurry.'

The frozen carcass of meat that she had brought up from the cellar stood on the table between them.

'It's thawing. . . . You'll need something, for the blood,' he suggested hesitantly.

Judith reached for a metal tray and Gordon seized the opportunity to help her. His hands briefly touched hers as they manhandled the tray together. She placed the meat on it and put a gauze fly-cover over it, whilst he perched heavily on the table edge, watching her as she moved around the kitchen. She seemed almost tirelessly efficient.

'Does it bother you, my being here?' he asked tentatively.

'Why should it?' she asked.

'My "ex" used to hate it. Being watched in the kitchen.'

Judith made no reply.

'One can't always assume these things. That one's welcome, I mean.' His voice had a slight edge to it.

Still Judith said nothing and, although Gordon tried hard, he found it impossible to decipher her expression.

'I'll say when you're not,' she replied at length and Gordon relaxed slightly.

'Where's Vic?'

After a short pause, she replied, 'On an errand.' She was

kneading some floury dough now and Gordon found the process quite soothing.

'I see he's getting into more of the old D-I-Y.'

She looked up at him questioningly.

'The sauna,' he explained.

'Except he's not doing it himself, is he?'

'Home improvement then.' He smiled at her.

'It's not for a home, is it? He intends to charge for it. He's even putting a lock on the outside to make sure of it.' Her voice had become oddly detached.

'He does his best you know, Judith.'

But she didn't reply, and Gordon noticed that there was a sudden rigidity in her expression and bearing. She continued slapping and moulding the dough. 'Is *that* why he goes out every night?' She asked drily.

'It didn't used to be that way, did it?' She was silent and he looked at her curiously. 'Do you ever regret it? Not having children, I mean.'

'I regret giving in over it.' Her voice was bitter and Gordon hesitated. Then abruptly he changed the subject.

'You really love it, don't you? Cooking.' He paused. 'It's a pleasure watching you.'

'We all like doing things we're good at.'

'You're certainly that.' Once again Gordon decided to change the subject, conscious that he might be sounding too enthusiastic. 'You know what you need, Judith? A microwave oven. Seriously now, it would halve your workload. Well, the catering side, anyway.'

'It might also halve our bank balance,' she replied ruefully. But Gordon was determined to be firm.

'Not if I arrange a decent discount . . . say 25 per cent? Why not? I'd get the benefit, wouldn't I? Being one of your regulars.'

She said nothing and he couldn't tell how interested she was. 'I'd even throw in some interest-free credit. How's that?'

'What is this? An after-hours sales pitch?' she asked harshly.

'Just a friend trying to do a good turn.'

19

She looked up at him, rather disconcerted by his sincerity.

Digging into a pocket, Gordon produced a brochure. 'Choose the model you fancy. You can have it for a week's free trial. Fair?'

She took the brochure without speaking.

'Just look at some of those cooking times . . .' he insisted. 'Think of the time it'll buy you. No strings, no catch, I promise.'

Judith stood, staring down at the brochure and he moved closer to her.

'Why not break the habit of a lifetime and trust someone, Judith?' The words came out in a rush and he saw a spasm of emotion cross her face.

'Who says I don't trust anyone?'

'Instinct.' He paused. 'It goes with the job.'

Judith kept looking at the brochure, as if she was wrestling with a confusion of emotions. 'All right,' she said with sudden decision. 'Thank you.'

'Good girl.' He put out his hand but she did not respond. 'An old habit of mine,' he said. 'To shake on a deal.'

Wiping the flour slowly from her hand she put it flatly into his. Despite herself, she let it rest there for a few moments.

'You ought to wear gloves to protect them,' said Gordon softly.

'I used to – when it mattered,' she replied.

'Judith.' Gordon said her name gently, with compassion, and she glanced up at him, a hesitant smile on her face.

The spell was broken as the front door slammed, and Judith quickly withdrew her hand from Gordon's.

Vic stood in the hall, pulling off his raincoat and looking blearily into the kitchen.

'Hey up, Gordon,' he said. 'You're wasting drinking time, lad.' He shambled away towards the lounge and bar. His territory.

Gordon followed him sheepishly, leaving Judith staring down at the brochure. Opening a drawer in the table she put it inside, then suddenly withdrew it again to give the title a closer scrutiny. It read: CREATIVE COOKING – THE HIGH-TECH WAY.

The lounge was clouded by a haze of cigar smoke and the male guests were lounging around the optics bar. Vic was in attendance behind it.

Helen was seated apart, in an armchair with her paperwork. Raucous laughter filled the room. Amidst the noise, one of the men slapped the bar for attention.

'Okay. All right. Try this one for size. Royalty's visiting this maternity home, see?'

'Ugh-ahem. Ladies present remember, Dennis,' Vic protested ironically, his eyes resting on Helen as he spoke.

'Aw, you could tell this one to your grandmother,' replied Dennis unrepentantly. 'Anyway, this girl's nursing a baby, see. Only the girl's got black hair and the baby's got this shock of red hair, right?'

Vic was still watching Helen as Dennis continued. 'So, Royalty says, "Does he take after his father?" And she says, "Dunno Ma'am, he never took his hat off." '

A chorus of groans greeted the punch-line – a sound which seemed to jar with Helen. She stacked her papers into a neat pile, put them away, rose and walked out.

Vic continued to watch her, openly appreciative, and Dennis leaned towards him. 'You'd have to thaw her out first.'

Vic smiled. His expression held a kind of raw anticipation.

'An early morning call, is that possible?' Helen paused by the kitchen door and Judith, leaning over her thawing carcass, looked up.

'Of course. What time?'

'Sevenish?'

'With tea?'

'Please.' Helen paused. 'It was a nice meal.'

'Thank you.'

'I can't even poach an egg myself. It makes one feel so helpless.'

21

'You work, don't you?'

'So do you,' Helen protested amiably.

Assuming that this was the end of the conversation, she turned to go but Judith interposed brutally. 'We didn't have this in mind when we started.'

Helen turned round again and saw that Judith was looking defensive. She smiled, and Judith continued, 'It was going to be a family guest house.'

'The age of Trusthouse Forte has put paid to that,' said Helen evenly and Judith gave her a glance, wondering if Helen was laughing at her.

'Still, you seem busy enough,' Helen added.

'Oh, yes. I'm kept busy.' There was the same defensiveness in her voice and she smiled with restrained politeness.

Quickly, Helen escaped up the stairs.

In the lounge, the atmosphere was deteriorating as the guests, half or even completely drunk, deposited themselves in armchairs whilst Vic crouched down by the video recorder. Only Gordon stayed seated at the bar.

When Judith slipped in to collect the coffee cups she was almost totally ignored, for the men's attention was absorbed by the television as Vic fast-forwarded a cassette. The speeding images seemed to consist mainly of a girl in slip and suspender belt revealing as much as possible to the viewer. Dennis shouted out an instruction to Vic to stop the tape. As Vic paused on a particularly absorbing moment, Judith went out with the tray. Gordon watched as she went.

While she was loading the cups into the dishwasher, Judith noticed a newspaper lying on one of the nearby surfaces. Slowly she stepped across to pick it up and saw the headline: RAPIST KILLS VICTIM NUMBER SIX.

A gale of drunken laughter came from the other room as she stood, motionless, looking down at the paper. Then, with some precision, she opened the table drawer and put the newspaper inside where it lay next to the microwave brochure with its own screaming headline: CREATIVE COOKING – THE HIGH-TECH WAY.

Switching out the kitchen light, she noticed that Vic's raincoat had fallen on to the floor underneath the coat rack. Wearily, she picked it up as another gale of dirty laughter reached her from the next room.

She stood there, holding it in her hand and the laughter persisted.

Judith could still hear that laughter as she lay in her single bed. Beside her was Vic's bed – empty as usual. Desperately, she switched on the radio to hear a woman's voice on a phone-in saying '. . . no point in free bus passes, unless those who need them get them, is there?'

'Thank you, Maureen,' said the DJ. 'On now to Jessica. Yes, Jessica?'

'It's about this . . . man. This rapist,' began Jessica.

'Uh-huh.' The DJ's voice was dull.

'I mean we're not just talking about rape here, are we?' The line distorted and her voice was drowned in a blur of static. Judith fiddled with the tuner and regained clarity.

'. . . or a woman's vigilante group . . . but someone, somewhere in this town is shielding this . . . animal, and that someone is probably a woman. . . .' Jessica's voice rose vehemently and Judith switched off the radio abruptly. Yet another gust of laughter assaulted her ears from downstairs.

An hour later, Judith lay in the darkness, fully awake. She was waiting for him, knowing he would come sooner or later, rigid with apprehension. Then she heard his footsteps coming nearer and the door opening. She heard shoes being removed, the zip of a fly, the rustle of clothes dropping, the sound of Vic's breath, wheezing, and his approaching footsteps. Judith closed her eyes.

'Judith? Love? You asleep?' Vic's voice was a surprisingly childlike whisper.

Judith lay frozen as he clambered into her bed, beside her.

'Judith?' He was pleading now but she didn't respond, and eventually Vic gave up. For a moment he lay heavily beside her and her fear mounted. Then he got out and into his own bed, where he banged and pounded at the pillow in sudden, frustrated violence.

Judith's eyes sprang open and her whole body began to shake.

The next day, Nancy's little girl Laura was back in the kitchen. As usual, she was perched on her stool, staring numbly at the bland screen of the television. A chef, cheerfully industrious, was performing on a breakfast show. His voice, determinedly breezy, chattered, 'And if, as they say, the way to a man's heart is really through his stomach, this is definitely one for those ladies with men on their minds. . . .'

In the dining room, Judith was serving breakfast and the men, sitting once again at their separate tables, were more subdued, far less aggressive than the previous night. Gordon was there, his eyes, as always, on Judith.

After a few minutes, Vic arrived to enforce his 'mine host' act as he paused by each table to give a passing nod and a greeting. He paused a little longer by Helen's table, and Judith, watching him, felt her body tense.

'Ms Cassady,' Vic murmured.

'Mr Hatton,' she returned formally.

'Sleep well?'

'I always do.'

'I can believe it.' He stooped to retrieve her napkin which had fallen to the floor and replaced it on the table beside her – every inch a gentleman. Then he ambled on to greet another guest. Judith felt the tension leave her.

A little later, Nancy was taking her ease on a guest's unmade bed, reading a magazine and smoking a cigarette. She should have been cleaning the room, but she reckoned that could wait: at least until she had finished the magazine. But at a sound she hastily stubbed out her cigarette, leapt off the bed and flung open the window. She had heard Judith's transistor radio, which Judith always carried on the bottom shelf of her trolley whenever she took clean linen to each room. As she entered the one which Nancy had been 'working' in, Judith caught a whiff of tobacco smoke and knew what her employee had been up to; but, as usual, Judith said nothing.

Her glance strayed to the open window as they both started to make the bed. The silence between them was broken only by the muffled sound of the radio on the trolley in the corridor. 'Finally,' said the DJ, 'the Westcombe Rapist. . . .' Both women strained to listen as they worked. '. . . have just confirmed a report that they now have the scarf that the rapist used to tie up his victims. The scarf is plaid, with red, white and black checks. If anyone knows someone who wears a scarf like that, who fits the description of the man the police are looking for, and has observed that the scarf is missing, will they please contact their nearest police station. All information will be dealt with confidentially. . . .'

'Makes you afraid to go out, doesn't it?' asked Nancy, but Judith stood stock-still, a pillow in her hands. She was breathing heavily.

'It does at my age, I can tell you.' Nancy didn't seem to notice Judith's silence. 'I'll tell you something else . . . I always keep Laura where I can see her an' all. . . .'

But even as Nancy spoke, Judith was leaving the room. She half ran down the corridor and hurried down the stairs to Reception. She paused, out of breath, as she caught sight of Vic at the Reception desk, reading the sports page. But she had eyes only for the clothes peg behind him. Vic's mac was there all right: where was his familiar plaid scarf? It was definitely not there. A chill stole over her as she carried on down the stairs into the kitchen.

There she found another mystery. The stool in front of the television set was empty. She panicked. Where was Laura? Then, through the window she caught sight of the child, playing in a corner of the small yard. Relief flooded over her, but the chill returned as Judith realised the implications of her relief. She tugged open the table drawer and the identikit picture stared up at her. Under it, the words sprang out: HAVE YOU SEEN HIM? The pain tore at her. Of course the picture was just like Vic.

In the cellar, Vic was talking to Jim while another workman nursed an electric drill which was noisily grinding and boring into the wall.

'Where's the thermostat?' yelled Vic.

'Bill, where's that thermo?' returned Jim, looking around him.

Bill tossed him the thermostat dial and he slipped it over a metal prong which protruded from the wall just inside the door of the sauna.

'And the heat control switch?' asked Vic demandingly.

Jim led the way through the door. 'There you go. Though I don't know why you want the two kept separate.'

Vic tapped the side of his nose smugly. 'Cost-effective. So the punters can't overstay their welcome.' He flicked the switch to the off position.

'Clever,' replied Jim.

'And I'll need a good padlock.'

'Right – I'll get hold of that for you,' said Jim privately cursing the extra work.

Vic meanwhile was looking round at the gradually emerging sauna. He had the air of a man well pleased.

It was evening. The men were again at their separate tables eating their dinner. Judith, now thoroughly alarmed after a day of brooding, though still not daring to acknowledge the full horror of her thoughts, was distributing the sweet. As she did so, she caught sight of Vic pulling on his raincoat in the hall. He paused, checked a pocket – and seemed to notice the absence of his scarf. Or did he? Was there really no hesitation at all? Was the whole thing some obsessive trick of her imagination?

A few seconds later, Nancy joined Vic, dragging Laura along by her side. Once again, as was his habit, Vic swept the child into his arms and the three of them headed for the door. After another second or so, Judith managed to collect

26

herself together, gathered up a few dirty plates and returned to the kitchen.

Judith's thoughts were in total confusion as she bent over the sink, her back to the door. She didn't see Gordon follow her in, and spun round terrified when he cried: 'Taraa . . . !'

He was carrying a large heavy box. Judith made an effort to stop herself shaking as Gordon said, 'Clear the decks then.'

Mechanically she cleared a space on the table on to which he reverently eased the box down.

'Open her up,' he said heartily and Judith started to tear open the cardboard box. He joined in and a moment later the microwave oven was revealed: narrow bands of gleaming chrome with a smoked glass door, looking both sophisticated and expensive.

'Plug?' he asked and Judith went to find one, while he busied himself with the oven. When she returned, he broke into sales talk.

'Right. Heat penetration of one and a half inches. Rotating plate for even heat distribution. You can put glass, china, anything in it. The heat will pass straight through to the food. Molecular structure you see. Microwaves vibrate the water molecules which generate the heat. The only thing you have to watch are these door seals. Make sure they don't get worn with use or you could get leakage of microwaves.'

'Is that dangerous?' asked Judith cautiously.

'Human tissue contains water, doesn't it? Just like animal meat. . . .' He paused and glanced at Judith's face. It had an odd expression that he didn't understand.

Judith was working through some paperwork at the Reception desk when Vic entered. He looked dishevelled and glassy-eyed. He saw Judith but did not greet her. As he pulled off his raincoat Judith said woodenly, 'They're waiting for you.'

Vic did not reply but she persisted.

'Did you go to the pub?'

He replied heavily, 'I did. Next question?'

But Judith could not think of anything else to say and miserably watched Vic walk away in the predictable direction of the bar. Finally she found her voice. 'Vic,' she began haltingly. She spoke quietly, wearily. He turned and waited for her. 'You don't have to take her home every night.'

'Correct, my dear,' he replied nastily. 'I don't.'

There was no more to say.

Dennis persisted, 'My point is,' he said, 'it must make it easier being a woman.'

Vic was behind the bar. Helen had made the bad mistake of sitting there and not at a table. 'Why?' she fenced.

'People are less suspicious of you, aren't they?' His speech was dulled by alcohol and, in comparison, Helen was cool and incisive.

'Are they?'

'Look – the whole business of selling rests on trust, right?' Dennis paused for effect but received only a cool smile from Helen and drunken laughter from the men. Somewhat blearily, he continued, 'A client trusts our assessment of a product. The foot-in-the-door shyster salesman is something we all have to live down. . . . Except, as a woman, you don't have that problem, do you?'

'Oh, I don't know. . . .'

'Come on. . . .'

Vic was watching Helen intently.

'Perhaps I have other problems.'

'For instance?' asked Vic, hungrily joining the conversation.

'Not being taken seriously. That my assessment of a product is inherently trivial, or simplistic.'

'Ah, but then you've got another advantage, haven't you? You can turn on the charm, flutter your eyelashes. Charm their wallets open that way.'

'That's not my style.'

'What is your style?' Vic's voice was curious.

'I treat my clients as my equal. Give them the facts, and

let them make up their own minds.' She sounded calm, confident.

'Does it get results?'

'Absolutely.'

'And you don't reckon the fact you're a woman makes any difference to your clients?'

'No.'

'You're sure about that?'

'I am.'

'Then you don't know very much about the male of the species, Ms Cassady.'

'Not all men are the same. And not all my clients are male.'

'But the majority are?'

'Possibly.'

It was as if they were playing a game of cat and mouse.

'You wear that outfit when you're at work?' persisted Vic.

'Or something like it. Why?' For the first time she sounded slightly defensive and Vic was quick to increase his attack.

'And the make-up?'

'Of course.'

'And you still think they don't notice you're a woman? You must have a very low opinion of your powers of attraction, Ms Cassady.'

Judith walked into the dining room as this exchange was going on. She began to arrange the tables for breakfast, listening as she did so.

'It's not something I think much about, one way or the other,' stated Helen firmly.

'So why dress like that?'

'It pleases me,' she replied.

'Why?'

By now even Dennis was beginning to become embarrassed, despite his drunken haze. 'Stop badgering the woman, Vic,' he said.

Helen was quick to reassure. 'I don't mind.' She turned back to Vic. 'Dressing well makes me feel good. It gives me confidence. Is that all right?'

'Because you know men are looking at you?'

'That doesn't mean they can touch.'

'Ah, so you admit the thought is in their minds.'

'Rather their problem, isn't it?'

The battle had been rejoined and all the men in the bar were fascinated as to who would win. Judith's thoughts, however, were running along other tracks.

'Suppose one of them, one of your clients say, decides to make it yours. Tries it on.' There was a slight leer in Vic's voice.

'Then I'd handle him accordingly.' A ragged cheer came from the men at the bar and she waited calmly for the noise to die down.

'The male ego, in my experience,' she said at last, 'is quite a delicate mechanism. One rejection, they don't usually try it on again.'

'Don't you like men, Ms Cassady?' The leer was still there.

'Some of them.'

'Sounds like it.'

She smiled up at him and this seemed to rankle.

'Is that funny?' There was a sharp edge to his voice.

'It's just the regularity with which that question pops up.'

'Really?'

'It's an assumption you all seem to make, if you think a woman isn't treating you with the respect you think you deserve.'

'I'm sorry to be so predictable, Ms Cassady.'

'And I'm sorry I have no stock answer for your stock question, Mr Hatton.'

Dennis exchanged an amused glance with one of his companions. It was unusual to see Vic so disadvantaged in a debate.

Helen waded back in. 'How about you? Tell me something? Do you like women?'

Momentarily, Vic looked too surprised by the question to answer.

'You see! It's that kind of question, isn't it?' She pressed home her advantage relentlessly. 'It's so general, it's meaningless.'

'My answer is the same as yours,' he said defensively. 'I like some of them.'

'Then we're quits.' She swallowed her drink and prepared to get up.

'Like to get the last word, don't you?' said Vic acidly.

'Whenever possible.'

'And when it's not?'

'I make a tactical withdrawal. Like now. I'll be checking out first thing. So I'll say goodbye now.' She put out her hand and Vic took it. He bent to kiss it, but Helen was too quick for him. As she withdrew her hand Vic was left foolishly kissing his own. Vic's companions roared with laughter as Helen smiled coolly and left the bar. Vic was not amused.

Judith was busying herself in the kitchen when the mortified Vic arrived to see the microwave oven gleaming on one of the work surfaces.

'What the devil is that?' He was angry already but the sight of the microwave made him even angrier.

'What does it look like?' asked Judith sullenly. Vic said nothing and she grudgingly elaborated. 'It's from Gordon. He's arranging a discount.'

'I'll bet.'

'He thought it would lighten my workload.'

'How considerate the man is.' After a pause he snapped, 'How much?'

'We haven't settled the terms yet. Not till I've decided if I want it.' For a moment she sounded like a hurt child.

'Good. Then you can tell him you don't. Home cooking is what we're known for, and that is what we guarantee to provide. They spot that thing, they'll think it's all . . . heated up left-overs. They can get that in a pub.'

'You should know,' Judith replied bitterly.

'You're very cute tonight,' he sneered, but she was not to be drawn into the row he wanted. 'Well, it's easily remedied,' he added.

She glanced at him.

'If you won't tell him, I will.'

'We're talking about a couple of hundred pounds, if that!' said Judith.

'Which I'm supposed to find?'

'You managed to find nearly two thousand for that wretched sauna.'

'Which will pay for itself in extra custom.' He smiled arrogantly, but Judith was not to be beaten.

'Which I'm supposed to cater for!'

'Keep your voice down.'

'Why? In case they discover "mine host" isn't the genial life and soul they think he is?'

They stared at each other in mutual hatred. Then, quite unpredictably, Vic appeared to give in. 'Look, I'm tired and I'm hungry and I'm not in the mood, okay?'

'Then I'll cook you something,' she said softly. She started banging about, collecting up food.

'Not in that thing, you won't!'

She ignored him.

'I said, I'm not eating it, Judith.'

'I'm not giving you a choice.' She placed a plate of cold food in the microwave but he sprang over to her.

'I'm not eating re-heated scraps like some . . . mangy dog!' He struggled to find the catch which released the microwave door, but Judith moved to stop him.

They began to struggle quite fiercely, both aware that there was something more than the microwave at stake now. Vic pushed Judith away but she flung herself at him again. The struggle was silent, intense, beyond words.

Then Vic hit her round the face and wrenched at her overall, tearing it open to reveal her bare shoulder. Their fight arrested, they stood panting, their eyes meeting in shock and hot aggression.

Gordon stopped short at the door, dirty glasses in hand, on his way in from the bar. He'd seen the two of them confronting each other: he took in Judith's bare shoulder, and the electric current between them. For a moment he stood on the threshold, so fascinated he was unable to move. It was animal combat, only temporarily halted.

All of a sudden Vic turned away to open the microwave door. He took out the plate of food but some of the bubbling juice trickled on to his hand and he dropped the plate, shattering it on the floor. Clasping his burnt hand – saying nothing, teeth clenched against the pain – Vic's eyes returned to Judith's face. As he dropped a cloth on the floor beside the spilt food and looked hard into Judith's eyes, Gordon stole quietly away. For a moment she did nothing. Then, slowly, she sank to her knees and began to mop up the mess, whilst Vic looked down at her in contempt as she crouched at his feet.

Half-an-hour later, Judith was sitting in front of her bedroom mirror, looking at her bruised and swollen face. Suddenly she sensed another image behind hers and for a moment could not identify it as it swept across her mind. Then she saw it again in the mirror – the battered face of the rape victim on TV.

The sound of approaching footsteps caused her to climb quickly into bed. Switching off the light, Judith lay with her eyes closed and her back to the door as Vic came in. She heard the sound of his clothes falling to the floor. Then there was a silence. Soon she sensed him moving towards her, standing beside her bed. Judith pressed her eyes tight shut, her body rigid.

Vic said nothing, he simply stood there. It seemed as if the sound of his breathing was filling the room. Slowly, he moved back to his own bed and she heard the sound of the springs and the angry beating of the pillow. Against her own will, Judith's eyes sprang open and she turned to look at him in the darkness.

A few uneventful days later, Judith was in the kitchen when she heard a scream in the hall. Rushing out into the Reception area, she found Nancy wide-eyed with shock.

'What is it? What's happened?'

Numbly, Nancy passed her the morning paper. 'That woman . . .' she said, 'that woman who stayed here.' There was a note of genuine fear in Nancy's voice as Judith glanced down at the newspaper. She saw a large picture of Helen's cool, perceptive smile. Above it the black headline blazed: RAPE VICTIM STRANGLED. Judith's hands involuntarily went to her own throat. Then she caught sight of Laura watching her from the doorway of the kitchen. Hurriedly, Judith returned the newspaper to Nancy and, with a warning glance in the direction of Laura, hurried back to the kitchen, trying to appear normal.

Laura was playing in the yard – some game that involved toy saucepans and the pretence of cooking – as Judith, her face still bruised, washed up at the sink. The voice of the television newscaster drew her attention reluctantly to the television. Behind him was a photograph of Helen. With that smile again.

'. . . last seen getting petrol, when a man approached her, apparently to ask for a lift. Two days later her unclothed body was found in a layby. . . .'

'Poor bitch,' said a voice and Judith spun round to see Jim the workman standing in the doorway, a broom in his hand. 'They say she knew him. That's why he killed her. . . . So she couldn't identify him,' he added bleakly. He glanced at her bruised face, and asked the inevitable question, 'What happened to you then?'

Judith did not reply.

'Where d'you want this?' he said, indicating the broom.

Judith mutely pointed to a corner. Then Jim caught sight of the microwave.

'Any good, are they?'

Judith said nothing. She looked as if she had fallen asleep standing up.

'Planned on getting the Mrs one, except she says they're unnatural. Cooking from the inside out. I keep telling her it's the only efficient way to do it. Still, not much I can tell you about cooking, is there?'

Judith moved to the door, still saying nothing.

'Wanta check her out now?' asked Jim a little impatiently. What the hell was the matter with the silly cow?

34

Judith turned to him questioningly.

'The sauna – do you want to check her out?' he repeated.
She nodded silently.

Jim tapped the thermostat. 'Tell your husband to keep an eye on that water temperature, first few times – build the heat up slowly. Or else the pipes will start complaining. OK?'

Judith nodded as she looked around at the interior of the sauna.

'It just needs a bit of running in.'

'Yes,' she replied and Jim started, realising that she had actually spoken.

'You don't want any teething problems.'

'No.'

'Obviously, I'll explain everything again to your husband. Give him a dummy run, sort-of-thing.'

'Thank you,' said Judith as she turned to go.

Back in the kitchen, Judith's attention was drawn again to the television set. A young woman was on the screen, standing outside some kind of public building. Other women jostled behind her, wielding a large banner which stated in crude capital letters: WOMEN AGAINST RAPE.

Fighting for the attention of the camera, the spokeswoman said in a rush, 'We just want to say this – if there's a woman out there, a sister . . . a mother . . . wife . . . who knows this rapist, for pity's sake – for all our sakes! Act now! Before he kills again!'

Judith glanced out of the window at Laura outside in the yard playing obliviously with her pots and pans.

Judith frowned. 'I don't think she's well.'

'Eh?'

Judith was standing in the corridor, holding Laura's hand and blocking Nancy's path as she came out of a guest room with a trolley of linen. Nancy quickly extinguished her fag and tried to concentrate on what Judith was saying.

'She was shivering. You'd better take her home.'

35

Nancy bent down to her daughter. 'What's up, eh? What you playing at?'

The child gazed up at Judith impassively.

'She's better off at home,' said Judith firmly. 'I can't take any chances . . . not if it's infectious.' She hurried on, sweeping up a bath towel from the trolley.

As Judith disappeared up the corridor Nancy hissed at Laura, 'What's got into you? Drawing attention to yourself again, is that it?'

The child shook her head dumbly but the suspicious mother was not appeased. 'Come on,' Nancy said in exasperation, dragging at Laura's hand. 'I'll sort *you* out.'

Vic was heavily asleep in their shuttered, shabby bedroom, as Judith entered. The smell of sweat from his unwashed body reached her as she stood looking down at him. She dropped the towel on the bed, saying urgently, 'Vic?'

He stirred slightly and she called him again, 'Vic?'

'Yeah?' He opened his eyes and gazed blearily up at her.

'You ought to try that sauna out.'

'What?'

'You ought to try that sauna out,' she repeated firmly. 'I'll make your breakfast.' She left the bedroom in a hurry. Vic lay in bed for a few moments and then drowsily dragged himself out.

Vic was really making a meal of his breakfast, as he usually did. He attacked his food with a concentration that Judith found both repelling and irritating. She sat watching him. Just watching.

When he had finished, Vic wiped his mouth and a small burp escaped. He rose slowly to his feet and Judith advanced to the table, collecting plates and carrying them to the sink. She suddenly realised that he was in the doorway, pulling on his mac.

'What about the sauna?' she asked abruptly.

'Later,' he mumbled.

'Suppose someone wants to use it?'

'Later.' His voice was predictably snappy as he escaped from sight, towards the front door.

Judith was uncertain whether she felt relieved, or alarmed. Then Vic's footsteps halted and he retraced his steps towards the cellar. As he passed the kitchen he gave Judith a furtive look and tugged off his mac. Then she heard him go down the steps into the cellar.

Several minutes later clouds of steam arose around Vic as he lay tentatively on the bench. Beads of sweat slowly began to form on his face.

In the hall, Judith bolted the front door and stood, listening intently. Apprehensively she walked slowly towards the cellar.

For a few moments, she stood outside the sauna. With a sudden movement, she reached quickly inside and then closed the door, firmly bolting it. Hesitating briefly, she checked to see that the heat control switch was in the 'on' position. It was.

Judith turned away from the sauna and hurried back to the sanctuary of her kitchen. There she began to pace up and down, a succession of terrible, confused emotions passing across her face.

After a few minutes, Judith took from her pocket the thermostat control she had removed from the inside of the sauna door.

Vic first realised that there was something wrong when the heat and steam built up to such a degree that he began to find it uncomfortable. He went to the door, reached up for the thermostat and found nothing. He searched again and again – and still found nothing.

The heat was becoming unbearable. He tried the door again but unbelievably it resisted all his attempts to open it. The clouds of steam grew dense as he began to beat at the door, hammering and shouting Judith's name over and over again.

She could hear him as she nervously paced the kitchen, watching the scalding steam rise from a pan of boiling potatoes.

Even when she put her hands over her ears, Judith could

still hear the sound of him beating on the door of the sauna. Nothing she did seemed to black out the sound. *Something must.*

Judith turned and ran into the lounge, switching the television set up full blast. But as she ran back into the kitchen she could still hear him, his voice shrill as he called her name. His hammering was thinner, feebler, but seemed louder in her ears.

Judith dashed round the kitchen, switching on the washing machine, the dishwasher, the television, the radio, even the Kenwood mixer. Anything, everything that would make a noise to drown the sound of Vic boiling alive in the sauna.

Judith looked good in black. Younger somehow and with more purpose. Gordon followed her into the dining room. He was wearing a black arm band.

Vic's funeral had been a dazed affair. The bizarre nature of his death had stunned the mourners. It was with almost incredulity that they had watched his coffin slide rapidly toward the flames.

Judith picked the local paper out of the letter box and automatically read the blazing black headlines: ACCIDENTAL DEATH VERDICT ON TRAGEDY OF LOCAL HOTELIER.

'The others'll be here in a minute.' Judith sounded as if she was dreading their appearance.

'I'll put the kettle on,' said Gordon, making for the kitchen, and leaving Judith standing looking up at the optic bar. Deliberately she went up to it and then frantically began to tear down Vic's extensive collection of girlie pin-ups. As she clawed at the glossy paper, Judith finally gave vent to deep, gasping sobs that shook the whole of her body.

Judith felt not quite calm, but calmer as she sat at the kitchen table, sipping tea. She looked and felt ill at ease, for she rarely sat down, and never with nothing to do. But, as Gordon busied himself with brewing more tea, she was forced to reflect although she already knew what decision she would come to.

'Well now, have you thought?' asked Gordon.

She nodded. 'I'm going to make some changes. Have the place redecorated, inside and out. Concentrate less on the commercial trade. Turn it more into a family guest house – afternoon teas, that kind of thing.' She spoke positively, almost bluntly and Gordon looked at her in some surprise.

'This is all very sudden,' he said.

'Not really.'

'Will you manage all that on your own?'

'Oh, yes.' She was confident and there was a strangely ironic note in her voice.

'It's quite an undertaking, Judith.'

But she did not reply and, after a while, Gordon hazarded, 'So, off with the old, on with the new, eh?'

'I told you once, I'd say when you weren't welcome, Gordon.' The statement seemed to reassure him. The front door bell rang and Gordon looked relieved. He wanted something to do.

'I'll see to them.' He went out into the hall where the first mourners were arriving.

With a sigh, Judith got up to take sandwiches out of tin foil and, as she did so, automatically switched on the television.

As the picture came into focus the newscaster said: 'Last night, the Westcombe rapist claimed his eighth victim.'

Judith reeled round incredulously staring at the television.

'Christine Banks, an unemployed secretary, was attacked and raped in a churchyard near her home. The police are looking for a thick-set man in his. . . .'

Abruptly, Judith switched off the television and her eyes moved to the local paper. Vic's photograph smiled disarmingly up at her. Judith grabbed at the paper and squeezed it close to her. She didn't understand her own feelings which were churning inside her. She screwed up the paper and threw it violently in the rubbish bin. Directly she had done this, the churning stopped and she was calm and at peace again.

Judith lost no time instituting changes at the hotel, and soon she had the workmen in, re-painting and refurbishing rooms that had not been touched for years. Only Gordon stayed on during the closure as work-mate. Now, as he entered the kitchen where she was making a cake, he said, 'No-one can accuse you of doing him in for his money. Hardly a sou there.'

Judith glanced at him. The contents of Vic's will had come as no surprise to her.

'Sorry, bad taste,' apologised Gordon, shamed, wondering if he had gone too far. But Judith said nothing and there was an uncomfortable pause.

'Do you think it's crossed people's minds?' wondered Judith finally.

'Don't be absurd – it was just a lousy joke.' He fiddled with some account ledgers on the table as Judith continued to mix the cake.

Gordon cleared his throat hesitantly and then said, 'I've been thinking about the re-opening – something you might have overlooked.'

Judith gave him a quizzical look and he immediately went on the defensive. 'Look, I know it's none of my business, but just hear me out, OK?'

'Yes?'

'Look, it's not what you had in mind, but Vic's built up quite a name for this place, Judith. I know you don't want the commercial trade back but. . . .'

'I want it to be *clean*,' she said passionately.

Now it was Gordon's turn to look at Judith in a puzzled way. She merely repeated doggedly, 'I want it to be clean.'

'But it is.' He was bewildered, but continued on his theme. 'Selling is a small world, Judith. A different world. And we look for something different. We're on the road so much, that we want a home-from-home environment. Families on holiday now, they're after something more lively.' He paused.

Judith was looking away as if she wasn't listening.

'Keep your options open, that's all I'm saying,' persisted Gordon. 'Let me spread the word around to the lads that you're open for business again. That way you've got a fall-back position.'

'They only came because of Vic, didn't they?'

'And the cooking.' Judith gave an impatient little gesture of disbelief but Gordon was insistent. 'You underrate yourself, you know.'

'Perhaps,' she replied. Then, with sudden decision, Judith said, 'All right, tell them. If you think I need them.' She got up to go.

'Judith?' She paused. 'If you don't agree, say so. Let's talk it through.'

But Judith seemed to have nothing more to say and Gordon spoke hesitantly, 'You make it sound like a – a surrender.'

Judith left the room.

As she passed by Reception, she saw the local daily paper lying folded on the desk and picked it up. Her eyes travelled instantly to a small black headline, which read: POLICE STILL HUNT RAPIST. Judith put down the paper, glanced towards the cellar door and almost ran into the dining room.

Here, the decorating was complete. A rather chintzy kind of colour scheme predominated with matching table-cloths. Judith walked across to the lounge where dust sheets still covered the optics bar and the furniture. She removed the sheet from the television set and switched it on. As she did so, she stepped accidentally on the video's remote control box and the video flickered into life. A girl clad only in a slip and suspender belt was tied to a bed, writhing about in a combination of pleasure and fear. Mesmerised, Judith continued to watch.

That night, Judith lay in one of the single beds. She was awake, still thinking of the video, unable to rid her mind of the erotic images. Suddenly, incredulously, she heard the sound of quiet footsteps. She heard them pause for a second and then move on. Listening to them retreating, she was aware of the empty bed beside her. She felt oddly disappointed.

The next morning, after a broken night's sleep, Judith stumbled into the kitchen to find Gordon stoking up the Aga.

'It was getting low,' he said by way of explanation.

Judith filled the kettle and he hovered near her, waiting for her to speak. Eventually he said, 'Better be making myself scarce, I suppose. . . . Calls to make. I'll be back Tuesday. Will you be all right?'

'Of course, why not?' she replied, surprised.

Gordon could not answer that. He couldn't think what had prompted him to ask the question in the first place. On his way out, he paused to touch the frills of her nightdress. 'Pretty,' he said.

Judith recoiled sharply, as he drifted passed her out of the room.

When he had gone, Judith went straight to her room, changed into a dress and returned with her nightie to the kitchen. She pushed the garment into the Aga, and watched as the flames licked at it with a curious expression of satisfaction.

Her feet lazily up on a stool, Nancy was sitting on a chair in the lounge, where Jim, now decorator, was painting a window frame. Unknown to them both, Judith was standing by the Reception desk outside, listening intently to their conversation.

'It could be anyone, couldn't it, if he's local,' said Nancy.

'Except they reckon he's not,' replied Jim. 'The police think he's not from round here. That he just visits.'

'He's an animal, whoever he is.'

'People aren't born that way though, are they? They get that way. Either because they can't get sex or they're made to think it's dirty.' He paused, then continued, 'Sex is natural, it's instinct. If you're made to feel it's unnatural, you behave unnatural.'

But Nancy's mind had moved to more melodramatic themes, 'They say there's a pattern to the attacks. Like how they're never on weekends. And he's always dressed smart, like for work.' She grinned at Jim. 'That lets you out.'

'You haven't seen me in my Sunday best,' he retorted and they both laughed.

Judith started to walk briskly back to the kitchen but she was interrupted by the front door opening. She noticed how smartly Gordon was dressed as he smiled at her and said, 'Your wanderer returns.'

A few days later, other wanderers returned: the salesmen were back, congregating around the bar, Dennis among them. It was like old times again, except that now it was Gordon behind the bar; he was the centre of their attention and he was loving it. In the dining room, Judith moved amongst the tables. It was the old routine – almost.

Later the same night however, Judith lay tensed in bed, waiting for the inevitable and unnerving sound of Gordon's footsteps. This time, there came a tap on the door and she went rigid with a combination of fear and anticipation.

'Judith?'

She lay there motionless.

'Judith? You asleep?'

Still she couldn't move.

Gordon's voice came again, rising a little in agitation. 'I've an early meeting. Can you call me? About seven?'

'Yes,' she replied.

There was a silence, as if Gordon wanted to say something else, but couldn't. 'Goodnight,' he whispered reluctantly.

'Night.'

The footsteps went on and Judith relaxed. She was utterly confused about her feelings.

The next day's kitchen activities had an air of contented

domesticity – at least on the surface. Nancy was pegging sheets on the clothes line, Gordon was at the sink washing up and Judith had just come in with some breakfast trays.

'You'll be late,' said Judith.

Gordon turned to Judith, almost guiltily it seemed to her.

'For your meeting,' she explained.

'Yes.' He pulled on his raincoat. Then he suddenly said, 'You don't know how lucky you are, Judith. You can earn your living without having to set foot outside your own front door. It can get pretty cold out there.' Gordon had obviously said more than he intended, and regretted it immediately. 'I'll see you later. Don't bolt the door, I may be late.' He hurried out.

The young couple looked exhausted as they arrived at Reception. They each cradled a young child asleep in their arms as Judith emerged from the kitchen to greet them. She was delighted at the sight of them – the family for which her family hotel should really be catering. An ideal fulfilled. From the lounge could be heard the subdued murmur of the men as they talked and laughed together.

'Good evening.' Judith's delight persisted.

'Evening,' said the man wearily. 'We're after a double room, if you've got one, with a cot.'

'For the one night?'

'Yes – we're on our way to the coast and hoped to do it in one hop, but you know how it is with kids. . . .' As he spoke he signed them in, while the woman walked towards the lounge, the child in her arms. 'Then we spotted your sign,' continued the man. 'That sauna looks promising.'

'Have you eaten?'

'Sandwiches might be handy.'

By now the woman was at the door to the lounge, her eyes wearily taking in the disreputable scene that presented itself within. The men were playing darts. They had pinned a picture from a glossy calendar on to the darts-board and were aiming their darts at the model's nipples and between her legs. Each time they scored, the men laughed up-

44

roariously. The woman watched horrified, and Judith, seeing her, tried desperately to intervene.

'I can serve the sandwiches in your room.'

'Whatever,' the man replied casually. His wife, however, was no longer interested in staying.

Turning from the door, she said grimly, 'That won't be necessary, thank you. Perhaps we'd better be pushing on, darling. We're half-way there now, aren't we?' She addressed Judith curtly, already en route for the front door. 'So sorry to have troubled you.'

'But we've just unloaded the car. . . .' protested the man.

'It won't take a minute to re-load it, will it?' the woman replied, a warning note in her voice.

Bewildered, her husband shrugged, but followed her out. They paused on the step and Judith could hear a muffled argument. Then the woman raised her voice, 'I don't want to stay there, it's not clean! I won't have the children stay in a place like that!' They hurried away to the car park, leaving Judith alone with her thoughts.

'Still up?' asked Gordon. Judith was sitting at the kitchen table, too full of despair and apathy even to make a cup of tea. Gordon put down his coat and his briefcase and asked, 'Too late for a cuppa?'

She started to rise, but he put his hands on her shoulders.

'I'll do it.'

Judith sank down again and he moved away to fill the kettle.

'Everyone tucked up for the night?'

She nodded and he sat back down beside her.

'How did it go? Your meeting?' she asked unwillingly.

'I talked too much. They're all half my age, the clients. Made me tired, just looking at them.'

They fell silent.

'Always so peaceful, this room. Vic used to say that too.'

She looked at him in surprise.

'Always said, though, that he used to feel like an intruder,' continued Gordon.

45

One of Judith's hands was resting casually on the table near him and he reached out and stroked the back of it with his forefinger. 'You've never made me feel that.'

Judith was mute, watching his finger on her hand. Gordon took this as encouragement, and pulled her hand into his. 'Poor old hands.' Judith didn't move as he brought her hand to his lips and kissed it. 'I'm going to hold you to your word, Judith. About saying if I'm not welcome. It must have been in your mind too.'

Judith said nothing.

'You're going to make me do all the running, are you? I don't mind. I prefer it.' He reflected, 'My ex-wife – now she used to take the initiative in this sort of thing. Never felt quite right somehow. Don't ask me why.' He caressed her hand, waiting for her to speak, but she didn't. 'What are you thinking?'

'Oh . . . whether that is what's really been in my mind.'

'You feel *something*, don't you? Admit it, say you feel something. You like me touching you, don't you? Holding you?' He slid a hand around her shoulders. 'Judith, admit it. . . . Say it,' he persisted. He was still touching her, stroking her. 'You like it, don't you? Say it.' His face was now only inches away from hers. 'You like it. Don't you? You like me caressing you?' He slipped his other hand into her dress and his fingers groped towards her breasts.

Judith sat frozen, like a statue. Gordon pulled her towards him and kissed her. She returned it with a passion which amazed him.

'Now tell me you felt nothing,' he said triumphantly.

Judith said nothing. It was as if she was afraid to speak. Gordon stood up and took the kettle off the gas.

'I'll go up and wait for you,' he said.

That night Judith felt that she was in a dream as she approached Gordon's bedroom door. She hesitated, raised her hand to knock, hesitated again, and then knocked. Slowly, the door opened to reveal him lying in bed. Without a word he opened his arms to her, but Judith spoke sharply, 'Not in here.'

46

He clambered out of bed and she led him back down the corridor to the room she had shared with Vic. Gordon seemed bashful now and awkward, so she guided him to the bed and kissed him. Then slowly she removed her night-gown as he watched, almost hypnotised. With a passion which startled him, Judith took him in her arms. She was taking all the initiative and this, too, surprised him. Delighted to have got through to her at last, he kissed her again passionately, and they fell on to her bed.

The television was on. 'The Westcombe rapist struck again yesterday evening,' said the Breakfast Television newscaster. 'The victim, a woman in her middle age, was attacked on her way home from work. A man, answering the description of the rapist, was seen leaving the area shortly afterwards. . . .'

Mechanically, Judith took the scrambled eggs out of the microwave as she stared blindly at the screen.

'If you have seen this man,' continued the newscaster, 'or know of his whereabouts, you are asked to contact the Westcombe police, telephone number. . . .'

The identikit picture flashed up on the screen as Judith put down the scrambled eggs. She noticed Gordon's raincoat which he had left lying on the chair, and picking it up, she stood with it in her hands, still staring at the screen. Then she turned and in a mad panic found her way upstairs to Gordon's empty bedroom.

Once inside, she found the bed unmade and his suitcase, half-open, on a chest of drawers. She paused, uncertain about the impulse which had brought her there. Then she moved towards the chest of drawers. Inside were a few clothes and some underwear. The suitcase contained a folded suit and some pyjamas. Under the pyjamas was a copy of a girlie magazine, a woman coiled seductively on a bed on its cover. Judith dropped the magazine as if she'd been burnt, and then she saw something else. In the side pocket of the case, neatly folded, was a red plaid scarf.

Gordon was wearing Vic's bathrobe and washing some dishes at the sink when Judith came downstairs.

'What are you doing?' she asked calmly.

'Helping out.'

'I don't need any help.' There was a disconcerting sweetness about her voice.

'It's Nancy's day off, isn't it?' replied Gordon.

'I don't need any help,' she repeated firmly.

'Sorry.' Gordon moved from the sink.

She didn't look at him when she next spoke: 'Haven't you some calls to make?'

'None that can't wait.' He looked at her rigid and unyielding back. 'Don't do it, Judith. Don't make me feel I've done something to be ashamed of.'

'It takes two,' she replied harshly.

'You just followed your instincts for once. Nothing wrong in that.'

Judith, as usual, had nothing to say.

'*Say* something,' Gordon rapped.

'And last night you found me so peaceful.' The harshness was in her voice again.

'Not upstairs, I didn't. I hardly recognised you.' He moved close to her in a last-ditch stand, placing his hand awkwardly on her breast. 'Is this really all you want? Is it? It's you that makes it degrading, you know. If I could just once crack that infernal will of yours. . . .'

'You did, remember,' she replied bitterly.

'I'm not talking about passion now – I'm talking about affection. But then you insist on confusing the two, don't you?' Gordon drew away from her. His voice was also bitter as he said, 'Surrounded by food, yet you starve yourself of the one thing that makes life worth living.'

'Is that a quote?' she asked sarcastically.

'No.'

'What a way with words you salesmen have.'

'I didn't hear you complaining last night.' He paused. 'Sorry, that was cheap.'

'No more so than I'm sure I deserve.'

48

Gordon tried one last appeal. 'What is it you do object to? My idea of love-making? Or my love?'

She turned to look directly at him. 'The memory of it.'

Gordon reeled under the impact of what she had said. Then abruptly walked out.

Gordon was dressing as Judith came into his bedroom and closed the door. He looked up at her, uncertain. She stood there, as if waiting for him to make the first move, which he dutifully did. Cautious at first, wary of rejection, he crossed over to her. Then hesitantly, he kissed her. He did not see the look of utter repugnance on her face but was aware that his kiss had not been returned.

'It's OK,' he said soothingly. 'We've got time. All the time in the world.' He was cradling her in his arms and she submitted like a rag doll. 'That's better. All nice and cosy.' He kissed her again, not passionately, but with real affection.

Suddenly she murmured, 'Gordon? There's something you can do for me.'

'Yes?'

'The sauna. The customers keep asking about using it.'

He looked down at her, puzzled.

'It should be checked out. Do you mind?'

'But –'

'It worries me . . . and it's losing money.'

Gordon sighed and released her. 'Your bidding. . . .' he said and reached for a towel.

Judith stole quietly down the steps of the cellar, reached swiftly inside the sauna door, then bolted it. Walking quickly up the stairs to the lounge, she turned on the television set as loudly as she could. Going into the kitchen, she turned on the television there, and all of the other equipment. Once the noise was as intense as possible she opened the table drawer. Inside was Gordon's brochure: CREATIVE COOKING – THE HIGH-TECH WAY. She dropped the thermostat gauge on top of it and gave a small sigh of satisfaction.

Gordon's fingers slid helplessly over the metal prong. The thermostat was not there. He tried the door as the heat intensified. After a few moments, realisation hit and he began to beat on it, shouting out Judith's name.

Up in the kitchen Judith was busy cooking while the vegetables bubbled merrily in a saucepan. She glanced at the screen and paused. A Ceefax caption read: WESTCOMBE RAPIST ARRESTED. Quickly, she scanned the details taking in the words 'confession', 'positive identification' and 'murder charge'. In great agitation, she rose and paced nervously up and down the kitchen.

Then suddenly, she ran out, tearing down the steps of the cellar to the sauna.

Steam was billowing under the door and she could hear Gordon whimpering inside. He had heard her and was pounding violently on the door. Judith raised her hand to unbolt the door but then she heard his voice, choking, gasping . . . 'Judith? Judith! . . . In God's name, woman . . . I love you . . . Why? Why?'

She froze in mid-action.

'Judith . . .' he gasped. 'Ju-dith . . . !'

But one word had stopped her in her tracks.

Gordon continued to entreat pitifully as Judith walked slowly back up the stairs. Once in the kitchen, she closed the door and leant against it. Then she went and peered at the bubbling vegetables. She was safe. At least for a while. Dimly she registered Gordon's voice still calling, but she was too absorbed in her cooking now to hear him.

Anthony Masters,
based on the television script by Paula Milne

LOST PROPERTY

The land was flat and desolate, with only a few bleak trees surrounding the pond and its wooden jetty. The lane that ran along one side of the deep, murky water and up past the old walled-in building seemed to lead nowhere. There were maybe a handful of houses at some distance; other than that, it was isolated.

Two gates were set well apart in a high wall of Cotswold stone. Both were made of spiked iron rails, a stone lintel above each one. Into the left-hand lintel had been carved the word *Boys*: into the other *Girls*.

The schoolhouse itself had also been built from Cotswold stone, as creamy-yellow as a faded school photograph. It was a small building, cold and run-down, that seemed to project a feeling of disappointment – defeat, almost – as if it somehow missed the sound of children's voices.

The high wall enclosed a tarmac playground, its white games lines now weathered and partly erased. The only activity on it recently had been from leaves that skipped in the downdraught before piling up against the two or three stone outbuildings at the far end.

There was only one upstairs window in the whole school complex, an upper dormer window that looked down towards the outbuildings and out across the hostile landscape. Otherwise the claustrophobia was unrelieved.

Highest point of all was the small bell-tower on the roof. Its bell was moving slightly in the wind, ringing faintly and spasmodically; inside, from the cloakroom, came the unrhythmic clatter of a flapping, open window. The rows of cloakroom pegs, empty of coats, were no more than four feet from the floor. Beyond them, their doors open, was a

51

row of cubicle lavatories, the pans tiny and near the ground. Above one cubicle, the window that was flapping on its hinges was also small. The old schoolhouse had been designed for small people.

But the footsteps that echoed on the flagstone floor of the corridor belonged to an adult. The woman who lifted the latch of the batten-door and entered the cloakroom was in her late twenties, slim, small-framed, quite pretty. She was dressed in winter clothes, with a heavy woollen shawl around her shoulders for extra warmth. On her hands she wore woollen gloves that had been cut off at the fingers, and she was carrying a clipboard that held a sheaf of well-worn papers.

Anne Forrest stood in the doorway and listened once more. She shivered slightly as the window clattered again, set her clipboard down neatly on a bench, and moved towards the source of the sound. Only by standing on the tiny lavatory seat could she reach the open window and slam it shut. At once, the high, thin sound of the wind disappeared.

The schoolmistress moved back along a corridor that was empty of furniture, her footsteps resounding on the bare flagstones. Only a pair of windows high up in the walls gave any sort of light to the shadows. She went into a classroom where the windows were longer and larger, but they too were high up, the kind that need to be opened by a long pole with a hook.

It was the only classroom in her school. Rows of small, old-fashioned desks, each with a blank sheet of paper and a pencil filled the room, and at the far end a larger, teacher's desk. To one side of this desk was a blackboard on an easel, and a tall cast-iron stove that was surrounded by a high, brass-railed guard. But, for all that, the room felt dank and unused. Young pupils had not occupied it recently.

Anne Forrest went over to the stove and put out her hand to touch it – but not as if she really expected it to be alight. As she did so, she slowly lifted her gaze, and studied the large picture that hung on the wall nearest her, a reproduction print that hangs in countless schools: 'The Gleaners'.

The staff room was not large. In one corner was a solid-looking table, too big for the room, surrounded by upright chairs; in the opposite corner, a mattress made up into a makeshift bed. John Forrest was sitting on the edge of it, warming himself by a battered electric fire. He showed no surprise when his wife opened the door.

Standing in the doorway, the schoolmistress cast her eye around the few personal bits and pieces in the room: items of his clothing scattered around in heaps. On the draining-board by the large, deep sink he'd put a packet of tea-bags, a bag of sugar, a cup and a kettle. Last item on her mental inventory was her husband himself, a man in his early thirties, tall, but of the same small-framed build as herself.

'That picture in the classroom,' she said, in a flat tone.

'Picture?' Forrest asked, his thin face set in an impatient frown.

'On the wall,' said Anne. 'Is that ours or does it belong to the school?'

Forrest shrugged and lifted himself to his feet. He obeyed the unspoken command to follow her meekly towards the classroom; his jacket collar turned up against the cold, his hands stuck deep in his pockets.

They studied the picture together.

'It was here when we came,' said Forrest without interest.

'Right,' said Anne briskly, and with a flourish of her pen she made a note on the clipboard list.

Forrest watched her. 'So what are we doing?' he sighed. 'Stock-taking yet again?'

Anne ignored this.

'I mean, what does it matter?' he said, the anger swelling. 'The school belongs to you.'

Anne's eyes did not leave the picture.

'Is there another one like it anywhere?' she asked.

'Possibly.'

'Then would you find it. And put it,' – she jabbed her pencil emphatically – 'on that other wall. . . . We need a balance.' With that, she turned and moved back towards the door.

'A balance,' Forrest muttered to himself.

Anne stopped, but not because she had heard him speak.

'And could we have a fire in this room. . . . Please.' The word was underlined with studied politeness.

Forrest glanced at the stove, then his eyes met hers.

'Why?' he asked wearily. 'Who comes in here?'

'I come in here,' she replied, with a wave of an arm that indicated her domain. 'I like to move around my school and I like to be warm. Apart from which, the place should be aired and it should be dried.'

She moved to the nearest desk and picked up the sheet of paper that was lying on it. 'Feel that,' she demanded.

Forrest did not budge.

'Damp,' said Anne, screwing it up. 'You can chuck the lot.'

Forrest kept his eyes on her for a moment, then strode towards the front row of desks.

'All right, then,' he said petulantly, collecting up the papers. 'You shall have a fire.'

A stack of worn and broken chairs lay outside the workshop at the far end of the playground. Inside, an old sandstone wheel was turning and, as John Forrest pressed the blade of his long-handled axe against it, the shrill grinding carried back across the playground and into the schoolhouse.

The room Anne Forrest was in had once been the head's private quarters. It was furnished with a divan-bed, an armchair, and Anne's personal belongings, but still looked more like a cluttered stockroom, with its boxes of stationery, pots of paint, paintbrushes, drawing-boards, and sticks of coloured chalk. In one corner were piled rush-mats, team colour sashes, netballs, and a medicine ball. Along the wall there was a table, that held numerous empty jam jars, a couple of empty fish tanks, shrimp-nets on canes, a microscope and slides. On a smaller table next to it sat an old wind-up gramophone and a pile of records. Beyond that, in the far corner, leant a maypole with ribbons.

Anne Forrest eased her way neatly around the clutter and placed her clipboard down on the divan-bed. The sound of grinding had become a rhythmic chopping. Curiosity aroused, she went to the dormer window to investigate.

John Forrest was swinging the long-handled axe, splitting the old chairs for firewood. He looked up in mid-swing, towards his wife at the dormer window.

For a moment she returned his gaze, then she turned, looked around the room, and moved away towards the boxes of stationery.

The classroom was warmer. The high, brass-railed guard had been moved aside and a stack of chair wood arranged close by. Forrest was feeding pieces of chair into the open mouth of the cast-iron stove.

When Anne Forrest arrived, she was carrying fresh sheets of paper.

'Now that's much better,' she said with satisfaction.

Forrest said nothing.

'So, have you decided what you're going to do?' she asked, moving up the aisles between the desks, carefully setting out sheets of paper as she went, one for each desk.

'When?' Forrest fed another piece of chair into the stove, then added, 'No.'

His wife did not look up from her task. 'You've made no plans, as usual?'

'Well, after two years of continually being told to leave, plans don't really enter into it.'

Anne adjusted the paper that she was carrying.

'This time I mean it, John.'

'All right then,' said Forrest wearily, 'you mean it.' He closed the stove lid and checked the fire door for air as Anne continued to distribute the paper.

'Is there enough chalk by the blackboard?' she asked.

'Considering that the blackboard is never used, yes.'

Anne ignored the remark. 'What about the waste paper baskets?'

'Still empty.'

Anne went on as if she had not heard him. 'Well, when you've finished the fire, you can put the clean roller-towels in the wash-room.'

'And what shall I do with the clean ones that are still hanging up in there?' Forrest asked, reaching for the fire guard.

'And how's the water level in the pond?' Anne continued in her schoolmistress tone. 'Have you looked lately?'

Forrest set the guard around the stove. 'It's quite high.'

'Good,' Anne said busily. 'I want to collect some wildlife samples this afternoon. They're always popular.'

Forrest glanced at his wife. She had finished laying out the paper, and was now tapping the remaining sheets into a neat and tidy package.

'Well,' she asked. 'Doesn't it worry you?'

'What?'

'The thought of perhaps being on your own when you leave here.'

'Of course it worries me. It always worries me.'

The faintest hint of a smile crossed Anne Forrest's face.

'But I expect I'll make do.'

'Yes, well, I can tell you now that I don't intend to stay here on my own,' Anne announced as she made her way back down the aisles. 'Not for long. I've a school to run.'

It was Forrest's turn to smile – a slight, tired, patient smile, that suggested he already had heard this conversation countless times.

Anne put her hand on the door knob. 'And *I* don't believe in making do. . . . So perhaps it's time you learned to pull your socks up.'

The smile broadened on Forrest's face. 'Pull my socks up! For God's sake Anne, you're not a teacher. You own a school but you're not a teacher. You never will be. . . . And no child will ever come here. Not in our time.'

There was a long moment before Anne Forrest replied, and when she did it was as if he had not spoken at all.

'When you've finished the towels in the wash-room, you can put a bit of polish on the entrance hall floor. That floor is starved of polish.'

Forrest touched his forehead, the tired smile still on his face. 'Yes, ma'am. . . .'

But Anne was already gone, the door shut behind her,

and the sound of her footsteps receded down the shadowy corridor.

Anne Forrest placed the surplus sheets of paper carefully back inside their box, then picked up her clipboard and began to make a further check of the inventory.

At first, deep in study, she did not hear the faint sound that came from outside, from down on the tarmac play-gound. It was the sound of a child playing a solitary skipping game, singing to herself: 'Dance, dance, wherever you may be. . . .'

Anne looked up suddenly. She stared at the window.

'. . . I am the Lord of the dance, said he. . . .'

From the dormer window Anne could see nothing but the open door of the workshop, with its stack of broken chairs and the long-handled axe propped against the wall.

'I'll lead you all, wherever you may be. . . .' The sound of singing, skipping persisted. 'I'll lead you a-all in the dance said he. . . .'

It was a small landing, with access only to Anne's private room. A short flight of stairs led from there down to a corridor lit by a small, narrow window. As she ran from the room, Anne paused to look down at the white-lined yard.

The skipping game was louder now. 'I danced in the morning when the sun turned black. . . .'

But still there was no child to be seen. 'How can you dance with the devil on your back. . . .'

Anne Forrest moved quickly along her corridor, towards a heavy door that opened out on to the playground. She shivered in the cold, drew the shawl tight around her shoulders as she looked across the tarmac. But there was no one to be seen.

Inside the schoolhouse, she met Forrest, his arms full of firewood.

'Did you hear that?' she asked.

'What?'

'There was a child out there. . . .'

They went out together into the playground, over to the spiked iron rail gates. Forrest stood in the open gateway

57

of the *Boys* entrance, Anne in the *Girls* entrance, both looking down the lane.

'I didn't hear anything,' Forrest said.

Anne stared at him for a moment. 'Well, I did.'

Forrest scanned the stark terrain, past the murky pond with its scattering of trees and up to the cluster of buildings in the far distance. But the child, if there had been one, had vanished into thin air.

'It was the sound of a girl,' Anne Forrest said. 'A small girl. Singing.' She was sitting on a tiny chair by the row of coat pegs in the cloakroom, watching her husband as he changed the roller-towels.

'Singing?'

'Yes. And playing some kind of a skipping game.'

Forrest didn't bother to hide his disbelief.

'It's true,' she said defensively. 'I heard it.'

'Probably some village kid having a joke with you.' Forrest emerged from the wash-room, two roller-towels under his arms.

'We don't know any village kids.'

'Exactly. All the more reason for them to play jokes.'

'Why?'

'I don't know,' Forrest shrugged. 'Because they don't come here any more?'

'That's not my fault.'

'No?'

'No.'

Forrest hung the towels on the nearest coat peg and sat down on one of the tiny chairs.

'Can I ask you something?' he said quietly. 'How much have we got left in the bank?'

'How much have *we* got left?'

'All right then, how much have *you* got left from your inheritance?'

'Enough,' Anne said evasively.

'There wasn't that much left over when you bought this place. And that was two years ago.'

Anne looked defiant. 'I said, there's enough.'

58

Forrest was not convinced.

'Anyway, you've done all right,' she said.

'Not exactly. I'm kept. But I work. . . . Work here,' Forrest said, as if thinking out loud. Then he added, carefully: 'I'm also your husband.'

Anne looked down at her hands for a moment, then up again. 'Which doesn't really mean anything any more, because the marriage is finished.'

'So you say,' Forrest observed wearily. 'D'you want some advice?'

'What?'

'Sell up.'

'No.'

'Then employ someone who's qualified to teach.'

'No,' Anne shook her head. 'You can't trust people. Just because they've had a bit of training they think they can organise everything – and everybody.'

'Like the two old dears who were running this place when you took over?'

'Yes. They would have been trouble. You could see it. That's why I kicked them out.'

'Well at least they had the place alive with kids.'

'And I've already said that's not my fault,' Anne protested sharply.

'Because the local authorities won't recognise this place any more. . . ?'

'Yes. . . .'

'Because, as far as they're concerned, it's no longer a working school, just a private dwelling. . . ?'

'They can think what they like. . . .' Anne looked down again. 'To me, it's still a school. *My* school.'

'But nobody comes here. . . .'

Anne Forrest got up from her tiny chair and retrieved the roller towels from the coat peg. She carried them to the door and started to lift the latch.

'Nobody likes us,' Forrest said to her back. 'They don't talk to us. Nobody wants us here.'

Anne turned around. 'Well, you're working, aren't you?' She seemed about to leave, then she hesitated, and added,

'Somebody *did* come to see us today. . . .' She nodded her head in the direction of the playground. '. . . Out there.'

Then, still carrying the heavy towels, she went out again on to the deserted tarmac. But there was nothing except the cold wind, blowing leaves into drifts against the stone outbuildings.

John Forrest approached the open door of his workshop. He selected some broken chairs from the pile inside, and threw them out on to the tarmac for chopping. Then he came outside, blowing on his hands to warm them. He reached for the long-handled axe that he'd left leaning against the wall, and momentarily froze: his axe was no longer there.

The small jetty jutted out only a little way from the edge of the pond. Old and rickety, the wooden structure had a couple of steps at its end – once used by those who had to draw their water from the miniature reservoir.

Anne approached the jetty from the schoolhouse, carrying a seed-tray loaded with empty jam jars. Setting the tray down, she selected two jars that had lengths of string attached to them, and walked on to the jetty. As she made her way along it, she had to side-step holes where the planking had rotted away. Holding the jars with their string attached in each hand, she could not grasp the handrail of the jetty. Her movements looked precarious; she seemed, suddenly, very vulnerable and childlike.

At the end of the jetty, Anne put down one of the jars before lowering the second one into the dark, muddy water, and it was then, in the distance, that she caught the sudden movement of a small figure, disappearing into the trees.

John Forrest was polishing the floor of the school entrance hall the old-fashioned way. Near him was a large tub of polish with a stick inside it and, in his hands, a long-handled polisher.

He heard his wife before he saw her, her footsteps resounding on the flagstones. Then the door opened and she appeared, the tray now laden with jam jars full of pond water. Forrest stared at her.

'Don't worry,' she said, 'I won't spill anything.'

She moved across the floor towards the short set of stairs that led to her private quarters. Seeing Forrest's interest in the jam jars, she said, 'Just some samples for the wildlife class.'

'Oh,' he said, going back to his work. Then he seemed to remember something: 'Did you take the axe with you?'

'Now why would I need an axe?' Anne kept her attention on the jars as she climbed the stairs.

'Well, have you moved it?' Forrest asked.

'No.'

'Only, it's gone.'

Anne stopped. 'What do you mean, it's gone?'

Forrest did not answer. Anne left the tray at the top of the stairs, beckoned him, and together they went, in silence, out to the playground.

She peered carefully inside the workshop. 'It's not in there?'

'No. I left it by the wall.'

Anne moved to where he was pointing, but there was no axe.

Forrest closed the workshop door. 'Oh well,' he shrugged tiredly, 'I expect it'll turn up.'

The only source of light in Anne Forrest's room was a small bedside lamp, casting eerie shadows around all the objects that cluttered it. The only sounds, those of the wind, the intermittent beating of rain on the window and, from time to time, the scratching of a pen as Anne, propped up in the divan bed in a nightdress, her hair tied back by a ribbon, worked once more at her school stock list.

Then there was another sound.

It was faint, but was quite definitely the steady, rhythmic tapping of metal and wood. Anne looked up from her sheaf of papers, and climbed out of bed, her shadow merging with the others as she made her way to the dormer window and drew back the curtains.

The sound stopped.

Anne peered out through the damp window, into the darkness. It was impenetrable.

Crossing the dark landing, she began to descend the stairs. Every few seconds, she stopped and listened, but there was only the sound of the wind and rain. She reached the hall light, and made her way along the corridor. Outside the door of the staff room she paused for a moment to compose herself, then opened it slowly.

'John?' she said in a low voice, peering through the partly opened door.

A lamp on the table was alight. So, too, was the battered electric fire.

But John Forrest was gone.

Anne looked along the corridor and called louder, 'John?'

There was no answer. Anne moved on down the corridor, treading carefully to soften the echo of her footsteps.

When she reached the cloakroom, she lifted the latch and went in slowly. Lit only by the hall light, the room was in semi-darkness, making shadows of the rows of coat pegs. Just feet away from her, there was a sudden, frantic, flapping sound.

Anne clutched desperately along the wall for the light switch, and found it.

The light came on to reveal John Forrest standing by the row of coat pegs, shaking out a wet plastic raincoat.

'Was that you outside?' Anne asked, trying to control her breathing.

'I was out there, yes.'

'Chopping wood?'

'What?'

'I heard a noise out there. Like someone chopping wood.'

'No.' Shaking his head, Forrest hung the wet raincoat on a peg. 'I hadn't locked the workshop door. It had blown open. . . .'

He opened the cloakroom door. 'That's probably what you heard. The door banging in the wind.'

Anne followed a few paces behind her husband as they walked back up the corridor.

'Did it wake you up?' he asked.

'I wasn't asleep.'

'Oh.' He stopped at the door of the staff room. 'Anyway, this place is full of noises. Needs a lot of work done on it to put it right. . . . You're going to have to spend money sometime.'

He opened the door of the staff room, then remembered something. 'By the way, I've decided to leave on Saturday.'

'Saturday?' Anne repeated, puzzled.

'Yes. Well, you seem to mean it this time, so I'd better go through with it.'

Forrest went into his room but did not close the door behind him. Moving over to the electric fire, he stooped to warm his hands. When he looked up, Anne was in the open doorway.

'So where will you go?' she said.

'I don't know. Stay with my sister and her husband for a while, I suppose.'

'You won't stand it there for long.'

'Oh, I know that,' Forrest sighed. 'Look, come in. . . .'

Anne stayed in the doorway.

'It's all right. I won't try what I'm not supposed to try any more. Just come in. Visit me.' He cleared an armchair and placed it by the fire. 'Here.'

Anne Forrest pushed the door to behind her and came into the room. She accepted his hospitality and sat down, leaning forward, palms out, to warm herself at the fire.

Forrest watched her. With the nightdress and the ribbon tied in her hair, she appeared almost childlike.

'Anne.' He said the word softly.

'Yes?' Anne did not look up.

'Let's both leave here. Go somewhere together.'

Without looking up from the fire, Anne shook her head.

'Just sell this shack and let's get out of here,' Forrest persisted.

'No.'

'We could go and live by the sea. You like the sea.'

Anne stared at the fire. 'Sometimes,' she said.

'And it wouldn't be that difficult to sell this place.' Forrest reached out for an upright chair, moved it towards the fire and sat down. 'I imagine quite a few people would go for it, tart it up, turn it into a private house.'

'It's a school,' Anne countered, eyes still fixed on the fire.

'You mean, it *was* a school.'

'No. It still is. It's bought and it's paid for and it's mine. And no one's going to change it.'

Forrest relaxed in his chair and watched Anne.

'You never liked going to school, did you?' she stated.

'No.' Forrest shook his head.

'Well I did. I loved it there. I never wanted to leave.'

'The best years,' Forrest smiled, a little bitterly.

'No. The safest years. I always felt safe at school. I've never really felt safe anywhere since.' As if to relieve her self-consciousness at having made the remark, Anne got up from her chair. 'The people around here, you say they hate us?'

'No, I didn't say that. I said, they didn't like us. They've no time for us.'

'Oh.' Anne looked towards the window. Then, folding her arms because of the cold, she moved towards the door.

'You wouldn't like to stay with me tonight?' Forrest ventured.

'No.' In the open doorway, Anne stopped and turned.

'What about the axe?' she asked. 'Have you found it?'

'Not yet.'

She hesitated a moment longer, then went out and closed the door behind her.

The sun shone into the room around the edges of the drawn curtains, bright and full of promise.

Anne Forrest lay awake for a moment or two longer, then climbed out from under the covers and opened the curtains. She switched on her electric kettle, and shifted some of the clutter so that she could reach the wind-up gramophone. Blowing dust specks from the surface of one of the old 78s, she placed it on the turntable, wound the handle, and lowered the needle. It was a scratchy recording, but the sound of a school choir singing 'Early One Morning' filled the room.

Anne hummed along with it for a while, then, still waiting for the kettle to boil, she went to the table where the jars of pond water had been set out beside the microscope. She took a slide, fitted it under the instrument, and peered into the eyepiece.

Anne went to collect more specimens that morning for her wildlife class: leaves, sprigs of grass and weed from around the edges of the pond, which she placed in a shallow basket.

She looped the handle of the basket over one arm and moved on to the unstable wooden jetty, peering over the handrail to study the surface of the water – unaware that she was being watched.

The girl was about ten years old. Dressed in cheap but warm clothes, she had the complexion of a healthy, country child who has spent a lot of time outdoors. As she peered out through the iron bars of the gate marked *Girls*, her eyes were fixed on Anne Forrest with an expression of casual, almost insolent, curiosity.

Anne slipped slightly when she was on the steps at the far end of the jetty and reached for the handrail to support herself. She walked on to the bank and began to make her way back up towards the school.

When she reached the gates, the child was no longer there.

Forrest was at work again with the tub of polish and the long-handled buffer-polisher when his wife appeared, the basket on her arm.

Sunlight was streaming through the high windows of the corridor, seeming to cheer it up. Anne, too, seemed in buoyant mood as she walked.

'So why aren't you outside enjoying the sunshine?' she asked happily.

Forrest did not reply, merely watched her as she walked over the freshly polished floor.

'Look at it,' she said, pointing up at the windows. Then she took the basket from her arm. 'And look at these. Buds. See?' She took some sprigs from the basket.

Forrest straightened, and leaned on the handle of the polisher. 'Yes,' he said, unimpressed.

'The very first buds,' Anne continued. 'So it'll be spring before we know where we are. Then summer,' She looked at Forrest. 'Well? I thought you liked the summer.'

'I do.'

'Then look happy about it. Think about those long summer holidays, with an empty school and no work to do.' She walked further down the corridor.

'I won't be here, remember?'

'Oh, yes. I'd forgotten. . . .'

The classroom, too, was brightly lit with sunshine. Anne spread out a large sheet of card on the teacher's desk and began to arrange her nature specimens on it, sticky-taping them in place.

After a few minutes, Forrest came in with a box full of chair wood.

'That's the last of those old chairs,' he remarked.

'You mean there's no more wood?'

'There's some logs. But they can't be split without an axe.'

Anne looked up from her work. 'Then we'll have to buy another one.'

'*You'll* have to,' corrected Forrest as he opened the stove.

'Me?'

'Yes. I can put together enough small stuff to last you till Saturday.'

Anne did not reply at first. Instead, she picked up the large sheet of card and carried it to the wall at the back of the classroom.

'Well, I've been thinking,' she said, starting to fix the sheet to the wall. 'I've come to the decision that Saturday is rather short notice.'

'Not for me.'

Anne ignored him. 'So I'll settle for a fortnight on

66

Saturday. All right?' She said it as if she did not expect any argument.

'No,' Forrest shook his head. 'Not this time.'

Anne stood back and admired her handiwork. 'That'll give you a chance to clean up that hole you're living in. It's *supposed* to be a staff room.'

'A what? A staff room! With no staff?' Forrest exploded. 'You stupid bitch!'

Anne returned his stare.

'I mean, look at that. You waste your time sticking that junk on the wall. And who's going to see it?'

Still, Anne stared. And there was a hint of menace behind her controlled calmness.

'And who's going to be writing on your tatty bits of paper?' Forrest snatched up a sheet of paper and screwed it into a ball. 'Eh?'

He threw the ball of paper away. 'And who's going to be looking at all those jars of stagnant pond water that you keep dragging in here? Eh?' He moved towards her.

'Nobody. Nobody. Never,' he said.

Anne's face held the same impassive expression.

'Nothing lives in that pond anyway.' He leaned forward and tapped Anne lightly and mockingly on the forehead. 'And nothing lives in your head. Not any more. Only this stupid, crazy place. And I don't want to live like that. I don't want to play that game with you.'

Forrest moved past Anne, into the open doorway. 'If we were rich I might have gone along with it, but you can't play that kind of game when you're poor. It stops being fun. And very soon, at this rate, you're going to be poor.'

He moved out into the corridor and Anne appeared at the doorway. She was still watching him.

'You see,' Forrest snapped, 'you still talk about school being the only safe place you've ever known. . . .'

'It was,' Anne cut in, quietly, still with the intent stare.

'Fine. But you're twenty-eight years old now. You can't use school and childhood as an easy way out any more. . . . You can't use it to avoid responsibilities or to shut off all the terrible things that happen in this world, even though you try to.'

Their eyes met and held for a moment, before he added, 'And you can't use it to avoid sex. Especially that. . . .'

A smile crossed his mouth briefly. 'After all, you're not exactly an innocent, now are you? You never were.'

On Anne's face there appeared a threat now, a trace of menace just below the surface.

But Forrest could not resist a parting shot, 'Oh, there's been a lot of black marks in the register for you, dear.'

And the smile was still on his face as he turned and walked down the corridor in the direction of the cloakroom.

Anne Forrest climbed the stairs to her room, moving quickly and with a very calm and determined look about her.

Closing the door behind her, she eased her way around the cluttered objects. From under a tambourine, she retrieved a key that had been hidden there – her key to the corner cupboard. Then she turned it in the lock, and rummaged inside the cupboard until she found the long-handled axe.

Anne's face still wore that same fixed expression, as she crossed the polished floor of the school entrance hall and entered the corridor. She walked quickly and purposefully along the echoing flagstones, eyes straight ahead; not once looking down at the object she was carrying in both hands. She pushed open the batten-door and strode into the cloakroom.

The door to the small recessed washroom was open. Forrest was stooping down washing his hands and face at one of the tiny, low-level basins. He did not hear his wife moving swiftly along the racks of coat pegs towards him.

Then, just as she appeared in the washroom, he straightened up from the basin, his face dripping with water, and turned and stared.

Anne was advancing towards him, one arm raised high above her. She hit out quickly, before Forrest had a chance to defend himself, bringing her arm down hard so that her long, lethal-looking cane slashed him hard across the face.

Forrest cried out and stumbled blindly towards her, trying to grab at it. Anne stepped back and hit him once more, across the arms that he was holding up to protect himself.

'Jesus! You bitch!' he shouted. 'You daft, stupid bitch!'

As Anne raised the cane again, Forrest lunged forward and grabbed it. Anne let go immediately and backed away from him. Forrest threw the cane to one side and ran after her around the racks, wincing with pain and touching his face as he moved.

Anne made for the door, but Forrest grabbed at her through the empty coat racks. Holding on to her tightly, he manoeuvred her along to the end of the rack. Once there, and still holding on to her, he turned her around sharply, forcing her back against the coat pegs.

'So what's this for?' he demanded, tilting his face so that the red weal was thrust at her.

Anne struggled. 'Let go of me, please.'

'Eh?'

'I said, let go.'

'I want to know why you did this,' said Forrest viciously.

'Because you asked for it. You deserved it.'

Forrest relaxed slightly, but kept his grip on Anne. 'Oh, I deserved it, did I?'

'For saying what you said to me, yes.'

Still holding her with one hand, Forrest felt his face. 'Because I just happened to mention sex?'

Anne said nothing.

'Is that it?' he insisted. 'Or lack of it, I should say. Because there hasn't been much of it around here lately, has there?'

Anne bit her lip slightly, but said nothing.

'Which, I suppose, is a lot different to the old days when you were putting it about all over the place.'

Anne started to struggle, but Forrest tightened his grip painfully.

'I mean, even I had to wait my turn in those days, and I was your husband. Then it all changed, didn't it? Because

69

someone left you some money and you decided to buy this place. Decided to buy back your schooldays. Buy back all that apple-for-the-teacher innocence. . . . Buy a bit of safety. Your kind of safety.'

'That's right.' Anne said it quietly. Defiantly.

'Well it can't be done.'

'I've done it.'

'No.' Forrest shook his head. 'You can't just wipe out all the bad things and the bad times by pretending to live in tiny-tot land. So . . . punishment.'

'Punishment?'

'Yes. Isn't that what I've just had?'

Still holding on to Anne, Forrest ripped one of her blouse sleeves down to the buttoned cuff. Anne stood stock-still, as if it was part of her defiance.

'After all, we have to set examples. Even to each other.'

Forrest jerked her around to face the coat rack and tied her torn sleeve to one of the pegs. 'Wouldn't you agree?'

She made no attempt to struggle. Kept her silence.

Forrest ripped the second sleeve then, forcing her arms wide apart, tied that sleeve to another peg. He stepped back to look at her.

'Six of the best, would you say?' She watched him walk back around the coat racks and pick up the cane. He grinned, and showed her the cane, slapping it against his leg for effect.

'Well,' he said, a little disconcerted by her lack of fear. 'I don't see why we should make it easy for you. . . .' And as he spoke, he reached forward and ripped open the back of her blouse.

Anne did not flinch.

Forrest began to undo her skirt. 'No favours. That's the motto of this school. Right?'

He tugged at the skirt and allowed it to fall. Then he slowly raised the cane – and checked himself, unable to deal the blow. . . .

At last, Anne was reacting to the situation. She was breathing deeply, her body moving gently.

Forrest stared at her, realising.

'Do it, then,' Anne said very quietly. 'If you're going to.' Then, with just a trace of impatience, 'Do it.'

But Forrest lowered the cane and dropped it to the floor. He reached forward, untied his wife's wrists, turned and walked to the door.

Anne Forrest moved slowly away from the coat rack, just the faintest of smiles on her face.

Alone with his thoughts, John Forrest walked out across the playground. Then he halted for a moment, and looked towards the gates. The *Girls* gate was open. Forrest peered out from it, then clanged it shut.

When he came back into the school, Forrest saw something else that stopped him in his tracks: a pair of child's gumboots, standing in the corridor. Forrest picked them up, looked at them, and put them down again. Then, shrugging it off, he walked down the corridor and away from the classroom.

Anne had been to her room to put on another blouse. Now she was in the classroom.

And she was not alone.

The girl was sitting in one of the small desks at the back of the classroom, very still. She returned Anne's stare.

'Do I know you?' Anne asked.

The girl shook her head.

'Well who are you? What's your name?'

The girl did not respond at first. When she did, her voice was slow and calculated, almost grown-up. 'Marian Price.'

'And what are you doing here?'

'The man said I could come in,' she lied.

'Yes, but what are you doing in this school?'

'Looking.'

'Well do you know that this is a private school, that it's private property?'

'Yes.'

'So where do you live?'

'Not far.'

'In the village?'

71

'The other side of it.' The girl was motionless in her seat.

'Yes, well, I think it's time you went home,' Anne said, going to the door.

Marian Price stayed put. 'This wasn't always a private school, y'know.'

'Well, it is now.'

'So where are the children?' the girl asked, with a hint of triumph.

'They'll be coming.'

'Oh.'

Anne waited by the open door.

'That man,' said Marian Price, 'is he your husband?'

'Yes.'

'What happened to his face?'

'He was chopping wood. It was an accident.'

'Did it hurt him?' the girl asked, still the same calculated tone in her voice.

'I expect so. . . .'

'Was he in pain?'

Anne squared her shoulders. 'Look, I really think it's time you went home. . . .'

The girl did not take the cue. 'When the children come, who's going to be sitting here at this desk?'

'I've no idea. Why do you ask?'

'Because this was my desk.'

'Oh, I see. You were a pupil here.'

'Yes. When Miss Palmer and her sister were the teachers. I liked them.' The girl studied Anne's face for a reaction. 'I liked them very much.'

She went on looking steadily at Anne for a moment longer, then got up slowly from her desk and moved into the aisle. She glanced at the wildlife card on the wall and looked back at Anne. 'You collected those things by the pond, didn't you?'

'That's right.'

'I know. I've watched you. That pond's dangerous, did you know that? It's very deep.'

'Yes. So I've heard.'

'Miss Palmer, she always wanted to get it fenced off. We

72

were never allowed near there.' The girl moved past Anne, into the corridor. 'Them tangly weeds in there, they'd pull you under. And you'd never come up again. Not alive.'

They went over to the pair of gumboots.

'I liked being at this school,' the girl said, tugging a boot on to her foot. 'I loved it.' She looked up sharply at Anne. 'I don't like it empty. And Miss Palmer and her sister, I loved them.'

Anne watched her put on the other boot. 'So where do you go to school these days?'

'Oh, in the town. A bus comes.' She stared at Anne. 'I hate it there.'

They walked together out of the school and on to the tarmac. Marian Price stopped and looked around her at the school playground with its faded white lines.

'I used to like this playground. I used to have my own corner. There.' She pointed. 'That was my corner. I used to skip there.'

The girl turned and looked back towards the school. 'Poor Miss Palmer.'

'Why do you say that?' said Anne, puzzled.

Marian Price looked up at Anne and held her gaze for a long moment. Then, without answering, she moved to the gate, opened it, and stepped outside into the lane. She half-closed the gate, and looked through the bars at Anne.

'I don't really want anyone sitting at my desk.'

Anne stared. 'Well, I'm sorry, but. . . .'

'When the children come,' the girl cut in – still slow, still calculating – 'and I find out who's been sitting at my desk, I'll hide somewhere. I'll wait.' She slammed the gate shut. 'And I'll hurt whoever it is.'

Then she walked a few steps away from the school before breaking into a jaunty skip.

Forrest was examining his face in the mirror when Anne opened the door and came into his room.

'That child. She was here.'

Forrest turned from the mirror.

'I talked to her.'

73

'You what?'

'She was there in the classroom. Sat at a desk. She even told me her name. Marian Price.'

'I saw a pair of kid's boots,' Forrest said.

Anne nodded. 'They were hers.'

'And is she still here?'

'No. She's gone home.'

Forrest relaxed and turned back to the mirror.

'That Miss Palmer,' Anne said. 'What happened to her?'

Forrest stared at her reflection in the mirror for several seconds. 'Didn't you know?' he said. 'She's dead.'

Forrest put the last of the chair wood on the classroom stove as he told Anne about the former headmistress.

'Her sister went into hospital, then into a nursing home. She's still there. The old dear more or less faded away when she was forced to leave here. Well, they were both too old to get another teaching job.' He adjusted the stove door. 'She'll never leave that nursing home.'

Anne shifted uncomfortably as she sat at one of the small desks near the stove, near her husband.

Forrest joined her, a desk or two away, and lit a cigarette. 'So Miss Palmer was left alone. When she hadn't been seen for about three days, someone broke into her house. She'd died in her bed. The coroner was kind enough to suggest that she'd taken an accidental overdose. But no one really believes that.' He shook his head slightly as he exhaled smoke. 'She killed herself. You see, the only thing they ever lived for was this school. Then you came and took it away from them.'

Forrest reached forward and knocked the ash from his cigarette into the ink-well. Anne rose from her desk and began to make her way along the aisle.

'So what about the stove?' Forrest asked.

'Split some logs.'

'And how am I supposed . . . ?'

'I've got the axe,' Anne said quietly.

'You?'

'Yes. I found it yesterday. By the pond.'

'By the pond?'

'Hidden in the long grass.' Anne went to the door. She stopped for a moment, to face Forrest. 'If you hate chopping wood that much then you only have to say so.'

'I didn't hide the thing,' Forrest assured her.

But Anne seemed not to care about his answer. She opened the door, and left the classroom.

Forrest shrugged and drew heavily on his cigarette.

Anne studied the ground and the long grass as she walked near the pond. When she reached the edge, she spent a while looking at the surface of the water. It was dark, and murky.

She examined the surrounding countryside, looking past the wooden pier-like structure that jutted into the pond, towards the village in the distance.

From where she stood, she could not see the main support posts of the jetty, could not see that wood had been freshly hacked from one of them, close to the water line.

Deep in thought, she wandered on to the jetty. She walked to the very end, side-stepping the holes in the planking as she went. She paused for a moment or two on the steps that led down into the water, then turned and started back towards the bank. She slipped slightly, exactly as she had done when carrying the two jars with string handles, and she leaned heavily on the handrail to steady herself – so heavily that she did not feel the structure's uneasy sway as she made her way back to the bank.

There was a suitcase on the table in the school staff room, into which Forrest was packing books and his other personal belongings.

The door opened. It was Anne, carrying the axe. She stared at the case, took a little while to realise. Then she held out the axe to Forrest.

'Thanks.' He set the axe down behind the door and went back to his packing. He noticed after a few moments that Anne was still there, still watching him.

'Thought I'd make a start on a few bits and pieces,'

he said. 'You see, it's Saturday the day after tomorrow.'

'I know.'

'Good.' Forrest smiled. 'Think you're going to be all right here on your own?'

Anne was asleep when the sound came, the faint, rhythmic tapping of metal on wood. She sat up in bed, and listened. The sound continued. It was like the sound of a woodcutter at work somewhere nearby.

Pulling on a dressing-gown, Anne moved downstairs. She unlocked the main door and peered out into the darkness. The sound had stopped.

The door to the staff room was ajar, and Anne looked in. A moment's pause, then she switched on the light.

The bedclothes had been flung aside. Forrest was not there.

Anne glanced behind the door. Wherever he was, he had not taken the axe with him.

Forrest approached from the direction of the cloakroom, wearing a coat over his pyjamas and carrying a torch.

'I heard it that time,' he said.

'Heard what?'

'That sound. Like someone chopping wood. Is that what you heard before?'

'Yes.'

'Well, it's stopped now. I've searched the yard and the playground and over by the pond. I can't see anything.'

'You're not. . . .' Anne found it difficult to say. '. . . Well, it's not you, is it?'

'Me?'

'Yes. Having a bit of fun at my expense. Trying to scare me.'

'No,' Forrest shook his head. 'I don't need to, do I? I'm leaving.' He moved towards his bedroom door.

'John. . . .' The gentleness of the word. 'I don't want to be here alone.'

'I thought you said you'd find someone to help.'

'Yes, but that takes time.' Her hand on his arm. 'Look,

76

it's not that I'm worried about anything, it's just – well, it's just that I don't like living alone.'

He moved, and her hand fell away. 'Sorry,' he said, 'but I've had enough of this place.' And he went into the room and closed the door behind him.

Anne closed the door of her room and went over to the window. She parted the curtains slightly and stared out at the darkness. She listened, but there were no more strange sounds, only wind blowing across the open land.

Anne went to the gramophone, wound it up, and put on one of her scratchy, school choir records. As it played, she moved about the room, looking at the objects in it, touching some of them, checking the pond water in the jars, rearranging the pots of paint on their shelf, straightening two or three ribbons on the maypole.

In the darkness of the school staff room, John Forrest lay on his untidy, makeshift bed. He was awake, and he was listening to the sound of the record.

Forrest was in the washroom recess the following morning, drying his hands and face with a towel, when he heard the shrill sound of a whistle from outside.

Putting on the dressing-gown that had been hanging from a peg, he went out from the cloakroom, into the corridor. Anne was at the far end, sporting a track-suit top, a grey, pleated skirt, white ankle socks, white pumps. Around her neck hung a whistle on a piece of cord, and in her hands she was carrying a netball.

'Come on,' she called cheerily, 'you need some fresh air.'

'Fresh air?' said Forrest, wearily, patiently.

'Yes. And exercise.' Anne threw the ball. 'Catch.'

The ball bounced down the corridor and Forrest caught it.

'So let's have you dressed and outside in the playground in five minutes.'

Forrest followed her down the corridor. 'No school today.'

'What?'

He tossed the ball back to her. 'It's Saturday.'

'Saturday?' she said quietly.

Forrest led her to the staff room. The suitcase and a large holdall were packed and waiting by the door. Another case lay open on the bed.

Forrest took off his dressing-gown and reached for a shirt.

'So how will you leave here?' Anne asked.

'I'll phone for a taxi.'

'Oh.' Anne fought to control herself. 'I've too much to do. Otherwise I would have given you a lift into town.'

Forrest picked up his trousers, held them against himself in mock modesty. 'That's all right,' he said. 'I'll manage.' Then he indicated the door.

Anne silently turned and walked away. Some way down the corridor she stopped, turned, looked back at the door to the staff room. Then she moved on, throwing the ball away as she did so.

Anne did not, at first, see what had been written on the blackboard. She was taking the cord and whistle from around her neck as she moved to the front of the classroom and sat down at one of the small desks. Then she looked up, and read it:

MISS PALMER'S CLASS. AWARD GIVING DAY.

In large chalked letters. In a child's writing.

Anne stared at the words, and at the large, flat book lying open on top of the teacher's desk. Putting two and two together, she went to investigate the contents of the small desk in the back row. Then she went to find her husband.

'It was supposed to be in the desk drawer there. It's the register. It always stays in the drawer.'

'So where was it?' Forrest was fully dressed now. Ready to go.

'On the top there,' Anne pointed. 'Look inside.'

Forrest looked at the open pages of the register. A name had been written in. It was the only name in the book. And the name had been marked off with a tick.

'Marian Price,' he read aloud.

'Yes.'

'And she's put her own name in here?'

'That's not all.'

Anne led him to the back of the classroom, to Marian Price's old desk. She lifted the lid. Inside were some well-used pencils held together with a rubber band, a shabby-looking exercise book, and a skipping rope.

'It looks as if she decided to come back here to school,' Forrest said. 'That kid must be weird.' Then he looked back at the blackboard. 'Award giving day?' he repeated, puzzled.

Anne and Forrest approached each other from opposite ends of the corridor.

'No?' Anne asked.

'No. She's not here anywhere.'

'Well, I think I've found out how she gets in.'

Forrest followed her back towards the cloakroom, to one of the cubicle lavatories.

'That window,' she pointed. 'I've found that open before.'

Forrest moved inside the cubicle and stepped up on to the small seat.

'The catch is rusted through. Comes clean away from the frame.' He studied her face. 'Like me to fix it before I go?'

'Please.' She meant it.

'If I were you I'd go and see that girl's parents,' Forrest said as he jumped down from the seat. 'Tell them what she's up to. Get them to keep the brat under control.'

'I will.'

Forrest nodded and came out from the cubicle.

'It's really not fair,' Anne said.

'What isn't?'

'That girl. She's beginning to frighten me.'

'How can she frighten you?' Forrest put his hand not much higher than his waist. 'She's only that high.'

Anne felt unconvinced, but was not sure what to say next. For something to do, she removed the games sash

79

from around her waist and shoulder and hung it on a peg.

'She can try to annoy, yes,' Forrest went on. 'But she can hardly terrorise you, now can she?'

'No.'

'So, be tough with her. It's your school.'

'Yes.'

Forrest went to the door, put one hand on the door latch. When he looked back at Anne she looked lost, like a child.

'Won't you change your mind?' he said with care. 'And sell this place? Move away from here?'

'Together?'

'If we could leave here, yes. We *could* perhaps stay together. Try to make things work again.'

'But I want a school.'

Forrest's jaw tightened. He gave an impatient sigh.

'Look, it was my money,' Anne reasoned. 'It was left to me. My mother never gave a damn about me when she was alive.'

'And you reckon you've made up for that, do you? By buying this place with what was left of her money?'

'Yes.' It was defiant.

'Then she must be having a good laugh up there somewhere,' Forrest said, opening the door. Then he relaxed slightly. 'Please. Buy something else, Anne. A long way from here.'

'What kind of place?'

'Well, why not a house with just a small classroom attached. Then you could still have your toy school.'

'And a home as well.'

'Yes. You see, this kind of place doesn't work. Not for you. It belongs to the Miss Palmers of this world.'

With that, he left the room, his footsteps receding down the flagstoned corridor.

But Anne stayed where she was for quite a while, just looking around her. Thinking.

Forrest's suitcase was outside the heavy side door of the school, on the tarmac. The door opened and Forrest appeared, carrying his holdall and a smaller case. He set them down.

'John?' He did not know where the call came from. He looked around.

Anne was standing in the playground. 'Shall we do that?' she said tenderly. 'Shall we leave here? Together.'

Forrest grinned, moved towards her, put an arm around her.

Anne smiled, and looked up at him. Then, still arm in arm, they walked back towards the open door of the school.

The main support post of the jetty had been chopped completely through. Its twin, too, had been hacked away close to the water line.

By the edge of the water, half-hidden in the long grass, glinting in the sun, lay a sharpened bill-hook.

Near it, quietly humming 'Lord of the Dance', sat Marian Price.

Man and wife, they walked together along the corridor.

'And, if it's just a one-room school. . . .' Anne began.

'It'll be simpler to look after.'

'Yes.'

'And I won't have to polish the damn floors. I can get a job, bring some more money in.' He broke free of her. 'Hey!' he ran forward, picked up the netball, and aimed it at her. 'Your turn to catch.'

'You . . . !' Anne stumbled as she caught the ball. She ran after him, ready to throw it at him in fun, but Forrest had moved quickly into the cloakroom.

Anne entered cautiously, holding the ball high above her head, ready to throw.

Forrest was hiding behind the door, and grabbed her arms.

'No. . . .' Anne laughed. Struggling girlishly to break free, she moved forward a few paces, dropping the ball. They ended up against the coat rack where Anne had left the sash. Anne relaxed, looked round at him.

'Of course, I could always do this again,' Forrest said,

reaching for the sash, tying one of her wrists to a peg with it.

'I was joking the last time,' Anne said, not struggling. 'Pretending.'

'Were you?'

'Well, not entirely. . . .' Anne smiled, as the other wrist was tied. 'But enough,' she struggled slightly now, a little afraid. 'Come on, John. This really is enough.'

Forrest stepped back.

'Look at you,' he said, amused.

'I mean it. The game's over. Now untie me, please.'

'Tell you what. I bet this kind of thing never happened in Miss Palmer's time.'

Anne tried to stay serious but dissolved into laughter.

'Sex play in the school cloakroom of all things. . . .' Forrest did not finish. The sudden clatter of the cubicle window cut him off mid-sentence. 'That kid. That bloody kid . . . !' He ran to the door.

'John . . . ?' Anne called, helpless in her bindings.

But Forrest was already too far away to hear her.

At first he had no clue in which direction the girl had gone. Then one of the school gates clanged shut.

'Marian Price? I want to talk to you. . . .'

Forrest ran out into the lane, guessing that she must have headed for the pond and the trees.

'Marian?'

No answer. He walked around the edge of the pond, saw no one. Then he noticed something on the jetty, on the steps at the far end. Marian Price's coat.

Forrest stepped on to the wooden pier and began to walk along it, side-stepping the broken sections as he moved. At the end, he bent down and picked up the coat. He looked at it, then at the dark surface of the pond. And it was at that moment that there was a heavy, sickening, creaking sound, and the wooden structure began to give way.

Anne Forrest was working at the knots with her teeth, and had almost untied one wrist. She stopped when she heard

82

the sound of footsteps approaching along the corridor outside.

'John?'

Silence.

'Stupid man!' she said, under her breath. She began to tug again at the loosened knot.

The sound of footsteps was outside now, had reached the door. They stopped, and there was a long silence.

'Will you hurry up!' Anne called impatiently, still biting at the knot.

There was a click as the latch lifted on the batten-door, a slight creak as it was pushed open.

Anne looked up, and her eyes widened. 'No!' she cried, a loud frightened cry, that became a scream.

But Marian Price walked relentlessly forward, the bill-hook held at shoulder-height.

Afterwards, when she had done her work, Marian Price walked back down to the pond. She watched Forrest's body for a while, floating just beneath the surface, tangled up in the weeds. And then she returned to her classroom, picked up the blackboard eraser, and slowly obliterated the words she had written earlier:

MISS PALMER'S CLASS. AWARD GIVING DAY.

Martyn Forrester,
based on the television script by
Peter J. Hammond

LADIES' NIGHT

'The Hunters' Club? Never heard of it.'

'Oh yes, *I* remember it – went there as a guest once. Terrible place.'

'Not an experience to repeat, then?'

'Once was twice too many!'

That was the way it might be spoken of in the more serious clubs, say in lazy reminiscence over coffee at Boodle's, or in the bar at the Garrick, or even occasionally at the Athenaeum. And mild argument might break out on whether the Hunters' Club still existed.

'Went bust donkey's years ago, some fishy business with the finances.'

'No, it's still there.'

'Where?'

'Same place, I believe. That little cross-street, what d'you call it, impossible place to find.'

'Who would want to!'

'Surely they were bombed out in the war?'

'Just for a while. They went back, though.'

'It must have been after that that they went bust.'

'Obviously. If they did.'

'Closed down by the sanitary inspectors, I shouldn't wonder. Place was crammed with trophies, y'know, stuffed animal heads all going mouldy.'

'Oh, it's gone all right. . . .'

But it hadn't. . . .

If any interest still remained, they might go on to personalities. 'Suppose it must have had a lot of characters once, big-game wallahs who shot all those things?'

'Endangered plenty of species!'

'Anyway they'd all gone the time I visited. Nothing in the place but bank clerks.'

'Oh dear.'

'Sad in a way, to see that. A club's terminal decay.'

'No wonder the finances got fiddled.'

'No wonder at all.'

'Wait a minute, though – wasn't there some terrible fellow in charge? One of the legendary monsters?'

'That's right, old Waley.'

'Colonel Waley, the Hon Sec. He ran the whole shooting gallery.'

'I like that. Shooting gallery, very apt.'

'Show, then. Anyway, he ran it.'

'He must be dead.'

'Oh yes, years ago. He was as old as the hills.'

'You saw him?'

'That one time. Oh yes. Frightening sight. I don't know what effect he had on the enemy but . . . etcetera.'

'Yes, he'll be dead by now. Dead as mutton.'

'Or one of his poor old tigers. . . .'

But he wasn't. . . .

Colonel Gordon Roberts Waley woke from a nightmare that often visited him, with variations, and found himself shaking with emotion, all in a sweat. He had just been five years old and weeping from Nanny Speirs' smacks. He had infringed one of her many rules, the one against greed. He was hungry and had grabbed a second cake at teatime before she could stop him. So he was beaten soundly on his bared bottom until he cried out with pain. That didn't stop her. It just showed her she was doing it properly and she struck twice as hard. Till little Waley shrieked and writhed about.

Then a most strange thing happened, as it always did in

some form. The brutal, panting, red-fisted Nanny Speirs changed into a lithe, brown-skinned girl.

Little Waley had become big Waley. And what the girl was doing to him with her deft hands was what he desperately wanted. She hurt him. She clawed him and pummelled him and bit him. Sometimes she was a black girl, or sallow oriental. They always understood his needs, with canes and leather strips and the like to furnish exquisite pain. Once he found himself with a white girl, or nearly white, and made the dire mistake of talking to her. Pitying himself for never having had a mother because she died when he was born, and his father hating him for it, and then all the dreadful Nannies. Nanny Clark and Nanny Larcombe and then Nanny Speirs, who was worst of all. And the listening girl's lip curled as he wept in front of her.

That one was the worst form of the nightmare. Because the white, or nearly white, girl would suddenly burst out of her nakedness into being Nanny Speirs, all dressed up. Grabbing at him in a rage for speaking out of turn. And starting to do things to him that the girls did, and were paid to do. But he was a subaltern now, Indian Army, and Nanny Speirs had no business to be coming after him.

'Damn her to hell!'

Colonel Waley swung his thin legs off the bed on which he had been taking his rest. 'Damn her!' Not at all clear whether he meant Nanny Speirs, or whichever girl he had just dreamt about, or even his mother for having started the whole trouble by dying.

All good stuff for a headshrinker, he knew. Nowadays nobody would think twice before running off to dump it in the lap of a shrink. But at the age of eighty-three he wasn't going to start.

He would cope till the end. He had found his psychiatrists' couches in the brothels, a good many of them. And he was grateful for the wicked little brown hands.

It was over now, anyway. All but the dreams that came on Mondays.

'Why Mondays, Colonel?' whispered the imaginary shrink.

86

And Waley knew the answer without his help.

'Because,' he sneered at the imaginary charlatan, 'because Monday is Ladies' Night!'

He rose to ready himself for the evening.

In the bathroom he rinsed the sleep out of his eyes. He soaped well into the deep wrinkles that patterned his cheeks. Even Nanny Speirs would have approved. He rinsed again and soaped again from his shaving-mug. He stropped the blade of his fine old cut-throat razor and set to work on his chin and jowls.

He felt better now. He enjoyed the bathroom because it was his own, all its mahogany and heavy porcelain and brass fittings. Exclusive, en suite to the bedroom. He could still chuckle at the squalls when it was built, the outcry over the cost. A resigning matter, some members had screeched. But in the end it had been they who resigned, not he.

The last weak rays of autumn sunlight made yellow patches on the wall.

There was an interesting principle in yellowness, Colonel Waley had observed. It was said that the afternoon sun's was caused by the low altitude, by having to strike through a lot of discoloration in the atmosphere. But what was that discoloration? What about the yellowing of old ivory, like the handle of the razor in his hand? He bared his teeth, all of them his own, at the looking-glass. He saw the same colour. He glared, and found it in his eyeballs. Only a hint, not enough to signify ill-health but to confirm the principle. Age brought a sort of gilding, the touch of a gentle and considerate Midas.

To complete his toilet he applied a dash of lotion to his hair, still thick and slightly grey. He went at it vigorously with twin brushes. He trimmed his white military moustache into line.

Crisp shirt now, cufflinks, Club tie. He took his trousers from the press and tested the sharp seam like a blade before pulling them on. From the wardrobe he chose a smoking-jacket of dark wine velvet, and checked in the long glass as he fastened the froggings across his chest. Never do to get

87

them crooked. Once he had, and was shamed to find them so at the dinner-table.

Another glance round for anything else that he might have overlooked. Yes, cigarette-case, quickly into his pocket. It was a friendly room, with much of his life in it. The big Sandhurst passing-out photograph over the mantel-piece . . . groups snapped at the happy conclusion of pig-stickings and tiger-hunts, in India long ago . . . the portrait, kept in its silver frame for convention rather than sentiment, of Miss Yvonne Carswell whom he had almost married in 1938. A narrow escape. Perhaps for both of them.

He touched his fingers to an object of much greater beauty, his prized Purdey shotgun. It was held level on a simple rack formed of upturned deer-hooves, subscribed by one of its own victims. He kept it loaded. The world had become a rougher place and you never knew.

He stepped out, a fine erect figure, to begin his nightly tour of inspection.

You had to walk carefully along the passage and the gallery beyond, to avoid the horns. They projected from the walls everywhere. The huge antlers of caribou, the lesser ones of native deer, the red and the fallow and the roe. Even the tiny spikes of a muntjac. Every set had its plaque. 'A. R. Harris, Alberta, 1901' . . . 'Brig. Wills, Reay Forest, 1923' . . . 'Lt. Cuthbertson, Wildspitze, 1895'.

Through the years he had learned to adjust to their presence, to incline his head at the right moment. Others had not, particularly after dark and with drink taken. So that elks had claimed victims long after death, and at times the First Aid box had been heavily called upon.

In the gaps there were tails and small skulls, all with their plaques. The hooves of deer, mounted singly, thrust out like hands to be shaken. 'Found Brockenhurst, taken 5th Sept. 1929, G. S. Norton. . . .' They could catch at your clothing and damage it if you were not careful.

Waley reached the wide staircase that led down to the hall. Here there was space for the biggest antlers and also for the heads. Tigers and lions bared their dusty teeth. Half a dozen snarling wild boars, several wolves, a polar bear, a grizzly. The jaws of a pigmy hippopotamus, the quite hairless head of some sort of ape.

But no sign of a single human being. Not a member about. Colonel Waley peered down into the Den, the curtained-off nook enclosed by the staircase. The old leather chairs were all empty.

He could see Bundock the hall-porter in his mahogany lodge. The man was frowning and gnawing a pencil over a sheet of paper, trying to look usefully employed. More likely it was his football pools.

Colonel Waley didn't trust him.

Bundock was a toady. This pleased the club members. And when he treated them to minor insolence that was only another side of the toadying, that pleased them even more. It was what they expected of a real club porter, one of the things they paid for. Bundock was an institution.

He had been with the Hunters' Club for countless years, yet never demanded a rise in wages. He took what they gave him and was grateful. Waley was certain he must be stealing, but it was something else to catch him at it. Bundock was cunning.

The Colonel made his circuit of the hall. Everything seemed to be in its usual order.

Glass eyes stared down at him. The mounted heads of two Siberian tigers and several elands. More skulls and antlers of every huntable species. There were far too many, of course. Members had been presenting their trophies ever since the Club was founded in 1883, and would have felt deeply insulted to have them refused. When it happened there had been bitter rows. One member had notoriously borne back a dozen gigantic stuffed bears, Kodiaks, and demanded room for them. From time to time the mouldiest and worst-preserved specimens were discreetly removed to the cellar. This was now crammed like a charnel-house with superfluous horns, crocodiles by the score, the entire hide of a white rhinoceros and a three-legged baby elephant.

'Evening, Colonel.' The hall-porter had stuck his head out of his cubbyhole, between a hippopotamus-tail and the

dangling head of a gharial, the thin-snouted Indian crocodile, shot in 1932 by Sir A. Barlow.

'Evening, Bundock.'

'Have a nice rest, sir?'

Waley ignored this, with its snide implication that he had
needed it. He turned instead to the Visitors' Book to see if
anybody had been signed in. Nobody had, yet.

'Not many in tonight, sir.'

Waley glowered. 'Ladies' Night, there wouldn't be.'

He slammed the book down and scowled round the hall
for something else to meet his disapproval, preferably
something that was Bundock's fault.

'Mr Monks is in,' offered Bundock. 'In the Bar, I believe.'

Waley ignored this too. Monks was always in, and always
in the Bar. On the other hand he was a loyal member,
totally dependable. A sort of sound drunk –

Then Waley saw something terrible.

'Who moved Eustace?' he cried. He pointed at the hall
table, where a stuffed animal stood. An entire creature for
once, with a bristly hide and a long snout. It had two
dangling ears, one of them almost adrift. Its head was quite
naked. It had once been an aardvark.

'He shouldn't be there!' shouted Waley, and set about
moving the animal himself, by several meticulous inches.

'No, indeed he shouldn't –'

'Who did it?'

Bundock put on his frown. 'I can't think, Colonel. No, I
tell a lie, it must'a been that lady. Must'a bumped him with
her parcel.'

'Lady?'

Bundock sniffed. 'I've not seen her before. Mr Tripp's
wife. She's coming back to stay the night . . . with Mr
Tripp, of course.'

Waley nodded grimly, remembering the arrangement
made.

'She left this,' said Bundock. He held up, as incriminating
evidence, a stiffened paper bag with a string handle. Silver
and pink diagonal stripes enclosed the words 'Flemyng's
Sale'.

Waley waved it out of sight. He could hardly bear to look.

Two shocks in rapid succession.

Suddenly feeling his eighty-three years, he lowered himself into a big leather chair nearby, the one reserved by custom for him alone. His hands trembled with an almost electrical current of anger.

The big front door swung open.

Colonel Waley stiffened and stared, expecting the worst, the appearance of the offending female herself. But it was only Leach. A pale, scholarly person, not a popular member. He stood shaking the rain off his umbrella.

'Now, now, Mr Leach,' teased Bundock. 'Don't drown us! Like a puppydog shaking hisself!'

Waley noted the illiteracy, carefully calculated no doubt to make the members feel superior. It worked on Leach. He grinned and thrust his umbrella into the great bronze stand in quite a manly way. And with a greeting to the Colonel set off towards the cloakroom.

'Leach!' Waley's voice halted him. Waley's beckoning finger summoned him back.

Leach remembered. He trotted apologetically over to the hall table and patted the stuffed aardvark, Eustace, on its bald head. Waley grunted his approval.

A little ritual observed.

Few of the members needed prompting. When Summerland and Greenhow came in shortly afterwards, though chatting together about overheads and interest rates, both paused to pat Eustace's naked pate. An automatic civility, just as they bade the Colonel himself a good evening.

He watched them as they went off towards the lower stairs, to the cloakroom and Ablutions. Sound fellows both. The sort to value the Club and everything that was special about it.

The Ablutions, for instance. A collection of sanitary equipment that would delight any connoisseur. All of it fitted when the Club was built, and quite unchanged. A row of massive, ancient porcelain urinals, vast washbowls and water-closets with mahogany doors. Shining brass everywhere. There was something strong and masculine about the Ablutions.

The women's Ablutions were very different. A disused pantry at the far end of the Club, converted with a quantity of pink plastic. Almost a year ago now. It would soon be the first anniversary of Ladies' Night. . . .

Mrs Evelyn Tripp did not trust her husband. That was why she had called at the Hunters' Club early that afternoon, ostensibly to leave a parcel with the hall-porter but actually to make sure she had been booked in.

Since then she had made a great many purchases at the autumn sales. She drove with them in a taxi to her husband's City office, to pick him up and give him no chance to weaken.

For the whole year of Ladies' Nights he had avoided asking her to the Club. The place where he lunched and dined several times a week, and quite often stayed overnight.

She sat impatiently in the taxi. An edgy, uneasy woman in her forties, with a strident edge to her voice as she ordered the man to wait. Her husband, James Tripp, appeared at last. His eyes seemed to wince behind his glasses when he encountered the parcels.

'You mean to take all those to the Club?'

'Where else?' said Mrs Tripp. . . .

Colonel Waley had found a natural victim. This was the girl-friend of one of the younger members, an uncouth person named Binns who described himself as a store manager. She was a pretty, plump little thing and very timid. On a previous occasion Waley had discovered his smile frightened her out of her wits. So he smiled at her.

'Oh!' She was all apology. 'I'm Ann . . . Ann Holroyd.'

'I know who you are,' Waley said patiently. 'We met last time. You know me.'

'Oh yes – Colonel – oh yes –'

She looked desperately round at Binns, who was grinning

self-consciously as he gave the stuffed aardvark two or three pats on the head.

'Oh yes –' she gulped, 'oh yes, you have to –'

She made a dive to do the same.

'No!' roared Waley. 'Not you!'

She nearly fainted.

Waley twisted his face into a smile of forgiveness. 'You're a – you're a guest,' he explained. 'You mustn't pat Eustace.'

'I'm sorry, I'm sorry –!'

She was actually wringing her hands. And her dolt of a boy-friend stood by and did nothing. Waley decided to rub it in.

'When's the wedding?' he demanded.

'Eh?' She goggled at him.

'To young Binns there? When are you getting married?'

'I – I – we don't –' Nothing could be further from her thoughts, of course.

'Take the plunge!' ordered Waley.

She bleated 'I – I'm just here for supper.' She looked wildly at Binns but got no help, just more feeble grinning. Panic struck. She was off, little feet carrying her at quite a clip in the direction of the Ablutions.

'Not that way!' yelled Waley.

And Bundock shouted from his cubbyhole: 'Can't go down there, miss!'

'Oh – oh, sorry –'

Like a small hunted thing, she swung back and veered towards the curtained nook at the foot of the stairs.

'Stop her!' howled Waley.

Binns started calling to her, and Bundock burst from his lodge. 'No ladies in the Den, miss! It's a rule!'

'I – I forgot –'

Bundock pointed firmly. 'Ladies' Ablutions through there, miss.'

He watched her scuttle gratefully off by a side passage. And turned to grin at Binns. 'They've got to learn, haven't they, sir?'

'Right, Mr Bundock.'

Colonel Waley watched the young tradesman make off

towards the real Ablutions. A wretch, he decided, who let his girl down and then turned cocky about it. Crawling to Bundock. *Mister* Bundock! Come to think of it, that provided a useful distinction. Proper fellows called Bundock just Bundock. But there were those who called him Mister, presumably because they were scared of him in some way . . . scared of what he stood for. Bundock the Institution.

Colonel Waley lay back in his chair. He hadn't really enjoyed that little scene as much as he expected. The Holroyd girl was hardly worth tormenting.

He dozed for a little.

When he looked up again he was rewarded. The Partridges had arrived.

Alan Partridge, an executive of some kind, was scribbling in the Visitors' Book. His wife stood watching, a young woman of about thirty with a curiously sensual face and what Waley had seen described as bedroom eyes. There was an unease in her that stirred Waley's curiosity. Perhaps her undergarments were too tight. More likely it was her husband's fault. Probably couldn't satisfy her. So he'd bought her that silver-fox coat instead, nearly down to her ankles, even if it meant a second mortgage.

'You always have to sign me in?' Yes, a husky peevishness in the voice.

'Rules,' said Partridge, and turned genially to Waley. 'Evening, Colonel.'

Waley considered. 'Forgotten something, Partridge?'

'I don't think so. Oh –'

Following Waley's nod, he turned to pat Eustace's head.

'Why d'you have to do that?' she asked. 'Another rule?'

'A tradition,' said Waley.

She turned. Yes, they were bedroom eyes all right. A score of years ago, or less, a lot less, he might have attempted her.

'Oh?' she said. 'You just do it?'

'Yes.'

'No reason?'

Amusement in her voice. Partridge looked alarmed.

'Oh yes,' said Colonel Waley, 'a very sound reason. This, madam, is the Hunters' Club.'

A lazy smile now. 'Yes, I know.'

Waley gave her the facts. 'Eustace there was a young aardvark, a harmless eater of ants. He was mistakenly shot during a big-game hunt by Major Wilfred Dawes in 1911. In Southern Rhodesia as it then was. Eustace . . . was not big game.'

Still the lazy smile.

'No,' she agreed.

'A sad error,' said Waley. 'We honour him still with our sympathy.'

'Well!' She gave a little laugh. 'I like that, it's quite fun.'

'Fun!'

Waley stiffened all the way up his spine. Partridge struggled to help. 'I suppose – that is, old traditions must get to seem a bit – well, I mean –'

But his wife wasn't taking the hint of danger. She was turning to give Eustace a closer look. Waley raised a warning hand and Bundock bobbed his head from his cubbyhole.

'All right,' she said, 'I'm not going to touch it.' Making a show of inspecting the creature and taking her time over it. She wrinkled her nose disparagingly. 'Not very well stuffed, is it?'

Waley couldn't resist that.

'If you want to get well stuffed, madam,' he ground out, 'you want to find somebody who can stuff you properly!'

She whisked round.

Her mouth was open and he saw she was actually blushing.

'Poor Eustace,' finished Waley, 'was unlucky in that too.'

A neat turn-off.

'Yes, poor old thing,' mumbled Partridge, as if he hadn't noticed. Or was pretending he hadn't.

She started away from them across the hall, pulling the silver-fox drapes tightly round her.

'Decent coat you've put on her back, Partridge. I like a

95

bit of fur on a woman. Not that damned battery kind, real fur shot with a gun.'

Partridge nodded dumbly.

'Alan!'

She stood waiting. When Partridge joined her there was a spat of furious whispers. She was hissing and accusing. Waley caught a moan from Partridge about it being business, and remembered him tagging after Greenhow trying to get some sort of introduction out of him.

'No, now! This minute!'

She swung round and made for the doorway, keeping her head high and her eyes averted from Colonel Waley. Leaving her husband to follow her. He grinned feebly at Waley as he passed.

'Sorry, Colonel, we have to leave after all. Something I forgot. Er – goodnight.'

He scuttled out after her.

Waley sighed. Considering some of the men they got, he could almost pity these women. . . .

There was a strict rule against females in the Bar. The nearest they were permitted to get was the Small Lounge, a cramped, bleak annexe. It was there that Binns had taken his tremulous little girl-friend.

In the Bar members watched appalled as Henry the barman mixed the cocktail she had asked for, a lurid mixture of red and yellow juices called a tequila-sunrise, and bore it next door with a beer for Binns.

'See that?' said Monks. 'My God!'

'Women!' said Colonel Waley.

He beckoned Monks over from his habitual bar-stool, to join Summerland and himself at a quiet table. This constituted an informal committee-meeting, or it would when young Foss the treasurer turned up. Committees and quorums were only what Colonel Waley declared them to be.

'Subject – Ladies' Night,' announced Waley. 'Had 'em for nearly a year, full trial period. It's been enough.'

'Every damn Monday, that's more'n enough!' Monks

agreed, spilling beer in his vehemence. He always drank beer, from some delusion of economy, but in quantities that had made him perfectly rotund and seemed to have diluted his wits. He called himself a company director, which of course meant nothing.

'It was just to attract more members,' pointed out Summerland, a retired architect who must have designed some dull buildings in his time.

'We didn't get more members,' said Monks.

'We got the women!' said Colonel Waley.

He gazed round the Bar. It was the warm heart of the Club, a place of tranquillity and good fellowship. The old Nile crocodile grinning in his place above the bottles, the tall dark paintings of stags being torn by hounds, and Bengal tigers despatched from elephant-back. The head of a finely-whiskered gnu above the doorway.

'I found hairpins,' said Monks thoughtfully. 'Stayed over one night. Hairpins. And a sanitary . . . whatsit. Bloody knocking shop.'

'They're allowed to stay the night,' said Summerland.

'What?'

'Members' wives, on Mondays.'

Monks looked astonished.

'Got to be married,' said Colonel Waley. 'I make sure of that.'

Monks had dropped into one of his vaguenesses. 'I never knew –'

'It was voted,' said Summerland.

'Not by me!'

'You missed it.'

'Where was I?' Monks was struggling with his memory. Waley gave him no help. Monks' shaky recollection had often come in useful, his name appearing on the minutes of many meetings he had not attended. It saved time.

'They bring all their things,' said Waley. 'Like that woman tonight, even her shopping, foisted it on poor Bundock!'

'No!' Monks was shocked.

'Relate everything to themselves, that's all they do. All

they're able to do. Giggling and sniffling!' Faint female sounds from the Small Lounge prompted this. The tequila-sunrise must be having its effect. 'They've no soundness in them,' cried Waley. 'No respect, no understanding of rules, or love of – of tradition! I want them out!'

The Tripps had arrived. James Tripp had fled straight to the Ablutions to escape the awful embarrassment of parcels. As his wife struggled with them, Bundock approached with the package she had left earlier.

'There we are, madam,' said Bundock. 'One more to add to your little collection. My word, we have been busy!'

It nettled her.

'Well, *I* have. Don't know about you.'

'Ha ha, get as good as I give, eh madam? Very nice. A bit of repartee makes the world go round.' Bundock swivelled on his heels as Tripp returned. 'Aha, the lord and master. Key to the bridal suite, sir. Number 4.'

'Thank you, Mr Bundock.' Tripp stood frozen-faced, staring at the parcels as if he had never seen such things in his life.

'Can you manage, sir and madam? No, the answer to that is you can't. Let me give a hand –'

Bundock seized some and started towards the stairs.

'Is he after a tip?'

Her hoarse whisper must have reached Bundock, Tripp knew.

'All this performance –' she added.

Bundock had heard and was offended. At the excuse of the front door opening he dropped the parcels and hurried to greet the newcomer. 'Ah, Mr Foss – the Colonel wants you, sir. Very important. In the Bar, sir.'

'Right, just shed my coat.' The slight, pale young man shot worriedly away.

Bundock made no further attempt to help the Tripps. He retired to his lodge and settled down to read a newspaper.

'You hurt his feelings,' said Tripp.

'What?'

'Our hall-porter isn't supposed to carry things. He was doing you a favour.'

There was nothing for it now. He started gathering up the packages Bundock had dumped. They were of awkward shapes and surprising weight. Two slipped out of his hands. He was trying to catch them when Foss reappeared, almost running. Tripp could have died of shame.

'Oh – good evening, Foss. Er, this is my wife.'

To his relief Foss didn't stop. With a quick 'Evening!' he disappeared along the passage.

'He had a handbag!'

'It wasn't a handbag,' Tripp explained patiently. 'It was a Filofax.'

Sniffing for signs of degeneracy now. And there would be plenty of other things for her to pick at, he knew. On the way upstairs she was pop-eyed at the heads and antlers.

'Good God, I didn't notice all these this afternoon! There were no lights on.'

'Rather impressive,' said Tripp carefully.

'Impressive? It's obscene!'

Tripp glanced nervously about, but there was nobody to have heard her. Bundock was out of sight in his cubicle.

'Most of the collection dates back to –' he began formally, but suddenly he couldn't remember. A blockage, perhaps, against telling her anything. 'Dates back – er, quite a while.'

His wife's mouth twisted. 'I can see that,' she said. 'Everything's filthy.'

Hugging her parcels to her, she climbed on. She reached the gallery and turned to look down, lips still curled.

'So this is it,' she said, 'your home from home!'

The bedroom was cold and gloomy. Two heavy old mahogany beds stood well separated, with a marble-topped table between them. There were photographs of former members with their feet on dead animals, but only a single set of antlers. 'Thank God for that at least,' said Evelyn. 'Thought I'd wake in the night and find a stuffed warthog looking at me.'

She looked sourly about. Everything in the room had

been put there by people who didn't care, for the use of others who didn't care either. Most of it belonged to some time in the past, like oddments from a junk-shop. Bronze ornaments in the form of rampant lions and tigers, but dull, badly made ones. The ancient gas-fire had cracked elements, and on the mantelpiece above it stood two brass candlesticks, long unpolished.

There was a big armchair at least, covered in withered leather. Seeing nowhere else to put the parcels, they piled them there.

They provided the only touch of colour in the room.

She sat down on one of the beds, which was as hard as she expected.

'Why?'

'What do you mean, why?'

'You know perfectly well what I mean why, James. Let's change it to how. How can you possibly choose to spend nights in a room like this?'

'It's not meant to be luxury.'

'It succeeds.'

He had to choose words carefully or they would be picked on, he could see. 'It's an amenity provided by the Club. Useful if I'm at work too late to get back to Amersham.'

'Well. At least I imagined you in comfort.'

'It's cheap.'

'Oh, good. Saving us money to take a holiday together!'

They had no plans to do so.

'It's sufficient.'

'You know, James, you never cease to surprise me. Isn't that said to be one of the essentials of a happy marriage? That must be what we've got!'

He turned to the window, refusing to let himself react to her. A vista of dirty stuccoed wall with fly-posters on it, not enough to take his attention away. The odds were fifty-fifty, he calculated, that she would now start on the subject of children. It was her way of talking about sex. She was obsessed.

'D'you think I'd have been a bad mother, James?' He was right, here we go! 'At least I'd have had something to do, it would have kept me out of the Community Association and the Old People's Welfare, bless them. If you'd run under a bus I could even have been a single-parent family, and tried that. Just one would have done. One little one. Just to know.'

Just one little one. That unborn, unconceived baby was a frequent visitor at recrimination-time. From the way she allowed herself to dote on him, and speculate on the future he might have had, Tripp had the feeling he would have grown up to be fairly nasty. So, all considered, it was just as well.

It was her own fault, anyway. The daughter of a senior partner, she had picked on him to marry as if she had a right. A marriage of convenience, or despair, when she was already too old.

'I should have married somebody else, is that what you're thinking, James?' It always startled him when she did that. 'People who are close often think the same things at the same time, don't they, James? So we have that at least, our only bit of closeness. Better make the most of it.'

'If you say so.'

Tripp tried thinking something deliberately, to see if she would pick it up. The thought that she was an idle bitch who had never had a job, or any life of her own, just enjoyed swanning round Amersham as a lady of leisure –

'Is there anywhere I can wash?'

He smiled to himself. No telepathy that time, my dear.

'Oh yes – the Ladies' Ablutions.'

'The *what*?'

'I'll show you. Along the passage and down the back stairs.'

'In the servants' quarters?'

'May have been once. Quite nice now . . . I believe.'

They arranged to meet in the Small Lounge, next to the Bar. He gave her particular directions. It was important that she should not go to the Bar itself, which did not admit ladies. . . .

In the Bar, Colonel Waley sat slumped in his chair waiting

for Foss. He had been appalled to watch two more tequila-sunrises carried into the Small Lounge for that silly young girl, with what results he could only imagine. Beside him, Summerland and Monks had gone maudlin, both on the subject of women.

'But my second,' mumbled Monks, 'she just ran off, the cow! Left me high and dry. Not a word. One day I met her in the street – with her new feller –' Finding he had slopped his drink on himself, he wiped it off. '– I said "Have you shown him all your tricks – that you got up to with me?" ' Monks chuckled. 'She didn't like that!'

Summerland was shaking his head, far away. 'I never felt a sense of loss. . . .'

'Then,' said Monks, 'Then I said to *him*, "Has she shown you all her little tricks – that she –" '

He spilled more of his drink in the excitement of his recollection.

'Just . . . of freedom,' mused Summerland.

Monks was dabbing at his waistcoat. ' "Got up to – got up to –" '

'The day after her funeral,' said Summerland, 'not till then. . . .'

Monks finished, 'Anyway, I never paid *her* any money!'

'. . . And the feeling of waste. My whole life in a sense. You understand?'

Summerland turned to Waley, who sat regarding both of them with contempt.

'You're bloody fools,' declared Waley. 'Ah, here he comes. Foss!'

Foss joined them, panting slightly. And Monks generously called for more drinks, guessing they would be slated to the Colonel.

'Now we're a decent quorum,' said Waley. 'Mr Treasurer, can we afford to abolish Ladies' Night?'

Foss blinked. He picked at the pages of his Filofax. The more he had discovered about the past finances of the Club, the more dreadful they seemed. A long history of waste. Dud investments and mysterious loans, the disappearance of assets. Most of it appeared to be Colonel Waley's fault.

'Well . . . I've tossed a few ideas round,' he said.

'Come on, young Foss!'

But it was Monks who leaned across the table with the air of a man to whom everything had suddenly become simple. 'Listen,' he said. He chuckled. 'There's something we always overlook.'

'What's that?'

'The Bequest!' beamed Monks.

Foss glanced at Waley. He said, 'The Calloway Bequest?'

'Right! You'd forgotten that, hadn't you, laddie? Old Calloway's entire fortune, every rupee he grabbed out of India – all left to the Club!'

Waley's eyes were on the table. Summerland murmured 'It *was* . . . most generous.'

'Well, then? We've still got that behind us!'

'Not exactly,' said Foss quietly.

'Why not!'

Foss tried to think of a way of putting it. 'Well . . . the Bequest was eaten into a lot. Through the years.'

Monks stared at him. 'But . . . it's a bloody fortune!'

'It's gone,' snapped Waley.

'What?'

'All gone, Monks!' Waley had no intention of having the matter pursued. 'Carry on, Foss – next?'

Foss licked his lips. 'We could merge.'

'With another club?' Summerland was shocked.

'Never!' said Waley.

'Bantam's have been putting out feelers.'

'Bantam's!'

'Surely that's a mixed club?' said Summerland. 'Women as full members!'

Foss could see from their appalled faces that it was a non-starter. He tried again.

'Raise the subs?'

Monks jumped. 'No!'

'Sell off part of the premises? The big lounge – the cold lounge as everybody calls it, rightly in my view. And of course the library. They're hardly ever used.'

'Foss,' scowled Waley, 'if your father had heard that

suggestion from the lips of his son —!'

Foss suppressed a sigh. His father's ghost was always being summoned up as a notable Hunter, yet the nearest he had actually got to it was being invited on occasional grouse-shoots by business acquaintants. But he had been Treasurer of the Club for a long time before he died, and had seen to the auditing of Waley's accounts. These honours had fallen to his son —

Suddenly, the sound of argument. Half of it shrill, female.

Colonel Waley was on his feet instantly.

A woman in a woollen twin-set, somebody he had never set eyes on, was squabbling with the barman. Leach and Greenhow looked on, shocked.

'Madam!'

Waley started towards her, his voice terrible.

'What are you doing here?'

'Looking for my husband,' she answered plainly. 'What's the matter?'

'Didn't he tell you? No women in the Bar!' Then, suspiciously, 'What's his name?'

'Tripp. Mr James Tripp.'

She stood up boldly to his rage, and now to his accusing finger as well.

'You're her! You're the parcel woman!'

Waley pointed to the door to order her out, and in the same moment Tripp appeared and froze there in horror.

'Tripp!'

'Colonel — Colonel Waley?'

'Show your wife to the Small Lounge.'

A man in agony, Tripp made an unfamiliar move. He tried to put his arm round her and guide her in a dignified manner. She shook herself free. He grabbed at her. They disappeared in an unseemly, muttering wrangle.

Waley and the rest listened keenly. It sounded as if she had deliberately disobeyed Tripp, but he was now reduced to pleading with her.

Colonel Waley clamped Foss's arm in a fierce grip.

'Listen to it, young Foss! That's why I never married. Oh,

I've had women – more women that I care to think about. But I never married 'em, never once. Use 'em and chuck 'em, that's what to do. Eh, Monks, don't you wish you had?'

'By God, yes,' mumbled Monks.

'Summerland?'

Summerland nodded.

Foss, who was closest, saw a strange look come into the old man's eyes. Almost a light. It was inspirational, he supposed. It was how Waley produced his effect on people. He could feel it himself, this very moment.

'Foss, you can forget your calculations. I'm going to save this club. I'll do it myself.'

'How?' whispered Foss.

'The old Hunters.'

That was nonsense, and Foss suddenly feared for him. As the grip on his arm tightened, he shot an uneasy glance at the others. 'They're all gone, Colonel,' he said.

'Men like your father.'

'He's dead.'

Waley shook his head. 'No! They had families, they were all strong, potent men. Fecund. I'll write to their sons, their grandsons. I'll appeal to them for their fathers' sake!'

'We've tried that,' muttered Summerland.

Colonel Waley smiled. 'Not the way I'm going to do it.'

'Well, I suppose there's no harm –'

And Monks chimed in, 'Have a go, Colonel!'

There was a swelling rumble of agreement from the rest. Even from Leach, who rarely joined in anything. Only Foss hung back, his hands clamped to his Filofax as a talisman of good sense and safety.

'They'll rally round, I know it! It's in the blood, you see. It's in *your* blood, young Foss, don't you feel it?'

Foss managed some sort of smile. It must have been sufficient because Waley beamed and turned expansively to the barman.

'The prime old malt, Henry – for all the gentlemen here –!'

The Tripps sat in the Small Lounge at separate tables made out of elephants' feet. Binns had just taken his girl away, looking as if she had been crying a lot and staggering against him slightly.

Evelyn Tripp could hear the noises from the Bar, the enthusiasm and self-congratulation led by Colonel Waley.

'He's mad, you know. As a hatter.'

'Oh no,' said Tripp. 'It's just his manner. I mean, he's a terrific character when you get to know him. In a sense he *is* the Hunters' Club. Would you guess that he's over eighty years old?'

'He looks it. Every minute.'

'Well –' Tripp was finding it hard to keep up the reasonable persuasion. 'Well, he is. But he's very sharp.'

'He certainly was with me!'

'We've dealt with that. But if you could hear some of his stories – I mean reminiscences, because they're all true –'

'Poor James!'

'What?'

'I can imagine you lapping them up.'

Tripp was suddenly full of foreboding. 'Perhaps we should leave.'

'Now?'

'Yes.'

'Drive all the way home? Oh, no. I've always wanted to know what it was like.'

'Well, now you do.'

'Not yet.' She gave him an icy smile and brightened her eyes at him in that way she had. 'Besides, I'm hungry. . . .'

The Coffee Room was long and dark and rather splendid. It had a high ornate ceiling, though this was much discoloured through time. There were elegant fluted columns, in need of repair. On the walls were tall oil-paintings of eminent past members, mostly in Edwardian clothes and uniforms, holding hunting-rifles. And many animal heads and skulls, and fine sets of antlers.

A long table ran down the centre of the room. Places had been set but they were so far unoccupied. By the walls there were smaller tables. At one of these Binns was trying to get some food into his tipsy girl-friend. He had made the mistake of ordering wine and she had suddenly gone into a giggly stage.

The Tripps sat at another side-table, the only others in the room. A waiter had just removed their soup-plates.

'You know what that was made of?'

'What?'

'That so-called soup. The nastiest commercial powder, with a few bits added.'

'You ate it.'

'Hardly any. Didn't you notice? You don't notice things if you don't want to, do you, James?'

'I quite enjoyed it,' said Tripp. He sat breaking his bread-roll into tiny, equal pieces.

His wife shivered.

'I can feel a draught.' Tripp ignored this. 'Why couldn't we sit in the middle? There's nobody there.'

'These are the guest tables,' said Tripp.

'Another of your rules?'

He explained quietly. 'It's the custom . . . in the Coffee Room, to seat guests at the side tables.'

She bridled. 'Coffee Room? Why aren't we in the dining-room?'

'This *is* the dining-room. It's *called* the Coffee Room.'

'How silly!'

'It's so in many of the older clubs.' Tripp permitted himself a tiny smile.

She frowned.

'When you come here on your own . . . you can dine in the middle?'

'Yes.'

Tripp began to pray that the meal would be served quickly and over before Colonel Waley and the others appeared. She was staring critically about.

'It's a depressing room,' she said.

'I don't find it so.'

'All those skulls and —'

He was not to be spared. He could hear their voices in the

107

passage, Waley's carrying loudest as usual. '. . . But nowadays a lot of young fellows have never even handled a gun, let alone possess one. And that, y'see, does something to their characters.'

As soon as he entered the room Waley caught sight of Evelyn Tripp. His face hardened. Ignoring her presence he made for his place at the head of the long table. The other members waited deferentially for him to be seated.

'A dinosaur!'

Evelyn Tripp's harsh whisper rang out clearly. Shocked faces turned at the long table. They could hardly believe what they heard.

But she was not looking at Waley. She pointed vaguely at one of the skulls on the wall.

'There, that one! I'm sure it is. A something-or-other-o-don, there's one in the Natural History Museum.' She turned to the shuddering Tripp. 'Now don't tell me they hunted those! The Club doesn't go *that* far back.'

Tripp whispered desperately 'You're mistaken. It's a kind of goat.'

'Oh? I'll just take a closer look.' She half rose from her chair and made a performance of screwing up her eyes and peering across. 'You're quite right. I can see a date. 1925.'

She glanced towards the long table.

Waley had his eyes on the ceiling, frowning as if in deep thought. But the working of his jaws showed his anger.

As she sat again Tripp splashed wine from a decanter into both their glasses. He glanced at his watch. 'I wish they'd hurry.'

'You're hungry too?'

'Er – yes. Quite.'

Colonel Waley suddenly snapped his fingers and called across, 'Tripp!'

Galvanised, Tripp swung round and nearly fell off his chair.

'Yes, Colonel?'

Waley beckoned. Tripp hurried across to him, apologies already forming on his lips. Waley put a hand on his shoulder and drew him close.

'We've been talking in the Bar,' he murmured.

Tripp gulped.

'Doing some planning, Tripp. On the future of the Club.'

'Er – planning?'

Waley actually smiled. 'We're going to need your expertise.' He spoke even more softly. 'Young Foss there, good trier, needs a helping hand. Depend on you?'

Tripp could hardly believe it.

'Of course, Colonel. I'd – I'd be only too glad – in any way –'

'Good man!' Waley clapped him on the shoulder in the friendliest way, then caught him by the sleeve. 'Your wife,' he breathed, 'looks a bit done up. See she gets some rest.'

'I will. Oh, I will indeed.'

Grateful for Waley's kindly nod, he started back to the side table. That had been the touch of a great man, he decided, the forebearance of a natural leader. It was the quality that drew people to the Colonel. In the Army the men must have worshipped him –

He found his wife hot with suspicion. She had heard nothing.

'What was all that about?'

Tripp smiled. 'Just Club business.'

Waiters became active, taking orders at the long table, bringing puddings to Binns and his girl, the main course to the two Tripps.

Evelyn poked hers about. 'James, what is this?'

'Boeuf bourguignon.'

'It's mince!'

'It's always like this.'

'If you were offered it at home you'd refuse to eat it. Wouldn't you?'

'Keep your voice down –'

'No talking in class!' she snapped. 'That's what it's all about – you're back at school! And all this – slops and gravy and custard and burnt offerings – it's school food! That's what they say and they're right. Prep school. Eat it all up or go to Matron – and God knows who Matron is in *this* place! Go to the Headmaster and p'raps he'll be cross or p'raps he'll just pat you on the head and say "Never mind, you did your best . . . Tripp!" '

The way she rapped out his name was so like Waley's summons that Tripp flushed.

'D'you know what the Colonel said about you?'

'What?'

'He was concerned. He thought you looked tired.'

She only glared. 'Oh, did he!'

A typically petty response, thought Tripp. He could hardly look at her. He turned instead to where Colonel Waley was presiding over the long table. Any other night he would have been sitting with them. He tried to listen to what Waley was saying.

'Now, gentlemen – to recap. Our task is this, to remake the Club in the image of its founders. As they, the old Hunters, would have wished.'

He raised his head and called across, 'Can you hear me, Tripp? You're included in this. Just because you've chosen to sit over there –' Faces turned and there were chuckles. '– doesn't mean you're out of it! Now, some of you may never have had a gun in your hands. No matter, not your fault if you missed a war. But you were drawn to this club because you recognised something in it, and something in you. Now I want your help. You are Hunters. We want . . . more Hunters!'

'Hear, hear!' called Monks, and started rapping his knuckles on the table. The rest followed suit.

'Bravo!' cried Summerland.

'We can do without clerks and counter-jumpers,' declared Waley. 'And money-grubbers and pipsqueaks!'

His listeners were instantly sure they were in none of these categories. Only little Ann Holroyd, woozy with the mixture of tequila and wine, prodded her boy-friend and giggled, because the old term was new to her, 'Jack, are you a pipsqueak?'

Binns shushed her.

'I think we know who we *don't* want,' continued Waley. 'We've got to decide who we *do* want!'

More enthusiastic rapping on the long table.

Before Binns could stop her, little Ann joined in, rapping her pudding-spoon and squeaking with laughter. This time Waley turned in fury.

'Get that girl out of here – she's drunk!'

Binns jumped to his feet to obey. He hauled Ann out of her chair.

'Let go of me –!'

'Out!' roared Colonel Waley.

Binns dragged her through the doorway, sagging helplessly in his arms and starting to hiccup.

'They can't take liquor,' remarked Waley, as he calmed. 'It's the extra fat in their bodies, soaks it up. Now, as I was saying –'

Evelyn Tripp hissed, '*They*? Who did he mean – *they*?'

Tripp pointed frantically to her plate. 'Have you finished? Let's go.'

But she cut him off with a gesture. She wanted to hear more.

Foss was asking helpfully, 'How do we – how do we recognise a Hunter?'

Waley smiled forgivingly. 'Your father wouldn't have put that question, young Foss.'

'Yes, well – after all, he –'

'He'd have *known*. Can I tell you a little story? Some of you've heard it before but –'

'Go on, go on,' cried Monks.

Waley leaned back in his chair. 'It was back in 1936. I was quite a young fellow then, on attachment in Berlin. I was invited to go shooting in East Prussia. My host was a chappie called Hermann Goering.'

He paused, knowing this usually sharpened interest. It did Evelyn's.

'He had his problems,' Waley continued. 'He was married to a Swedish woman, a neurotic invalid. But he'd just been appointed Reichsmarschall and he was celebrating. We shot 17 boar that day. Towards the end . . . I was standing near old Hermann when a huge tusker broke cover. Straight at us. He raised his gun – and it jammed!'

'My God,' said Monks.

Waley smiled. 'Mine didn't. Hermann turned to me and he said "Danke, mein Jäger." Those very words. Thank you, my Hunter.'

Those at the long table were deeply moved. The quantity of malt whisky they had drunk in the Bar helped.

Evelyn could hardly speak. She turned to Tripp and demanded, 'Did you hear that?'

'Yes.' He had been moved too.

'He saved Goering's life!'

It came out of her as a hoarse cry. She was on her feet, yelling on over the spluttered protests of Monks and Greenhow: 'D'you think that was a good deed, all of you?'

'You don't understand!' protested Summerland.

And passionately from Monks, 'They *never* understand!'

Even Foss's pale face had grown heated as he cried, 'It was a matter of honour!'

Evelyn spat it out, 'And what did you do for Hitler?'

The very name quietened them. Uncertainty crept in and they looked to Colonel Waley. He stood to face her and grind out his reply:

'Hitler, madam, was a vulgarian!'

So complete a riposte delighted them all. Knuckles rapped the long table loudly. She had to shout over the noise.

'Colonel – I thought you were senile!'

'Shame, madam,' cried Summerland. 'Oh, shame!'

'I was wrong! You're plain mad! You've been mad all your life!'

There was uproar.

They were all on their feet, shaking their fists. Waley himself pointed a shaking hand at her, trying to mouth a denunciation. But this time words failed him and he slumped back into his chair. He seemed on the verge of a stroke.

There was a rush. Evelyn found herself surrounded. She was being thrust violently towards the door by jostling, yelling men. Red, furious faces surrounded her.

'Foul-mouthed, vicious –!'

'Bitch!'

'Disgusting – slanderous –!'

'Throw her out!'

'Out! Out! Out!'

Her husband was beside her, but only to assist in her removal. In a moment they were both ejected into the passage, and he was clinging to her, not to support her she realised but to prevent her returning to the Coffee Room.

'I'm going back in there!'

'Evelyn – no!'

She tore herself free.

'Have pity, Evelyn!'

'You didn't stand up for me!'

'How could I? The things you were saying!' He moaned. 'You know what this means, don't you? I may have to resign.'

'I should hope so!'

'How can I face them?'

She stared at him, mouth open. 'You mean you'd *want* to – to come back to this – this awful – and that old – old – and those dreadful, lunatic, idiot – oh!'

Tripp drew himself up.

'It's my club,' he said.

She gave a grunt of disgust and marched off along the passage. He noted bitterly that she knew exactly which way to go. She had always had a sound sense of direction. Getting lost and wandering into the Bar had all been a pretence, just to start unpleasantness.

All his nerves were tightening with hatred as he followed her. . . .

Bundock had heard the distant shouting. It had begun while he was helping Binns and his sozzled bit of jail-bait to a taxi.

He peered up from his cubbyhole and saw the Tripps hurrying along the gallery, one after the other. Short, barking words passed between them. Not what you'd call a loving couple, reckoned Bundock.

It might yet be an interesting evening. . . .

In the Coffee Room, Colonel Waley was making a remarkable recovery, fighting off compassionate hands. For a moment they had feared for him.

'I'm all right, I've survived worse things!' he snorted. 'Bring me pen and paper!'

Foss grabbed his Filofax.

'Not that stuff, Foss! Proper pen! Club paper!'

The members looked at each other. They knew what this meant. . . .

Tripp closed the bedroom door and stood with his back against it, as if he had no wish to come further in. Like everything else now, the room was being changed by her presence and made wrong and ridiculous. It had been plain and adequate but not any longer. He tried for a moment to get into her mind – not by telepathy but by imagining. She might have been pleased if the room had demonstrated luxury. Those swagged curtains that looked like knickers, which she had hung all over their house in Amersham. Wall-to-wall carpets, colour television, an automatic tea-maker.

If they telepathised now – was there really such a word, telepathised? – if she could read his thoughts she would throw herself on her knees before him and beg his forgiveness. And cry in terror.

Instead he watched her light a cigarette. At least her hands were trembling.

'It may not even have been true,' he said.

'What?'

'That anecdote.'

'About Goering?'

'Yes. He changes it.'

She drew heavily on the cigarette. 'It doesn't matter. They all *wanted* it to be true, that's what I hated.'

After a moment he said, 'Why did you come here?'

She put weariness in her voice, he could hear her doing it. 'I wanted to go to the sales. It fitted in.'

'Oh, did it?'

'And more tomorrow, an early start –'

'You're lying!' cried Tripp. 'You came to spy!'

114

She glared back at him.

'All right! I wanted to see for myself . . . just what your hidy-hole consisted of! I wanted to know what this wonderful place was that you've been running off to all these years! Better than your own home!'

'Yes!' cried Tripp, stung. 'It was. It *is!*'

'You never talked about it. My Club, the big secret! You never invited me here, even when they started Ladies' Night. Even today, I had to ask you. And d'you know what I found?'

Tripp winced. 'I know what you're going to –'

'A broken-down museum with little boys playing in it! Not even a school, because a school is where you might learn something, and none of you want to learn anything at all – just suck up to an old madman!'

'Don't –!'

'You should all be in short trousers. Even those soaks in the Bar!'

'Those are my friends!' choked Tripp.

'Calling yourselves Hunters. Hunters! – you're not even *men!*'

Her manner suddenly quietened, and he knew this would be worse. She came close and studied him as if he was an object she had the task of describing. Quite detached.

'*You're* not a man, James. Just . . . something I'm . . . stuck with. Now and then when you're not at your Club.'

She sat down on one of the beds.

She sighed. 'There now, I've said it.'

As if it had been in her mind for a very long time.

In the silence there came a sound of footsteps, moving rapidly along the passage.

Something was pushed under the door.

An envelope.

The footsteps retreated. Tripp picked the envelope up. It was made of heavy paper and carried the Club crest. He opened it and took out the short note in Waley's writing.

'What's that,' she asked, 'the bill?'

Tripp looked as if he might burst into tears.

'What is it, then? Have they chucked you out?'

115

He made a curious sound in his throat, like an attempt to laugh that went the wrong way. A kind of thin cawing. She got up and peered over his arm to see for herself.

'No need to resign!' She laughed aloud, partly because he himself seemed to be trying to laugh and partly because, in a hysterical way, it seemed funny.

Tripp turned.

Without any warning he snatched one of the brass candlesticks from the mantelpiece and hit her savagely on the head with it.

She yelped. She nearly went down. She twisted blindly away from him and there was blood spurting. Blood in her eyes and she couldn't see.

He had to go on. He struck again and again. She was on the floor, crawling and groaning. The brass candlestick whirled and thudded as if it didn't know how to stop.

She wasn't moving now.

Tripp stared. He didn't know what had happened. He muttered softly. If it had been words it might have been to say sorry, wanting her to get up. But he couldn't make words.

And she didn't answer.

He dropped the candlestick. And backed away, trembling all over, towards the door. . . .

In the Coffee Room an interesting conversation had developed over the meal. It was about the special skill of shooting tigers from the swaying back of an elephant. Interesting at least to Colonel Waley, who was the only one who knew anything about it.

The door opened. Bundock burst in, wild-eyed.

'Apologies for the intrusion, gentlemen. Colonel –'

'What is it, Bundock?'

'Mr Tripp, sir. He's killed his wife.'

Consternation at the table. Summerland gasped. Monks' mouth slowly opened to disclose the food inside. Leach choked on his.

Instinctively they all looked to Waley. His eyes were squeezed shut. His lips trembled. He might have been struggling with a violent visitation of grief, but it was nothing of the kind. He was fighting to suppress a smile.

To control himself he spoke sharply.

'Where?'

'In their room, Colonel.'

'He still there?'

'On the stairs, sir. Kind of stuck.'

'Right, Bundock. Get rid of the servants. Rest of the night off, they can clear up tomorrow. And, Bundock –'

'Sir?'

'Careful what you say.'

'Rely on me, sir.'

Bundock hurried away to the kitchen. Luckily there had been no waiters in the room to hear it.

Summerland whispered, 'We'd better see –'

'Indeed we had!' Old Waley almost sprang to his feet. . . .

They found Tripp crouching at the top of the stairs. His hands were clamped tightly to the banisters and he was weeping.

'Tripp!'

The wretched man blinked tears out of his eyes. He hardly seemed to recognise them.

'Tripp – what happened?' But Waley got no response. 'Monks – Greenhow – help him down to the Den and get a drink into him!'

'Right. Come on, let's have you.'

But Monks needed all Greenhow's help to tug the whimpering man's fingers free and unstick him from the balusters.

The others hurried on.

Waley found the bedroom door still open. He looked inside and saw Evelyn Tripp's body crumpled on the floor. There was a great deal of blood splashed about. The other members pressed behind him to see.

'Oh my Lord,' said Summerland. 'What a mess!'

Waley seemed to be looking for clues. He moved into the room and stooped.

'Better not touch anything,' warned Foss.

'What are you talking about?'

'Well, I mean – evidence.'

To Foss's alarm, Colonel Waley deliberately bent down to retrieve the note and its envelope. Both of them were spattered with blood.

'Colonel!'

'Here, hold these.' He pushed them into Foss's hand. Horrified, Foss crooked his fingers to avoid contact. But worse was happening. Waley was searching again. When he stood up he was holding the heavily bloodstained candle-stick.

'The weapon, I think,' he said.

Foss was appalled. 'You – you can't just – carry it about –!'

'Why not?'

'Well, I mean – your – *your* fingerprints are on it now!'

'Of course they are,' said Waley. He looked at his hand and the blood on it. He grinned. He wiped it on Foss's face – forehead and both cheeks – in a deft ritual gesture. 'How's that, young Foss?'

'Let's get out of here,' muttered Summerland nervously.

Foss was frantically rubbing his face with the back of his hand.

Waley produced a handkerchief. He did not offer it to Foss. Instead he started wiping and polishing the candle-stick.

Foss goggled. 'Colonel Waley – what about the police?'

'Well,' said Waley coolly, '*what* about the police?'

He plucked the envelope and writing-paper back from Foss's clawed hand. And pocketed them as he went. The others followed. Only Leach hung back for a moment to peer at the bloody shape on the floor. He had not had much to do with women's bodies, dead or alive. He was curious . . . and then suddenly sad. He turned and trotted out after the other members.

Tripp was in the Den. Monks and Greenhow had almost carried him down the stairs, helpless as a sack. Now he was slumped in one of the old leather armchairs and Monks was feeding him whisky from a glass, just like a baby. Tripp gagged and spluttered.

'My God!' said Waley.

'He couldn't keep a grip on it,' explained Monks.

Then Bundock came hurrying along the side passage. 'Staff all gone, Colonel,' he reported. 'Seen 'em out meself, the back way.'

'Good man. Lock up here too.'

Waley held up the candlestick in front of Tripp's eyes.

'Tripp – you hit her with this?'

Tripp stared blankly at it. Then memory came back with a rush. He stiffened and stared round in sudden alarm.

'Want to tell us about it?' asked Waley. 'You might as well.'

The other members crowded to hear, sitting on the arms of chairs or leaning over the banister rail.

Tripp whispered, 'She went on and on about –'

'What about?'

'The Club.'

The listeners exchanged quick glances.

'She said things. . . .'

'She would!'

'About me . . . and all of us.'

'What?' demanded Monks.

Waley waved this aside. 'We don't need to know, Monks. A lot of vicious hysteria, no sense in making him repeat it.'

Tripp looked grateful. 'And then . . . and then something happened . . . and I . . . and I didn't know what I was doing . . .'

'You had a blackout,' said Waley firmly.

'Yes! That was it, a blackout.'

'When things become too much, Tripp.'

'And all of a sudden she stopped saying anything because I . . . I'd hit her, I suppose.' Tripp frowned. 'There was a letter.'

He struggled with his memory. Colonel Waley fished the envelope and paper from his pocket.

'This letter?'

'Yes . . .'

Waley tore the letter in two. And then in four. And dropped the bits in an ashtray.

'Forget it, Tripp.'

Tripp tried to understand. 'You mean – I –?'

'You're a member in good standing!'

Tripp was too overcome to do more than nod his gratitude. Waley patted him on the shoulder.

'Better burn it,' said Foss uneasily.

Waley shrugged. 'If you think it matters.'

'It might.'

'Very well, go on then.'

Foss busied himself with applying his lighter to the scraps of paper. Not everybody felt this was the right thing to do.

'Destruction of evidence?' wondered Summerland.

'Yes,' said Foss. 'I never thought I'd be doing – doing this –'

'Finish it,' ordered Waley. 'We've *all* got to do this. We've got to save Tripp.'

Tripp cried in a faint voice, 'Save me?'

As if he had only just become aware of his peril he trembled from head to foot. Waley grabbed the glass of whisky from the table and clamped Tripp's hand round it.

'Now drink that!' he ordered. 'Hold it and drink it by yourself!' He watched Tripp do it, straight down. 'Fill his glass again!'

Monks did so, licking his own lips.

'We all need one,' said Waley. 'Bundock, raid the Bar. Get plenty.'

'Right, Colonel.' Bundock hurried off.

Waley beckoned the others aside. 'Tripp here has done something he never thought he'd do. Nor did I, I never thought he'd be capable of – anything like that. Of ridding himself of . . . of. . . . That's why I sent that note.'

He nodded at the smouldering remnant in the ashtray. They saw Tripp finishing his refilled glass at a gulp and reaching for more.

'Now he's restored to us,' said Waley. 'We have a clear duty.' He lowered his voice. 'You do realise, gentlemen, it goes far beyond concern for Tripp? If this scandal breaks it would destroy the Club. No question about it.'

'Yes –' breathed Summerland.

'It would!' said Monks.

'The Hunters' Club, pilloried in the gutter press. They'd wipe their naked girls off page 3 to make room for us. You'd all be there – Summerland – Monks – Foss – Greenhow – Leach. And those fuzzy little photos that make people look like criminals.'

'By God they would!' said Monks.

'So – do we have a choice?'

'No choice!' declared Summerland.

When Bundock returned with bottles and glasses they all grapped for them. Even Tripp poured for himself without help or prompting. His aim was poor.

'Help yourself, Bundock,' said Waley. There was no alternative. The man had to be included. 'You're one of us now.'

'Rely on me, sir.'

'Now,' said Waley, 'we've got to get rid of . . . that thing upstairs. And soon. In a few hours there'll be problems with rigor mortis.'

A chilling note of reality.

'Suppose she's reported missing?' worried Greenhow.

Waley snorted. 'Who by? Tripp?'

'Relatives.'

'Um. She got any relatives, Tripp?'

But Tripp had sunk into a new state of helplessness, a drunken haze. Monks shook him and demanded 'Any relatives?'

Tripp tried to focus. He nodded.

'They live in Midhurst. My . . . my dear father and mother. . . .'

'Not yours,' snapped Waley. 'Your wife's!'

'Oh . . . she lost both of them.' Suddenly Tripp began fighting for accuracy, through the fumes. 'She's got a sister called Charlotte,' he announced.

'Where does she live?'

'In Australia. She married a man . . . a man called Leslie Harper and they're not doing very well. Not a very good marriage, Evelyn thinks. They don't even send Christmas cards.'

'All right, Tripp.' Tripp relaxed back into his stupor. 'No problem there. So let's have ideas, positive and practical.'

'Use the back door?' ventured Summerland.

'Obviously.'

Greenhow frowned. 'We can't just carry her out.'

'Ah – half a mo' now,' said Monks. 'I was reading a whodunnit the other day. They wrapped a body up in a rug. How about that?'

Bundock chimed in. 'Use the carpet in the room. I mean, it's all . . . marked now. Better gone.'

It was agreed that Monks should bring his estate car round from the multi-storey car park and back it into the lane. There they would load the body. They would all come with him to help, all there was room for.

'Find some sort of wood or something?' Monks wondered. 'Bury it there?'

Summerland shook his head. 'Dogs!'

'What about a road repair?' suggested Greenhow.

'That's it!' cried Monks. 'I passed a place on the way in – all dug up, about a mile of stupid little bollards – I knocked a few over, I can tell you –! That'd be the place!'

He refilled his glass.

Greenhow looked at the others. 'Is *he* going to drive?'

'Why not?' Monks pulled vaguely at his tie and dabbed at his dishevelled jacket.

'If we were stopped –!'

'*I'll* drive!' said Summerland firmly.

Monks started to argue. 'Wait a mo', Summerland, you don't know the car. New model, I don't want anything to happen to – I mean –'

But another objection had occurred to Greenhow. 'Of course there might be security men on the site.'

A short, concentrated silence.

Foss cleared his throat. 'I suppose Tripp could just plead self-defence?'

'Against a woman?' Waley snorted.

Leach was whispering, 'I didn't really mind her. At

122

supper, when she said all those things . . . she reminded me of mother. A bit.'

The silence was longer this time.

Then Bundock put in.

'Losing heart, gentlemen? No need. I can tell you what to do.' He was the focus, instantly, of fervent attention. 'Get her in the car, run her down to dockland.'

'You mean the river?' Summerland shook his head. 'Oh no –!'

'Oh *yes*, sir. You just got to know what you're doing. Pal of mine kept a pub down that way and I learnt a few things. A lot more goes on than gets into the papers. Never discovered. There are . . . certain places for it.'

Colonel Waley found he was seeing his hall-porter in an entirely new light. All suspicions were now confirmed, of course, the man had certainly been stealing. On the other hand. . . .

'Bundock,' he said, with respect, 'could you take us to one of those places?'

'I think so, Colonel.' Bundock's fawning and insolence had both vanished. He spoke with authority, in charge of the situation. 'Now what we'll need are some really heavy weights.'

He glanced about the hall, clearly dismissing most of its contents as useless, all the antlers and stuffed beasts. He went quickly to the massive bronze umbrella-stand beside the front door. He hefted it.

'About right,' he said. 'And there's another in the Ablutions. Those ought to do the trick. Now if I can just lay hands on a bit of rope –'

He disappeared into his lodge.

There was a rush of excitement among the members, the quite false feeling that Bundock had solved the whole problem for them and taken it off their hands.

'So now we do it!' said Colonel Waley. Faces grew grim again all round him. 'Eh, young Foss?'

Bundock emerged with a fat coil of rope in his hand, old and dirty but usable.

'Here we are, then.'

He started up the stairs. He got halfway before he found he was alone, and turned irritably.

'Come along, gentlemen!'

Waley first, they started after him. Steeling themselves in their different ways. Monks's puffy face was clamped into resolution. Foss held his Filofax tight to his chest, like a protecting teddybear. Leach shivered. No shirking now, no skulking behind the door. The testing time.

It was when Colonel Waley collided face-to-face with Bundock in the doorway of the room that he knew something was very, very wrong.

'She's not in there, sir.'

Waley pushed past him. And stood stock-still.

'Not possible!'

Where Evelyn Tripp's body had lain there was a pool of blood, now soaked into the carpet. Nothing more.

'What's happened?' cried Summerland.

'She's gone!'

They all came pushing in to look. Bundock was already ransacking the wardrobe. Greenhow threw himself down to peer under the beds.

'No sign of the body,' muttered Monks, 'just like a whodunnit!'

Then they were all nervously arguing. Had somebody taken it – but who *was* there? Or could she possibly have been alive? The state she was in, she couldn't possibly have got far –!

Colonel Waley pushed past them. In the passage he found Tripp, who had been forgotten down in the Den and had made his way up the stairs, mostly on hands and knees.

'Evelyn –?'

'She's not dead!' Waley yelled at him, as if somehow that was Tripp's fault. He found his stupefaction of a moment ago turning to icy rage. There was some trickery going on, some typical female deception. He yelled 'Bundock!'

Bundock appeared from the room. He no longer had his coil of rope. He was just the hall-porter again.

'Colonel –?'

'Bundock, if she gets away she'll destroy us! The back door?'

'Locked, sir. I've got the keys.'

'Right, right.' Waley turned to the others. 'We've got to find her! Try the other rooms – try everywhere! Get moving!'

The Hunters ran.

They threw open the doors of the other bedrooms. They switched on the lights. They called her name and looked into likely hiding places, searching for any clue. Waley made for his own private suite to make sure it had not been invaded.

Summerland and Greenhow tackled the Coffee Room, where the abandoned meal still lay on the long table. Even the columns offered no concealment.

Foss tried the Bar. Peering about, all he found was a half-empty glass on the counter. He gulped the whisky in it, moved on to inspect the Small Lounge. It was equally empty.

Monks was in a dimly-lit service passage. He was steadying himself against the wall when he was aware he had touched something disagreeable.

'Agh!'

Bundock rounded a corner behind him. 'Found something, sir? That's blood – where was it?'

He inspected the spot.

Then he yelled at the top of his voice, 'Colonel!Colonel Waley, there's a trail here!'

'By God, yes,' agreed Monks. 'Blood all over!'

The message passed quickly, shouted from room to room and along the passages. By the time Summerland and Greenhow arrived, breathing hard, Colonel Waley was already demonstrating the bloody handprints to Leach.

'She was moving in this direction, see? Tell by the way they point.'

'Poor soul!' said Leach in horror.

Then Bundock, who had run ahead, came puffing back. 'All down the back stairs, Colonel –'

'The kitchen?'

'I looked. Nothing, sir.'

'She's gone to ground somewhere,' decided Waley. 'Hiding up in some damned cupboard! We'll have to quarter the whole place – store-rooms and so on. Got to track her down and –' He broke off. 'You hear something?'

It came from the distance, a faint, fearful voice.

'That's Foss!' said Waley. He called back, 'Foss, where are you?'

But instead of an answer there was a sound that none of them could ever remember having heard before. A heavy, booming slam somewhere deep in the bowels of the Club.

'What on earth –?' spluttered Monks.

Waley was already on the move, pushing angrily past the others. In a muddle they all turned, back the way they had come. Rounding the corner they nearly ran down the wretched, staggering Tripp, who had just got that far.

They found Foss in the hall, peering nervously down the cloakroom stairs.

'You've seen her?' demanded Waley.

Foss shook his head. 'But – but she must be there. I saw some marks on a wall and I – I was looking round – and then – it sounded like –'

'Yes, we all heard it,' said Waley. His face was very grim. 'She must have doubled back and got past us.'

The breathless members gathered near, trying to take in the appalling fact.

'In the Ablutions!' Monks was the first to say it.

They exchanged glances. Each one waited for somebody else to take the lead in this totally unexpected situation. Once more it fell to the Colonel.

He led the way down in careful silence.

At the foot of the stairs he came to a halt and pointed. There were smears of blood. The sort of streaks that would be made by somebody putting a hand to a still copiously bleeding head and then grabbing to steady herself. Waley moved on through the cloakroom, past the rows of pegs on which were a few hats and coats and the occasional furled umbrella.

The door to the Ablutions was shut.

Massive and old, panelled in dark mahogany, it was a formidable barrier. Colonel Waley tried its brass handle. He rattled it hard.

'Locked!'

Monks cried indignantly, 'Never been shut before! Never!' And glared round as if to defy argument about it.

'Mrs Tripp!' called Waley. 'We know you're in there – open this door!'

He put his ear to it and listened.

'Lying doggo,' he murmured. Then he shouted again, 'You fooled us once – you can't fool us again! It won't work!'

Monks yelled, 'Come out of there!'

They listened again.

'Not a sound,' murmured Summerland.

'She's shamming!' cried Monks.

Colonel Waley bellowed, 'Woman! If you defy me I'll have to smash this door down! It's a good door – too good to waste on you!'

'Far too good!' agreed Monks fiercely.

'I'm not going to start counting up to fifty or give you three minutes to surrender! Nothing like that! No promises, no time allowed. When I give the word we'll come in and take you!'

There was a clatter on the cloakroom stairs. It was Tripp, falling headlong before Bundock managed to grab him.

'Tripp, come here!'

Tripp found himself being bundled along from hand to hand.

'Your wife's inside – *you* tell her!'

Tripp struggled to grasp what Waley wanted of him as they swung him to the door. He could only judge by the red, angry faces.

'Evelyn –'

'Louder, Tripp!'

'Evelyn, they mean it. You'd better give up.'

Waley had moved away for a quick instruction to Bundock, who hurried off up the stairs.

Tripp cracked. 'Evelyn, I'm sorry,' he whimpered. 'I

don't know what came over me – I didn't mean to hurt you –'

'Bloody fool!'

Waley grabbed him and flung him away from the door.

'She did no harm,' piped Leach. He seemed to have been moved by Tripp's distress.

'She did! She came here to insult us!' Waley's eyes bulged. 'Came to belittle everything – all our traditions and our customs that she couldn't understand!'

'I tried to tell her –' whispered Tripp.

'She came to make fun of our manhood!'

That did it.

'A spy, a bloody spy, that's all she is!' yelled Monks.

'Jeering at us –!'

'No business here –!'

'Get her out!'

Suddenly they had turned into a tiny mob, drawing mania from each other.

Waley put his face to the mahogany and roared through its thickness, 'You want to betray us! You want to destroy us! But you won't! Oh no you won't – madam!'

In a fury the members flung themselves at the door, knocking and slapping and hammering on it. Hoarse, incoherent cries came from them. Monks was gibbering with fury. Greenhow had lost his spectacles and his very blindness helped his rage. Even Foss was shrieking, beside himself, though he still clutched his Filofax in one hand. And sober Summerland was snarling. But then –

'Stand back!'

It was Colonel Waley, holding the shining Purdey that Bundock had just fetched.

At the sight of the shotgun the members sprang aside. Waley levelled it at the door and fired. The explosion was deafening, painful, in the confined space.

The lock was shattered.

Waley was first into the Ablutions, still holding the shotgun at the ready. The others crowded behind him.

'Where is she?'

'More tricks –!'

128

'She's here all right,' said the Colonel steadily. There was blood everywhere. Great streaks of it along the tiled walls and the floor. One of the wide hand-basins was full of a watery crimson, where she must have attempted to wash some off.

Waley moved cautiously towards the row of water-closets, a hunter prepared for attack by a wounded beast. He held the gun ready to fire. And Tripp realised what he intended.

'Oh no – Colonel –!'

But it was only what he himself had nearly managed to do.

'Got to put her down,' said Waley. 'Won't feel a thing.'

He kicked open doors. He prodded one wide with the barrel of the gun. No sign of his quarry.

'She's gone!' cried Foss.

'How? There's no way!' from Summerland.

They ran to search for themselves, banging doors and yelling. At the end of the row Foss found a window open. The others rushed to see.

'No, she couldn't,' said Monks, 'it's too small.'

'Yes, she could!' Foss knew he was right, by the red smear on the ledge.

Then a moment of violent confusion.

'She's here!'

Waley had turned to find one of the water-closets locked, though they had just looked there. He smashed the door open with the butt of the Purdey. A squeal of fright and Leach was discovered, trousers round his ankles, ridiculous. He had been taken short.

Waley turned, dully.

'That window, eh?'

Foss nodded. He showed them, and there was no more doubt. They stood silent, waiting for Waley to suggest the next move. The lane . . . the darkness outside.

Then –

Above in the hall, the doorbell rang.

'Somebody –' said Bundock.

They all looked at each other. It rang again. Followed by

129

a sharp knocking, as if somebody was hitting the front door with a stick.

'Better go see,' said Bundock. He waited for Waley's nod. From above there was a furious banging on the door. It had to be answered.

They started slowly through the cloakroom, nobody anxious to be in front. Except Bundock, whose duty it was to answer. The impatient ringing of the bell and the knocking were now continuous.

Bundock made for the door and opened the spy-hole. He turned, shaken.

'Police! It is, sir, I can see the uniforms.'

'Open up,' said Waley.

He still held on to the Purdey. He would face them man to man, surrender honourably if it had to be.

Bundock threw the bolts back. He turned the key. And swung the heavy door open.

A woman entered, and then another.

Both were in police uniform, with shining badges and their hats trimmed with striped bands. Both wore personal radios. The first was a sergeant. She was what the Hunters of old might have called a fine figure of a woman. Her face was strong, even attractive, but it was hot with anger now.

She spoke into her radio. 'I'm inside the place. There's quite a line-up here. Check the back.'

She came to Colonel Waley and said, 'I'll take that.' She jerked the drooping Purdey out of his hands and tossed it to the other girl, who broke it expertly open.

'I'm Sergeant Gallagher, Special Rape Detail.'

'Rape?' Leach cried in horror.

But standing there holding his trousers up, he did not impress her.

'I can assure you –' began Summerland.

She ignored him. 'We've found a woman outside seriously hurt. Managed to give her name as Mrs Tripp, Elaine or –'

'Evelyn!' said Tripp.

'Don't say anything yet. There'll be time for all your statements. And there'll be charges. Quite a lot, I'd guess.'

The Hunters shrank from her contempt.

The drunken Monks. Tripp, who was trying hard not to be sick. Leach, clutching forlornly at his trousers, and Foss trembling all over. Summerland, totally lost. Myopic Greenhow. And Colonel Waley, all of a sudden incredibly old.

Sergeant Gallagher's radio crackled and she answered it briskly.

Outside, there was the wail of an ambulance arriving.

Then more women police.

Waley had heard of these new squads. His heart raced in horror as he watched them move in. Young, quite personable women, all of them. They were taking over the Club. They were on the stairs and in the passages, crisp in their blue uniforms and striped hats and dark stockings. They conferred in quick, light voices. A couple headed for the Ablutions, the scene of –!

As if the whole place belonged to them. In total possession now.

Colonel Waley groaned. Cruel hands seemed to be forcing through the wall of his chest, searching out his heart to crush it and stop it working. The hands, it seemed to him, of Nanny Speirs.

Breath whistling, he managed to cry it out, the most terrible word in the world:

'Women!'

Nigel Kneale

WINDOW, SIR?

Raining as usual.

A misty rain slanting in from the sea and dripping off the slated roofs of a small Welsh town. Something to do with the geography of the place, the way the clouds broke onto the mountains behind.

It rained in summer too, but then there were tourists to liven the place up, pack into the fish and chip shops and bring money to the pockets of the landladies. Of course, it had been better in the old days just after the war, when real money was to be made. It wasn't the same now, what with package tours to Spain and Greece. Still, summer was better than winter.

And this was winter.

Every morning, at 8.30 am, Perry left one of those small slated houses as he had done for forty years. Breakfast, cooked by himself, inside him, the dishes washed, dried and put away: sandwiches, made the night before, usually luncheon meat tucked up in grease-proof inside his pocket.

Down identical back-streets of grey houses Perry walked to his identical work. He wouldn't have stood out in a crowd, although if you looked at him carefully – but nobody did – you could see from the studied neatness of his old raincoat, from the precision of the crease in the scarf he wore tucked into it, the way he moved his arms, thumbs down the seam, that Perry had been in the Army once. Well into his fifties now he was, with a belly, flat-footed, but somehow you could still guess he'd been a soldier . . . a foot-slogger. Infantry. Poor bloody infantry!

Down a back-street of identical houses, dark roof-slates

132

shining in the rain, the shop waited to be opened, as it had done every day but Sunday for forty years. The lop-sided barber's pole gave colour to the otherwise grey slate and brickwork. The old-fashioned lettering of VINCE AND PERRY · GENTLEMAN'S BARBERS was peeling. But then sea-air is hard on paint-work.

Inside, yellowed paint sweated slightly with damp. The styling photographs on the wall curled at the edges, out of date, their colours faded: showing Tony Curtis hair-cuts with DAs. A litter of tattered girlie magazines spread across the bench. Three empty chairs stood there in front of three empty sinks. And above the chair by the window and the one next to it, hung two framed photographs. Vince and Perry in their Army days, circa 1945, two young hopefuls.

The frosted glass door opened, rain blew in, then the door shut. The shop-sign turned from CLOSED to OPEN. Perry took off his raincoat, deftly shook the rain from it, reached for the hanger, flicked the scarf from his neck and draped it over the now hung coat, crease still intact. All this without thought, as always. Expressionless, he turned to check his appearance in his mirror, pushing his damp hair back at both sides with his hands, though he scarcely seemed to see himself. He turned again, found the string for the wall heater without looking, and tugged it. The heater broke the silence with a small humming noise as it warmed up. Perry stood beneath it staring into the middle distance.

Somehow out of juice.

From the opposite direction down similar streets, trying to keep his polished brown shoes out of the puddles, walked another man. Same sort of age, same sort of clothes, also inclined to corpulence but with a jauntier look about him. He had a soldier's walk, though a little stiff.

Vince, once the young swaddie with a way with the girls. He'd had a lovely wife in Mollie. She'd died back in '68 from cancer. After that he'd taken to going down the club in the evenings: always enjoyed a laugh and a joke, had Vince.

In the shop Perry's motor engaged suddenly. He pushed

open the door to the dark cubbyhole, rummaged through shelves of unused stock and found the tea-caddy. Rinsed yesterday's tealeaves from his pot, then pulled Vince's two used tea-bags from the sink, picking them out by the strings – Vince's bloody tea-bags. Suddenly Perry leant over and retched violently, just as Vince crossed the road in front of the Fun Palace, giving it a glance. The Palace reminded him briefly of better times, of playing the slot-machines after de-mob while they planned it all. They'd make a bloody fortune, Perry promised, wonderful position, no over-heads, and hair-cuts always needed. Back in '46 that was, before Molly died. Never had taken her on that holiday. His face hardened: no use regretting things now. Jingling some coins in his pocket he turned the corner, whistling tuneless-ly through his teeth.

Perry was laying out the tools of his trade: razor, scissors and electric clippers. Each piece of sharp gleaming metal set in its particular place, ready for his hand. His daily, soothing, surgical ritual. Picking up the scissors he indulged himself in a practice cut, snip-snapping the air. Then suddenly his motor cut out in mid-flourish.

Vince turned down the back-street where each window was draped in nylon lace, each the same. With apprehension he checked out the three or four pedestrians splashing through the puddles towards him. All familiar faces. All seen many times before. He stooped to pick up their pint of milk from the shop doorstep.

As he was stirring tea in the cubbyhole, Perry heard the door open, and knew it was Vince. Without glancing up he knew Vince was straightening the OPEN/CLOSED sign, knew it from the absence of any sound after the door had closed. Rigid, he stood listening, spoon in one hand, seeing nothing but what was on the inside of his own head.

Flinging back the cubbyhole door, Perry leaps towards Vince, the scissors he brandishes in one hand sharp and shining – Fix Bayonets, Charge! – the milk bottle flies from Vince's grip. Stab, twist, turn and out. Perry pulls back the scissors red with blood as Vince staggers clumsily against his

134

chair. The spilled milk lies in a wide pool on the floor between them.

Sitting in their respective chairs, waiting for their first customer of the day, Vince and Perry drank their tea, and read their papers, as they had done for forty years. Sometimes Vince would glance out of the window. Perry knew the repetitiveness of the movements of Vince's head – from shop to street, and back – without needing to look. He stared at Vince in the mirror, waiting for the moment when Vince would lift the tea-bag from his mug by its string and drop it into the wastepaper basket. There it would seep deep into yesterday's tissues. A disgusting habit. Perry made his tea in a tea-pot, like God meant him to.
    Perry's eyes followed Vince in the mirror.

Pleased with himself today isn't he? If he has to whistle through his teeth, why can't he bloody whistle something musical, like? He's tidying up the magazines now, is he? Weren't they tidy enough already then, Mr Vince, Sir? And you won't find out which one I took home last night, because I put it back, didn't I now! Turning off the fire is he – just because I put it on – Oh, and looking out of the window. Must be nice that. Wish I could look out of the window, all light and airy with a view – not that you could call it a view, the fronts of bloody boring houses and dogs shitting.

Perry's body tensed as he saw the first customer approaching, across the road. Before Vince even said them, words screamed in his head.
    'Number One. Kelly's Eye,' Vince said cheerfully. He picked up his cloth and dug in the box for a paper tissue for his first customer.

The cloth tightens around Vince's throat. Cups, pots, tea-bags and caddy fly as he struggles to free himself. Vince's face turning purple, his tongue protruding, his breath rasping as his legs kick. Behind him, Perry's knuckles knotted in the ligature, straining to choke the life out of the other man.

135

Vince turned on the radio, just as Perry knew he would. He knew what Vince would do, before Vince did himself. Music and chatter filled the shop, as it would fill it for the rest of that day, like the day before, as it would the day after. As it was in the beginning, is now and ever shall be, world without end, Amen. Perry was sick, fed up with it. Perry was fed up and *sick*.

So the barbershop swung into motion, into its daily rhythm that seldom altered. Perry and Vince working side by side, snipping, trimming, patting, combing and reaching for the mirror. Handing the customer a tissue, shortly followed by the customer handing them the cash. Working on reflexes established by years after years in the business.

After the initial rush of customers there would be a lull. If the odd customer wandered in before the next rush, it would be to Vince's chair that he went. The chair by the window. Perry would sit redundantly on the bench watching Vince's reflection in the mirror.

Window, Sir? Chair by the window? Certainly Sir. The customer would have a bloody heart attack wouldn't he, if he wasn't at the window. Mr Vince . . . Mr Window, Sir.

Once in a while, Vince and Perry were visited by a travelling salesman from Cardiff. The salesman flashy, young, confident, and in a hurry, wouldn't have bothered with the visit at all, had it not been that their shop was on his way to Aber and he fancied Ceinwen at the CUT AND BLOW. Hardly worth the petrol for the Toyota was it to sell six dozen combs?

Vince would deal with the salesman, just as Vince dealt with everything. Of course he would defer to Perry, who'd be sitting on the bench, once again staring at nothing, but Perry knew it was pretence. Vince was patronising him, laughing at him.

The salesman drummed his fingers on the chair arm.

'Tell you what – six dozen the tortoiseshell, three the nylon, three the steel.'

Dear, oh dear, he thought as he glanced round, this place could do with modernising. . . .

The salesman thought a lot of modernisation. These two old sods gave him the creeps, and the shop had an unpleasant, backward sort of feel to it. A coat of paint, some nice bright colour, bit of modernising: it would work wonders.

Now the old boy was on about the Teddyboy wars. The what? How the Teds bought up all the steel combs and filed down the tails. Murderous that was, a steel comb in your guts. Fish hooks sewn into their lapels too? Very nasty.

Kinky was he, the old boy? The salesman flicked imaginary dust from his new-look suit. So they were only taking two dozen nylon now? Blow this visit in the future! How to get out without more reminiscences of the sixties, the fifties and the bloody forties? Spooky old sods, he thought, pushing the door to behind him with an air of relief. Oh well, Ceinwen next call!

Back to business for Vince and Perry, Perry and Vince. Perry shampooing a customer's hair – unusual someone wanting that – watched Vince in the mirror.

Vince whistling some infuriating tuneless whistle through his teeth again, while carefully sweeping hairs from the linoleum, with that attention to detail which was driving Perry mad: every day for forty years.

'Char? Char? Cuppa?'

Perry heard the call for tea-break from a long way away. Where was he really? And who was the man calling him?

'Brew-up? Brew-up? Time for Brew-up.'
Yes Sir, No Sir, three bags full Sir. Trained not to think. Not trained for anything but boring old brew-up, boring old war!

Yes, it was Vince who did the organising. Vince who ordered the stock, announced the tea-breaks, the time of annual shut-down. It was Vince who told the jokes, turned

on the charm. Vince in the window seat, words pouring out
of his mouth, endless repetitive drivel. . . .

How's the Brother? (Sister, Wife, Mam, Kid)?

Sorry (Glad) to hear about the marriage (birth, death,
job, weather)?

Heard the one about the Vicar (Actress, Englishman,
Irishman, Scotsman)?

Bla, bla, bla, on and on in an endless stream.

Vince looked out of the window as he worked, and Perry
looked at Vince in the mirror.

*Oh, very cocky this morning, isn't he? He's had a good
bloody laugh out of me, him and his pals, him and his
cronies . . . Window, Sir? Joe Muggins here never gets a
look in, never even got a squint out of the window in forty
years. Turn and turn about, he said. In front of my bloody
sister! Let him deny that. Turn and turn about . . . I'll have
the window see, the first month: then turn and turn about.
Only fair, only bloody fair, isn't it? Something to look at
instead of old ears and backs of heads all day. Him this
month, me next. Only fair . . . Now try and flog him a
comb. . . .*

Vince pulled the cloth from his customer's shoulders with a
flourish and a professional smile.

'Nice comb? New line?'

The customer pulled a face that indicated No Sale, and
Perry allowed himself his thin I-told-you-so smile.

So the day went on. Slowish up to dinner time, but steady,
oh yes, steady. So things had ticked over since they started.

Usually one of them worked over dinner; the other
relaxed on the bench eating sandwiches. Turn and turn
about, only fair. They would reverse their positions without
a word, and then the other would relax on the bench, eating
sandwiches in an identical place. The two of them were
interchangeable to a casual glance.

Each day Vince and Perry trod the same paths on the
worn lino, from chair to bench, bench to chair, chair to
cubbyhole, cubbyhole to door. How many miles of foot-

slogging did those worn paths represent? Poor bloody infantry!

After dinner, another lull. Sitting side by side on the bench Vince and Perry – Perry and Vince, sharing the depression of that time when their working day went limp around them.

It would usually be then, at the lowest ebb of energy that they'd get the difficult customer. A kid, say, with a solicitous mother who would stand by the chair and get in the way. It was always Perry who got that one, of course. Mr Vince wasn't nearly so quick with his – Window, Sir – then, was he? Oh no, Mr Vince did the accounts then. Perry would manoeuvre around the mother, trying to keep Vince in view, as if he couldn't let the man out of his sight for a second, however much he'd grown to hate him.

In the cubbyhole Vince would crouch over his heavy old-fashioned calculator, the kind that required its handle to be yanked down for each computation. And, as always, Perry would flinch at every whirr of the handle, every click of the mechanism.

Vince was in charge of accounts and stock. Vince with his head now stuck in the stock cupboard at the end of the cubbyhole. The cupboard contained everything needed for the orderly running of a barber-shop: Shelves crowded with items ranging from replacement brooms to a spare leather strop.

With typical fastidiousness, Vince ran his fingers along the shelf, picked out a container of talcum powder, removed it, set it down on the sink, and padlocked the door twice.

Perry's eyes noted each single, small movement. He knew every individual key on the key-ring that Vince returned to his pocket, but never once in forty years had Perry's hands touched one of them. He peered sideways in the mirror as Vince re-filled the talcum powder puffers and handed his own across, without a word.

After the lull, the storm. Suddenly eight customers appeared in the shop. Two in the chairs, and six squeezed up on the bench, their heads bent into the girlie magazines, hoping their neighbours wouldn't notice which bit they were looking at. With no time for thought, Perry and Vince looked almost happy. Their trade became a skill, performed with bravura. Perry was as near to surfacing reality as he ever was. The tune in the head was on his lips as he hummed something approaching 'Men of Harlech', and speeded up his rate of work to match his partner's.

Vince and Perry both knew without looking at the clock what time it was. The shop grew greyer and dingier, the corners darker as the short winter's daylight faded. If there had been a sun out there, it would be rolling over the horizon into the sea. But there was no sun, just the persistent misty rain over the slate roofs.

Silence save the chinking sound of Vince bagging that day's takings, tongue between his teeth, as if he was about to shovel the whole amount into his mouth and swallow it. He counted it neatly into piles. Copper, silver, notes. Perry stared at the dark reflection in the window and signed the paying-in statement in the leaking biro. Vince pulled on his coat, and taking the tattered brown case that had carried the cash for forty years, he left the shop, turning the sign from OPEN to CLOSED as he shut the door behind him without a word.

Perry in his chair continued to stare in the mirror. The shop grew dark round him, but he couldn't bring himself to put on the light: he thought better in the dark these days. He was aware of feeling ill, and wasn't sure why. He ran his fingers back through his hair again in the familiar gesture.

Vince cowers rigid in his chair (the chair by the window), his whole shocked concentration on the sharpened tail of a metal comb only a hair's breadth from his eye. Perry holds the comb.

   'Comb, Sir? Nice comb? New line?' Jab, goes the comb, jab, jab, jab.

'Cuppa? Cuppa? Char? One bag or two?' gabbles Perry's voice, gab, gab, gab.

'Nice steel comb, sir. Would there be anything else, sir?'

Vince cringes into the chair, back arched, eyes bulging, unable to escape the sharpened tail of the comb.

'Window, Sir? Chair by the window, Mr Vince's chair by the window? Certainly, Sir.'

Jab goes the comb towards the soft jelly eye.

Mr Vince always had the chair by the window, the nice view of the street. Nineteen forty-six Mr Vince had the window, first day we moved in, rent twelve and six a week, a month after de-mob, make a fortune man, make a bloody fortune we will.

Jab, jab, jab, so near the jelly-fish eye. The tentacles of blood flow down that face. Like a slippery ball was it, or more like a peeled grape? Jab goes the bayonet, jab, jab, jab. Just once, just that bloody once!

Perry's hands stalled in mid-jab, as they stalled with the scissors earlier. Scissors! Now there were scissors in his hand.

Mr Vince Window – Sir sitting in his chair, but with Perry telling the jokes this time. Mr Perry with the bla, bla, bla!

'This chap see, only got one eye and loses the glass out of the other. Man in shop can't do anything for him, he's out of glass eyes. Tell you what, he says to the chap, the brother's a fair hand with wood-carving. He'll fix you up with a temporary one, paint it up, look like new. Wooden one? says the chap, no good to me at all. How the hell would I see through it?'

Be anything else, Sir? One of these?

One of these in your face, Sir?

Perry sat there in his old chair, scissors in hand, lost in motionless reflection until, far away, a sound brought him up to the surface again. As the cubbyhole door opened he stared down at the blades still grasped in his hand, then thrust the scissors back in their accustomed place. He stood up and quickly pulled on his raincoat, placing the creased scarf inside it, slid a tatty magazine deftly from the pile on the bench and turned into the half-lit shop.

'Dear God, you frightened me, Mr Perry!'

Morved stood there, with a dust-pan and brush in one hand, her other clasping at the frilly neck of her pink nylon blouse.

Silly old bugger, she thought angrily, giving me a fright like that, creeping round the shop in the dark.

Perry looked right through Morved as if he hardly recognised her.

'Well, then . . . off now, then,' he said with an effort.

Morved look him up and down. Sixpence-in-the-shilling he is, she thought to herself. No ambition like. Not like the other one, Mr Vince. He was different somehow. Something could be made out of him. Morved knew this for Morved knew about ambition. It lay within her, tightly wound.

She looked at Perry with a flirtatious little smile. There was something she meant to ask. 'Was it "walls" tonight? Mr Vince said something about walls being on Wednesdays.'

Morved hoped it wasn't. She hated cleaning bloody walls. Why couldn't they put their hands in their pockets and buy a pot of paint? Miserable pair of misers. Morved hated misers.

Perry stared dumbly at her for a moment.

'I'm afraid I wouldn't . . .' he trailed off again, still looking through her.

Bloody barmy, Morved thought. She wished there was more light in the shop.

Perry brought himself to with an effort.

'You'll have to ask the great man himself. I just do haircuts' . . . Perry's voice trailed off but surfaced again inside his head.

Private soldier in this two man army, me. Poor bloody infantry.

142

Unexpectedly, Perry smiled at her, or rather his face cracked in the middle somewhere. He gave her a jaunty mocking salute. All those years fighting Jerry, now it was the 'enemy within' that he fought. Perry the walking wounded saw Morved's quick little eyes flick to his saluting hand. Embarrassed, he turned abruptly, slamming the magazine back on the bench and left the shop shutting the door behind him.

She waited for a moment, staring after him. So that was what he did with his evenings, she thought; she'd often wondered. Tentatively, she picked up the discarded magazine, let it fall open, checked there was no one in the street, and peeped inside.

Well! she thought, scrutinising pink bosom, legs, white suspenders and black stockings. Well. . . ? she thought, as she inspected herself in the mirror. Middle-aged, though she wouldn't admit to it, Morved had her aspirations, and still dreamed of better things to come.

Life had dealt her a blow, hadn't it? Leaving her with Jim. Married him for his bloody money and now he was a cripple. Morved, with the head on her shoulders, who'd dreamed of a band-leader or a business man, now stranded in a boring little Welsh town with a cripple. No wonder she was plump and bored to death.

Wouldn't anyone be? Heaving about a cripple for twenty years or more? She ran a hand slowly, experimentally over her bosom and her stomach. Still plenty on top girl, she thought, bit too much below though, but nice legs.

Look after yourself girl, thought Morved. She meant it and she meant to. She always had the latest clothes, latest hair-styles, and spent plenty on both, hadn't she? Morved believed in spending money. With a start she dropped the magazine back on the bench and picked up the dust-pan and brush. Spooky old shop. She didn't know why, but she'd never liked being here alone at night. There was this feeling about it.

Morved started cleaning. She didn't do the walls.

Another day.

Perry had even less recollection of how he came to be standing there than usual. He couldn't remember swallowing his breakfast, putting on his coat, or closing the door. He had not even noticed the sallow sun which showed up greasy finger-marks on the blank windows of that small Welsh town.

Now he stood before the mirror, still in his coat. Before him, he saw this ordinary-looking man begin to cry. Tears ran down grooves in the face and trickled onto a scarf, making dark blotches. Inside himself, Perry felt an uncontrollable grief take hold as the man before him was wracked by sobs so heavy that his body shook. He watched, as the sadness inside gripped harder then slowly passed away. Together they stood there he and this man, now tired and at peace after the storm. Poor bloody infantry.

Vince had been down the club the night before. Just a few drinks with his cronies. Not too many, mind. He felt jaunty. After all the sun was nearly shining and Vince felt almost young – young at heart at any rate. He didn't think of Molly so much now. Time passes and there might be someone else one day. Who knew? thought Vince, as he marched cheerfully down the back-street to the shop.

He paused to check the window display, pint of milk in one hand. He still wasn't sure about the arrangement of new combs: were they at their best advantage between the rubber goods advertisement and the hair preparations? The shop-front was peeling, but today he noticed it and he reminded himself to ask Perry about re-decorating the outside and the interior, something he'd been meaning to do for a long time. Time for a good clear out.

Perry didn't care much for Vince's mood, as he flicked away dust which the sun showed up on the shelf. He responded with sarcasm to the idea of painting the shop and even when Vince brought him his tea, for the first time in years, couldn't bring himself to drink it. Revulsion clawed at Perry when he realised that elation was sweeping through

Vince. It was as if their emotions were the balance, teetering on a see-saw.

They sat in their chairs, staring at each other's reflections. Vince toasting Perry expansively as if it were a celebration, Perry's feelings crawling back into their lair.

'The point being,' insisted Vince, sucking out a bit of breakfast bacon from his back teeth, 'the point being, inside five or ten years we'll be thinking of retiring. . . .'

'So. . . ? Perry compressed all his biting scorn into the word.

'So the place needs a lick and a polish. You never know who mightn't come in and make an offer.'

Conversation this, but it was a reflection of each other in the mirror they addressed, and not flesh and blood. They'd been standing shoulder to shoulder for too long to talk face to face. This was the natural way of dealing with each other.

'Oh yes "such a wonderful position, isn't it? Bound to make a bloody fortune, no overheads." Nineteen forty-six you said that, didn't you? "Make our bloody fortune man. Stands to reason there's always going to be hair-cuts needed." Oh yes.'

Perry's face was contorted with sarcasm. He could hardly bring himself to look at the object of his contempt.

Vince was about to protest, when their first customer came in. Perry leapt in first for a change.

'Window, Sir?'

He grabbed his tea and swilled it down the sink as the customer made for Vince's chair.

'Just tell me when to clear out, that's all,' he hissed at Vince, still attempting to keep a professional smile on his face for the benefit of Mr Jenkins, a regular.

'If it'd be more handy like, for me to throw myself under a train, just tell me, won't you? I shouldn't like to get in anyone's way, me.'

Again he flashed a precarious smile at Mr Jenkins, who frowned as Perry rushed into the cubbyhole, slamming the door behind him.

Vince fussed over Mr Jenkins, tucking the cloth into his

neck, soothing him with patter. Mr Jenkins had a profitable business down the Arcade so there was no harm in keeping on the right side of him. But Mr Jenkins had already taken a decision to make the inconvenient trip to Aber for his next hair-cut. Mr Perry looked very wild, he thought.

Inside the cubbyhole Perry started to shake. He placed his hands flat against the wall to stop them trembling, then threw back his head and howled silently.

Vince kept looking anxiously at the closed cubbyhole door. And Mr Jenkins began to wish that another customer would come in through the frosted glass door.

'Oh, Mr Vince . . .'

On an impulse Vince set down his scissors and made for the cubbyhole.

'Shan't be a . . .' and he disappeared inside.

Well, this would be something to tell them down the club, thought Mr Jenkins. Whatever were the two of them up to in there?

Vince puts up a brief clawing, kicking resistance, and seems almost likely to get away by dragging himself into the toilet cubicle leading off the cubbyhole. But Perry keeps hold of his leg and wrenches the despairing man out again, stunning him with a blow that sends him reeling against the sink.

Perry takes his advantage by pulling open the doors of the stock cupboard, grabbing Vince and stuffing him into the space between the shelves and the door. The items on the shelves crash to the floor, as tins, cans and odds-and-ends fly everywhere, but Perry keeps stuffing in the injured man, as if he were a large, limp rag doll. When he finally gets all of the man inside, Perry scrabbles for the padlock.

As he pushes the door to, something gets in the way: Vince's twitching hand sticking out of the gap. Perry crashes the door on the wrist as hard as he can, but the fingers keep trembling. He leans his whole weight against the door and looks around for something to help him. By the sink is an old blunt butter-knife, one of the stray pieces of cutlery collected in the shop over the years. The knife is only just out of reach

of his hand, but as he lessens the pressure on the door to grab
the knife, the door inches open. . . .

Vince opened the cubbyhole door and looked in.

Perry was standing by the sink, stalled again. Vince felt a
sort of restrained fondness for him. After all, they'd been
together all those years, foot-sloggers through war, foot-
sloggers through peace.

'Not got anything on tonight, have you?'

Well he wouldn't, would he? Not Perry! Vince tugged the
hair on the back of his neck, a military shortness, with
maybe a quarter of an inch too long for an old soldier.
Something needed to be done about that.

'After hours could you. . . . I'd appreciate it. There's a
club dinner prize-giving tomorrow night see, and I thought
I'd make a bit of an effort. . . .'

Mr Jenkins, draped in the white cloth, peered across at
Vince with empty curiosity.

Perry barely heard Vince's request, though he took it in
somewhere in his head, and Vince turned back to the shop
just in time to catch Mr Jenkins' interrupted question.

'Got the message from Ada did you? Morved can't come
in tonight – husband's ill again. Did you hear?'

Dusk. The sun rolled under the horizon of the sea, just as
always. Only difference, today you could see it. The shop
sign was turned to CLOSED and Vince relaxed in Perry's
chair, his eyes shut, glad to get the weight off his aching
feet. From inside the cubbyhole he heard the faint sound of
retching, and the clanking chain to the old cistern. Vince
smiled gently.

Perry emerged dabbing his lips with a tissue. He advanced to his chair, tucked the cloth expertly round Vince's
neck before setting out the tools of his trade. Scissors,
razor, clippers: the instruments shone in the light cast by the
street lamp outside. He did a swift sharp practice-cut, snip-
snapping the air, reached across to plug in the power for the
clippers, and was about to start when he noticed Vince's
eyes were open, watching him.

147

'Do you know –' said Vince, 'You can throw in a shampoo tonight.'

Perry didn't query the change from routine. He set the scissors down, put the rubber plug in the basin and watched it fill.

He nodded at Vince to dunk his head in, paused for a moment in his lathering, staring at the bare flesh of the neck presented to him, then reached for the sprinkler hose.

As Perry reached, Vince jerked awkwardly as if there were something in his eye. His hands grasped blindly along the shelf for a towel or tissue, and as Perry plunged his hands deep in the sink to remove the plug, Vince's fumbling fingers dislodged the clippers. They fell into the soapy water with hardly a splash.

A bang and behind him Perry arched back.

Vince gazed at his reflection in the darkened window as he casually towelled dry his hair. He may have heard the scream. The chair beneath him gave a series of small jerks. There was a faint drumming noise on the floor.

After he'd finished with his hair he telephoned the police and reported an accident.

Winter had turned into a grudging Spring, infiltrating the small Welsh town, whose few thousand inhabitants read with an interest verging on the inquisitive of the accidental death of Mr Perry of VINCE AND PERRY · GENTLEMAN'S BARBERS. It had been reported briefly in the small print of the *Aber and Afon News*, which observed that Mr Perry had seen active service in the last war. It observed too, his successful long-standing partnership with his comrade, Mr Vince and offered condolences to Mr Vince on his bereavement which – the sub had felt – finished the paragraph off nicely.

As he stood there in his overalls in the barber shop two weeks later Mr Vince did not look bereft. Whistling through his teeth, he dropped a tea-bag into his mug. Continuing to whistle, he casually slung Perry's old tea-pot into the bin where it landed with its spout snapped off

148

amongst the tissues. Finding that the sugar basin needed refilling, he opened the padlocks to the stock cupboard. At that moment, he heard someone tapping on the frosted glass door, and quickly pushed the stock cupboard shut.

The survivor held open the door gallantly as Morved swept in. Just out walking, she said, but she didn't look as if she was going far, not on those heels anyway. Vince hoped she wouldn't stay but she didn't look easy to shift, standing four-square in the shop staring at the unopened paint tins. A strong woman, thought Vince, as he fetched her the cup of tea he'd hoped she'd refuse. He'd been looking forward to doing a bit of painting by himself, making that fresh start.

Morved's little eyes missed nothing. Flick they went to Perry's chair, flick to the photograph of Perry above it. Flick to the girlie magazines on the bench. She declined Vince's offer of sugar.

'Got to mind the figure,' she said, patting her back-side, 'What's left.'

Vince felt uneasy at the remark. She took no notice of his various attempts at conversation, lingering over the three chairs, pausing by each in turn. He himself seemed unable to find a suitable place to sit. He turned to the middle chair, Perry's, but shied away from it at the last moment. She was watching him in the mirror and he feeling uncomfortable in his own shop, tried to cover the feeling by assuming a casual pose. It didn't fool Morved not for one minute.

Nothing fooled Morved, not any more. She'd been fooled once, when she'd married Jim, and that was enough. Hadn't it ruined her life? She, a dreamer of dreams, buried alive in a wet, dull little town that came to life only in the brief summer months when the trippers came. Her husband, a cripple that she had to heave up and down the stairs and on and off the toilet seat. Lucky she was strong wasn't it? She the dreamer of dreams had dreamt of the good life, the life of candle-lit restaurants, dance-band music, trips to the Costa Del. . . . So Morved was waiting her chance. She knew only too well, life was about grabbing that chance while it was there.

Vince and Morved were sitting side by side. Vince in

Perry's chair, Morved in Vince's. Quite cosy like, he thought happily as he passed her another biscuit from the caddy. Sad for her being stuck with a cripple for a husband, a young woman like her too.

She had a way of making you talk she did, sitting there beside you snuggled up in the chair. Asked just the right questions in just the right way somehow. And he enjoyed it, talking away about the old days and early years, working all the hours God sent, trying to build up the business. No chance of getting away from it, not even for the match on Saturday, couldn't risk losing their regulars.

He'd had Molly then of course, but what prospects had old Perry had of getting a girl? It wasn't even a business where there was a chance meeting now and then, not like working as a barman or a bench hand at a factory. Monastic like, it was.

All at once Perry had turned round and found himself with a corporation and fallen arches. He knew sixteen blue jokes, and twenty-five ways to start a conversation about the weather and not much else, so no wonder he'd turned to girlie magazines in the evening. At least those girls didn't expect glamour.

Morved had a way with her all right, thought Vince, dunking a biscuit in his tea. He hadn't talked so much for years. They were just the right questions asked in just the right way. Well now, should he risk asking her one. About Jim?

'If you can't stand him, why don't you leave him?' His voice wasn't as casual as he'd have liked.

Morved smiled gently, concealing her sense of triumph. The conversation was going as she planned.

'What would you do if you was me. Kill the old cripple?'

Vince's new-found confidence left him abruptly. He finished his tea and got to his feet.

'I have to be getting along,' he said briskly, hoping his change of tone would indicate an exit. But it didn't. Morved remained in the chair.

'Kill him, or wait for a stroke of luck, like something electrical doing it for me?' She watched him carefully in the mirror. 'Drop a toaster in the bath one Friday night? Accidental-like? That'd do the job for me, wouldn't it?'

Vince whistled desperately through his teeth, to conceal rising panic. But Morved wasn't fooled, not Morved.

'Better still, easier at the inquest like, if Jim was in the bath and I knocked something flying accidental like, something electrical off the shelf. . . .'

What was she getting at – what was she trying to say? Her with her questions, just the right questions.

'What you come here for? What are you saying?'

All she was saying, announced Morved, coolly and calmly, was that she wished for a man with courage; a man who could do something out of the ordinary when called on. That was all she was saying.

Morved glanced at Vince. She knew her man: all she had to do was lick him into shape, grab the chance while it was there. Life was about taking chances. Gently does it she thought.

'Bloody clippers,' she said soothingly, 'Them two wires could have touched any time.'

'Any time,' said Vince, regaining some equilibrium. 'So the chap at the inquest said. . . .'

'Any old time at all.' Morved smiled.

Vince, relieved, bent over to open a tin of paint.

'Could have knocked them into the sink any time . . . any time Perry was shampooing.' Morved still spoke soothingly as she made her way quietly to the door.

'Any old time at all. . . .' She noticed his body as it tensed over the paint-tin.

'Funny it had to be the only time in twelve years that you asked for a shampoo with your trim.'

Morved didn't show up again that week. It meant he had to clean the place himself, but it saved cash and killed time in the evenings, for he didn't exactly feel like going to the club these days.

Instead he sat in his chair staring at the books. He'd gone over and over that conversation with Morved. Did she know, or didn't she? If she did – and he was sure she did – what would she do?

Better she doesn't come in, thought Vince, with those knowing little eyes; those questions she asked and the way she asked them. He'd have to get rid of her, give her a couple of week's money. He'd take it round himself, that very evening. But somehow he couldn't manage it.

The routine in the shop remained oddly unchanged. He snipped and trimmed, patted and combed, smiled professionally at his customer's jokes and offered a few of his own, accepted condolences with the correct degree of regret, but his eyes were drawn to the shabby street more often, and with more apprehension than before.

She came in late, just before closing. Vince finished off the customer in the chair and closed the shop early, took two weeks' money out of the till, and told her to go in a voice harsh with nerves.

Morved didn't take the money. She sat on the bench looking deflated and sad.

Jim had been ill. She'd wanted to stay away a few days to avoid the gossip. Ah, those Welsh tongues! Morved sighed and looked out of the window at the grey houses that were trapping her.

She turned round again to face him. Backlit by the street light, she looked soft and vulnerable. What was she after now?

She told him she wanted him, Vince with the fallen arches, the flabby belly and the bad back. There she was, standing there all soft and feminine, telling him she wanted him!

All she asked was a cuddle now and then, maybe the odd meal out, even the physical if he wanted it. She wasn't bothered. Time was passing and she was lonely, that was all. Not much really was it. . . ? And, yes, he felt she knew, of course she knew, that he'd killed Perry.

Morved and Vince – Vince and Morved sat on the bench, side by side, for nights in a row. They didn't speak – too

152

much to say somehow. It would be dark outside but he didn't put the light on, he thought better in the dark somehow.

They couldn't prove a thing. She couldn't prove a thing. Was she sitting next to a man she knew was a murderer? In the dark? And back he would return to the same point each time. She knew. She must know. Then one night, in that concealing, confiding dark, Vince confessed. It brought him the relief of the confessional, to share the guilt. And now they were conspirators in it together, he and Morved. Weren't they?

For years he'd been planning it. Years of plans and not telling a soul. The schemes he'd thought of: blowing him up, drowning him, poison. Then he'd found a phrase in a book somewhere, one of those detective stories he some-times read. 'It wasn't the string, it wasn't the knot. . . It was the untying of the knot.'

Vince smiled, 'Simple, see, nothing tricksey-dicksey. I had to make sure no-one could untie the knot, so it had to be something domestic, familiar and just the two of us.'

Morved's eyes met his in the half-light.

'You're a very clever man,' she said admiringly. 'A very dangerous man.'

Vince felt drawn to her, drawn by her sympathy, her admiration for him but still he remained on guard, watchful.

'Only to Perry, you keep that in mind, to no one else, ever again.'

Morved moved towards him.

'There's depths in you,' she said as she leaned over him. Morved the cunning. Morved the sultry. He could smell her scent – she wore a lot of it.

'You're a very cruel, ruthless dangerous man.'

Morved opened her mouth before she kissed him.

She came again on Sunday, to help paint the shop. They'd all be in chapel so no one would see, no one would guess. Vince did the painting, while Morved fussed about the tea.

Vince had been thinking since their last meeting. His

attitude to Morved had changed. She wasn't against him, she was *with* him. She hadn't run away once knowing what he'd revealed to her. Vince was no longer alone.

He felt lighter, brighter from relief and now he'd told her so much, he must tell her all. Morved was his friend, his ally, his partner. Oh and more, much more!

At the moment when he judged it was right, gathering his courage, Vince handed Morved the keys to the stock cupboard. He couldn't bring himself to look at her, so deep was his shame, waiting as she opened the doors and looked inside. Puzzled, she moved one or two items on the shelves, then turned to him.

'Don't you want to know why I did it?'

Morved looked at him, expectant, smiling. What more could there be? she thought. There's excitement, there's gossip now!

'It was '52, 1952 . . . it was my month to handle the stock.'

He stopped, searching for his next word. Go on, go on bach! thought Morved.

'Whatever made me do it I don't know . . . but I took fifteen bob for myself. Fiddled the books.'

Still without looking at her he moved the items on the shelf, and from behind them he drew out another set of ledgers. The duplicate books. He thrust them into her hands.

'Of course, I had to do the stock myself next month, but instead of putting the thing right, I took another fifteen bob.'

Looking at a fixed point on the floor Vince unpeeled the guilt of forty years.

In all that time he hadn't embezzled even two thousand pounds. He hadn't had a holiday, not even when his wife was alive. All that time, night after night, sitting up with the figures, trying to find a way through, find out exaclty what he had stolen, find a way to cover his tracks.

Morved opened a ledger. She trembled, as she turned over page after page, a spider's web of figures, the spider's web that had trapped poor Vince.

Page after page, month after month, for forty years Vince couldn't take even a half-day, because he had to balance the takings and bag the cash himself; and all the time, do it twice. Two sets of figures to keep, the fake ones needed to be straight, or as straight as possible. All those years, knowing that when they came to sell up those books would be opened. Knowing that he was cheating – had cheated – old Perry. Perry, his pal, his partner, the man with whom he opened the bloody shop.

'I'd have died of shame if he found out. I'd have died with them talking about how I'd been cheating my pal all those years.'

Ah, those wagging Welsh tongues!

Vince appealed for her understanding.

'Can you understand? I'm not a dangerous man . . . I'm not a cruel man . . . I'm a thief. That's all.'

Vince appealed to Morved for her comfort, her forgiveness.

'Morved. . . .'

Morved knew his needs. She understood and she didn't move towards him, just yet.

'I'm a killer and a thief.' Vince was almost in tears.

Morved waited a little longer before speaking. Let him earn her forgiveness, her comfort, her understanding, she thought.

'But you got away with it. Forty years of thieving, and then you got away with murder.'

Vince bowed his head.

'Come here,' said Morved at last, taking him in her arms, a mother with a small child, very much in charge now. Cradling him against her, swaying from side to side, she eased and soothed him.

All he needed was a bit of loving, a bit of understanding, just to give him his confidence back. It's up to you girl, she thought, to get him through this now.

Oh, she could do that: Morved, the spinner of webs, the dreamer of dreams. What was needed was a bit of flattery to make him feel strong, make him feel dangerous again, that was all men required. A bit of flattery, a bit of motivation

155

and he'd become the man she was looking for, the man to take her away from all this. Not quite what she'd expected mind. She'd imagined more of a dance-band leader, maybe a rich business man. Never guessed it would be a killer and a thief. Here was her chance – the one she was waiting for – and she was taking it.

They stood clasped together, she soothing and whispering, cradling him gently in the dark shop.

The wagging tongues had plenty to occupy them. Over the next weeks the town observed the changes in VINCE'S GENTLEMAN'S BARBER SHOP. It changed colour from dirty cream to green, and from green, through cream to orange. The regulars weren't sure they didn't prefer the original, finding the bright orange hard on the eyes. Not only that, pot plants displayed in rows of plastic 'Wedgwood' jardinières replaced the comfortable mess on the shelves. Far too like their own front parlours for comfort. Worse still, the girlie magazines that once littered the bench were replaced by equally glossy household magazines.

Vince wasn't entirely sure about the transformation of the shop, nor the transformation of himself. He was waiting impatiently for Morved to finish doing her make-up in the newly-papered cubbyhole: the paper was a violently flowery mauve.

Vince wore a new suit, a loud herring-boned cloth. Gone was the photograph of Perry, gone was the early photograph of Vince, banished to the flowery cubbyhole where it hung, out of the way, on the stock cupboard door. In its place above the sink hung a cheap watercolour of uncertain school in a gilt frame.

These alterations were symptomatic of the subtle changes in the relationship between Morved and Vince. She had moved in slowly, first with suggestions, then with demands and within weeks had achieved the moral takeover of Mr Vince's shop, and of Mr Vince himself.

Morved emerged at last from the cubbyhole, dressed in spangly mauve with low-cut cleavage. Mauve was the colour this season, in the Welsh seaside towns, at least.

Briefly she checked her eye make-up in the mirror above the sink. Perfect match. She glanced round at Vince, staring in the mirror again as if he didn't recognise himself.

'Well?' She tapped her foot.

Vince knew his orders. Shambling over to the till, he took out some cash, and was about to close the drawer when he caught her eye and took out more. He put it in his pocket. He didn't look too happy about it, but he already knew better than to protest.

It was a take-over, complete with no conferring. His shop, himself and now his money. And Vince was uneasy about it.

Every morning, killer, thief, adulterer or not, he went through the daily grind, as usual. Every morning picking up the milk from the door-step, opening the door, turning the sign from CLOSED to OPEN.

Tugging the string to the electric fire over the bench, Vince would stand there immobile, his motor stopped. Perry's old habit.

He went through the ritual of making the morning tea, but one morning reaching for the tea-bags he saw something beside the sink which shouldn't be there: Morved's cheap flowered make-up bag. He snapped it open and looked inside. A mess of stained cotton wool, a mascara brush, a tube leaking orange make-up, and something else that he shut his eyes to. Morved! He was overcome by nausea, as Perry had been at the sight of the tea-bags. He held the thing as far from him as he could, as if he were about to vomit.

Staring absently at himself in the mirror in front of Perry's old chair, he drew his hands back through his hair, in Perry's gesture. His thoughts were far away waiting for the answer to the question he'd yet to ask.

More and more, he looked out into the street, staring straight through his customers as if he were looking past them at someone else. They watched him ever more disconcerted, having to wait for him to remember their names, or notice their presence.

157

Ah, those Welsh tongues.

Can't think what's come over Mr Vince these days, seems nervous like.

Maybe Mr Perry's accident got him down? Accident, was it?

Those fancy clothes he wears. . . .

Had to wait a good minute Thursday before he noticed I was there in the shop.

Stares right through you he does. Gives you the creeps!

Can't think how he manages to cut hair, always looking into the street like that.

Watching for someone is he? I wonder who?

We don't see him down the club much. Wonder why?

Mrs Harry Bach saw him in that posh restaurant in Aber you know, the one that calls chips something else.

Sure it was him, she said. Wonder who was with him?

Now you mention it. . . .

The shop-sign was turned to CLOSED as another day ended. In Vince's mirror Morved's mouth contorted in a circle as she applied her vivid lipstick. Vince watched repelled, wondering why this was necessary. The discontented mouth was always demanding now – and no, Morved wasn't happy to go to that boring old French place in Aber again. Just a bloody old steak house it was!

Time was, and not so long ago, when Morved had got a thrill out of giving the old-bugger-her-husband the slip on some silly pretext. Hurrying up the narrow, dark streets, slipping into the narrow dark bed that she shared with a murderer, a thief! Holding hands on the dark drive to Aber in Vince's old car. Now she wanted him to buy a new one. Something sportier, a two-seater. Morved wasn't content and Vince was far from happy as he stood watching her, leaning on the broom. It was he did the cleaning now.

He knew before she did what she would say next and, sure enough, she started on about that poor-old-bugger-her-husband. Always hinting, never quite letting him off the hook.

'The old bugger, the old cripple, coughing and farting all

day like the Co-Op horse. Looking like he's going on for ever.'

Vince watched her mouth in disgust. The language that came out of it.

'You through yet?' She turned to him, impatient at the familiar vacant stare on his face.

She flounced to the till and took out some extra cash. Seeing Vince watching her in the mirror, she deliberately put her hand in again and took out some more. She shoved it in her purse and put the purse into her new hand-bag.

Vince was behind her.

'Can I wash your hair?' he asked her softly.

Morved wasn't sure she'd heard him right.

'I'd like to give you a shampoo.'

'Don't be daft,' Morved said. 'We booked a table for half-past. You did book, didn't you? We're not going to have all that again.'

Once he'd 'forgotten' to ring, to save his money, hoping the restaurant would be full, the miserable old miser: she didn't like misers.

'I don't mean now, I mean sometime, can I give you a hair-wash?' Vince smiled nervously, shifty as a bad child.

Morved frowned. She didn't like this latest suggestion, and she was going to put a stop to it. Just let him remember what he was.

'You don't want to say them things, even joking . . . I just gone all hot and prickly. . . .'

Anyway, it was disgusting, a man wanting to wash a woman's hair. Was he kinky or what? And in Perry's sink! Morved gave a shudder. What was the matter with him, coming out with a thing like that?

'I asked, that's all. I just asked.'

'Well you know what happened to asking, don't you?'

In charge again, she looked significantly at the cleaning things. Was he going to stand there all night with that broom? She stared after him as he shuffled into the cubbyhole, as it occurred to her for the first time that perhaps she didn't know him as well as she thought.

159

The balance of their relationship was changing again. It was Vince who did the asking now. Vince who put on the pressure, but Morved was hard to shift.

'Let me, let me wash your hair.'

'Drop it, will you.'

But he didn't drop it. Every time they met he asked again, cajoling and wheedling. Morved uneasily averted her snip-snapping eyes; she wasn't going to show her growing fear of this man she once thought predictable and mundane. For a while it gave their relationship a renewed excitement. They took ever greater risks, and once Morved came to the shop in broad daylight, and sat in his chair, the chair by the window.

Vince leaned over her.

'I find you a very dangerous, attractive person.'

And he bent towards her. She could smell his toothpaste. There in broad daylight, for anyone to see, he kissed her.

Morved found that exciting.

For a time.

Vince worked on her, just as she had worked on him. Vince and Morved. Morved was becoming less certain, and the shop was beginning to give her the creeps again, maybe even more. Well, it always had. Nothing to do with being haunted, just that it felt odd. She couldn't define it but she felt it with her Celtic instinct for the oblique, felt the thing hinted at.

But she'd seen her chance, she'd grabbed it. She'd spotted her man, worked on him, improved him and taken him over. He was her way out, her means to an escape. . . . Then with the old bugger's cash, and her determination, she would leave, free. For who knows where, maybe Cardiff . . . maybe even London. . . ? Anywhere except where she was. But she was much less certain now.

'No, I told you, and it's staying no.'

He was at it again. Asking her to his place to do it this time. Oh, the cheek!

'I got a husband, and besides you done it to your best pal.'

Better alive with the old cripple than dead from the demon barber!

'You got to trust me. I'm trusting you. I told you everything.'

So he was trying a new tack now, was he?

'Which I didn't ask for, did I?' Morved asked unhappily.

'I put myself in your hands,' he came back.

'What about me – getting involved with a murderer?'

'We got to trust. This is a life-long thing now. You do realise that?'

She was beginning to, only just beginning to and it was time to cut her losses, to re-group, re-plan. In Perry's words, live to fight another day.

Vince checked the shop. No customers. He beckoned her into the cubbyhole, and gently shut the door.

'Stand to cash in when he snuffs it, do you?'

Morved didn't look at him.

'You know who I'm talking about. Be able to move away would you, forget this place, forget me?'

Morved didn't speak. Oh, he was sharp, this man she no longer knew.

'You just say the word. You drop the hint . . . I'll finish him for you.'

Morved's eyes flicked to his face. Her hand clutched at the neck of her familiar pink nylon blouse.

In the distance she heard a customer calling 'Shop!'

'Say the word and he's a dead man, that old cripple, that old bugger. You're free of him . . . and me,' Vince hissed.

He put on his professional smile: his teeth even, white and false. Alone, Morved leant her head against the stock cupboard. It was tempting; it offered her a way out. Morved, who believed in taking the chance when it came, wondered whether to take this one offered by Vince.

Vince trod the small grey streets, the same route every day. Poor bloody infantry! He never went to the club now. Didn't see much of her either. He was becoming obsessed by the small, the domestic. He spent minutes watching water in the sink, would put his hands in and move his fingers, closing his eyes and letting his thoughts run through his head, oblivious. Stand there, he would, with a black plastic bin-sack in front of him, and run his hands up and down it, his face vacant, thoughts elsewhere.

Vince stood in the closed shop working out his various alternatives. Checking the possibilities in his head. He hadn't bothered to switch on the light: thinking came easier in the dark.

Someone was knocking on the street door and he switched into full alert, seeing the shape of Morved through the frosted glass. Silently he stepped into shadow, away from the light of the street lamp. He heard the key turning, and the noise of the outside world passing as she opened and gently shut the door behind her. From the shadow, he saw her place a letter on the shelf in front of his chair. She tiptoed back to the street door like a large fluffy moth in that pale Angora she wore when she wasn't bothering much. It suited her better thought Vince, than all those fancy sparkling clothes. She looked cosy and vulnerable.

Morved abruptly stopped, remembering another part of her errand. She turned in the direction of the cubbyhole. She looked very white as she flitted quietly across the darkness of the shop.

Reaching the cubbyhole door and fumbling towards the light switch she was so close to Vince that he felt her breath brush his face. Morved paused, listening. No, she hadn't heard anything.

Don't be a fool girl, get on and get it over quick. The sooner you're out of here the better. She took her hand off the switch. It was better not to risk a light.

Like hide-and-bloody-seek this, thought Vince, or blind man's bloody buff! He listened to the noises inside the cubbyhole. He knew what she was doing in there, as her hands searched for her plastic make-up bag.

She knew exactly where it was, slung on the draining board between the Squeezy and the mugs. Had he moved it? No. She stuffed it in her skirt pocket. It was an old one, so it didn't matter if it made the pocket baggy.

Now for the cardigan on the cubbyhole door. It was a good one, she wasn't leaving that behind. Cost money that had – not her money, mind, but even so. . . . She slipped it from the hook.

Vince waited. He felt rather than heard her come out from the cubbyhole. She stopped, peering around her, caught in the street light again, and Vince knew what she would do next. She flitted to the till and opened it.

Vince stepped softly behind her, watching over her shoulder as she flicked out first the notes, then the silver, ignoring the copper.

'Helping yourself to that week in hand was you?'

He spoke softly but his voice sounded loud in Morved's ear. In her shock she spilled the coins noisily all over the floor. They ran and circled and settled on the lino in the pause that followed.

Vince stood in the half light, her letter in his hand.

'Oh Morved. . . .' There was regret in his voice, even tenderness. 'Why couldn't you have told me to my face you'd had enough?'

Morved clutched the remaining money.

'I got to go. I got a sick husband.' She thanked God for a strong heart or she'd have certainly collapsed.

'You're not taking up my offer then? You don't want me to kill him ?'

Vince sounded almost kindly as he stared down at her.

Morved sounded Welsher in her fear. Her voice lost that practised refinement she'd worked so hard to get.

'I'm through with all that, I got to go. I told him where I'd be,' she added.

Morved was cunning, but not cunning enough for Vince. He'd read too many detective stories to fall for that one.

They stood there facing each other in the half light, Morved and Vince. Vince was blocking the door.

She began to talk breathlessly; partly out of panic, partly because it was her nature to talk. As she talked she watched for that chance, and Vince watched her watching for it as her Welsh voice filled the dark between them.

There was something about the shop that she couldn't get

163

straight even now, something still unexplained. What was it? She scrutinised Vince, playing him mentally to find his weak point. Hadn't she always been able to find the weak point in a man?

'Every day that I've been here, every time I've looked around . . . something here isn't right. There's something I should have asked about.'

Vince advanced towards her slowly. He let his hand drop on the chair, the chair in the window.

'Well now. . . .' His eyes didn't leave her face. Slowly he moved again, placing his hand on Perry's chair.

'I wonder what. . . .'

He reached the third chair, the unoccupied chair in the corner. He raised his hand but this time paused and looked at her, saw her eyes fix on his raised hand as he slowly let it drop.

Morved took a moment to realise then her face stiffened into a gasp: *why were three there chairs for two partners?*

There had been three of them once, Vince and Perry and Harry. Demobbed together they'd been thrown into peace just as they'd been thrown into the war, they struggled to come to terms with civvy life, boredom, law and order.

Vince and Perry and Harry, the three bloody musketeers. They'd come home to Wales when all the shouting was over and mooched around the town, the pubs and the arcades. It was peace after the storm, anti-climax after the fight. Not that they'd seen much fighting. Boring old war. And peace was just as bad. Vince paused. He noted that Morved had moved. She'd inched herself in front of the cubbyhole. He started up again, conversationally.

It was then that they'd got the idea of the barbershop, there playing the slot machines down the Fun Palace. There would always be a need for hair-cutting, nothing to it; that's what Harry said. Harry was a bit of a wide boy, Harry laughed at everything, couldn't take life seriously. Always poking fun at poor old Perry he was, Perry who took life too seriously.

They opened the shop and worked all hours God sent,

apart from Harry. Harry didn't pull his weight even at the start. He got into the habit of drinking, more out of boredom than anything else. Peace was even more boring than war.

'Harry was a Welshman.

Harry was a thief.

Harry went to my house and stole. . . . That was about the sum of it,' said Vince, seeing Morved snatch a glance at the butter-knife on the drainer, gauging her chances of reaching it.

So Harry went for a walk one night and never showed up again. Fell off the harbour wall, some reckoned. . . . Just kept walking, according to others.

Vince and Perry took down his picture and never mentioned his name again for, of course, he hadn't fallen off the harbour wall, had he?

'I came back to find him helping himself to the float, just like I found you. We was both fair scrappers, and he put up one hell of a fight but I got on top. I did have a temper, in them days.'

He looked down at Harry's chair regretfully: tired and old and sad. Poor bloody infantry.

Her eyes flicked again to the knife.

'You can trust me, you know that,' she said soothingly, but he wasn't listening.

'I'm stuck in this bloody shop till the day I die, it's been round my neck forty years and it might be around it another twenty.'

Vince seemed to have stalled again, gone down the muddy road of self pity, and now suddenly Morved was in the cubbyhole, the knife in her hand.

'Harry's still here.'

Vince appeared in the doorway and she backed away against the stock cupboard.

'How could I let the place go? Let strangers move in? Harry's in there.' Vince gestured towards the stock cupboard behind her.

'Two and a half bags of cement I had to use that weekend. Reckon that's what did in my back.'

165

Morved straightened up away from the cupboard, away from Harry, who'd taken to drink because peace was too difficult. But who would have drunk and thieved his life away anyway, even if he'd never known a damn war.

An inch or so further from Harry, meant an inch or so nearer Vince.

But he'd turned away from her, apparently forgetting her again, looking out of the window into the street, this habit he had looking onto the street.

He never could give up that window seat. Now and then Perry would mention it, joking like but he had to have it. He knew the resentment Perry felt: turn and turn about, the promise never kept. He knew he was letting down his old mucker, his pal but what could he do? For forty years he'd been on the look-out . . . for the police . . . for Harry's family to come for him. He hated the bloody window seat, never could get warm. But he'd stayed on watch – with no one to relieve him – for forty years.

'And the next twenty,' he turned slowly from the window. 'How ever long I'm spared, I'll be frightened they're coming for me on account of you too now.' Vince felt tired of the trap he had sprung. Tired and sick.

'I told you,' her voice was shrill in her fear, 'I'm no push-over. I'm a strong woman. You'll have as big a scrap as you had with him. You'll get a surprise if you try it on with me.'

Vince smiled a small regretful smile.

'Unless I got an advantage. Well, I do have one. I've had a fair bit of time to put some thinking in, figuring exactly how I'm going to finish you.'

They faced each other in the back-street barbershop, Morved and Vince. And at some final moment, no one ever knew exactly when, he moved towards her in the dark.

Caroline Hunt,
based on the television script by Ron Hutchinson

HIDDEN TALENTS

The tiny white cross was whiter than mere white, and although the grass had grown over the square patch of earth and weeds clung to its base, the cross looked as if it had been placed there only days before.

Madelaine Mary Hargreaves
aged 8 years
Suffer Little Children To Come Unto Me
December 15th 1969

'I'm so sorry sweetheart, I should have come before, but I just couldn't, I just couldn't.'

Florence Hargreaves felt rain seeping through her cheap woollen coat. Her feet were icy cold where graveyard mud had splattered up her ankles, and she pushed her hands deeper into coat pockets. It had been a long time, a long wait. She'd wondered if she'd be able to find her. Things had changed. New paths had been made, and she'd had to pause to get her bearings.

Under advice from her doctor, Florence had been moved to a new housing estate, less than a month after police found what remained of the girl.

The nightmare of waiting, not knowing where her daughter was, had taken its toll. So that when the police eventually found her daughter's pitiful body in Sniggery Woods, buried under a crude grave of leaves in a ditch, Florence had sighed with relief.

'At last, thank God.'

The police officer who broke the news, wrote later in his report that the mother seemed in a uneasy dream. How, he'd asked afterwards, could any mother thank God on being told that her child's body had been found? He was very young.

The same doctor gave Florence *Diazapam* to help her through the burial – the sad, forlorn funeral – and also paid an unscheduled call to her house a few days afterwards. Florence had been well dressed, even pleased to see him, and offered him a cup of tea. It became apparent though that not all was well when Florence carefully set three places at the table. Madelaine would soon be home from school Florence announced and would he like to see her also? Her voice was totally matter of fact.

The social worker went round next and discovered that Florence had not yet been back to work, either at the paper shop or at the school where she cleaned in the mornings. Florence, confronted by the social worker, assured her that life was fine, her daughter was well again now, and would soon be able to restart her piano lessons. She showed off a photograph in a wooden frame.

'Madelaine's very talented, you know, Mr Southall her tutor has said so. Shows a real flair, he says, and can pick up a tune by ear. Lovely isn't she? Pretty girl, although I shouldn't be saying so myself.'

She shouldn't have been, and the doctor and social worker arranged for Mrs Hargreaves to be admitted to a 'rest' home. They never mentioned what it really was, and to Florence it was just somewhere where she could rest.

A year later, Florence began to face the fact that her beloved daughter was not coming back. She cried, then wept as grief that had been hidden beneath a shell of fantasy gushed out.

She needed the rest, her husband had deserted her, and she'd been working day and night for her daughter to go to that small private school . . . for those piano lessons. Madelaine had been Florence's sole reason for existing, and when the girl died Florence's tenuous hold on reality became no hold at all. It was a long time before she was able to live normally, though it was easier to carry on once the home and the doctors had finished with her. They had decided it would be better for Florence if she moved to a new housing estate, away from her tragedy, away from her memories.

Her past sorrow was forgotten, too forgotten; so that when the new estate suffered subsidence and the council had to find the tenants somewhere else to live they had, without any thought, moved Florence right back again. Right back to Madelaine.

Florence tore at the grass with her bare hands until the cross stood uncluttered. She would return the following day with flowers, daffodils were Madelaine's favourite.

Sitting at the top of a double decker bus Harold Southall checked over his shopping and knew that he had forgotten something. He didn't worry about it though, as quite often he did it on purpose because at least that got him out of the house. There was only one stop to go, one more stop before they passed the graveyard. As always he felt his chest tighten and he would know with one flick of an eye the exact position of Madelaine's white cross.

Years ago he had brought her flowers every first day of the month and placed them by her tiny cross, until his mother found out and put a stop to it.

The bus rumbled and slowed with a jerk. Two women stood outside the graveyard gates, umbrellas up and with loaded shopping bags. They waved the bus down to a stop.

Sitting up on the top deck, Harold's mind muttered to itself, any minute now, you'll see her coming up now, just a few more yards.

Without thinking Florence turned towards the sounds of the stopping bus, and stared. The rain was coming down hard now, and the bus was blurred. Her hair was dripping with water, hanging in rats' tails around her hollow cheeks. She made no effort to wipe the rivulets from her face. She could even feel the rain dripping from her fingers.

Harold craned towards the window and, as the bus jolted forwards almost twisted his neck. That woman . . . the woman standing by Madelaine's grave. There was a woman by the white cross. He pressed his face hard against the cold window pane, then rubbed foolishly at the rain dripping down the other side of the glass in the hope that he could clear it, but his breath only made the window misty.

'Mrs Hargreaves,' he said slowly, 'Mrs Hargreaves.'

The two women from the bus stop bundled their way up the stairs, shaking their umbrellas.

'Eh, eh you know your shoppin' bag's open love?'

Harold turned to them defensively and shrank back in his seat . . . he could see their mouths moving, but he couldn't hear what they were saying.

'Shit, shit, batteries, I forgot me batteries.'

The two women plonked themselves down in the empty front seat, raised their eyebrows at each other and began to gossip.

Harold frantically stuffed his groceries back into the bag, as the ringing in his ears grew louder and louder, until even the rumbling sounds of the old red bus couldn't be heard. The bells sounded loud as St Mary's, and in desperation Harold pushed his way off the bus, dropping potatoes behind him. He just had to get off. He couldn't hear, he couldn't hear anything but the bloody bells.

Harold had left the bus two stops early, so now he had to walk through the pouring rain. Swearing busily, muttering about forgetting his ruddy batteries he made his way home: but running in a small section of his mind, running all by itself like a picture show was that haunting face, that half-seen sad staring face at the graveyard.

'Mrs Hargreaves was at the cemetery.' He repeated it slowly, tasting it.

Harold stood at the back door in his sodden mac clutching his shopping bag. The kitchen door led into a scullery off which was the main kitchen area itself. Not that it looked like a kitchen any more . . . far, far from it. The room was dominated by a battered Jacobean four poster bed, its posts crudely sawn off to allow the monstrosity to be brought into the room. There were old dressers against the walls, tables, easy chairs, cupboards and a wardrobe; the whole room turned into a living bedroom of almost unbelievable clutter. There was not a space on any flat surface without its untidy pile of dirty dishes, objects, ornaments or crumpled papers. The bedside table was crammed with photographs, magazines, chocolates and again the invariable mound of squalid crockery.

Nellie Southall, her huge bulk seeming even vaster beneath an array of blankets, eiderdowns, shawls, cushions and pillows, sat waiting with a face like sour thunder. She always timed his shopping expeditions, and he was well over twenty minutes off schedule.

'I'm soaked to the skin,' he said sadly, getting his complaint in first.

She looked at him. She too was sodden. She could have held on, but out of anger had drenched the bed. 'Well I'm soaked too and that's *your* fault. Where the hell have you been? Did you get my hair dye? Harold, did you get my hair dye? The right colour this time?'

She sighed theatrically. He looked such a fool rooted to the spot, standing there in his dripping mac still clutching his shopping bag. Angrily, Nellie began to peel off the numerous cardigans wrapped around her bosom, and over went a half eaten box of Cadbury's creams. She swore, then heaved her bulk over to retrieve them. When she looked up he was still in the same position.

Nellie raised her voice. 'Clean sheets Harold, I'll need clean sheets and a nightie, Harold?'

He couldn't hear her, didn't intend to hear her. He dumped the bag on the fridge top, knocking over an empty milk bottle that fell unbroken with a clatter on to the floor to join a row of other dead and dirty milk bottles.

Nellie struggled on, and as her heart began to thud she paused to gasp for breath, then shouted again for clean sheets.

It wasn't clear whether Harold had heard. All the same he moved like a mechanical toy soldier, still in his raincoat. First he pulled an old screen around the end of the large bed, then reached up to a pulley above the old black fireplace. He held a nightie to his cheek, it had dried, then chucked it on to the bed and went to get the dried sheet. The ironing board had been up in the same position for at least five years, not that he ever ironed anything. Every day of his life for five years he had to step round the thing, but

171

had never thought, never bothered to take it down and put it away.

Harold carried across the rumpled but dry sheet, and heaved off all the top blankets and rugs from the bed in one pull. He pulled a top greyish, once white, sheet from Nellie on to the floor, and tried not to look at Nellie in all her squalid, untidy glory.

Thick woollen bed socks, layers of nightdresses and shawls. Legs as swollen as her body, as if she was a bag filled with water. Harold shoved his mother on to her side and eased the acrid smelling wet sheet from beneath her.

He had the exercise of bed-changing down to a fine art. The clean sheet was already folded lengthwise down the middle, so he laid it flat and rolled her over on to the clean side, then moved round the bed, pushing her forwards as he pulled the rest of the sheet over the bed. He tucked it in, flipped the top sheet back into place and heaved over the rest of the covers. He then handed her the nightdress, and pulled the screen right round for Nellie to change, in privacy.

Harold stood staring blankly at the screen, still in his sodden raincoat.

'She was at the cemetery,' he said. 'Mrs Hargreaves, I saw her standing. Like a ghost. It was her, she was at Madelaine's grave.'

Nellie's heart, already thudding from the effort of changing, banged even harder, as if pushing through her chest. Her voice was loud, hoping he would hear. How many times, she asked bitterly, had she told him never to go there? Never to go to Madelaine's grave again?

Harold wheeled the screen away, without answering, and pushed it back into its dirt-filled corner of the kitchen.

'I told you not to go up there, I've told you that, Harold, Harold can you hear me?'

She knew he couldn't, from the way he stood holding his hand protectively to his deaf aid.

Three times, louder each time, she asked if he'd got his batteries, but he remained silent. Then with the dirty sodden sheet bundled in his arms, he took it into the scullery and shoved it into the washing machine.

'Where are you going . . . Harold?'

He opened the back door and muttered that he couldn't hear, couldn't hear and then was gone.

Nellie's heart slowed to its normal erratic pace and she leant back to pick up an ever-present mirror and stared at herself. Her roots needed doing now.

She began to unbraid her long plait of red hair. She used to be natural red, of course, but that had faded so now she just brightened it up. Problem was, Harold could never remember that it was *Light Auburn* and he'd bought her back some terrible shades. Nellie admitted to herself that her hair was a strange mixture of auburn and chestnut but, more important, showing through the colour was that two-inch grey parting.

Soft bugger, she thought as her stomach rumbled, must have forgotten the dye as well.

Nellie flicked on the television, her lifeline, and flicked from channel to channel. She hated afternoon television and never could find – there never was – anything of interest.

It was dark when Harold trudged back home, new deaf aid batteries in his pocket. Not many people bothered to say 'hello', or acknowledge him; although he would occasionally get a brief nod or a small wave of recognition. Over the years neighbours had stopped bothering. The shopkeepers in the local stores were friendly, though his shopping lists were a source of amusement rather than profit . . . two chops, not a lot of fat, four slices of bacon. He was actually a pest, with his meagre smallest possible packs of butter; a nuisance because he was back the following day with yet another neat, small list.

The storekeepers would always mention the weather, and invariably asked after his mother from habit but, due to his apparent deafness, they rarely received a reply. Oh, Harold heard them but simply couldn't be bothered to talk. So they gave knowing glances and tuts – such a sad dejected, defeated man – and felt comfortably sorry for him.

The road he trudged down was in the most respectable area of Waterloo or rather it had been once; now many of the big houses had been turned into flats. Number fifteen stuck out like a smashed thumb with its overgrown garden, grass almost as high as the side fences, a front doorstep thick with rotting leaves; and curtains always drawn at the front of the house. The once elegant frontage was peeling back like skin and the pebble-dash showed big wounds through to the brick beneath. The roof had slates missing and even the garden gate hung itself by one rusted nail.

The front hedge was more than eight feet tall and totally out of control, hanging over on to the pavement. Residents complained regularly to the Rates and Environmental Health but nothing was ever done; number fifteen remained standing, just – decaying, year by year.

As Harold had turned into the street he noticed, exactly opposite number fifteen, a large furniture removal van. Now two men were carrying a wardrobe into the house opposite. Harold lifted the gate to walk up his path . . . and as he turned to shove it back into place, his eyes met those of Mrs Hargreaves.

She was staring blindly across the road, face as forlorn as it had been at the graveyard. Then she followed the removal men back inside the house, into the house opposite number fifteen. Harold burst into the scullery, so agitated that he merely gabbled, pointing unhappily towards the hall.

'She's moving in,' he said at last. 'She's moving in opposite, I'm telling you, I've just seen her.'

Nellie switched off her television and yelled at him to shut up and calm down.

'Who? Who are you talking about? Who's moved in?'

Who? Harold was shaking. He looked as if he was going to cry.

Nellie pursed her lips and shouted for him to sit down next to her. 'Have you got your batteries in . . . can you hear me?'

But he just sat there frozen.

Nellie had to jerk his face round to make him look at her, and his wide eyes were as frightened as a child's.

'Now you listen to me,' she insisted. 'It's in your imagination. There's no Mrs Hargreaves and there's nothing to be afraid of . . . I'm here, Harold, I'm here and no one's going to hurt you. Just go about your business and, whatever you do, *don't* go near that graveyard, promise me.'

Calmer now, he shuffled into the scullery and threw his wet raincoat over a chair. Suddenly he turned and broke from the room and, though Nellie shouted after him, he slammed the door shut on her.

She waited. Already she knew what was coming and lay back in the mounds of pillows. 'Oh dear God, no,' she said. 'No.'

The notes began. Repeated. The same piece of music, over and over again, Nellie punched the volume button to loud to block out the tinkling repetitive tune from Harold's piano.

The music room was dark, its heavy velvet drapes always drawn and dusty. There was only one small light on, a fringed Victorian glass lamp standard. All of the carpets had been rolled back and the piano raised up on bricks, on top of the bare floor boards. By this method, Harold was able to hear his notes a little more clearly, the echo effect and the vibration helping him.

His fine delicate hands moved lightly, lovingly over the keys and his eyes closed. He loved this piece so much but somehow he had never been able to finish it.

Harold could see her clearly now, in her neat white cotton frock, with golden curls caught up by a ribbon which was also white.

She was not a beautiful child, but she had talent, a dazzling smile and such a laugh that it was like a breath of fresh air.

Madelaine used to come every Tuesday and Thursday for her lessons. Harold had been a student then, at Liverpool University, and, at first, he had taught her to supplement his meagre grant but soon he actually loved those afternoons. With Madelaine he wasn't shy, he didn't stumble with his words and he used to be able to chatter away to her,

175

telling her all his dreams, as if he were the child.

Harold had such dreams then, and they were not as many now believed without hope. He had won a scholarship to a music academy. He had won the Musical Association's Pianist of the Year award playing one of his own compositions that had impressed the judges with its flair and imagination.

Harold was, everyone said, extremely talented. He was also exceptionally, unusually even unnaturally shy and reserved, finding it difficult if not impossible to make friends – or for that matter even acquaintances. Then Madelaine had come into his life, and those two afternoons a week he lived for and looked forward to, working out easy pieces for her to practise, encouraging her with an excitement and an energy few ever saw.

The child was talented and she also loved music. She had once made him sit still in a velvet-covered chair, saying she had a surprise for him. So he had sat down and, straight-faced, had waited for her to begin. Her tiny hands hung for a second over the keys and then, to his astonishment, she began to play from memory one of his own pieces, as yet unfinished.

Harold played that same piece now, and felt her with him in the room.

Nellie's screech of a voice suddenly broke through his dreaming and Harold thumped the keys in anger. There was someone at the front door, she shouted, she'd heard the letter box bang.

Harold leapt into the hall, flung open the kitchen door and yelled back that there was no one at the door.

'Well there's something on the mat, I can see it. You get out there an if it's from the Church tell 'em that if they're beggin' we need a new roof, never mind those buggers.'

The large brown envelope was addressed to Harold Southall. Puzzled, he carried it back into the kitchen.

Nellie peered through her glasses her hand out, wanting to know what it was. The single sheet of cheap paper said, in a fine spider's web writing:

Dear Mr Southall,
I know how fond of Madelaine you were and I thought you might like to have this.
Yours sincerely,
Florence Hargreaves.

The envelope also contained a large blown-up photograph of Madelaine staring back at the camera, and Harold began to shake as he looked into the face he had pictured just as clearly in his mind not two minutes before.

He stared at his mother who was scrutinising the note, then crossed to the mirror, examined what he had become and looked down at the photograph. He could have wept.

He'd grown so old, thin and wizened. And she was just the same, all these years later, just as she was then.

'Well, of course she is you great soft bugger. She's dead. Now give it here, put it back in the envelope and shove it through her door, if she's opposite. Give it back.'

Nellie tore the note into tiny pieces, but Harold wouldn't give up the photo. He was too busy pressing his body back against the dresser willing himself to disappear.

'She knows,' he said frantically. 'She knows. That's why she's come back here. She's coming after me, she knows.'

Nellie had to scream to make herself heard above the hysteria in his voice. She needed to get him close to the bed, so she could grab him.

'People said at the shop they'd moved her here because of subsidence,' Harold told Nellie, 'but that was a lie, she's getting at me.'

Nellie eventually coaxed him within her reach and pulled him down beside her. Her fat ringed hand gripped his own tight, as she snapped at him that the woman would have no option. If the council had decided on it, then there was nothing anyone could do.

'I'm the one the police talked to,' she said bitterly. 'Not you, they came to me, an' you open that stupid mouth of yours and they'll be back. Are you listening to me?' She shook him. 'I lied for you, so keep your mouth shut and give this photo back. I know why she's sent it over.'

Harold wriggled out of her grasp and edged round the bed. Sometimes when he saw his mother he hated her so much he would have liked to batter her heavy face.

'Well,' he said, 'go on, know all. Tell me why you think she's here?'

Nellie could have clouted him one. He had that cocky silly expression, and when he had it he looked like his father; but then he was his father all over, weak, spineless and just as much a soft fool.

'She's bound to want to try and be friendly isn't she? Because who's left round here that she would know, eh? You tell me that? She went funny in the head, didn't she? Asylum case, put her away, and that's where they'll put you if you carry on like this.'

Harold slumped into the broken armchair. The seat was piled so high with newspapers that his legs didn't reach the floor as he sat kicking at the chair, looking with loathing at his mother.

'She never knew nobody when she lived here before,' Nellie stated fiercely. 'She was always hanging around, just like her at the back, that Judith's mother.'

Harold listened in dreadful fascination as Nellie launched into one of her dramatic stories. About Judith who used to live close by, Judith who had been chasing Stanley, just like all the girls chased Stanley.

As if on stage, Nellie carefully retold the story about how she'd come home from the pub an' heard from Stanley's own room all these grunts and groans. Up she'd gone and banged on his door.

Nellie roared with laughter as she recalled her youngest son how even then, she couldn't help but notice, he was so well endowed. No wonder all the girls were after him.

'Harold, I swear I'd have been after him meself if he wasn't my son. You know what I mean? God, he was a looker was Stanley; they were all around here after him.'

Harold was off the chair in a second on to the bed, yelling in fury, demanding to know if she was insinuating that Mrs Hargreaves and his precious Madelaine were *after* Stanley?

Nellie sighed, pushed him away . . . God he was so

178

stupid. It was not Mrs Hargreaves she was talking about, but her at the back, Judith who'd drop her knickers for an ice cream cornet.

'I said to Stanley, I said Stanley I'd hop it love if I were you. That one Judith's after the altar job, and what you were up to in your room with her could get you there with a shotgun.'

Nellie's bellowing laugh made Harold hysterical. 'He left because he stole your money. You told him to get out! You screamed the place down because he stole all your savings. It had nothing to do with her at the back.'

Nellie's moon face crumpled, and she plucked unhappily at the bed-clothes. It was true, course it was; but sometimes she made up these stories as an excuse. Her Stanley had stolen her savings, all those hard-earned tenners from singing at the local pubs. Harold didn't have to remind her. It had broken her heart.

Harold immediately recognised the swing in emotion and saw her big painted doll's eyes fill with tears. He knelt on the bed, would have liked to hold her but as always she shoved him away.

'Ma,' he said plaintively, 'why don't we sell this place, move someplace small? We don't need this huge house. We could get away from here, from her across the road, just you and me.'

She slapped him hard, angrily saying that this was her home and she'd never leave it. All the antiques, all the valuables from her husband's family were here in this house. And they were going to stay there. They were hers and no one was going to take them away.

'Why'd you do that Ma? I'm only saying we could move away and find someplace nice.'

Nellie picked up the ever-present photograph of her beloved Stanley, touched it and replaced it next to her bed.

'I want to be here if he comes home, that's why. I want to be here. The only way you'll get me out is in a box.'

In a box . . . Harold felt the old pain of jealousy cut through him. Always Stanley, even now after all these years she still loved Stanley more than she'd ever loved him. It was odd. . . .

'Ma, all those years ago, why did you lie for me, to the police? Why did you do it?'

Nellie lay back and closed her eyes. It was a terrible thing she had done, something she could never forget, never forgive, deep down in her heart. 'Because, so help me God, you're my son.'

She heard the door close and the piano start up, and she didn't have the energy to flick on her television switch to drown the sound. She lay there and thought not of Harold or of Madelaine but of Stanley. Why had he done that to her?

Nellie had never really been much of a mother when they were kids; she knew that but she had reasons, her own reasons.

Married at sixteen to their father, a man she'd been so impressed by. He'd had such class, such dignity. He'd been outside the stage door waiting most nights. She was on tour with *Sound of Music* playing one of the children, only sixteen and a half, and how he had impressed her. He'd taken her back to her digs. True he wasn't the first, she never said he was, but he was the one who got her pregnant.

Walter Southall had no real intentions of marrying his 'little actress', but she had forced him and as she saw his large and splendid house filled with family antiques she really believed that she was set up for life. She could pick up her career after the baby – but instead of that she'd blown up like a balloon, and had never – even after long diets – been able to lose weight again. Doctors, expensive doctors, said it was glandular: whatever, her perfect adolescent figure had gone and with it her hopes of stardom.

Her husband proved to be weak, dominated by his mother. And when, at long last, his mother had died the fortune Nellie was expecting proved mainly debts and only a few hundred pounds. So she'd worked in pubs as a singer – not that she really needed to, her husband's job would have sufficed – but Nellie still hungered for applause and eventually found it in the cheap pubs and bars. She also drank, and on many occasions never came home for nights on end.

Later on, one of those nights she had been away with one of her men, Stanley had come home and she'd missed him. He never returned and wrote only once after that. For twelve years there had been silence.

During those twelve years Nellie had been treated for a heart tremor, and using that as an excuse had taken to her bed. Here in this kitchen-bedroom she still performed for Harold. And here, more importantly, she could watch him, could monitor him. She wanted always to be sure where he was, in case *it* ever happened again.

Nellie wept. Harold, that simple twisted replica of her husband. Harold who had done that terrible, terrible thing which he had made her part of, because God help her, she *was* his mother.

Harold wept, unaware his mother was crying silently in her kitchen. Then he crept up the stairs. Always, when he reached the top, the dark corridor, he paused. This was where Stanley used to boo out on him and terrify Harold. Night after night, he had been too terrified to go upstairs to the toilet in case Stanley was there.

Harold paused and listened. As he couldn't hear the television, he presumed his mother was asleep, so he tip-toed along the landing towards the room at the end. This was Stanley's room, forever forbidden territory but Harold was going to go inside.

The door creaked slightly, unused for so many years. Harold paused, wondering if his mother had heard. He turned up his deaf aid and listened, not a sound. The door creaked again, but by then he had slipped into the inner sanctum.

The stench of the room made him wrinkle his nose. Airless and stale, shut up just as Stanley had left it. The bed had its sheets thrown back, you could even just make out the impression of the body that had slept there. The room was littered with dirty football socks, muddy boots, old jock straps; all flung off and left where they fell.

The light bulb had gone, so that the room was lit only

by a thin crack of light from the street lamp outside.

On the wall were faded posters, The Beatles, and scrawled across in Stanley's childish writing, 'To Stan, With Love from The Beatles', the same boyish scrawl with messages written by himself were on a Rolling Stones poster. Stuck to the open-doored wardrobe was a huge coloured picture of Elvis . . . it read 'Good to know you Stan.'

Stanley's drum kit had cobwebs hanging from the cymbals. A guitar left on its side was thick with twelve years of dust. Harold crept round the darkened room, touching, remembering. As he reached the windows that overlooked the front of the house his heart stopped.

Mrs Hargreaves, like a ghost, was standing in an unlit window exactly opposite outlined in the street lamp and, at first, she appeared to be completely naked. Harold hid himself behind the curtain and watched through the crack. She lifted her hand. 'Dear God,' he mumbled. She must have seen him. She was waving. A pink underslip clung to her scrawny body and, to Harold's horror, she started to dance . . . her arms held up as if to a partner. Suddenly she clicked on the light and he could see her clearly, dancing in her underslip. So thin. He could see even at this distance the hard outline of her nipples. Harold started to drag Stanley's wardrobe across the window frame to block out the sight, to block out the window, to hide her. If he ever came into the room again he didn't want to see, didn't want to remember that window opposite.

A scream came up from below, Nellie announcing that *Come Dancing* had started. Watching the dancers whizzing round the screen, she looked up briefly to the ceiling, hearing the dragging, thudding noise of the wardrobe.

'Harold? . . . *Harold*, what are you doing up there? *Harold*?'

He came in with a familiar sly expression on his face, and Nellie knew instantly that he had been up to something.

'I've told you not to go in his room. You leave his room as it is.'

Harold giggled and hopped around the room, dancing a

waltz in time with the formation team on television. 'Leave it as it is.' He started his annoying childhood habit of repeating everything she said, like a malicious parrot. And Nellie was so angry she threw her book at him.

'She's watching this place naked, I just seen her,' he said unhappily.

Nellie flicked the television off and made a grab at Harold as he waltzed past again. He switched moods as fast as she switched channels.

'You always loved him the best, didn't you?' Harold stated. 'Stole all your savings and yet you still love him the best. . . .'

She made no answer, waiting for Harold to turn. Slowly he gave her a funny clown-like droop of his shoulders, and a soppy grin. But it didn't work, not this time. She'd had enough of his antics and was going to put a stop to them, now and for ever.

'Do you blame me? Well tell me, do you blame me . . . You?'

He began to do an old music hall routine they'd practised when he was a kid, pointing to himself, pointing to her, and strutting around like Charlie Chaplin.

'You think every time you walk out that door I don't worry myself sick, well Harold?'

'Well Harold?' he mimicked her, repeated it, and her temper rose again.

'If it wasn't for me you'd be in Broadmoor.'

Now she had him and he dropped his funny walk and snarled that if it wasn't for him, she'd be rotting in the geriatric ward at Sunny Brook. 'There's nothing wrong with me, Mother, it's you that's sick.'

They started to go at it hammer and tongs, throwing any and every word that they knew would hurt . . . and Nellie won, as she always did. 'I'm not the one that's got a doctor's certificate that says *Mentally unstable* . . . that's you.'

Harold kicked at the great bed with its chopped off posts, shouting that he was deaf, that was all, just deaf, and there was nothing else wrong with him.

'Deaf?' Nellie snorted. 'Mentally unstable . . . sounds

like deaf to you? No, falling off that moped like that, made them write what they did about you. Why they threw you out from that college. . . ? *Mentally unstable.*'

Nellie knew she'd won, beaten him as always. And she should have left it there but never before had he insinuated that she should be put into a home, so she took it one step further.

'An any more mention of me being put into a home and I'll show them. . . .' Too late she knew she should have kept her mouth shut. Knew it but it was too late, it was out, she'd almost said it.

Harold was on to it like a bird of prey. He lurched against the bed, shook the shorn-off pillar of the four poster. 'Show them, show them what?'

He knew she'd burnt his clothes. She said she had burnt his clothes, had she been lying? In a frenzy he began to search the kitchen, not yet knowing what he was looking for. Just that perhaps she'd kept something back, something that had belonged to Madelaine, something that would incriminate him.

Over went dirty china, unused drawers were pulled out, scattered as he rampaged around the kitchen until there was nothing else left to throw on to the floor. He dived under the bed and dragged out all Nellie's theatre scrapbooks and her make-up box and tipped it all out, whilst Nellie wept and shouted that there was nothing, she had nothing, she never kept anything.

Harold stood over the bed and ripped apart her beloved pictures of herself in the *Sound of Music*. As he bent down to search again even further beneath the bed, he hit his head and his deaf aid was torn out. The ringing started again, and the bells began clanging ever more loudly inside his brain. . . .

'I can't hear,' he sobbed. 'I can't hear . . . Ma? Oh Ma, I'm sorry.'

Nellie wouldn't let him near her; just shoved him away and looked broken-heartedly at her treasured keepsakes. 'Get away from me. Get away from me, you sick, sick madman.'

Harold couldn't hear her. He just saw her mouth open and shut. He wanted her to hold him, love him. Confused and frightened, he held his arms out begging her but she swiped them away.

'It wasn't me,' Harold pleaded, 'it was Stanley. . . .' He suddenly stood stock still, shocked.

Nellie didn't strike him, didn't even bother with her scrapbook or her precious photographs. Simply looked at him with uncontrolled loathing and disgust. Harold went to kiss her, wanting her to forgive him but she couldn't bear him to touch her.

'Don't you ever,' she said, 'drag Stanley's name into your filth. Get out and leave me alone. It's bad enough having to live with what you did, but leave Stanley out of it.'

Harold hadn't heard what she'd said, but he felt it. Shuffling his feet, unable to hear her abuse, with the bells still clanging, banging still in his head, his mouth crumpling up like a small boy's, he left her.

Nellie's heart was thudding, the whole of her chest felt as if it was about to split open . . . she swallowed more of her pills and lay back breathing deeply as the doctor had taught her to do.

She could hear Harold slowly moving up the stairs, hear him cross the landing above, then she heard the creak of the door to Stanley's room.

It was starting again and she knew she would have to put a stop to it . . . he was going crazy. She knew the signs, knew them, but it had been such a long time since she'd seen him behave like this that she was frightened.

Nellie needed Harold, needed him almost as much as he needed her. They were tied together by shame and need. Nellie held the trump card, though she prayed she would never have to use it.

Slowly Nellie's heart began to beat normally, and knowing that Harold was upstairs she dragged her heap of bedclothes aside. She would keep *it* close to her: if he got worse she would have to use it to control him, to keep him chained safely beside her.

Nellie grabbed hold of one of the bed's posts and hauled herself up into a standing position. Her bloated legs quivered but she dragged herself, step by step towards the wardrobe. She had to stop, gasping, before she could edge close enough to the wardrobe door. As she gripped the handle the door swung open and the full length mirror was overfilled with her reflection.

'Dear God,' she whispered, 'Look at me. This is what I have become.' Her own ugliness made her sway and like her son her mouth trembled. Gone was the girl who had been so beautiful, so slim. In her place was this fat food-stained old hag. The creak of the floor boards from above made her move as quickly as her bulk would allow. She fumbled in the hat section of the wardrobe and there, behind her old picture hats, she grabbed a newspaper-wrapped parcel and then tottered back, falling heavily on to the huge bed.

Harold sat in the darkened room. He held one of Stanley's football boots, still with the caked mud dry between the studs.

Stanley had played a good game that afternoon, scored two goals, and the policeman who had come to interview Nellie had remarked that Stanley could go far. It had been coincidence only that the policeman's son had been playing in the game with Stanley that afternoon.

In a jagged nightmare of jigsaw-puzzled pictures, Harold saw Stanley shaking with fear and crying for help, for his elder brother to help him. Harold had done more than just help him, and Stanley had run away leaving him, Harold, to face the music.

Harold tried ripping the football boot apart, but he couldn't so he turned his fury against the posters, ripping them from the walls, kicking out at the drum kit until it rolled and banged across the floor. 'You're coming back you bastard, you shit, you son of a bitch . . . like it or not you're coming back.'

Below Nellie heard the banging and quickly rewrapped the newspaper parcel. The child's rabbit with its dark stains, its chewed ears where the little girl had bitten them.

Nellie looked with loathing up to the ceiling . . . he was in

Stanley's room again. She'd have to put a stop to that as well.

'You try putting me in a home, Harold, and I'll have you, we'll see who'll be sent away.'

Then the piano started up again, the same tune, over and over, until Nellie put a pillow over her head to cut out the sound.

The bed was littered with her letters and with newspaper cuttings from her days on the boards but she was too exhausted to put them away. She slept eventually, a deep troubled nightmare sleep while Harold played on, and slowly began to laugh to himself. He had an idea . . . and he was certain he could make it work.

His plan was not yet completely formed but when he crept into the kitchen he suddenly knew exactly what he would do. There on the bed were a bundle of airmail letters. Letters that Stanley had written over fifteen years before, still neatly wrapped in pink ribbon. Letters that Nellie lovingly read and re-read, hoping, always hoping that there would, one day, be another one. Well there would. In fact she was going to get one soon. . . .

Harold crept to the bed and eased one of Stanley's letters from within the pink ribbon. He was just about to slip out of the kitchen when he saw Nellie's spectacles on the floor where they had fallen. With one quick step Harold crushed them until he heard the glass splinter, then he quietly left the room.

Harold carefully copied Stanley's writing, taking hours to form each loop, then sat back and surveyed his work, well pleased.

'Dear Mother,' he read.

Harold tittered and added the final touch. 'Dear Mother and Harold.' He licked down the envelope, took off his shoes and crept down the stairs, placing the letter on the door mat. He had smudged the date stamp and pressed the envelope so that it looked fresh. He had to cover his mouth because he wanted desperately to giggle out loud.

Nellie woke up to the smell of bacon frying and Harold

busy preparing her tray. 'Plop,' she looked at the closed kitchen door.

'That's the paper come, Harold, the paper lovey.'

Harold placed the tray on her bed and smiled, then opened the door wide and wandered up the hall. She stared uneasily after him. The paper covered the airmail letter completely but he knew it was there.

'Eh Ma, you won't believe this,' Harold called, 'but there's a letter. Good God . . .' he smiled slightly, 'it's amazing, you'll never guess who it's from. Well . . . I never . . . will you look at this it's a letter from Stan the Stud.'

Her breakfast forgotten, Nellie pressed herself back on to her pillow and shook her head. He had to be playing one of his silly games, it couldn't be true. He handed her the air-letter and opened up his newspaper, watching her all the time from behind it, grinning like a cat with stolen cream. Nellie searched distractedly for her glasses but couldn't wait, so she tore open the letter and held it almost to her nose.

'Is he coming home then? Eh? Coming home, is he?' He hadn't expected to feel anything but glee, but seeing her there holding the letter to her vast chest, the tears rolling down her cheeks, he had a moment of doubt, almost of compassion.

She couldn't even answer him, just nodded, her chins wobbling, the tears dripping down her moon face.

Stanley had even written the time and date of his arrival, which was soon. There was a lot to do to prepare for Stanley's long awaited homecoming. Nellie made copious lists of things she needed. New hair dye, make-up, special food, even champagne. The news had given her a new lease of life. She sang and laughed, and was so happy she hardly yelled at Harold once.

Harold, too, was busy. He cleaned the house from top to bottom and was up with a can of spray polish by eight in the morning. She didn't even have to ask him, he seemed as overjoyed as she was. They sat together at night discussing what food they would need, and both agreed that Stanley's room must be aired and clean sheets put on his bed.

Harold was out to the shops every day now and Nellie didn't even have to time how long he took. In and out he went; there and back without dawdling, the fridge stocked, back out again to the off-licence, nothing was too much trouble for him. He even got the right hair dye and sat with her, helping her to do the parting and as she couldn't see without her spectacles, which had disappeared, she depended on him to make sure it was a good even colour.

At the local shopping centre, an Indian store had opened up with groceries and anything else the family could fit on their shelves.

Harold chose carefully three silver threaded scarves; a pink one, a bright red one and a blue. Then he saw a carved knife with a leather sheath, so he bought that too. At the toy shop, an American baseball cap with *Bronx* written on it took his fancy, so he got that too, along with some tissue paper and sticky tape. Finally, Harold had everything he thought he would need.

As Harold passed the telephone kiosk, he giggled. Stanley had been surprised to say the least . . . so surprised that he'd been unable to talk, but he'd listened, certainly he'd listened. His voice had hardly altered. Harold wondered what he would look like . . . it had been a long time.

So amused was he at his detailed arrangements, that Harold began to whistle. All the same when he reached the garden gate he averted his eyes from the house across the street. Mrs Hargreaves was there – he knew it, could feel it, just as he could always feel the presence of Madelaine in the house – but Mrs Hargreaves wasn't going to catch him peeking.

Harold was whistling as he entered the scullery. Nellie was watching television as usual, squinting at the screen, surrounded by crumpled blouses and boxes of beads and necklaces. She was still preoccupied with what she should or shouldn't wear for Stanley's homecoming. Nellie was no longer worried about Harold: since the letter had arrived, he'd been happier than she'd known him for years.

Harold, his purchases under his coat, wandered out into the hall, telling her he'd put tea on soon; first he just had to finish clearing a few things in the bedroom. 'He'll not know he's been away, Ma, his room's lovely.'

Harold carefully wrapped each item in the tissue paper and put everything into an old suitcase. Only a day to go . . . thank God. He was almost ready. Harold had begun to make sure the kitchen door was closed to the hallway at all times, telling Nellie he didn't want the dust getting to her sickly chest. And there was a lot of dust as he moved all her furniture from the hall into the lounge: her cabinets, her paintings, her carpets, and then he rolled the stair-carpet downstairs inch by inch.

'What's all that hammering goin' on Harold?' she shouted.

Harold shouted back that he was fixing a few pictures back in place, nothing more. It wouldn't take long. Then he stood back and surveyed his work, nodding with quiet satisfaction. The hall was empty, down to the bare floor boards, not a cabinet, not a painting to be seen – the place was empty.

That night Harold couldn't sleep for excitement. It would soon be over, not long now. Nellie tossed and turned. She wanted to, was sure she *should* wear the pink blouse but was worried about Stanley seeing how fat she'd got: perhaps if she draped the embroidered shawl round her shoulders it would hide the extra pounds?

The day started sunny and the bowl of fresh carnations on the table looked lovely. She nodded and her chins wobbled. Harold had certainly worked hard. The place was polished and reasonably tidy; anyway, as tidy as it ever had been. He had put out crisps, titbits to eat and two bottles of champagne on ice. He also bought bottles of sherry and whisky, just in case Stan didn't like champagne.

'Are you washed and changed Harold?'

Harold was filthy, his hands and his frayed cardigan still covered in stains, dirt and dust from all his removal work.

'Yep, I'm all ready,' he said. 'What about you?'

Nellie was behind the screen, had been behind the screen all morning getting herself made-up and dressed for the occasion. She'd insisted Harold leave the screen around her, to surprise him.

The Mickey Mouse alarm clock ticked, whirred and pinged, its alarm set for three o'clock. Stanley's letter had said he would arrive at three-thirty prompt.

'All right,' she said, 'I'm ready, you can take it away.'

Harold wheeled the big screen away from her bed, and not until the screen was back in its place did he turn to get the full effect. He gaped, then had to bite his lip to stop himself from laughing.

Nellie sat with her hair crimped and curled in a huge bun, but without her spectacles she'd made it cockeyed. Red hair dye was still evident around the edge of her forehead; her face was thick with panstick make-up, rouged at the cheeks and with bright blue eye shadow; and thick long false eyelashes finished off the vision.

'Well,' Nellie demanded. 'How do I look?'

He couldn't speak, he just stood there, she picked up a hand mirror and squinted into it, complaining that without her glasses she'd had a hell of a job.

'You look staggering Ma, absolutely staggering. Years younger. Good God, it's amazing.'

Nellie primped, explaining that it was her stage make-up. Bracelets jangled and the fat ringed hands fluttered. She was shaking and so nervous that it touched him.

'You sure I'm alright? You don't think this lipstick's too young for me do you – it's Sweetheart Pink – I'm alright am I?'

Harold's voice caught in his throat. For a fleeting moment he wanted to run to her, hold her; but he looked away, feeling himself want to cry.

'He'll fall in love with you Ma.'

Then Nellie realised that Harold hadn't changed and shouted at him to go and wash, peered at her Mickey Mouse and told him that he'd just enough time. Harold was almost at the door when her voice caught him again, cracking with emotion. He couldn't face her.

191

'He's my Madelaine, he's not got any older. I still see him every day like he never left. Oh God I'm so scared . . . he is coming isn't he? Tell me he's coming.'

Harold left the room in silence and, having placed the suitcase that Stanley would need on the front step, closed the door quietly. Then he slid his arms into a jacket and went back into the kitchen.

'Get that off you soft bugger,' Nellie ordered. 'Get it off this minute.'

Harold stood there framed in the doorway wearing a black penguin jacket from his father's old evening suit. The cut was far too large for him and the sleeves covered his hands, flapping. A white handkerchief was draped over his arm, and he bowed.

'I think Mother,' he said formally, 'that I am *very* suitably dressed. This is, after all, a very auspicious occasion: I mean the lad *is* coming home, all these years later.'

Harold then dived for the crisps and filled his mouth, chomping like a rabbit. Poured himself a double scotch and downed it in one: felt it burn the back of his throat, warm him right through his body. He had another.

'Ah, don't drink Harold! Don't drink before he comes.'

Harold poured her a glass of sherry and tangoed across to the large four poster, bowing and dusting the bed with flicks of his handkerchief. The glass was crystal, delicate and full, and grudgingly Nellie took it. Harold grabbed a quick look at the Mickey Mouse clock. Stanley was late. It was three-thirty now and he still hadn't arrived. Diving back for more crisps, Harold shovelled in a huge handful, while Nellie lay back, sipping the sweet, sticky sherry.

'Oh I remember these glasses,' she said, in her best theatrical posh voice.

'I said to her – gave it to her straight – I said, "Look here, no one's been up before, and this is no cushion I got stuffed in me drawers. Your beloved son did it and he's going to marry me" That's what I said.'

The glasses matched a set of champagne glasses Nellie's mother-in-law had given her. God, Nellie thought. How she'd hated the woman who'd tried to get her precious son

192

to pay Nellie off. Get rid of that wretched theatrical and her unborn baby.

Harold had heard it all many times before; could mimic each word, knew exactly what was about to follow. He began to mouth along with Nellie as she talked.

'My whole career ahead of me it was, up the spout because of him, and I blew up, blew up like a balloon. That was your fault, Harold, you did that to me. Before you, a man's hands could fit round my waist.'

Nellie turned to see Harold standing, hands on his hips, mimicking her, and she downed her sherry in one gulp. He was there with a refill before she could speak and, close to, she could see he was sweating, his face red, the skin blotchy.

'Don't drink any more,' said Nellie, 'Ahhh, Harold don't get drunk before he comes.'

Harold waltzed past the bed and whipped up a carnation, turning with it stuck between his teeth.

'Here you go, Julie Andrews.' He tossed it to her. 'Stick it behind your ear.'

Nellie muttered blackly that in her day, she could have given Julie Andrews a run for the money, but stuck the flower in her hair all the same and sipped more sherry, her finger sticking out from the glass. Harold stood at the end of the bed, nudging its rickety frame with his knee, pushing it so that it rocked.

'Give us a tune Ma. Come on, one of the old ones. Sing for us the way you used to, give us all a song.'

She refused. He was beginning to get on her already shredded nerves. But Harold just kept going on about a song, until he saw her put down the glass. She coughed, at the same time announcing that she wouldn't sing, her voice had gone. He knew that she would though, knew she'd start. Always the trouper.

'Go on, go on,' he encouraged her, keeping one eye on the clock; knowing that at any moment Stanley would appear. Any time now they'd hear that knock on the door. He covered his mouth to prevent himself from laughing aloud.

193

Nellie was still preparing herself, eyes closed, hands slightly lifted in front of her.

'When you walk through a storm
hold your head up high,
and don't be afraid of the dark, at the end of the road is
a golden light.'

Harold stopped wanting to laugh. It wasn't funny any more. There she was, an ungainly mountain of fat, looking ridiculous, and yet there was that perfect voice. It was as clear, clearer than a bell, but there was more. She sang with such emotion, such sweetness it destroyed him.

He knew he had to break that moment, had to, before he cried. He began to do his Elvis impersonation, swinging his arms and thrashing an invisible guitar.

Nellie, irritated, raised her voice, and as she did so the bell-like clarity went. The louder Harold got, the louder Nellie got until her voice sounded as it used to when she sang in the smoky, noisy pubs – loud, hoarse and crude.

'Walk on, walk on
with hope in your heart and
you'll never walk alone.'

Still singing at the top of his voice, Harold was suddenly aware she had stopped, aware she was staring blindly towards the kitchen window. Harold turned, and there he was. Stanley had come home.

Harold leapt to the door and dragged Stanley in, yanked the suitcase out of his hands and, when Stanley put his hand out to shake, Harold grabbed him by the shoulders and kissed him.

'Eh, don't be so formal, come in. Come in and look, look there she is, there she is, just as you remember her, eh. . . ?'

Harold enjoyed seeing Stanley unable to speak, frozen to the spot, staring with horror at his mother. Staring towards what looked like a parody of a pantomime dame, fat arms outstretched towards him.

Harold popped open the champagne and, talking non-stop, poured three glasses full, scurried to the bed to hand

194

Nellie one, then back to Stanley. Stanley took his glass, stared at Harold, his eyes frightened.

Harold picked up his glass, about to make a toast but Nellie got in before him, glass raised. Using her poshest voice, adoring eyes looking towards Stanley, she whispered, 'To my son.'

In silence they all drank, and then Harold rushed to Stanley with the bottle and poured more, spilling it over Stanley's hands. With the white handkerchief he swiped briskly at Stanley's sleeve. Stanley was at a loss, his eyes staring at his mother.

'What's in the case Stan, what's in the case?'

Like a robot, Stanley picked up the case, opened it and took out the presents in their tissue paper.

'Good God, the lad's brought us presents. Bloody hell, Ma, it's an Aladdin's cave.'

Stanley was about to cross to the bed with the presents when he noticed Harold's name on one and handed it to him, which resulted in a shriek of delight from Harold. Stanley was just about to hand the others to Nellie when he saw that there was yet another one for Harold.

Harold unwrapped the gifts, talking without stopping as Stanley gave the last parcel to his mother. He handed it to her at arm's length, not wanting to get too close. Harold had opened his parcel containing a baseball cap and put it on . . . too big, the peak hung round one ear. Clown-like he looked up at Stanley.

'This from America, is it? Bloody hell Ma, the lad's been to ruddy America and this, what's this? A knife, Indian is it? My God, they're from all over the world. No wonder we've not heard from him, if he's been on the other side of the Atlantic.'

Nellie held up the cheap Indian scarves as if they were treasures, kissed each one in turn and draped them over herself. Stanley hovered, as if unsure what to do next. Suddenly he took from his coat pocket a square, neatly wrapped packet.

'Eh what's that? Stan, what's that?'

Nellie received it, smiling. Her pink lipstick beginning to

run in lines around her mouth. Harold like a hawk, turned to Stanley. 'Eh what's that? What's in the packet, Stan?'

Stanley coughed, said it was something he'd done himself when he was in. . . .

'In . . . what you say. . . ? In. . . ? In where?'

Stanley moved away from Harold and quickly said it was done on board a ship he'd been in. He looked over to Nellie as she carefully unwrapped the parcel and puzzled, squinted at it. A small picture was done in chalk of a neat sailing ship at sea.

'Oh it's lovely,' Nellie said. 'What is it, oils?' She wiped the painting with her finger and promptly smudged the billowing sails. Stanley dived for it quickly but it was ruined. Harold grabbed the picture to have a look for himself . . . this wasn't what they'd agreed.

Nellie held her arms up towards Stanley. 'You always were the talented one, Stanley. Come and sit by me.'

Harold snapped that Stanley certainly was the most talented, and he tossed the smudged picture on to the floor, whipped out his new knife and with a kung-fu scream hurtled towards Stanley, the knife held out to Stanley's throat. The move made Stanley swing round instinctively and he cuffed Harold hard across the head, on to Harold's bad ear.

Stanley knew he shouldn't have done it. He went immediately to hold Harold, who'd crumpled up in a heap howling, holding his ear.

'Get out', Nellie screamed, and shouted at Stanley that he should never have given Harold the knife.

'Get out, will you, Harold,' the woman shouted hoarsely. 'Go on you bugger, get out.'

Harold backed away from Stanley, still holding his ear, then dropped his hands as if the pain had been an act.

'Eh Stan,' he said, 'give her a big kiss, a down-the-throat job. She'll like that. You'd like that wouldn't you Ma?' Stanley was sweating. He rubbed his scalp nervously, already regretting his part in the plan. Nellie again told Harold to get out and, with drooping shoulders, his baseball cap still awry over one ear, Harold plodded to the door.

'Hello, Ma . . .' he heard Stan say behind him.

Harold hovered at the door, hearing the soft deep voice. He turned to watch. Slowly Stanley moved round the bed and sat, distancing himself. Nellie stared at him with hungry, desperate eyes and put out a hand, which Stanley reached for, held, then bent his head and kissed.

Nellie couldn't hold in the tears. They poured down her cheeks as Stanley played the old childish game she remembered. He turned her hand over, palm upwards, traced the centre with one finger and then looked into her face: lifted the palm closer, closer, until he kissed it with a lover's long, lusting kiss.

They moved into each other's arms, no words necessary, and held each other. Nellie kissed his neck, but he felt suffocated . . . it was her heavy scent, a scent he'd never been able to forget.

Harold removed the baseball cap and let it fall from his hand. Never had she held him like that or kissed him with such tenderness. Never had he, even as a child, seen or felt that adoration. He bowed his head and closed the door silently behind him, as he went in to play his piano. She'd never loved him, he knew that as he hit the tarnished keys, not like she loved Stanley, not ever. Well it didn't matter now. . . .

Stanley had, eventually, to ease Nellie from him. She clung so tightly that in the end he had to be quite rough. She watched him walking slowly round the room, shimmering within her tears, and still she could not believe it was true, that he was home.

Stanley felt sick, sicker than he had expected. He took out a filter cigarette and lit it, his hands shaking. He dragged, heavily, on the cigarette and wished that the room was not so stifling, as he pulled at his black nylon polo neck sweater.

Stanley was still handsome – that was obvious – his definite features, his black hair going grey at the temples had made him, if anything, better looking, even distinguished. Nellie ate him up with her eyes, loving the glint of the gold looped earring in his right ear, his looks, his smart suit.

In her shortsightedness, Nellie couldn't see the seedi-
ness, the fugitive tiredness. She saw the wandering gypsy
but Stanley, in reality, was washed-out, something inside
never whole. He was one of life's walking wounded. Unknown to her, his eyes betrayed him: unable to look her in
the face.

Memories were coming in, closing in. Stanley sniffed;
then crossed to the old mahogany desk, bent down on his
knees and sniffed at it like an animal. The tobacco his father
used to smoke, sweet caramel, he could smell it now
clinging to the desk.

What was really eating him up was her heavy scent, the
strange strong musk smell she always wore and that always
clung to her.

Stanley poured himself a stiff drink and downed it in one.
Then had to have another, and another until he saw the
shaking in his hand stop. Throughout, the damned piano
kept playing; playing something he vaguely remembered.
He looked towards the closed door of the kitchen. Nellie
followed his eyes and nodded.

'Gets on yer nerves after a while, doesn't it?'

Slyly, Stanley asked her what had happened about
Harold's music. All he'd ever heard as a boy, was how
talented Harold was; what he was going to do with the
music scholarship, how famous he'd be.

'Nothing. He's deaf, can't hear what he's playing. I think
that's why he plays the same thing over and over. Doesn't
really know what he's playing.' She shrugged, forgetting
Harold.

'Come and sit by me, Darling. We've got chicken and
mash potatoes and we'll crush up the carrots the way you
like them.'

But Stanley wouldn't sit down. He paced the room,
muttering about the money that had been wasted on Harold
and his music. For what? It all came to nothing.

'Harold seems . . . a bit nutty to me. All right is he?'

Nellie felt Stanley's coldness, and feeling it unnerved her.

Of course he was all right, she said, just a bit deaf, 'cause
he'd had this fall off a moped. Stanley's remorseless pacing

198

up and down the room, his nervousness was flustering Nellie.

'You shouldn't have done it, cut the posts off this bed.' Stanley announced suddenly to Nellie, 'It's lost all its value. Dad'd turn in his grave if he saw what you'd done, Jacobean this was, you know.'

Nellie was really getting jumpy now, Stanley wasn't to be allowed to know he'd come home to an invalid. She jerked her thumb to the door, at long last the music had stopped.

Its sudden stopping coincided with Stanley seeing, stuck there in the frame of her dressing table mirror, that photograph of Madelaine. He had to go for another drink, fast . . . his whole body shaking.

'What the hell is that doing there?'

Nellie squinted down at the mirror, unable to follow his train of thought or see what he meant. Stanley ripped down the photograph.

'What's this here, this?' He shook it.

Nellie lay back, lazily wafted her hand. That was Harold's. She was slightly puzzled at the desperate way he stared at the photo.

'It's that girl, Madelaine. You know, the one they found up in Sniggery Woods.'

He knew all right. Stanley decided then and there to go through with it. Harold had been right. He looked at Nellie and said, 'She's moved in opposite . . . her mother.'

Nellie nodded.

Stanley banged his glass down. Shit, he was blowing it. He had to get out of the room. 'I'd better go find Harold,' he said bleakly as he walked to the door.

And Nellie, confused by his anger, his coldness, held out her fleshy hand to him and had to ask her question. 'Why did you stop writing to me?'

Stanley swung round to face her, his eyes angry . . . how could she ask that, ask it now? As he yanked open the door, she called out to him, 'I forgave you. You know that I wouldn't have. . . .'

'Told the law, eh?' Stanley snarled at her, his face vicious. He was a stranger, and his words confused her, 'Wouldn't have told the law eh? That right is it? Just a threat was it? Well it worked Ma, I kept well away, didn't I?'

He slammed the door so hard that the pictures shook. Now Nellie was even more confused. She would have forgiven him for taking the money. She rubbed behind her ear trying to remember. Course she'd threatened to call the police, course she had. . . .

She jumped, her whole body shaking as sudden impatient footsteps ran up the stairs, across the ceiling . . . bang, thud, bang . . . so loud, so heavy the ceiling trembled and its light bulb swung.

'Stop it,' she called, 'Stop it.' She could hear him shouting, shouting out for Harold, and the next minute the kitchen door to the hall was flung angrily open.

Stanley, like a madman, stood there screaming at her, 'The bloody place has been stripped. There's nothing in the whole house, it's empty, the place is empty.'

Nellie moaned for Harold, but Stanley was yelling that Harold had gone, had pissed off.

'No, no, he can't have, all my valuables, my antiques, my *capo di monte* collection.'

Stanley actually jumped on her bed, banging his fist down beside her as he shouted and shouted so loudly she had to put her hands over her ears. 'Harold's gone. He's pissed off. Don't you understand friggin' English. Harold's gone and he's taken everything.'

Nellie froze in horror . . . it couldn't be true, she wouldn't believe it. The next minute, Stanley had her in a tight grip, his fingers digging into her fat shoulders, shaking her.

'The house, who gets the house? *Who owns this house?*'

Stanley was off the bed, leaving the kitchen door wide open so she could see the floor with its bare boards, its furniture gone, the whole hall stripped down to the bones. Stanley opened the front door and screamed out, 'It's for sale, for sale. Look, there's a bloody *FOR SALE* notice up.'

Nellie's arms fluttered, her weak heart lurched inside her

chest and she couldn't talk. She pointed frantically to her pills, mouthing to Stanley to pass them to her.

Stanley slowed his pace and walked over to her bedside, picking up various half empty pots and jars. 'These them? What do you want, this? This the right one?'

Nellie held her hand pressed to her heart and gasped, gritting her teeth, as blood pounded so loudly she could hardly hear and pain shot from her shoulder, down to her left arm, deadening her quivering fingers. Stanley carried the pills into the kitchen and picked up a glass. He was in no hurry, his eyes watched Nellie.

'Come on,' Stanley gritted his teeth. 'For Jesus' sake, come on, come on.' She'd flopped over the bed, and Stanley stared, thinking this was it. He ran to the bedside and dumped the water down. Nellie was gasping, like a fish drowning in air. Pointing, gulping, trying to make him understand she wanted something from beneath the bed. 'Box, box, box.' She was repeating it blindly, over and over.

As Stanley placed the pills down she grabbed one and stuffed it into her gasping mouth. Heart and pain were merging into one. She shook her head defiantly, gritting her teeth. 'Box,' she ordered.

'This, it's a make-up box. You want this? Make-up, that what you want?'

Nellie's fingers scrabbled at the box and Stanley helped her open it. She pushed aside the top layer of pansticks and began to claw at the newspaper in the under tray. 'I kept this, kept it. Give this to the police and they'll find him, they'll have to bring him back.'

Nellie unwrapped the parcel, unaware that Stanley had frozen with fear . . . she held up the toy rabbit, shaking it so that its ears flopped. 'He had it with him, that afternoon.'

Her voice was bitter. 'He took her up to the woods. It was him . . . Harold . . . I lied for him.'

Silently Stanley's mouth open and shut. This was his nightmare. One shock Harold had promised, just one shock would kill her. And she was killing him with that thing. Shaking it before his face.

201

'No, you know,' Stanley stated wearily. 'No, it wasn't him. . . .'

It was Stanley's face, bleak and tired, that told her, nothing else. His face. She knew, but dying and with her dying breath rattling, she wouldn't believe it, couldn't. She lay back and held the pitiful toy in her arms like a baby and the world went hazy around her.

Stanley was down on his knees. He was weeping, repeating over and over that she knew, knew it had been him, she'd known it all along.

He buried his face briefly into her bed-clothes. Then still sobbing, looked up. Her eyes were clouding. 'I never touched her, I swear Ma, believe me, Ma.'

She wanted her heart to stop, she wanted to die. Nellie couldn't see Harold standing there by the door listening. He crept to her bed, shoved Stanley aside and pressed his imploring face closer and closer to his mother. 'You had to know Mama. You had to know. It wasn't me it was Stanley.'

Stanley tried to get close to her, to tell her what had really happened, but Harold fought him off, pulling the toy rabbit from Nellie's arms.

'Get away from her,' Harold snarled, 'Can't you see she's dying. . . .'

Angrily Stanley pushed Harold away, and enfolded her great bulk in his arms. He wanted to shake her, make her hear him. But behind him Harold's sing-song childish voice kept on telling him that it was too late, too late . . . . she was dead.

Harold walked swiftly out of the hateful room, leaving Stanley heartbroken as he looked down into those sad, reproachful but empty eyes. He wept as he knelt beside her, breathing in the heavy musk scent that he remembered, that he'd never forgotten.

Harold was playing calmly now, surrounded by rolled up carpets, cabinets, paintings, all the things he'd stripped from the hall and stairs. He was playing Madelaine's tune, running his hands skilfully along the piano. Stanley hovered in the background, then lit another cigarette and walked slowly to his brother's side. There in front of him, standing where the sheet music should have been on the piano music stand was Madelaine's photograph. The toy rabbit sitting on top.

Harold smiled softly, happily. He was going to finish this piece now, he told Stanley quietly, and added that he felt it would benefit from harp and violin, perhaps even a flute. To Stanley, he seemed unconcerned by what had just taken place.

Stanley sat next to his brother on the double piano stool, and Harold ceased playing. It had been her perfume, Stanley said, that was why he had got so upset.

'Ahh, but it worked didn't it Stan? Just like I said it would.'

Stanley was in control of himself now and unanswered questions began to flicker across his mind . . . he hit a single piano note. 'She never thought it was me, did she? She always believed it was you . . . that letter she wrote to me all those years ago doesn't make sense.'

Harold shrugged his shoulders mockingly, like a naughty boy, and grinned. Stanley looked at him with a sidelong glance, then gripped him by the collar.

'You wrote that letter, didn't you?' Stanley's voice was harsh. 'It was you who said she'd tell the law if ever I showed my face back here . . . *You*.'

Harold wriggled out from the grip, and pranced happily round the piano, all the while reminding Stanley how good he had been at forging Stanley's writing, even when they were at school.

Stanley looked helplessly at his elder brother, shaking his head. Why? Over and over again . . . why? Why had Harold done that to him, why?

Many times he had wanted to come home, needed to come home and never dared. Stanley's life was a wandering mess of petty thieving that landed him in and out of jail. And when he *was* released, he'd never had anyone, any place to go home to.

'You always knew where I was, and you never, never told her. Why?'

Harold was standing in the shadow of two cabinets containing Nellie's *capo di monte*, his gaunt face stiff, his mouth a thin tight line.

Quietly Harold told Stanley, without emotion, about the accident, his fall from the moped. How Harold knew where Madelaine had been buried, in a ditch just down from the slope by Sniggery. He knew exactly where, because that had been where he'd buried her. Every night on his way home from college he passed that spot, that tiny grave in which the police had found her. And on one of those nights, caught in his headlamp was a wounded rabbit, his back half squashed, flattened into the road. But the creature hadn't been dead. It was still alive and it was screaming, a high-pitched terrible scream.

'I lost control and I fell. I hit my head, Stan. That's why I'm deaf.'

So? Stanley shrugged. He didn't see why this should have anything to do with him. Harold crept from his dark corner, out of the shadow, moving closer and closer to his brother.

'She was still alive when I found her,' Harold told Stanley. 'She was screaming, she didn't sound like a child more like a trapped animal.'

Stanley clamped his hands over his ears. He didn't want to hear this, didn't want to believe it was true. But Harold wrenched the hands from his brother's ears, and he wasn't hysterical. He was calm, and his eyes fierce, burning with anger.

'She was broken, crawling round in a ditch where you'd left her and I held her and promised to take her home; but it was too late, so I buried her to hide what you'd done.'

A clock could be heard between the silence, ticking. Stanley stared helplessly into his brother's face and knew he was being told the truth. He tried, nervously, to reach for Harold's hand but Harold pulled himself away, as Stanley said, 'So help me God, I never touched her. It was an accident . . . I never touched her, Harold.'

Touched her? Harold erupted into a fury, kicking hard at his brother; screaming that Stanley had gone out and played a good game of football. Knowing what had happened, he'd gone out and scored two goals, knowing that the little girl was in that state. He never touched her? Stan the Stud who had his hand up every girl's skirt in the neighbourhood?

'You liar, You liar, YOU LIAR.'

Stanley tried at first to fend off Harold's wild punches, all the time trying to tell him what really happened. Then, in anger, he swung Harold against the door, cracking Harold's head so hard it silenced him.

'Can you hear me? . . . Harold?'

Harold nodded.

Stanley with head bowed and eyes staring at the floor, told Harold what had really happened that afternoon. How Madelaine had left early for her music lesson with Harold, how he'd met her in the street on his way out to the match.

'It was Christmas, remember?' She said she'd never seen a real Christmas tree growing. She was such a little kid – only eight wasn't it? – an I told her that up in the woods she could see for herself . . . all the trees waiting for Santa. So she sat on the crossbar of my bike an' I took her up there. It was on my way to the match and. . . .'

Harold inched closer, never letting his eyes move from Stanley's face. 'Go on, he said, Go on. Then what? Go on, Tell me.'

Stanley fended off Harold with his right hand while shuffling slowly backwards all the time. It was *the* game, he told Harold. He'd started to fool around playing the game.

Harold knew instantly what *the* game was. Stanley had played it often enough on him – jumping out on him when he was going to the toilet, or leaping out of the dark coal shed.

'The bear, you did the bear.'

Stanley growled, seventeen years of anguished guilt building up like a volcano about to explode and erupt against Harold. But he wasn't quick enough.

Harold kicked him hard in the balls and Stanley roared, arms held out like claws and again Harold kicked. Stanley went wholeheartedly into *the* game as a release, screaming as he pulled the sweater up and over his head, arms held up and, with fingers bent like a bear's claws, he gave chase.

The game that had terrified Harold as a child was now played out for real, as Stanley chased him up the stairs, in and out of the bedrooms.

Stanley caught Harold and brought him down midway on the stairs, falling over each other and crashing into a heap, with Stanley on top of Harold. He still growled and lurched forward as if to bite his brother's neck, but his whole body was wracked with sobs.

Harold held his younger brother tightly, and the sobs went on and on, shaking his brother's body until he was cried out, exhausted.

'I was so scared Harold,' Stanley whimpered. 'I didn't mean any harm, I was chasing her, that's all . . . she ran, she was playing too, and laughing, then she lost her balance and fell down the slope. The truck didn't even see her. The driver just drove on, he didn't stop.'

Harold rocked Stanley in his arms: allowing Stanley time to release his shame, to tell Harold how he had run away, on to the football game. He'd been unable to tell anyone else but Harold. As always, he'd turned to Harold and, as always Harold had helped him.

It had been Harold who went up to the woods that night, Harold who had taken the blame within the house: a house that had virtually stood still since that day.

'I ran away Harold, because I knew I'd have to tell. I couldn't bear the way Ma looked at you, so I stole her money and ran, I couldn't face it . . . I couldn't tell her it was me.'

Harold cradled his brother, patted his head and told him it was all over, they would be all right now. Stanley lay back on the stairs and sighed.

'What we going to do about the house?' he asked. 'Best thing to do with her, Mrs Hargreaves, being opposite is to sell, split it between us. You could go to a place where they'd look after you.'

Oh no. Harold was up on his feet, hand on his hip, wagging his finger. 'Now don't talk silly, this is my home and I love my things. I mean that *capo di monte* collection's worth a fortune. We're staying here Stan, together, you and me. And if you don't like it . . . well . . . I'd have to tell, Stanley. I'm sorry but she'd have to be told – I mean she's across the road, she's there.'

Stanley stared at Harold, but Harold was already giving him instructions to move the furniture back in place while Harold went to get their food ready.

'I'll put the chicken on, and mash up the carrots just the way you like them. Come along, go up and wash. Your room's just as you left it.'

Harold scurried through to the kitchen, and Stanley could hear pots and pans clattering. Slowly he got to his feet and went into the music room. He picked up Madelaine's photograph and tore it into shreds, then he grabbed the rabbit and ran, just as he had run all those years before.

In the kitchen, Harold now humming his Madelaine tune, put on the already peeled potatoes, and began to pull a plastic bag of giblets out of the chicken. Behind him, as if sleeping, lay Nellie with a crumpled sheet draped over her face.

Stanley shut the front door silently, lifted the lid off the rubbish bin and stuffed the rabbit inside. But in his haste to leave, to get away from that house, he didn't put the lid on properly and it clattered to the ground. He froze, waited and then ran to the garden gate, unhooked the string and bumped straight into a woman waiting on the pavement. Stanley tapped her elbow and apologised. He then ran, ran as fast as he could down the darkened road.

Mrs Hargreaves stared after him, and wondered who it was and what he'd been doing. Perhaps he was a thief. She walked up the path and she picked up the bin lid, meaning to replace it: but poised with it above the bin, she saw something else.

For a second time the bin lid clattered. Not that Harold could hear. He was humming to himself. Already he'd decided that the music would, more than likely, benefit most from a clarinet or oboe and not, as he'd first thought, from a flute. Conducting serenely to himself with a wooden spoon, he missed both the sounds outside, and the rising tap, tap on the door.

Mrs Hargreaves kicked at the door, kicked with all her force and it burst open. Harold wheeled round shocked, and instantly stepped back as she stood in the dark staring, glaring at him.

'Stanley? . . . *Stanley*?'

Harold moved further and further back into the kitchen and she followed, so quietly her footsteps made no sound. Stanley. He knew Stanley had gone so he turned to Nellie for help.

'Ma . . . Ma! Oh God, Ma, she's here.'

The mound in the bed was silent, as were Mrs Hargreaves' footsteps. Slowly she came towards him. Harold pressed his hands to his deafaid, he couldn't hear, she terrified him. Mrs Hargreaves – her eyes no longer empty, no longer haunted – accused him. She gave Harold the rabbit. Thrusting her child's toy in to his arms. His deaf aid bleeped, and Harold could hear the sounds of the police siren screaming along the road.

Lynda La Plante

EVENSONG

Louise swore several times, mildly, as she pulled up weeds, raked out stones. There was no fear of being overheard, not on a weekday. The row of dismal little gardens was deserted, everyone out at work or watching films on video. 'Come on up, damn you,' she urged, tugging at a piece of concrete lodged in the wet soil. She supposed that builders found it more economical to dump their rubble in the earth rather than transport it to some tip.

She carried the offending lump to the bins at the back door and then realised that the bin men would almost certainly refuse to dispose of it. She took it into the garage instead. She'd have to get Keith to take it a walk some-where; possibly he could drop it over the railings by the council offices, on top of all those bedsprings and rusty cookers flung among the daffodils.

'Naughty, naughty,' she reproved herself, and picking up the cricket bat returned to the garden. She'd forgotten to put on her wellingtons and her shoes were saturated. Still, there were other things more important than physical health.

'Blast you,' she muttered, as she knelt by the border and unearthed a length of piping and a crumbling brick.

It wasn't as if she was a country person at heart, or even that she was particularly interested in growing things, simply that it was necessary to spend as much time as possible out of doors. She didn't put it into words, any more than Graham did, but the house was hateful. It was too small, too ugly. She could feel its presence behind her, a box made of red brick with the second lid of the grey sky clamped above its chimneyless roof.

When she woke in the mornings from bad dreams, opened her eyes to the coffin-like dimensions of the cream-painted bedroom dark with furniture, she felt she was still asleep, still caught in nightmares. The wardrobe inlaid with mother-of-pearl which had illuminated the landing of her parents' home, flashing silver in the sun on summer afternoons, now blotted out the light. Year by year, the tables and the chairs, the bookcase and the sideboard which had furnished her childhood, grew more oppressive, more threatening.

Graham had suggested that they put it all into store. 'Though I don't expect we shall be here very long,' he had said, ten years ago. She had pretended that she couldn't live without the Chippendale desk, the George III library stairs, her parents' bed with its cluster of wooden grapes on the headboard.

'I know they look out of place here,' she had told him, 'but unless you feel strongly about it I should like to keep them. I need them.' And of course he hadn't felt strongly about it. How could he? It would have been her money, that small and dwindling inheritance left to her by her father, which would have paid the storage costs.

They couldn't afford such costs, any more than they could have afforded to buy new furniture to put in place of the old. It was Graham who always referred to it as her money; she herself would gladly have given it to him, had tried to, but he wouldn't hear of it. 'I couldn't touch a penny,' he often said. 'John meant it for you.' It was only one of a number of small deceptions they practised, this pretence that the money was for her use alone.

Remembering that the rambler rose needed staking against the wind, she went on hands and knees further down the garden to attend to it.

Beyond the house the long corridor of the road was deserted too, save for a few cars parked at intervals along the kerb and the dust-cart abandoned under the lamppost. A child's swing creaked above a patch of scuffed lawn. It was half past three in the afternoon. And then an ordinary

210

young man came round the corner from the direction of the High Street and began to walk down the road, nudging the privet hedges with his shoulder as he passed, for earlier it had rained and he took pleasure in the way the leaves sprang back, spattering the pavement with drops.

When he drew level with the church he stopped and looked across at the house, at the board nailed to a post beside the gate. On it was written in Gothic lettering 'Vicarage'. Underneath, daubed in white paint, were the words 'God is out. Call again'.

He walked up the side path to the church and entered by the vestry, leaving the door on the latch behind him. The oval door into the church was ajar; someone was playing the harmonium. On tiptoe he moved cautiously round the cheap wooden table with its dusty water jug and its pile of parish magazines, and peered through. He had a clear view of the two of them, the man seated at the harmonium, the girl standing beside him, her hand resting on his neck. The music stopped.

He dodged back instantly, flattening himself against the damp raincoat hanging on the wall behind him. He heard the girl say in a complaining voice, 'But we're not doing any harm,' and then the Sunday school hymn began again. He ran out of the vestry and down the path and looking neither to right nor left crossed the road to the vicarage.

When he pushed open the door the chimes rang out. Even before they had finished striking he was down the hall and into the living room. He noticed nothing but the handbag on the table. He was taking a £5 note out of the leather purse when he heard a dull clopping sound. Beyond the French windows, in the square of garden, he saw a woman wielding a cricket bat in both hands, stomping a stake into the earth beside a rose bush.

The young man put the note into his pocket, the one in which he kept his knife. He watched as the woman flung down the bat and began to take off her gardening gloves. He took out the knife and flicked it open as the woman turned, one hand rubbing the small of her back, and approached the house.

She came in through the French windows. She looked first at the table and then at the young man. 'How much have you taken?' she asked.

'I never touched your bloody bag,' he protested.

'It's no good lying, Keith,' she said. 'I know exactly how much I had.' She left the room and he heard her moving about in the kitchen, running water into the kettle. He stuffed the £5 note into the handbag, not bothering to replace it in the purse, and sitting down at the table began to jab with his knife at the papers covering it.

Louise returned carrying a tray with two cups and set it down in front of him. She said, 'Do stop that. They're Graham's notes for his sermon.' Her tone was matter of fact, without emphasis.

'You've left his cricket bat out,' he told her.

'Damn,' she said.

'He'll do his nut,' he warned her.

'He won't be back for another hour. He's gone to visit old Mr Syme at the Cottage Hospital.' She bent down to switch on the electric fire.

'That's good of him,' said Keith evenly.

'I'll put it away after I've had a cuppa,' she said, and went out into the kitchen to make the tea.

He called through to her, asking where her cousin was, but Louise didn't reply. He knew she had heard him. He stared at the photograph in its ornate frame on the wall behind the door, frowning. 'Where's your cousin?' he repeated, when Louise came back with the teapot.

Louise said that Pamela was at the hairdresser's. She didn't look at him. She took her cup to the armchair by the fire and sat down, positioning herself sideways so that she was facing the photograph. As always when gazing at the image of her father her expression softened. He was standing in a garden holding a cricket bat over his shoulder, smiling at the camera. The photograph had been taken before she was born, when he was a young curate in Surrey.

'How long is Pamela going to go on staying here?' Keith asked.

'Until she's ready to leave, I suppose,' said Louise, and

she made a little gesture with her hand, signalling that he should keep quiet.

Sullenly he drank his tea. He knew he should offer to go out into the garden and finish whatever job it was that Louise had begun. It was what he was here for – to help out, to make himself useful. He had promised yesterday that he would clean the windows, but he hadn't got round to it. He didn't expect he'd get round to it today either.

He said loudly, 'I never knew my Dad. He scarpered before I was born.'

'Rubbish,' said Louise. 'Graham met him when he went to see your probation officer.'

'Well, we've never got on. He's a bad tempered bastard. It wasn't like you and him. I never got no attention.'

'I'm not deaf,' she said, and she leaned back in her chair and closed her eyes. Defeated, he flounced out into the garden, slamming the doors behind him.

Louise felt guilty, but only for a moment. God knows, these days she seemed to spend more time with Keith than anyone else. She thought how dangerous it was, this craving for attention which everyone had, herself included, as though it was some drug which once given could never be withdrawn. She supposed it all began in infancy. 'I never got none,' she said out loud, mimicking Keith and speaking to the photograph.

Of course it had been a disappointment for him, having a daughter when he had wanted a son. Not that he'd really shown it, just that she had always known deep down that she was second-best. When she had met Graham, her father had been almost pathetically pleased at her choice. She suspected that he was also baffled that someone like Graham should find her interesting. She had overheard him telling her mother that he was a catch, though Graham had only recently come down from Cambridge and had neither money nor prospects.

Her father had done his best to ensure that Graham was subjected to the full range and intensity of his friendship, lending him books, employing him as a temporary secretary when he went to the ecumenical conference at St George's

Chapel in Windsor, introducing him as his prospective son-in-law to the Bishop of Chichester. He was doing it for her, of course, just as taking Graham to the Test Match at Lords on her birthday had been mostly for her benefit.

He had married them and paid for the honeymoon and telephoned Graham every morning at the hotel in Broadstairs. Once he had asked to speak to her, but there must have been some electrical fault because when she picked up the telephone the line had been disconnected. He had hung on for three years waiting for a grandson to be born, and when she hadn't obliged he had died. The local papers had written briefly about his work in the parish, and at length about his days as a county cricketer. He had left a letter for Graham in his desk. Graham hadn't told her what was in it, and she didn't suppose she would ever know, for the letter had since been lost, if not destroyed, and besides, it had all happened twenty years ago and no longer mattered.

She got up and put the cups on to the tray. She could hear Keith outside in the garden, whistling 'There's a friend for little children above the bright blue sky'. It was almost dark and the rain was falling again, streaking the windows.

When Pamela came in her hair was flattened to her head. She said she'd had to walk back from the hairdresser's, and she hadn't taken an umbrella. 'What a waste,' said Louise.

At a quarter past five Hilda arrived. She was already crying as she came through the door. Pamela, who was typing at the table, gave her an insincere smile. Ten minutes later Mr Mahmood called at the house. He was wearing his best suit, his only suit. He said he had an appointment with Graham. He was clearly appalled by Hilda, and nervously paced about the room, tugging at the points of his striped waistcoat with plump fingers encircled with thin gold rings.

'My father also was a cricketer,' he said, standing on tiptoe to examine the photograph. 'He learnt the batting in the British Army. Is the vicar playing the game also?'

'No,' said Louise. 'He used to, but not any more.'

'Ah, well,' observed Mr Mahmood. 'He is a very busy man. He is helping everyone.'

'In what way is he helping you, Mr Mahmood?' Louise asked. She was twisting the strap of her watch round and round on her wrist.

'He is getting me rehoused.'

'Really,' Louise said, and added, 'How nice.' She took a Kleenex tissue from the box on the table and handed it to Hilda.

'I am living on the Bayham council estate and it is not a nice place,' Mahmood confided. 'My neighbours are posting me shit through the letter box. Mr Sinclair is talking to the council and getting me a little house of my own . . . possibly with a garden.'

'I see,' said Louise. She was aware that Pamela was watching her.

Mahmood began a detailed description of the sort of house he had in mind. Four bedrooms would be enough, though probably later he could do some extending, as he was handy with the nails and the hammers. If it had a porch he would hang a name plate from it on chains. His uncle was a sign-maker in Bermondsey and would make him one cheap. There must also be a shed for his bicycle. At the moment his bicycle was living in the bedroom and it was catching at his trousers whenever he moved.

'I am a very lucky man,' he enthused, 'meeting so good a vicar. He is a very kind man.'

'He is certainly a well intentioned one,' said Louise, and managed a smile.

Shortly afterwards Graham came home. He apologised to Mr Mahmood for keeping him waiting and said he had been unavoidably detained. Depressed as he was, he was still charming.

Mahmood was overcome. He protested that it was not a question of Mr Sinclair being late, rather that he himself had presented too early. Wearily Graham told him to come through into the front room. He had given up calling it the study. For a time he had referred to it as the Surgery – Louise had advised against it – until that woman with the

215

dyed red hair had insisted that he examine her for gallstones.

'How was Mr Syme?' asked Louise. 'Is he any better?'

He was disconcerted, and showed it. What a fool I am, he thought, jeopardising my peace of mind, my happiness. And then it occurred to him that he had not been happy for years.

He was saved from an outright lie by Hilda, who at that precise moment began to utter thin little screams. It was only an effort of will which prevented him from covering his ears to blot out the dreadful noise of her misery.

'I am anxious to finalise things,' said Mr Mahmood, unexpectedly pushy, the skin under his hopeful eyes the colour of plums.

'There, there,' Graham murmured, patting Hilda awkwardly on the shoulder. He took Mahmood by the elbow and escorted him from the room.

After a cup of tea and a biscuit Hilda recovered sufficiently to remember the children waiting for her at home. When she had gone Pamela said she didn't know how Graham stood it.

'Graham,' cried Louise, exasperated.

'I'm not at all sure that it doesn't make her worse, pandering to her, letting her sit here and wail like a soul in torment.'

'She is in torment,' said Louise. She prowled about the room, arms crossed, hugging herself. At last she said, 'I wish he wouldn't do it. It's so unfair. He shouldn't promise people like Mahmood that he'll help them. It's damaging. It's almost cruel.'

'You're unfair,' Pamela accused her. 'You can't resist knocking him, can you?' She knew she shouldn't say such things aloud. Louise wasn't a complete fool. All the same, she couldn't bear Graham to be criticised. 'It's part of his job,' she said, 'helping people. Just as it's your job to encourage him.'

'Who does Graham know on the council?' asked Louise. 'He has no authority, no influence.'

'He needs your support,' Pamela shouted.

'Dear God,' said Louise, and fearing she might strike the girl she left the living room and marched in the dark about the tiny kitchen. It was unjust of Pamela to suggest that she wasn't supportive. Who had succeeded in getting Syme into the Cottage Hospital when the social services had told Graham that the old man wasn't a priority case? Who supervised Keith, made his lunch, thought up jobs for him to do, listened to his whining complaints about his parents, his excuses? And in the end it would be her who would be left to cope with Mahmood.

She knew exactly what would happen, because it had happened before. First, Mahmood would give up his rent book; then the phone calls would begin, calls which Graham would avoid. And then one afternoon, depend upon it, the poor deluded Mahmood would trot up the path, homeless, dispossessed, followed by a wife and numerous children.

Picturing the scene with frightful clarity, tears welled up in her eyes. She leaned against the sink and stared into the darkness. She saw Keith's face pressed to the window, his nose grotesquely squashed against the glass. 'Go home,' she mouthed, and ran back into the living room and drew the curtains. Pamela was still sitting at the table.

'Keith's out there,' Louise said. 'Spying on us. He never leaves me alone.'

'He doesn't like anybody but you,' said Pamela. 'You can't blame that on Graham. He did try to get him a job.'

It was true, thought Louise. He had tried. But then, who but Graham would think it was possible to find employment for a boy like Keith.

'What did Keith do?' asked Pamela.

Louise proceeded to tell her, though she omitted certain details, such as the blood on the floor, the smashed spectacles which had become embedded in the bridge of the nose. The man behind the counter of the corner shop had almost died. Not from the blow on the head but from the vomit in his windpipe. He had been drinking all day. And it was all for a packet of cigarettes.

'Poor Keith,' murmured Pamela. Her blue eyes were tender with misplaced sympathy.

'Don't be ridiculous,' Louise said. 'You're as bad as Graham. There are thousands of people with backgrounds every bit as deprived as his and yet they manage to live perfectly ordinary, decent lives. They're the ones you should be sorry for.'

'I wish I understood about violence,' said Pamela. 'I often feel angry, but never murderous. I wonder what stops most of us from harming each other?'

Louise didn't reply. Nothing stops us, she thought. Nothing at all.

The following morning the hospital telephoned to say that Mr Syme had died in the night. When Pamela went through into the front room to see if Graham needed her to type letters, she was shocked at his appearance. He looked terrible, as if he had suffered a personal loss. He sat there, drawing little squiggles on the blotter on his desk. He told her to leave him alone.

Louise told Pamela not to worry, that he would be all right in a day or two. 'He hardly knew him,' protested Pamela.

'What has that got to do with it?' said Louise, and she smiled and went upstairs to make the beds.

Pamela waited until lunchtime. She knew that Graham had an appointment with the social services department, and she hid in the garage. When he saw her his expression altered. Before, he had looked sad, now he was irritated.

'I must talk to you,' she said. 'There's something I want to discuss.' He said that he was too depressed, that the last thing he needed was a discussion. She had thought it all out, rehearsed the words of comfort, and now it was her turn to be annoyed. 'I want to help you, dammit.'

'I don't need your help,' he said, fitting the key into the lock of the car. She came towards him and he backed away down the garage, putting distance between them, as though she was contaminated with some virus.

'I don't mean any harm,' she said. 'We're friends.'

'We're not friends, Pamela, and you know it.'

'You're always preaching about love,' she accused.

'Not this sort I'm not,' he said.

'Are you frightened of Louise. Is that what's depressing you?'

'I refuse to discuss Louise,' he said. 'You know nothing about it.'

She stood there, close to tears, and watched as he opened the car door and struggled inside. He wouldn't look at her. On other occasions he had said that she mustn't cry, that he couldn't bear to see her unhappy. She was such a little scrap, he had said. Such a dear little scrap, why, his heart melted just hearing her voice.

She turned away from the car and walked down the garden, devising schemes, thinking up ways of gaining his attention. Perhaps she could draw a picture of that old man who had died, and leave it on Graham's desk. She had once done a pencil sketch of the view from the back window and he had praised it. He had said that talent was a gift from God. But then, she didn't know what the old man had looked like, and in any case she was no good at faces.

She went miserably indoors and found Keith in the living room with a plate of sandwiches on his knee. The television was on.

She watched as he pulled the cheese from the bread and gobbled at it. He wasn't all that much younger than she was, thought Pamela. They were of the same generation. She could probably understand him far better than Louise. If she got to know him, gained his confidence, he might come to rely on her. Graham would be pleased.

She leaned forward and switched off the television.

'What's the bloody game?' Keith said.

'I thought we might have a chat.'

He was looking at her legs and hurriedly she smoothed her skirt down over her knees. 'It's silly,' she said, 'seeing each other every day and not really talking. Don't you think? I'd like to know more about you.'

He seemed amused. 'Find me interesting, do you?' he asked.

'I just wondered what sort of things you liked doing. What sort of hobbies.' He laughed at her. 'I'd like us to be friends,' she persisted. 'I'd like to know you, find out the sort of things that interest you.' He stared at her, licking the crumbs from his mouth. 'Don't you want to know things about me?' she asked.

He said pleasantly, 'I do know things about you, as a matter of fact.'

She was surprised, and pleased. 'Do you?'

'I reckon I do. You're an outgoing sort of girl. Full of life, a good sport.'

'Is that what you think?'

'Sure I do. And you're bright with it.'

She could feel herself blushing. She murmured some kind of denial.

Keith was enjoying himself. 'Yes, you are,' he insisted. 'I can tell. Just because I bashed some old bloke on the bonce it doesn't mean I'm thick.'

'No,' she said politely, less sure of herself. 'No, of course not.'

'And I can tell you like people. All sorts of people. Wanting to talk to me, for instance . . . that proves it.'

'I do like people,' she said eagerly. 'You're right. I really do.' He waited a moment, and then he said, 'Of course I'm right. And you like messing about in churches . . . with blokes.' He thought she was going to faint. All the blood left her cheeks.

'Now me,' he said, 'I'm your opposite side of the coin. I don't like people at all, or very few.' He put down his plate and turned on the television again. It was a wildlife programme, something to do with smaller animals being hunted by larger ones. There was a distant shot of a dusty horizon and a herd of cow-like beasts. The commentary was promising. It is only a matter of time, the voice said, before the weakest member of the herd will fall behind the rest of the pack.

He was still watching television at seven o'clock that evening, though earlier he had hosed out the garage and disposed of a lump of concrete. Louise and he were watching Channel Four news when Graham came home. Louise said she would make him an omelette, but he told her not to bother. He wasn't hungry, and he had a headache. Besides, there wouldn't be time. Mrs Crombie was coming.

Keith got up and made for the door. It was obvious old Graham was in a bad mood.

'Turn the television off, will you,' Graham said.

Keith returned and did as he was told. He was just going out of the door when Graham shouted, 'Pick up the tray, please. Louise isn't your servant.'

Humiliated, Keith picked up the tray and dropped it on to the table. 'No,' he said, 'She isn't, you bastard. But don't you get a kick out of thinking she's yours.'

He slammed the door behind him with such violence that the photograph on the wall slipped sideways on its cord. Louise righted it, and stepped back to see if it was straight.

'Shall I tell him not to come here any more,' Graham said. She didn't reply. 'I don't appear to exert much influence on him, do I?'

Still she remained silent. He stood beside the table and fiddled aimlessly with the papers. Suddenly he hit the surface with his fist, scattering the cutlery on the tray. A fork bounced to the carpet. 'What do I ever achieve,' he said. 'I might be invisible for all the effect I have.'

Louise bent and picked up the fork. Graham turned and clung to her. 'I don't influence anyone, do I? All I have is good intentions.' He moaned. 'I couldn't even manage to say goodbye to old Syme before he died.'

Louise stood passively in his arms, her hands at her sides. 'You meant to, dear,' she said. 'You meant to.' She let him ramble on. It was always better to let him wallow in his self-pity.

'When I think of the ideas I had,' he was saying, 'the plans. Do you remember John telling me I'd be a Bishop before I was thirty?' She didn't remember, although she had heard it from him often enough. It was time to put her arms round him, to pat his back as though comforting a

221

child. She was looking over his shoulder at the picture on the wall. 'Oh, God,' he said, 'this ugly house, that ugly church, these wretched people.' And he let out a groan of terrible, indulgent despair.

'That's enough,' said Louise. She disengaged herself from his arms and busied herself with the knives and forks. 'I detest self-pity,' she told him. 'And so did John.'

He said she was quite right, as always. He wiped his eyes with his sleeve and murmured that he didn't know what he would do without her. She must tell him what to do about Keith. There had been a moment back there, God forgive him, when he had wanted to strike him.

Louise said it was all a question of time, of having confidence. Keith would never amount to much but they must be patient. She took the tray to the door. Graham was already humming to himself, his self-esteem restored. 'Perhaps you should have struck him,' she said. 'It's one of the few gestures he understands.' Graham looked shocked. Taking pity on him, she said, 'No, of course you shouldn't. The remorse would have outweighed the satisfaction.'

An unusually large number of parishioners arrived that evening to ask Graham for his advice. Sidney came, and Mrs Crombie brought a friend. There was even a young boy, the sort with a punk haircut, who said he was thinking of getting married. Mercifully, Hilda was absent. Louise was glad for Graham: it would make him feel worthwhile, having so many people who depended on him.

She was going into the kitchen to put the kettle on for the third time when she noticed Pamela crouching on the stairs. 'Can't you find anywhere else to sit,' she asked. 'I prefer it here,' said Pamela. 'Any objections?'

Graham was showing Sidney out when Louise came back into the hall with the teapot. She heard Pamela say, 'If you don't let me talk to you I just might smash a few windows.' She pretended not to have heard and called out from the living room that Mrs Crombie was next if Graham was ready.

'Keith saw us in the church,' said Pamela.

'For God's sake,' hissed Graham. 'Lower your voice.'

He called out, 'I'm ready when you are, Mrs Crombie.'

'He made me give him ten pounds,' shouted Pamela. Louise was helping Mrs Crombie up the hall. The old woman was leaning on her, breathing like a horse. 'How nice to see you,' said Graham, and taking her arm he almost pushed her into the front room and closed the door behind them.

Pamela was shaking. She wasn't sure how much Louise had overheard. She couldn't think which was worse, Keith knowing, or Louise. Trying not to whimper, she went into the living room. Louise smiled at her. She was talking to a young boy with pink hair. He was fingering the silver snuff box that stood on the mantelpiece.

'It's pretty, isn't it,' said Louise. It belonged to my father. Mr Sinclair keeps his stamps in it.' She took it from him and slipped it into the pocket of her cardigan. Then she poured Pamela a cup of tea, still smiling. She didn't hear, thought Pamela. All the same, her hands continued to shake, and her cup rattled in its saucer.

Later, when Mrs Crombie and her friend had gone, and the punk boy was in the front room with Graham, Louise began to talk about Hilda. She said that she was relieved that she hadn't come, but also worried. It wasn't like her to miss her tea and biscuits and the opportunity of a weep in public. She hoped she was safe.

'Is she a battered wife?' asked Pamela. Sometimes the woman's arms had been covered in bruises.

'Not in the way you mean,' said Louise. 'Her husband walked off with a younger woman. She's just very depressed.'

This is a dangerous conversation, thought Pamela, and in spite of it she said, 'I don't see the point of people hanging on to each other against their will.'

'No,' said Louise. 'I don't expect you do.'

'I mean if someone falls in love with someone else, then it's useless trying to pretend that nothing's happened. I mean, once love has gone, it's absurd to think that it can be resurrected. I think people should be more honest with each other. It's better for everyone in the end.' Suddenly

Pamela was weeping, and shouting through her tears. 'Oh, I know you don't agree, Louise. You're all for duty and self control'.

'You're right,' Louise said gently. 'I do believe in duty. I was brought up that way. I can't claim any credit for it.'

'Well, it's bloody hard on other people I can tell you,' Pamela said wildly. 'It's stifling. We all have to creep round feeling inferior. Your disapproval is killing . . . killing –' In the hall the chimes rang as Graham showed the punk boy out of the door. 'You've ruined bloody Graham,' Pamela shouted. She waited for Graham to come into the room. She wanted it over and done with, everything out in the open. And then he was standing there, his face bleak, his frightened eyes staring at her. 'Is anything wrong?' he asked inadequately.

'Oh, Christ,' said Pamela. 'He can't even think for himself any more. He's just all twisted up about whether you'll approve.' Then she was running for the open door, pushing Graham aside with her arm. He staggered and fell against the wall, jerking the picture from its nail.

The next morning Pamela apologised to Graham. 'I don't know what came over me', she said, when Louise had gone out shopping. 'I must have been mad. It was just that I was so worried about Keith seeing us in the church together like that.'

'There was nothing to see,' he said dismissively. 'I shall ask him to give you the money back.'

'I may have been mistaken,' she admitted. 'I think he only borrowed it. Please don't mention it to him. I shall feel terrible.'

She was nothing but a trouble-maker, he thought. He told her about the picture falling off the wall and said that he would take it into town to have the frame mended and the glass replaced as soon as he had the time. She begged him to let her see to it. And pay for it. After all, it had been her fault, pushing him like that. But first she would type his letters ready for the post.

Keith turned up early for once, though he spent over an

hour in the kitchen making himself rounds of toast. Louise was in the garden, building a rockery. He rapped on the window and waved at her, but she turned away instantly, as if she was sick of the sight of him.

When he had eaten he filled a bucket with warm water and went round to the front of the house to clean the windows. Graham was rummaging in the drawers of his desk, a frown on his face. There was a neat pile of addressed envelopes on the windowsill. Presently he snatched them up and left the room.

He couldn't understand what had happened to the snuff box. He needed some stamps. Surely he had seen it on the mantelpiece only yesterday. He, too, banged his fist on the window to attract Louise's attention, but she immediately moved further down the garden, her back resolutely turned on him. He remembered that he had left his raincoat in the vestry. Perhaps he had absentmindedly slipped the snuff box into one of the pockets. He left the house by the front door, ignoring Keith, and crossed the road to the church.

Pamela was unlocking the boot of the car when Keith came up the path carrying his bucket. He stood in the entrance of the garage and looked down at the picture propped against the wall.

'Were you going to clean the car?' asked Pamela. She tried not to sound nervous.

'How did this happen?' he asked, squatting down and examining the photograph.

'It fell,' she said. 'Graham knocked it down. I'm taking it to be reframed.'

'You get in,' he said. 'I'll put it in the boot.'

Pamela got into the front seat and felt the car rock slightly as the boot slammed shut. In the mirror she saw Keith going down the path and into the house. She reversed expertly out of the garage and felt a bump as she backed on to the path by the bins. He must have left his bucket in the way, she thought, and then beyond the bonnet of the car saw the picture lying face down in a slick of oil.

The photograph was damaged beyond repair. The face of the man had been shredded by the broken glass.

Louise heard Pamela's cry of rage, of hatred. 'Damn you,' she was screaming. 'Damn you.' Sometime soon, thought Louise, I shall have to ask her to leave. She watched as Pamela ran into the house like a madwoman. Perplexed, she looked at the car parked outside on the path.

When she went into the garage she thought at first it was a rag lying there on the oil-stained concrete, and then she noticed the shards of glass. She turned the buckled piece of card over with her foot and stared down at the photograph. The face of her father had gone. All that remained was the handle of the cricket bat clenched in a blackened fist.

The snuff box wasn't in the raincoat pocket. Graham tried thinking back to the last time he had seen it, the last time he had needed stamps, but he couldn't remember. He went out into the empty church and stared hopelessly at the cross above the altar, at the flowers withering in the vases. He thought of Louise and then of Pamela. Thank God he had resisted the temptation to do more than kiss her. But then, the sad truth was that he hadn't been tempted. Even that small fall from grace had been denied him.

Suddenly he heard a noise coming somewhere from the left of the church, a soft footfall. He knew who it was. He ran across the aisle as if he was running for the crease, his face contorted, and hurled himself into the vestry. Keith was halfway to the door. Graham jumped on him from behind, seizing a clump of his black hair in his fist, forcing him to his knees. He was calling the boy names, dreadful names. He was tugging his head back on his neck as if he would tear it from his shoulders. 'You rotten lump of shit,' he was slobbering. 'Give me back my snuff box. Give it to me.' Gathering saliva in his mouth and gobbling like a turkey, he spat full into Keith's upturned, terrified face.

Louise was standing facing the house when Graham came stumbling up the garden towards her. She stood quite still, her eyes blank. 'Louise, help me,' he pleaded. He was holding out his hands to her as if he was drowning.

226

She stepped back from him in disgust. 'Get out of my sight,' she said. 'I shall never speak to you again,' and she, too, held up her hands, fending him off, her fingers smeared with oil.

She kept her word. The house was as silent as the grave. After almost a week Pamela could stand it no longer. There was something wrong, she felt, something beyond the matter of the picture. It had something to do with Keith. She had seen him that morning, lounging against the fence as Graham went down the path. Graham had spoken to him, though she couldn't hear what he said. And Keith had laughed. And then Graham had come back into the house and he was crying. He had gone into the front room and locked the door behind him. It was Keith that was poisoning their world. She would write to him and tell him what he must do.

She sat down at the table in the living room and began to write. She felt inspired.

Dear Keith (she wrote),
I cannot stand by and see a family destroyed. You must know that it would be better if you stopped coming here. Graham believes that he is doing you more harm than good, and it is dreadful for him.

You must tell Louise that it was you who put the photograph for me to drive over. In some way, she holds Graham responsible.

Try to be brave. You must tell Louise the truth. We can't go on like this. You must tell her you're leaving. If you don't tell her, I will. Believe me, it's for the best.

Pamela

When she had read it over to herself she thought it wasn't long enough. A little too abrupt. She began it again and covered both sides of the notepaper, and had to use another piece for the last part, which she left unchanged.

When it was finished she put it in her handbag and tidied up the table. She found the silver snuff box under a pile of bills and replaced it on the mantelpiece. The telephone rang in the hall.

Keith had been outside the French windows, watching

227

her. When she left the room he entered and listened for a moment to the murmur of her voice. He opened her handbag and taking out the folded letter thrust it into his pocket. He heard the click as Pamela replaced the receiver and slipped out again into the garden.

Pamela knocked on Graham's door. There was no reply. 'That was Mrs Crombie,' she said. 'She says you promised to run her and Mrs Haley to the OAP's Bingo night.'

He unlocked the door and stared at her. 'That was Mrs Crombie,' she said again. 'I heard you the first time,' he said. 'I don't have to leave for another half hour.'

'You rest,' she said. 'Things will be all right now. I'll call you when it's time to go.'

She sat on the stairs, gazing at the locked door, rocking backwards and forwards.

Keith took the letter to show Louise. He told her it was important. She said she wasn't interested, either in a letter or in him. She was tying the rambler rose to the fence with a length of wire. The cricket bat lay on the grass at her feet.

He walked away from her to the other side of the garden, the letter still in his hand, and crouched down behind the privet hedge.

Sitting on the stairs, guarding Graham's sleep, Pamela indulged in fantasies. She would tell Louise that it was she who had destroyed the picture. Graham would overhear and be moved by her selflessness. You dear one, he would say, or something like that. And then she'd tell him that she was going away, so that he and Louise could grow close again. He would beg her to change her mind, or better still, offer to come with her. And of course she'd say he couldn't.

She felt sad but also relieved. I will go away, she thought. I don't really want him to leave Louise. It would be nice if before she went she could patch things up between them. Perhaps she should talk to Louise now, tell her about the letter she had written to Keith. Louise would be pleased with her, and then when she went to wake up Graham she could tell him that everything was truly all right.

'Louise,' she called excitedly, as she opened the back door into the garden.

Louise was trying to hammer the rose stake deeper into the ground. The bat was heavy and she didn't seem able to hit the wood squarely. There came to her a memory of a holiday in Hastings just after the war when her father and she had played cricket together on the sands. It was a child's bat she held, and her father was shouting at her to swing it from the shoulder. She shut her eyes because she was frightened of the ball. 'Loosen up, Louise', he told her. She could hear his voice quite clearly now, and she turned as he called her name again and swung the bat with all her strength.

When she opened her eyes, Pamela was lying face downwards on the grass. One of her shoes had come off.

'Drop it,' said Keith. She stared at him blankly. 'Drop the bloody bat,' he repeated. She let go of it. 'Take off your gloves,' he ordered, and when she made no move he tugged them from her hands. 'Walk away,' he said. 'Walk away. Don't look round.' He had to take her by the shoulders and set her off down the garden like a clockwork toy. 'Stay there till I tell you,' he called. 'Don't look back.'

First he took the bat and the shoe to the garage, and then he returned and gripped Pamela under the armpits, dragging her across the grass. He had to leave her beside the car while he went into the house to fetch the keys from Graham's raincoat in the hall. He opened the door of the car, bundled the body on to the back seat and laid the shoe beside it. He ran into the house again and took the raincoat to cover her over. He shut the car door, and carefully balanced the cricket bat against it. The letter, he thought, the last page of the letter, and taking it from his pocket he unlocked the car again and thrust the single sheet of paper into the glove compartment beneath the dashboard. Then he slipped into the house for the last time and left the keys on the windowsill in the hall.

Graham woke five minutes before he was due to pick up Mrs Haley. He had another headache. He picked up the

229

cricket bat by its handle and placed it carefully outside the garage, propped against the fence. As he reversed the car down the path he saw in the glare of the headlights two figures standing in the dark garden, facing away from the house.

'It will be all right,' Keith told her. 'It wasn't your fault. I expect she said something to annoy you.'

'I'm frightened,' said Louise.

'That old bloke in the shop,' he said, 'the one I bashed . . . when I asked him for fags he said hadn't I heard the word please. He looked at me as if I was dirt.'

'I'm frightened,' she repeated.

'It wears off,' Keith said. 'It isn't our fault. We was driven.'

As he was approaching the corner, Graham passed Mr Mahmood and his family. He waved at them and drove on.

Mr Mahmood was wheeling his bike. From the handle-bars hung various carrier bags and a frying pan. Behind him, in single file, walked his wife and four children, each carrying a suitcase.

Beryl Bainbridge

PARTNERS

The black stockings had been Eric's idea. In the early days of what Marcia called their 'relationship', when she was still living in the bed-sitter just off the Broadway, Eric had shyly and tentatively suggested one evening that she ought to think about wearing something a bit sexy. Not vulgar, he'd added hastily; not like a woman in a cabaret.

Marcia's sister, who had been a nurse before she married a Norfolk pig farmer, had said it just went to show that all men were retarded. Nurses, Lorna had observed, wore black stockings and Eric had probably been comforted by one when he was a little boy and become fixated.

Marcia had been impressed. She was three years younger than Lorna.

Sixteen years later Marcia was still wearing black stockings. There were times when they made her feel degraded. Many of the suburban bakers who dropped into the office were leery and dirty-minded, and couldn't resist letting on with a smirk that they knew all about Eric's affair with the secretary-cum-book-keeper who wore the black stockings. On these occasions, Marcia would seriously think about exchanging them for the pale tights of her youth. She thought about exchanging them too each time Eric told her the affair had to end because it wasn't fair on Helen. But that would just be to spite him; and she never went through with it because he might take it as a sign that she'd accepted the inevitable. He would be relieved and Marcia didn't see why he should be let off so lightly.

Did she really love him? She often pondered the question when she glanced up from her typewriter or calculator and stared at Eric's back through the dusty glass partition that separated their working areas. He'd always sat with his back to her. Perhaps it was because he didn't want her to see his acute misery and despair. With his back to her he could pretend to be dealing with invoices while fantasising about what life could have been if he'd resisted his father's pressure to go into the family business.

He'd always hated it. On the odd occasion when he and Marcia had managed to slip away to a hotel for a weekend, and got in with a crowd at the bar, he had never revealed that he was a yeast merchant. 'Company director,' he'd snap in a tone which implied that the questioner had seriously breached etiquette and good manners.

No, she didn't love him. Not today anyway. Not in fact for the last nine months. Not since he'd launched into yet another of his 'this-has-got-to-end' speeches.

Marcia stabbed the calculator. Orders were up from Daphne's Crunchy Loaf; Mrs Pamela Parkin's Perfect Cakes were down by nearly two hundred pounds which was serious but understandable. The cakes were like granite. Mrs Parkin was really the bankrupt Frederick Parkin trading under his nephew's wife's name.

She looked through the glass again. What was he doing? What was he thinking? Well, she'd know soon enough. She had been accurately interpreting his moods from the doodles on his blotter since she was twenty-two and first come to work at Ashtons.

She had come as a temp for two weeks because Mrs Bartlett, who'd been with the firm when Eric's father was alive, was in hospital for a minor op. They'd opened her up, found it was everywhere, sewed her up again and sent her home. On the night she died Eric had asked Marcia to stay on, and then seduced her.

Lorna had told her to leave at once. It was unhealthy. She would waste her life because Eric would never leave his wife. Men always said they would, but once they'd got you into bed they had second thoughts and started talking about loyalty and how much they respected their wives. Marcia had wondered how she knew so much, living isolated in Norfolk with only her dull Colin and three hundred pigs to talk to. But then, she had been a nurse.

Marcia was looking at the back of Eric's head. No, she definitely didn't love him today; though she would have to admit if pressed that he still had a fine head of hair. Perhaps that was all she had ever really liked about him. She'd once seen a French film about a man falling in love with a girl's knee. She hadn't really understood it, but one of the bakers' sons who was going to university had said the director was a major figure, and who was Marcia to argue with that?

The alarm buzzer on Eric's digital watch sounded. Marcia stood up. Eric silenced the alarm, took a pill from a silver snuff box and swallowed it with water from a carafe on his desk; by which time Marcia was standing at his side, waiting to show him the monthly figures.

She could now see what he had been doing for the last half hour because photos of Dan and Cheryl's wedding were spread over the desk. Dan was Eric's brother, the small firm's only traveller. With his assumed suburban accent, cheap jokes and fondness for alcohol he did a good job. Why he had suddenly got married at the age of forty was a mystery. And why to the little tart? That was how Marcia always thought of Cheryl.

The wedding had been absurd. Dan, with his drinker's paunch, his ill-fitting hired tails and a tuft of hair standing up like Tin-Tin, had been surrounded by baker cronies, boasting that he hadn't got to bed until five. Cheryl, in a wedding dress from Oxford Street, had invited a lot of shrieking girls. It should have been fun but it had seemed forced, lacking spontaneity. Eric hadn't helped, bossing people around and organising horribly posed photos, barking at everyone to make their way to their cars, and dishing out maps showing the location of the house, which everybody knew anyway because they were all Ealing locals. Helen had done most of the food and kept telling people how tired she was. Eric had sidled up to Marcia at the reception, having waited until the baker's son who had made it to the university went to get another two glasses of sparkling wine.

233

'Well,' he said. 'That's Dan snared. And not before time.'

Marcia was feeling particularly spiteful. 'She must have something. But what? Cunning?'

At the church, before stepping into the hired white Rolls, Cheryl had done something unforgivable. She'd aimed her bouquet straight at Marcia. It had caused much suppressed mirth. Half the guests knew about her and Eric, and the younger ones undoubtedly thought she had one foot in the grave.

Marcia was still smarting from the humiliation three weeks later. She placed the list of figures on Eric's desk. He had been looking at a wedding photo of Cheryl which, even Marcia had to concede, made her look quite pretty.

'They'll be in Lago di Garda today,' said Eric enviously. 'The fourteenth?'

'I don't remember being shown an itinerary.'

She tried to direct his attention to the monthly figures. After all, it had taken her two days to prepare them.

'Are you interested in these? You were in profit last month.'

'. . . about ten miles from Verona. And then on to Pisa. Some people, eh?'

He took a pen and slid it down the column of figures. After twenty-five years it was an easy, routine exercise but Marcia had worked hard on the figures and he always rewarded her with his full attention.

'Yes, these are better. Excellent, Marcia. Well done.'

It was all so shallow, reflected Marcia. When they were making love he didn't feel the need to be falsely polite. Well done?

'Is Albert back from the Watford round?'

'I think we'd have heard the van scraping the yard wall.'

Eric was worried about Watford. Two bakers who had accounts with Ashtons Yeast had muttered dark threats about moving to the International Yeast Company, one of two or three major combines poised to mop up what remained of the tiny opposition of small family run wholesalers.

Eric was brooding on this when he heard Albert's van pulling up in the yard.

It was nearly lunchtime. Helen stood in the dark, tiled Edwardian hall looking at the grandfather clock whose hands stood at five minutes to one. In four minutes she would go upstairs and ring down to the yard office on the internal phone to tell Eric and Marcia that lunch was ready. She had a good view of the yard from the master bedroom. She could see the yeast vans coming and going; she could see Eric talking to the roundsmen. She couldn't see into the office or the roundsmen's rest room, but that didn't matter. She had always known about Eric and Marcia; always known that the affair would burn itself out. For years she had longed for the day when Eric would say that he'd decided to leave Rotary. Rotary nights were when he and Marcia 'did it'.

Ten months or so ago when Eric had announced that he had resigned, Helen had said, 'Oh dear, what a shame, because Rotary do so much for charity.' She had pretended to accept his explanation that they weren't, in his opinion, doing enough, which was why he'd been forced to resign. It was a matter of principle, Eric had said. Helen had agreed that principle was everything and let the matter drop.

The Edwardian family house was separated from the yard by a little strip of garden where Helen grew her herbs. The brothers' parents had lived in the house and when they died – mother following father within a few months – Eric and Helen had moved in. Helen hadn't bothered to change things very much; and Eric hadn't complained. At first it had surprised her. Then she realised that he simply didn't care.

Looking down on the yard from the bedroom window Helen could see Eric with Albert, the roundsman. It looked as if they were arguing.

'They've elbowed us, Mr Eric.'

Albert was cantankerous and these days spoke to his boss with the confidence of someone who had only three months to go before retirement on a decent pension.

'Both shops?'

'You can't blame 'em. They can get the stuff cheaper – 90p a box, and if you want my opinion –'

Eric retorted quickly that he didn't. But he felt obliged to justify Ashtons' record.

'Who else gives such a flexible service? Immediate delivery, no delivery too small.'

'Get out,' said Albert. 'Get out while you've got the chance. I was here with your dad in the 'thirties. Had to stay. Nothing else. You've got capital, assets. Go and do something you want to do.'

He turned into the roundsmen's rest room and closed the door behind him.

Eric was astounded. His watch alarm sounded again. As he jammed his finger against it he sensed Marcia watching him from the office doorway. She walked towards him.

'What was all that about?'

Eric was looking puzzled.

'It shouldn't have gone off then,' he said. 'The alarm wasn't set.' He was still thinking about Albert's outburst.

The lunches were a tradition continued by Helen in honour, she said, of the boys' mother and father. In their day, life had been more leisurely. There wasn't the same competition or fight for survival, so it hadn't mattered if the office telephone was unmanned for over an hour in the middle of the day.

Marcia had often told Eric that three courses at lunch every day could kill a man of his age. She suspected there was a more sinister reason for Helen's insistence on maintaining the tradition. Sitting there like a matriarch with the hostess trolley beside her, for one hour of each working day she had complete control.

'The peas are delicious, Mrs Ashton,' said Marcia. 'Is the mint from the garden?'

'From the herb garden. Yes.'

'And the potatoes,' muttered Eric for want of anything better to say.

'The potatoes are from Cyprus.'

'Ah. Seems an awfully long way to send a humble spud.'

'Eric has never understood the garden. He hasn't the faintest idea of the thought that goes into running a home, have you Eric? Everything happens as if by magic. Until he hasn't got a freshly ironed shirt in the morning and then! Oh dear me!'

Marcia wanted to scream. It was always the same. The chance of finding a new topic of conversation each day with a woman who only cooked, cleaned and gardened was slim. She had once asked Eric what he and Helen did in the evenings but he had told her not to interfere.

'How was your morning, Marcia? Both of you?'

'We lost two shops. To IYC,' replied Eric gloomily.

'The International Yeast Company,' added Marcia. Helpfully, she thought.

'Thank you, Marcia, but I do know what the initials stand for. Eric's father always said they would try to swallow us one day. Of course that was long before you joined us.'

It was a nasty little put-down, a reminder that Marcia was not family, merely a hired hand.

'When Dan comes back . . . Dan the road man, with his smile and his jokes, will ride into Watford, with Cheryl perhaps, and Watford will be charmed. Watford will soon come to heel.'

Marcia banged down her fork.

'Is something wrong, Marcia?'

'You make it sound like a Western.'

Helen accepted the challenge.

'You will have some more, Marcia. You'll have some more, *both* of you.'

From the landing window, Helen watched Marcia and Eric return to work. Instead of going into the office Marcia disappeared into the street, and Helen was curious.

Eric stopped to supervise Albert loading a van with boxes of sour-smelling yeast.

Washing-up next, thought Helen. She went back down to the dining room and trundled her hostess trolley into the kitchen.

In the yard Albert was contrite. 'I was out of order this morning, Mr Eric. Sorry.'

'You're late, Albert. I'd quite like to hang on to Ruislip if you don't mind.'

When the van had driven away the suburb was quiet; it was early closing day. Eric looked at the surrounding houses, the sightless windows. He looked at his own house and felt unhappy. The sound of footsteps on the pavement preceded Marcia's return. She stood by the yard gate smiling sardonically.

'I had a good idea at lunch. Why not start smoking again?' She held up a packet of Silk Cut. 'What a wheeze, eh?'

Self-pity overwhelmed Eric. He glanced up at the house, then across at Marcia.

'Come here.'

She hesitated before moving to him. There was something in the tone of his voice that she recognised.

'Come with me.'

'Where?'

'Come.'

He took her elbow and propelled her to a door which looked as if it might lead to an outside lavatory.

It was the roundsmen's rest room where Albert and John and young Fred ate their sandwiches and read the *Sun*; a dank, nicotine-soured place furnished with a springless sofa and a couple of London Transport seats salvaged from a local tip.

Eric pressed his mouth hard against Marcia's. He knew how she dressed and she knew where he started, and her body yielded.

'But why, Eric?,' she couldn't help murmuring. 'Why start it up again?'

Half an hour later Eric was fighting post-coital guilt.

'Why?'

'I needed to.'

'Therapy?'

'Sorry. Wanted to.'

'Thank you kindly sir she said. Without wishing to appear

ungrateful I rather resent being told every eight months or so that "this has got to end" and then being practically raped on Albert's sofa.' She looked at him, and softened. 'Is it really on again?'

He nodded, but he still didn't look very happy.

'This thing between us – whatever it is – is to continue. You will start coming round to my flat again?'

'Yes.'

Marcia lit the first of her cigarettes. Knowing that it annoyed him, she blew a cloud of smoke at him.

'It causes so much unhappiness.'

'To you? If you'd rather we didn't . . .'

She had anticipated this and she chipped in quickly, 'I'm not exactly overwhelmed by offers at the moment.'

She might have been, she reflected ruefully, if she had taken Lorna's advice and got out all those years ago.

'Will you come round this evening? You can use the old excuse. Rotary night.'

'I'll try.'

Marcia was about to suggest that he set his watch alarm just in case he forgot, but she had second thoughts. You could push your luck too far.

The next morning in the master bedroom, Eric stood in front of the cheval mirror putting on a crisp, freshly ironed shirt. Deciding that it was not up to standard he discarded it and reached for another in the wardrobe.

'Why are you going to Rotary again?'

Helen stood in the doorway, holding a plastic laundry basket neat with pairs of Eric's socks and piles of his underpants.

Eric was careful not to look at her. 'It's a duty,' he said in as casual a tone as he could manage.

'I thought you'd had a disagreement with them.'

'Which is why I pulled out for a few months. To teach them a lesson. Must go . . . Appointment with the bank manager.'

When he had gone, Helen picked up the discarded shirt which she had ironed so carefully the day before, and with a strength which amazed her when she thought about it later, she ripped the cotton from tail to collar.

Then she walked downstairs, passing the stained-glass window and the portrait of Methodist grandfather Ashton, crossed the hall and went into the kitchen. She had laid out the crazed vegetable dishes after breakfast; an oxtail had almost defrosted and oozed blood. Next to it lay a black-handled kitchen cleaver.

Helen picked up the cleaver and brushed her thumb against the blade. Yes. She took it through into the dining room.

When Eric came into the office from the bank, Marcia watched him through the glass partition and wondered how long it would be before he looked at her. Eventually she received a brief smile. She returned it, and then beckoned.

'It was good last night?'

'Yes.'

He hated talking about it. It was something you did. Putting it into words, discussing what the other person liked was distasteful. He had read somewhere that women were more basic than men. Years ago a roundsman had told him that he'd heard a girlfriend and three of her friends discussing men and sex over coffee and biscuits. The roundsman had said that their jokes about bodily functions and anatomy were worse than anything he'd ever heard in the public bar of the Rose and Crown.

'How's Helen this morning?'

'Fine . . . fine.'

'Not even a teeny bit suspicious? You didn't hear her on the phone to one of your mates' wives discreetly checking on whether Rotary met last night?'

The thought had often occurred to him. It was worrying but so far he had got away with it.

Marcia was determined to wind him up. 'Has the wife of dear old Freddie or Charlie or Johno gorn an' blown it?'

'Helen wouldn't do that.'

'I would. Perhaps she's too thick.'

She should have known better. Criticism of Helen was

definitely out of order. The relationship had slipped smoothly back into its old rut. They both recognised the fact and brooded on it a while.

'She'd rather not know,' said Marcia, and started attacking the calculator. Eric watched her. He felt miserable and, as always, guilty.

'You're bright, Marcia. Why on earth did you stay here all these years?'

'Because of you, darling.'

It was malicious, but there was also some truth in it. It had the desired effect of increasing Eric's guilt. Why shouldn't he suffer too?

Eric stared around the office. The gas fire with the broken filament spluttered. They had been talking about redecorating for years but had never got round to it. Eric's father had always said that the secret of making money was simple: keep the overheads down. The reason Jew Boys were always going bust was because they showed off with fancy carpets and Venetian blinds. Father had been embarrassingly anti-Semitic.

'I wonder . . .' began Eric.

Marcia was hopeful. Was it possible that he was about to suggest something new and exciting? Were they about to cut loose and run away together?

'Would I have chosen to be a yeast merchant and bakers sundriesman if my father hadn't been one before me?'

'Oh, don't start feeling sorry for yourself. That's too pathetic for words.'

Secretly, though, she agreed that it was a boring life for him. The yeast came in from one of the combines. Ashtons put their own label on it and sent it out again. In, out, in, out. But Marcia liked to think that in most respects she was a realist – what else could Eric do?

'I wanted to do fine arts.'

'I know, I know. And you're being boring.'

It was an old whinge of Eric's. Totally unrealistic. The telephone rang. It was one o'clock, but it wasn't Helen on the internal to announce that lunch was ready; it was Dan phoning from somewhere in northern Italy to tell Eric that

241

he and Cheryl were coming home from their honeymoon two weeks earlier than planned.

Eric and Marcia were late for lunch. Helen was forced to put it back in the oven to keep warm. When at last she was able to wheel in the hostess trolley she looked at Marcia and was sure the ugly bitch's lipstick was smudged. Helen knew why. 'Ugly bitch!' Wouldn't that surprise them all! 'Such a charming woman. Such a refined lady. Do give my kind regards to your lady wife.' Helen had overheard such comments from the hall as Eric ushered his business friends from study to the front door.

The trolley scraped against the sideboard causing the lid from a vegetable dish to slide to the floor. Eric turned from examining and straightening his little collection of water-colours. He picked up the lid and as Helen took it from him he was sure her hand trembled.

She took her place at the head of the table. For once Eric had an easy topic of conversation.

'Dan and Cheryl will be home tomorrow.'

Helen frowned. 'Two weeks early? Why?'

'He didn't say. Probably bored. You know Dan. You didn't tell us what was on the menu today.'

'No. Because it's not very exciting.'

Eric shrugged. 'Well. It's only lunch.' It was a tactless thing to have said he realised, as Helen almost spat her words at him, 'Lunch is what I do. Lunch is what I'm good at.'

Marcia eyed her warily. Had the old cow smelt a rat? Christ! That would kybosh everything. She didn't fancy traipsing the streets looking for a new job at her age.

'Eric is going to Rotary again, Marcia.' It was said innocently enough. She appeared to have calmed down. Even so the colour drained from Eric's face.

'How is the local business community?' Helen continued.

'Ah . . . much the same. New in-take. Some younger blood. Always interesting to hear what young people are coming up with.'

Even though she was worried, Marcia still found time to

242

reflect that Eric could be horribly pompous.

'Dan and Cheryl . . .' continued Eric, but Helen was not to be diverted.

'Are the younger Rotarians more charitable than the older lot? Rotary does a lot of work for charity, Marcia dear. It used to be such fun in the old days when Eric took me to Ladies' Night.'

Marcia did not take kindly to being patronised by Helen.

'Next time we have a ladies' do you and I will be there, Helen,' promised Eric. 'We'll make a night of it.'

Neither did Marcia like being excluded by Eric. 'We'll trip the light fantastic, what?' Now he was over-doing it.

And Marcia decided enough was enough. 'Rotary meet more often now, don't they Eric? Isn't it *three* evenings a week now?'

Eric was furious.

'Once. It was always once. It will always be once!'

A brussel sprout rolled off Helen's serving spoon into her glass of water where it floated. Like a little green turd, thought Marcia. Nobody attempted to remove it.

'Do you think Dan and Cheryl will have children?' asked Helen. 'They should have children. It would be so nice if this house echoed with young footsteps like when Eric and Dan were young.'

Had she finally fallen off her trolley? Marcia wondered.

'I'm glad you're going out in the evenings. You need to get out to the Rotary and squash . . . and whatever you do. *Both* of you.'

Eric didn't dare to look at Marcia. Then it came.

'You bitch. Bastard. Fucking swine! Filth!'

Eric had never heard the voice before. It was as shocking as the words.

'You think I don't know? Haven't always known? The filth . . . pornography . . . the writhing and screwing each other on the floor . . .'

She was standing now. Her hand groped blindly at the cushion on her chair.

'I can smell her on you!'

Her body slackened. The corner of her mouth drooped.

The arm that had been stretching to the cushion hung limply. Helen was looking at it with a clouded, befuddled expression.

'Can't . . . can't move it.'

She fell backwards. Eric scrambled over to her and held her head up clumsily.

'The cushion, on her chair. Quick!'

Marcia's eyes widened when she saw, concealed beneath the cushion, a black-handled kitchen cleaver.

Marcia stood smoking under a 'No Smoking' sign in the long hospital corridor. Eric was frowning as he walked towards her, and she wondered if it was because the news about Helen was grave, or because she was smoking and he would be guilty by association when the smoke detection alarm sounded and security men started to arrive.

'Well?'

'A stroke. Put that out please.'

Marcia ground out the cigarette with the heel of her foot.

'Is she conscious?'

'She just stares at me, but no movement, no words.'

'Did the doctor say . . . what caused it?'

Eric shook his head. He wore his guilty look, and Marcia knew more or less what was coming.

'All those things she came out with before . . . Now she's just lying there, her eyes on mine, accusingly.'

'Eric, it is not your fault. Just because . . .'

She had to stop because a gentle-looking hospital porter was wheeling an old man down the corridor. The pensioner's flies were undone; he hadn't shaved for two or three days and saliva ran down his chin. The porter was telling him how much the hospital food had improved since the new chef had taken over. The old man plainly wasn't interested in food, but felt obliged to respond. Bubbles of spit were all that he could manage. For some reason Marcia felt a sense of shame. She envied the young porter his important job, but knew she could never do it.

Eric was pursuing his own guilty thoughts.

'If I'd known that she knew that you and I . . .'

'Oh thanks a lot.'

Marcia stormed down the corridor. Outside by the ambulance bay she lit another cigarette. An ambulance sped away into the night, blue light flashing. The siren would begin to scream as soon as it reached the High Street. Marcia wondered what sad little event awaited its arrival.

She sensed Eric at her side.

'Come on,' he was saying, 'I'll buy you a drink.'

Two days later Dan, Cheryl and Eric were seated at the dining table.

'I can't believe it – I just can-not believe it,' said Dan, shaking his head.

He was wide and expansive. Often one couldn't be sure that he wasn't merely talking for effect. He turned to his trim little wife, who was busy thinking that the room was cold and drab.

'Can you believe it?'

'No,' said Cheryl. 'I can't believe it.'

It was said without much thought or interest. She wasn't particularly intelligent, thought Eric. But she was a pretty little thing, and he suspected that what she lacked in intelligence was amply made up in sharpness and cunning.

'She looked so healthy,' Dan was saying. 'All that work for the wedding. The little pasties . . . the jellies . . .'

No one had been taking much notice until jellies were mentioned.

'We never had jelly!' Cheryl wasn't going to let her special day be reduced to the absurd status of a kid's party. Dan ignored her.

'You don't think she overdid it? We could easily have got caterers in. It was Helen who insisted on –'

'It was a stroke,' said Eric firmly. 'It can happen to anyone, at any age.'

He thought he said it with a certain authority, then realised that he had unconsciously imitated Helen's specialist.

The door opened. Everyone looked up. Marcia was wheeling in the hostess trolley.

245

'Look at this. Terrific! Keeping up the old tradition, eh Marcia?'

Marcia smiled at Dan. 'It's not up to Helen's standard, I'm afraid. Just soup and delicatessen. I'll serve the soup and then you can help yourselves.'

Cheryl's eyes glittered as she watched Marcia standing in Helen's place at the head of the table. What a cheek! For all they knew Helen was on her death bed and there was Marcia, Eric's mistress (it had taken her all of four days to wheedle that out of Dan), taking over. And no doubt hoping for a phone call from the hospital to let them know that Helen had passed on.

'Why did you two come back early?' asked Marcia, ladling out the soup.

'To be honest, Marcia, eight weeks would have been just that little bit too long.'

Now Dan was playing up to her.

'It might have been for some,' snapped Cheryl.

'There's a limit to the number of churches and pictures of the Virgin and Saint this, that and how's-your-father you can take in. When you start thinking if it's Tuesday it must be Tintoretto you begin to get a little bit homesick.'

'Homesick for Ealing Broadway. Terrific, isn't it,' said Cheryl to Eric, who was sitting opposite.

They didn't sound like a pair of newly-weds, thought Marcia. They weren't even pretending, and she was pretty sure she knew what their problem was.

'Not many of us of course – apart from Eric – have Cheryl's appreciation of the fine arts. Did you know she got O level art, Marcia?' Dan sniggered as he said it.

'A level.' Cheryl glowered at him.

Eric thought it was becoming embarrassing. 'How long before you move into the new house?' he asked, hoping to change the subject.

It did nothing to alter Cheryl's mood. Eric noticed that the corner of her mouth drooped slightly. She looked disappointed: in a few years it would be her permanent expression.

'The way the builders are going, about three years I shouldn't wonder,' said Cheryl moodily.

'Then you'll just have to get behind them, won't you?' said Marcia.

Cheryl felt she was being talked down to by some jumped-up book-keeper with ideas above her station.

'Are you sure – what with all your work over at the yard – you can spare the time to do the lunches, Marcie?'

'*Marcia!*' The rebuke was sharper than Marcia had intended. 'I just stop at the delicatessen on my way in, and put it in the fridge. Eric's given me a key.'

A key! The husband stealer had her feet under the table and her own key to the house. Well! Cheryl would soon put a stop to that!

'But I've so much time on my hands. And let's face it . . . I'm family now.' She smiled sweetly at Eric. 'Right, Eric?'

Eric was aware that Marcia was looking extremely tight-lipped and wasn't too upset. During the past few days she had begun to irritate him. She was forever asking him if she could wash his underwear or take things to the cleaners. They could easily have slipped out to the local Italian for lunch. He would have enjoyed it after years of English stodge, but when he had suggested it Marcia had starting wittering on about the importance of tradition, and maintaining standards. It had sounded horribly false on the lips of the woman who for years had ridiculed his way of life.

Eric looked across at Cheryl. The corners of her mouth no longer drooped. Why had he thought that she looked disappointed? She was pert, vivacious. Her eyes were sparkling humorously.

A couple of weeks later, two ambulance men carried Helen's wheelchair over the front doorstep and carefully set it down on the hall tiles. Eric opened the study door. That morning he had made up the divan and adjusted the aerial of the new Boots black-and-white portable television. Helen's specialist had said that it might be some months before she would be able to climb stairs.

'In here, please.'

He fussed and tried to help but only got in their way as the two burly and experienced ambulance men wheeled Helen into the study, plucked her from the chair as if she were no heavier than a feather, laid her gently on the divan, covered her up, and arranged the pillows. Then they said 'night night, darlin' ', and left.

Helen's eyes were open but unblinking. Disconcertingly, she was staring past Eric's shoulder.

'What would you like for you supper?' he asked.

She gave no sign that she had heard him.

'You must eat. Nothing too fatty, the specialist said. But you must have something.'

He glanced through the window at the yard, and wondered if Marcia had bought the cake.

She was standing in the office doorway holding a be-ribboned cakebox. When she had offered to buy a cake for Helen's birthday, she had imagined handing it to Eric on the day with a warm smile before sending him off to the hospital. It was designed to look like a magnanimous gesture which might have stopped Eric snapping at her all the time, and implying that what had happened to Helen was her fault.

Marcia hadn't bargained for Helen being sent home quite so soon.

She stood on tiptoe and could see a light in the study. When she thought she saw some movement she wondered what was happening. It was only Eric crossing to the door.

Dan was lurking in the hall. The brothers conversed in hushed tones. They had never been close, not even when they were teenagers. Eric had acted the goody-goody. Dan still remembered him tut-tutting when Father said that he had driven past a coffee bar in the Broadway and seen Dan sitting under a rubber plant with an unsuitable girl.

But an illness in the family tended to draw people together.

'Well?'

'Nothing. She won't talk. Not a syllable.'

Dan wondered whether it was physical or sheer bloody-mindedness. Perhaps Helen had nothing left to say to Eric any more.

'The doctor said she should be able to talk. She should be able to use her right hand.' He looked bewildered, and Dan felt sorry for him.

'She'll get it back, with the remedials and physio-whatsits.'

Although Eric thought that his brother was probably dissembling, he took heart. 'How was your day?' he asked.

Dan held up a cheque between index and middle finger. 'I've got Watford back. And I've upped 'em. Five per cent.'

'Well done, that man. Where's Cheryl?'

'Upstairs. Writing a filthy letter to the builders. She looks like a little waif but she's tough. Is she tough!'

The thought seemed to worry him. Eric grinned brotherly solidarity.

'You can still pick 'em. And has he picked them over the years! I stopped counting when you were twenty.'

Dan returned the grin. Eric thought he was attempting to look boyish, but he didn't. He was nearly forty and it just looked silly and conceited.

Later, Dan, Cheryl and Eric stood at Helen's bedside. Marcia, not being family – Cheryl had reminded her yet again – waited in the dining room.

She had listened to a dismal rendering of 'Happy Birthday', and was quite glad that she had been excluded from the gathering.

Dan extinguished the candles with one blow, which was what one would have expected, thought Eric, as he sliced the cake on the marble stand.

He put down the knife and Dan placed a slice of cake on a plate on Helen's stomach.

'You'll manage a taste or your Uncle Dan will be very cross.'

He removed the tiny candle and smiled encouragingly. Helen stared, sightlessly, it seemed, over his shoulder. For once Dan was at a loss for words.

'Let's leave the girl to get a bit of shut-eye. Okay?'

When they had left the room Helen's head moved for the first time. She looked at the cake stand.

Although it was raining Marcia declined Eric's offer of a lift home; the bus was so quick, and she was sure the family had plenty to discuss.

'Take some cake.'

It was Dan who suggested it.

'I don't really –'

'You bought the damn thing. Take some cake before you go.'

'Okay Dan. Thanks. Night all.'

Before she closed the door behind her Marcia heard Cheryl's Acton twang, 'Dear Marcie. Such a kind woman.'

Marcia slammed the door with a force which she knew they would not be able to ignore.

The study door was open. Light from the little room spilled into the hall. Marcia tapped gingerly on the door. There was no answer. She tapped again, and entered.

Helen was propped up against the pillows, the cake on its plate still untouched on her stomach.

'Dan insisted I should take a piece of cake, Mrs Ashton.'

There was no response, so Marcia crossed to the cake trolley. As she folded a slice of cake into a napkin she thought she saw Helen's eyes move.

'It looks good,' said Marcia. 'Have you tried some?'

There was a sound of something brushing against crisp linen. Helen's right hand appeared from under the bed-clothes, grasping the cake knife. She slashed out wildly at Marcia scoring her shoulder and upper arm. Blood splashed on to the bed-clothes, a few flecks spattered on Helen's forehead.

Marcia reeled back. She dropped the little wedge of cake, and staggered into the hall, clutching her shoulder and screaming.

Eric was the first into the hall. Followed quickly by Dan and then Cheryl.

Marcia's arm was pumping blood on to the tiles and the Edwardian panelling. Cheryl sat on the stair and screamed.

Dan hurried into the study. Eric picked ineffectually at the shoulder of Marcia's blouse.

In the study Helen lay very still. Her hand still grasped the blood-stained cake knife.

When Dan returned to the hall there was a puddle of blood on the tiles. Cheryl was still sitting on the stairs, head in lap and whimpering. Eric was trying to staunch the flow from the wound in Marcia's shoulder and arm.

'Sorry, Eric,' said Dan. 'Sorry, everyone.'

Three pairs of eyes focused on him. He held the cake knife, wrested from Helen's fist.

'Helen's dead.'

Eric's watch alarm sounded. It hadn't been set.

Even though a cold drizzle had begun to fall the day before, there was a good turn-out for Helen's funeral. Many of Ashtons' older customers were there, plus a sprinkling of relatives. A dowdy lot, thought Marcia, in the shiny and worn mourning clothes.

Dan, Cheryl and Eric were in the first stall. Marcia knelt behind them with Albert and John and the other drivers.

Although she hadn't wanted to go to the funeral – the six stitches in her shoulder and arm were not due to be taken out for another eight days – Marcia resented being shoved in with the drivers as if she was merely a lowly employee.

A remote vicar, hired for the day (after their father died the brothers had stopped pretending to believe) mouthed platitudes: '. . . beloved wife of . . . prominent member of the business community . . . support of family and friends . . .'

Marcia wondered if anyone was listening. Would anyone miss Helen? Would Eric? It wasn't as if a blazing light had been extinguished. Helen had had few friends and no children. Marcia felt a twinge of . . . no, not sadness. Regret, perhaps. Regret for such an empty life.

For some odd reason the organist was playing 'For Those in Peril on the Seas'. Perhaps Helen had had interests and connections that none of them knew about.

A few weeks later Cheryl stood at the landing window. It had stopped raining at last. But the wind sent scraps of yeast wrappers over the yard where the rain still lay in puddles.

A van drove in from the Watford round. Its new long-haired, sharp-faced driver climbed from the cab.

Albert had retired the week after Helen's death. They had held a little party for him in the drawing room. Cheryl had made cucumber and egg sandwiches, and there was sherry.

Albert had almost ruined the occasion when he said, suddenly, 'I suppose this is when I get me gold watch.'

Eric and Dan had – after a lengthy debate – settled on a cut glass rose bowl, which Albert would be able to share with his wife. Although the brothers had got the bowl inscribed, it was cheaper than a Rolex and Albert hadn't even tried to conceal his disappointment.

Cheryl turned from the window as the hall clock struck one. Marcia and Eric were crossing the yard to the house for lunch.

Dan joined them later. He was in one of his boring moods, thought Marcia. The three of them sat at the dining table, with Dan droning on.

'It's all health today. We've got a health industry. High fibre. It's the brown bread brigade who'll be the salvation of us little suppliers.'

Cheryl wheeled in the hostess trolley.

'And how's that for a sweet little supplier?'

Cheryl grinned and then announced that there was strawberry tart, Black Forest gâteau, cheese or fruit.

'Bloody hell,' said Dan. 'Helen's three courses were bad enough for the waistline.'

'If you don't like it go back to work.'

'I didn't come over till twenty-past one.' He looked at Eric. 'We've got a problem in Cricklewood.'

'Then go and sort it out,' suggested Cheryl. She bestowed a glacial smile on Marcia. 'I'm sure we don't want to lose Cricklewood . . . wherever it is. I'm sure the phone will be ringing. I'm sure someone should be answering it.'

Marcia snatched her handbag from the table and stormed from the room, banging the door behind her.

'Do I hear the sound of plaster dropping from the ceiling?' said Dan.

But after he'd given Cheryl a quick peck on the cheek Dan followed Marcia back to the office.

Eric smiled awkwardly at Cheryl.

'I think perhaps I ought to –'

'Nonsense. You get in much earlier than the others in the morning. And all that book work you do!'

She picked up the cheese knife and gave him a warm, almost motherly smile.

'Don't you want just a little taste of the runny end of the Brie?'

He couldn't resist it. Or was it her? He nodded and Cheryl put the cheese on his plate and pushed the bread basket towards him. She watched him eat for a moment or two.

'Spoilt, aren't you. Did Helen spoil you?'

'I . . . think she probably did.'

'What are we going to do about you. Don't you get lonely?'

'At times.'

'What are you going to do about it? You're still a young man.'

'Well . . . early days.'

Tears welled and trickled down Cheryl's cheeks. Eric wondered if she was crying for him and his loneliness, or for herself. The poor child had had a rotten homecoming, what with the dreadful incident with Marcia and Helen's death.

'Why did Helen do that, Eric?'

Although he had been thinking about it, the question still caught him off guard. He shrugged helplessly. He suspected that Cheryl already knew why and wanted to talk about it. There was still a bloodstain on the hall panelling which he had twice seen Cheryl scrubbing. It was now a dirty pink colour, but she would never shift it entirely. It would be there until he died: a permanent reminder of the mess he had made of his life.

Dan was on the telephone to the Cricklewood baker. Shamelessly he kidded the man along by hinting that deliveries had only been erratic because of family problems, and deliberately made the problems sound trivial, provoking the baker to reply that they were no concern of his, he had a business to run and Ashton's inefficiency was losing him income.

It was then that Dan announced in a hushed and reverential voice that the problem he had referred to was a death. His brother's wife's death. He was smiling at Marcia as he said it.

There was a longish pause, and then Dan was saying that a wreath was a very nice thought, even though it was a rather late one: Helen had been cremated over a month ago. Yes, an obituary had appeared in the trade press but there was really no need to apologise. Yes, he would make the delivery in person.

He was still smiling at Marcia when he hung up.

'Cricklewood bends the knee.'

'Very clever.'

She walked behind the partition and sat at her desk. Dan followed and watched her working the calculator.

'What's the matter,' he asked. Things not going the way you hoped they would when Helen died?'

Marcia's fingers trembled so much that she had to lay her hand on the desk.

She answered Dan with a question. 'Why did you marry her?'

'Cheryl? It will seem strange to you, but Cheryl and I do . . .'

'Don't. It's too embarrassing.' Marcia lit a cigarette, then blew a cloud of smoke at him hoping that it would annoy him as much as it annoyed Eric.

'Why did you come back early from your honeymoon?'

'Glutton for punishment. And I was worried about the business.'

'That all?'

'What else?'

254

'Just that you've had so many girlfriends over the years. One has often wondered why.'

'There's nothing wrong with me in that department.'

She blew another cloud of smoke at him, then smiled. 'How quickly you catch on.'

The pleasure she took in seeing the angry tightening of his jaw was short-lived because she glanced through the office window at the house and immediately began to think about Eric still sitting at the dining table with Cheryl.

'What's going on over there?' she asked moodily.

'Cheryl is making a point of being kind to Eric. He's been through a very bad time.'

'You're a bit like the Kennedy brothers with your hand-me-down women.'

'You silly jealous cow.'

'Without the glamour. A couple of suburban Kennedys. Is Cheryl happy, in that department?'.

Dan smirked and ran his fingers over the back of her hand. 'You should know.'

She lashed out and her nail caught his cheek. He touched it and stared angrily at a spot of blood on his fingertip.

'Mad bitch. You've sat here in your black stockings for sixteen years. You wrecked Helen's health. . . . You've torn Eric in two. Just clear off out of our lives and give us some peace.'

He had meant to wound and he succeeded. Instinctively he backed a couple of paces when Marcia opened her desk drawer and he saw what she was holding: a black-handled kitchen cleaver.

'Nasty little thing, isn't it.'

'It's a kitchen thing,' he said, eyeing her warily.

'A very sharp kitchen thing.'

Marcia explained how she had found the cleaver under the cushion on Helen's chair on the day of her stroke.

'The day she came out with a lot of filth about me and Eric.'

'Which just happened to be true.'

He was still watching the cleaver gripped firmly in Marcia's hand.

'You're missing the point. Helen wanted to kill me. We've all very conveniently written off her cake knife job as stroke-induced dementia. Only it wasn't. She'd been planning to kill me. Over the lunch table. With this.'

She swished the cleaver under Dan's chin, dangerously close. 'And you dare to call *me* a mad bitch!' she said, jabbing the cleaver at him so that he backed again.

'For Christ sake . . . put it away.'

He couldn't take it in. He didn't want to. He just wanted to go. He was about to use the pretext of his urgent delivery to Cricklewood but he didn't need to, because Eric was in the doorway asking him to come and inspect a dent in the new roundsman's van which he was sure hadn't been there that morning.

Marcia put the cleaver back in the drawer. She slipped her blouse from her shoulder and was still examining the livid scar when she saw Eric behind her, reflected in the mirror. She didn't turn; she didn't pull the blouse back to hide the scar. She wanted him to look at it, was pleased when he closed his eyes briefly.

Eventually Eric pulled the blouse back on to her shoulder to conceal the disfigurement for which he felt responsible.

'Decidedly damaged goods,' said Marcia.

'It will fade. You need some sun. A nice long holiday in the sun, eh? You must be owed at least six weeks.'

It sounded like an invitation. For a few seconds Marcia was happier than she'd been for a long time.

'You and me? A holiday in the sun . . . together?'

But that wasn't what he had meant. He was obviously trying to send her away on her own, she thought bitterly, and wondered what changes he'd make while she was away. Would he re-marry? Would there be a bright-eyed 22-year-old usurper sitting at her desk when she returned?

'What's to stop us going together? Apart from a bit of gossip. Small businessmen thrive on it . . . but nobody believes half what they hear.'

'But it would be true. The gossip, I mean . . . in our case.'

It sounded more promising, thought Marcia.

'You mean if we went together we would be picking up the threads –'

'No', Eric said sharply.

'Then there wouldn't be much point, would there.' She turned away. He was a sadist, she decided. Marcia was damned if she would give him the pleasure of seeing how hurt she felt.

'Can't you understand? Any time we spend together now – after those two dreadful events . . .'

But he couldn't leave her stranded, high and dry. Not after all these years. 'We'll just have to give it time.'

'For appearances' sake?'

He nodded.

If it was for appearances' sake, thought Marcia, there was hope.

'Heaven preserve me from the shopkeeping class,' she said. 'Are we going to let them spoil things for us, darling?'

She folded an arm around his neck and kissed his eye, his ear, his mouth. She was in desperate need of warmth, of comfort. She drew away from him, essayed a smile, and said in a tarty voice, 'Sure there's *nothing* I can do for you, sir?'

'Well . . . not here,' said Eric.

He had smiled briefly and Marcia decided it was best left at that for the time being.

Was there any particular reason why Eric was gadding about with Overton? The black Mercedes had dropped Eric off at the yard, and although a fine rain had begun to fall Eric had turned up his jacket collar and stayed chatting to the dark-suited man behind the wheel.

Marcia had heard Eric laugh and thought it sounded sycophantic. Overton was the managing director of the International Yeast Company, and to him Ashtons were very small beer indeed.

Marcia had been walking across the yard to get her bus when the Mercedes swept in. She had backed into the doorway of the roundsmen's room. When she thought about it later, as the eighty-three bus jerked its way up Hangar Lane in the rush-hour, taking her home to her one-bedroom flat in The Ridings, she wasn't sure what had prompted her to spy on Eric. Perhaps it was instinct, or habit after so many years of watching for danger signals.

She often wondered if married women also spent their lives on the look-out for tell-tale signs or was it just the inevitable lot of the mistress?

And what would Eric do now that he was free? Marcia had put in a lot of time. She smiled at the vulgarity of the expression, and went further: a lot of bunk duty.

If there was any justice, she thought, as she got up and rang the request stop bell, Eric would soon be hers. And sod the tradesmen and their gossiping wives.

The next day the family were again at lunch with Cheryl in firm command at the head of the table, dishing up from the hostess trolley.

'Marcia's delicatessen was a very practical idea,' said Cheryl, 'But . . .'

'But?'

'All gong and no dinner, Marcie,' she giggled. 'Seriously . . . additives, Marcia. Poison. E this and E that. Permitted colouring. Ugh. Heart disease, bowel cancer and impotence, I shouldn't wonder. And we don't want that!'

She giggled again and looked at Eric. 'Do we, Eric?'

'I should say!'

'It all comes down to what you were saying the other day, Eric.'

She paused while she spooned lentils on to Dan's plate. 'If things are wrong in our lives we must act decisively. Change them.'

Dan and Marcia were both contemplating the mysterious conversation that had taken place between Eric and Cheryl. What was wrong in Eric's life, wondered Marcia.

But Dan had decided to say nothing to Eric until Marcia left the office to catch her bus to The Ridings.

Then he straddled a chair and stared steadily at his brother.

'What changes?'

Eric opted for a look of innocent enquiry.

'Changes,' insisted Dan. 'You're making some changes round here. What changes!'

Although Eric had only spoken in the most general terms to Cheryl, for some weeks now he had been planning to make a radical change in his life.

He took a small watercolour from his drawer and passed it to Dan, who looked at it and frowned, not knowing how he should react.

'Very nice. Romney Marsh, is it? Something like that?'

'Something like that,' said Eric, removing the painting from Dan's hand. 'I could never make it as a painter.'

'No,' said Dan carefully, 'you're a yeast merchant.'

'Today. Tomorrow . . . or soon after, I shall be an art dealer.'

The moment Eric said it Dan realised that he had known it was coming. 'You'll never do it,' he said. 'You'll never make a go of it.'

'We'll see.'

'You'll need capital, assets.'

'And that is why I'm glad the subject has come up. You had to know, sooner or later.'

He replaced the picture in the desk drawer, and without looking at Dan said casually, 'I'm going to sell the business.'

Pretending not to have noticed that Dan's mouth was open or that Dan was looking very foolish, Eric told him about arranging a meeting with Overton of IYC. Overton was very keen to impress his multi-national bosses. He had made Eric an offer in order to mop up one of the last of the small wholesalers. A handsome offer which Eric could not refuse.

'How much?'

'Three hundred thousand.'

Dan wasn't impressed. It would leave him and Cheryl with a paltry hundred thousand pounds, because Father had left Eric two-thirds of the shares.

'So I get . . . and you . . .' He could barely control his anger. '*And* you get the house!'

Eric looked at him coldly. 'Father knew what he was doing. You were always good at your job. A good road man. But your private life left a lot to be desired. Didn't inspire confidence. Whereas I . . .'

'Married young,' Dan sneered.

'Yes. There was a stability about me.'

For a moment, as Dan leapt from his chair, Eric thought Dan was going to hit him. Instead Dan leant across the desk, his colour rising. At such an unusually close proximity, Eric could see the mass of broken veins in his brother's nose. He must have been knocking it back with customers for years now; definitely a drink problem.

'You hypocrite,' Dan snarled. 'All these years with Marcia . . . and half the women I've had when I'd finished with them . . . but when the old man was alive, what was it then? "Don't let Father know!" And I didn't, did I? I covered up for you. Whatever I've done it's been in the open. Not sneaking up the hill to Marcia. Not borrowing *your* flat for an afternoon quickie.'

Eric recoiled from Dan's anger and from the sour smell of whisky. Dan must have started drinking early in the day, and secretly. There was only ever water at lunch.

'I've sat at this desk for twenty-five years. That's long enough.'

Dan slumped back on to his chair. He was busy with some mental arithmetic.

Cheryl came from the en suite bathroom wearing a T-shirt nightie that revealed the little pubic triangle.

'Market's not exactly flooded with jobs for people of your age.'

She sat next to Dan on the bed. She looked sullen, and Dan thought her reference to his age was unnecessary. He started to wonder why she had married him. Was it simply for the security that was fast disappearing?

'He'll be all right, won't he,' she said, petulantly. 'He's got this house and two-thirds. Oh yes, he'll be fine.'

'Married the wrong one, didn't you.'

'I want to have babies.'

They'd met at the tennis club. Dan wasn't a member, and had kept announcing that he was only there for the beer.

Cheryl was twenty-seven and getting a bit panicky about marriage. Something always seemed to go wrong at the last minute; perhaps she was just unlucky. She had lived in the suburb all her life and although she had heard of Ashtons she had never met either of the brothers. Rumour had it that they were rolling in money. Their father had always lived modestly. Not like Dan who had ordered three bottles of pink champagne and told Cheryl that he didn't believe in doing things by halves.

'He likes you.'

Dan's deep sense of injustice was growing, presaging a sleepless night. 'He's always liked my . . .'

'Women? Thanks.'.

The last thing she wanted this evening was to have his whisky-soaked affairs paraded before her.

'I wonder she didn't try to kill him,' said Dan.

'Helen?'

'Yeah. She knew what a hypocrite he is.'

Dan glanced at Cheryl. She looked like a child who had just been told that the treat was cancelled.

'You're right.' Suddenly she was smiling. 'He likes me a lot.'

She got into bed and drew her knees up to her tummy. She had her back to Dan, but he knew that she was still smiling.

Dan opened the top drawer of Marcia's desk. The kitchen cleaver lay snugly if incongruously among the neatly arranged bottles of Snopake and Baby-Bio and the boxes of paperclips. He slammed shut the drawer when he heard Marcia coming in. Her surprise and suspicion at finding him on her side of the partition was quickly dispelled by a tirade of abuse about Eric's meanness. She thought he was drunk, and was worried when he said that he was going on the road for a few days.

'Should you, in your condition?'

'When someone cheats on you, Marcia . . .' He raised his shoulders and hands: an imitation of Jewish despair.

'Who's cheating on you, Dan?'

He jerked his thumb in the direction of the house.

'Eric is, over there, having a little heart-to-heart with my wife who is beginning to think she married the wrong brother.'

Almost relishing the iniquity of it all, Dan expounded on why Eric and Overton had been meeting. The business was sold to IYC. He'd only found out a couple of days ago, but he was pretty sure that Eric had taken Marcia into his confidence, weeks before bothering to tell his own brother and partner.

He seemed surprised when Marcia said she knew nothing about it.

'Nothing?'

'Nothing.' She had sat down. She looked as if she might be in shock.

'He's an even bigger bastard than I thought,' said Dan.

With some surprisingly deft work on Marcia's calculator, Dan estimated that after sixteen years service Marcia's redundancy money amounted to about seven thousand pounds. He tugged half a bottle of Bells from his jacket pocket and proffered it. She shook her head, so he took a swig himself and put the bottle on the desk.

'We had some good times once, didn't we, you and me? Remember?'

He stood behind her, resting his hands on her shoulders, and massaged gently.

'Dan . . . I'm frightened. He's . . . sacking me. That's what it amounts to.'

'It's worse than that. He's had the best of you and now he's tossing you on the scrap heap.'

Gently he stroked the nape of her neck.

'Don't.'

'You still want him? Forget it, love. He's got another fish to fry.'

'And you're going away? Leaving them . . .'

'He's sacking me too, isn't he? I've got to lean on a few creditors. I'm going to need every penny I can rake in.'

He walked unsteadily to the yard door.

'What about lunch?'

Marcia would do anything to stop him going.

'Lunch? don't you understand anything? It's all over. It's the end of an era.'

He almost fell into the yard. Marcia was worried for him. She could imagine blue lights flashing on a motorway; the cab of an artic on its side; a Rover with its front crushed.

Cheryl served lunch at five past one. There were herrings with yoghurt. Black-eyed beans and lentils. Fruit or low-fat cheese for dessert.

'Where's Dan,' asked Eric, but only because he felt he ought to.

'On the road somewhere. Always on the road some-where, isn't he?'

She didn't seem to mind, thought Eric. He was enjoying being alone with her, even though he was feeling a little guilty because he hadn't asked her where Marcia was.

'While you're tucking in, have a look at this. Something I've found.'

She was holding a small watercolour. She propped it against the carafe and eagerly awaited his opinion.

'It was in the junk shop next to the wholefood shop.'

Just as Eric was about to pass judgement, the telephone rang in the hall.

'Excuse me. Won't be a mo.' She went into the hall and snatched the receiver from the cradle. She knew it would be Marcia wondering when lunch would be ready.

'Lunch is half-eaten,' snapped Cheryl. 'Go down the Broadway and get yourself a sandwich. I'm not your bloody skivvy.'

She slammed down the receiver and returned happily to the dining room where Eric was still examining the watercolour.

'Eric. *Mister* Eric! You haven't eaten a thing.'

She took the painting and told Eric to eat up. They would look at the painting quietly and at leisure that evening because Dan was on the road, and that was no bad thing because Dan could be a bit of a philistine when it came to fine arts.

'Eat up now, please. You must be back at work by three at the very latest.'

Eric decided that he rather enjoyed being bossed about by her. He went back to the office and sat with his back to Marcia. She knew that he was only pretending to work.

He sat at his desk for nearly three hours, occasionally moving a piece of paper from one pile to another, and then back again.

The town hall clock struck five. In the yard John's motorbike started up. Marcia listened to the sound of the engine ebbing away. It was lighting-up time, and it was beginning to rain heavily. Her bus would be steamed up, its young conductor prowling aggressively up and down the aisle clinking the small change in his fist.

Marcia didn't want to go home. She stood up and walked around the partition to Eric's desk. He had heard her coming, and when she arrived at his side he held a pen poised over an invoice which Marcia immediately saw was two weeks out of date.

'Are you coming round tonight?' she asked.

'Not Tuesday, is it?'

'Does it have to be Tuesday now? Does it still have to be Rotary night?' She knew that he hadn't deliberately intended to hurt her; but he couldn't have succeeded better if he'd tried.

'I'll never understand you. Are you just a cold fish? Is it as simple as that?'

Eric's phone rang. Marcia returned to her desk. She listened to the rain as she put on her coat and was thankful that she'd remembered to bring her umbrella.

Eric glanced over his shoulder. Cheryl was on the line and he wanted Marcia to leave quickly. Cheryl sounded very unhappy.

'This house gives me the creeps. I'm all on my own here . . . Dan's away . . . could you get away a bit earlier?'

Marcia saw his right shoulder hunch and suspected it was because he didn't want her to hear who it was on the other end of the line.

'Pop into the off-licence,' said Cheryl. 'Get a couple of

bottles. Not that German rubbish. Something dry and French.'

Eric doodled on his blotter as he listened. He hung up, turned and mouthed, 'See you in the morning', at Marcia, grabbed his coat and left before she had time to respond.

All that was left for her to do before catching her bus was to see what he had written on his blotter. 'Two.bottles . . . Macon?' One too many she thought as the phone on his desk rang again. Before she had time to say, 'Ashtons Yeast', a voice piped, 'And one more thing, darling . . .'

'Yes?' said Marcia crisply.

'Oh sorry, Marcie. Eric must have left already.'

Marcia banged down the receiver.

The grandfather clock struck the half hour as Eric let himself into the house, carrying a plastic off-licence bag.

'Cheryl!' He called. 'Cheryl, I'm home.'

The house felt empty. He went into the dining room, peeled the blue tissue paper from the bottles and placed them on a tarnished silver tray. As he did so, he thought he heard the familiar creak of step fourteen on the stairs. It reminded him of returning home after ten when he was in his teens.

In the yard Marcia, umbrella open and heading for the bus stop, glanced up and stopped when she saw Cheryl pass the landing window. Seconds later a bedroom light came on.

In the hall Eric thought he could hear the sound of someone sobbing. Was it Cheryl? He hurried up the stairs. Cheryl was standing at the cheval mirror in the window bay, dabbing her eyes with a Kleenex.

'What is it? Cheryl . . . what's the matter?'

She turned and seemed surprised but relieved when she saw Eric in the doorway.

'It's this house . . . there's blood in the hall . . . can't get it off . . . can't get rid of it . . .'

He hurried over to her, stretched out his arms. She was so vulnerable he thought, as she collapsed against him, limp as a rag doll. Stroking her hair, he murmured comforting endearments until she gently drew away from him for another Kleenex. After a final little sniff and dab at her eyes she smiled bravely.

'Did you get the wine?'

'A very expensive and superior Macon.'

'All Dan does is chuck down pints. Pints of whisky. Know what you're doing, don't you. Man of the world, Mister Eric.'

She'd perked up quickly, Eric thought. But he was still surprised by what came next.

'Shall I get it? The wine? Shall we have it . . . up here?'

Her eyes had the mischievous sparkle that he'd always found so entrancing.

'Why not?'

When she left the room to fetch the wine Eric took off his jacket and loosened his tie. He was smiling and humming softly. By repositioning some of the furniture, introducing a pot plant here and there and changing the lighting Cheryl had made the room look much prettier. It felt warm too. She was a natural home-maker, he thought, as once again he heard the familiar creak on the hall stair, followed unexpectedly by the sound of a car and the yard gate closing.

He crossed to the window and looked down, but there was no one to be seen. Just the silent yard with its row of transit vans lit by the sickly glare of a sodium lamp Eric had installed to deter burglars. Again he thought he heard the stair creak. That would be Cheryl returning with the wine.

He turned expectantly and was grinning broadly when the door opened. His jaw fell as the cleaver sliced through the air at his head and split his ear. He moaned softly and fell to his knees. When he tried to look up, he could see only hazily because his eyes were filling up with blood. He lifted his hands to shield his head and the cleaver severed his index finger before embedding itself in the crown of his head. When he rolled over on to his side all that could be seen was the tip of the little black handle.

When Dan reached the landing, a bedroom door opened and Cheryl came out. She was pale and her whole body was shaking violently. He took her hand.

'Did it work? For Christ sake – did it work?' He tugged her towards the door of another bedroom.

Marcia was still staring wildly at Eric's body when the door opened. She saw Dan with his arm around Cheryl, and she shook her head. She couldn't think of anything to say, so she shook it again. And then again, and again.

'Why, Marcia? Why?' asked Dan.

A split second later Eric's watch alarm sounded.

Seated at the dining table, Dan was thinking that the house felt warmer these days. Cheryl had worked wonders with the antiquated heating system. It was odd, but she was far more mechanically minded than he was. In fact she was far cleverer than him in all sorts of ways. And, he reflected, as she piled his plate with organically grown vegetables, he was even getting used to the healthier diet.

'How does it feel to be the sole proprietor?' She was sipping water and smiling at him from the opposite end of the table.

'It feels terrific,' said Dan, smiling back, admiringly.

'And the owner of a lovely house?'

'It's just great.'

'We'll have babies, won't we?'

'At least five.'

Cheryl quivered with happiness.

After lunch Dan paused briefly in the yard. He looked around, proudly tossing a bunch of keys in his hand.

When he entered the office the phone was ringing.

'Ashtons Yeast . . . well! Long time no see. Yeah . . . we must, we really must . . .'

He leant back in Eric's old chair and put his feet on the desk.

'Sure . . . married, settled down . . . but there's always the odd Rotary night . . .'

Cheryl was standing at the landing window looking down on the yard. It had started to rain again.

Nicholas Palmer

OTHER JAVELIN TITLES

Reference

1703 3	Protect Yourself *(Also available in hardback)*	Judd Whitelaw	£5.95
1929 X	British Trivia	J Converse	£2.95
1663 0	How to Buy a Used Car	Tom Askem & John Yates	£5.95

Mind, Body and Spirit

1758 0	Graphotypes	Sheila Kurtz	£2.95
1787 4	Self Hypnosis	A B King	£1.95
1719 X	The Other You	Andrew Laurance	£3.95

Puzzles/Games

1612 6	50 Daily Telegraph Brain Twisters	D.St.P. Barnard	£1.95
1782 3	The International Sporting Trivia Quiz Book	James M Riley	£1.95
1736 X	Take the IQ Challenge	Philip J Carter	£1.95

Humour

1916 8	Nudge Nudge Wink Wink	Nigel Rees	£1.95
1877 3	The Royal Bedside Book		£2.95
1751 3	Sling Your Hook	Roy Carr	£1.95
1885 4	Cooking for Sexcess	James Chatto	£1.95
1862 5	The Compleat Cricketer	Jonathan Rice	£2.95
1868 4	Everybody's Doing It!	Max Hodes	£1.95
1709 2	How to be a Commuter and Survive	Nigel Farrell	£1.95
1590 1	How to be a Tourist	Ged Neary	£1.95
1759 9	'I'm Sorry I'll read that again' Scripts	Graham Garden & Bill Oddie	£1.95
1708 4	Mrs T's Bedside Book		£2.50
1698 3	Really Nurse!	Roger Brook	£1.25
1791 2	Warning! This Computer Bytes	Kipper Williams	£1.95
1731 9	World of Donald McGill	Elfreda Buckland	£3.95
1633 9	The Young Fogey Handbook	Suzanne Lowry	£3.95

Sport

| 1559 6 | Mike Patrick's World of Speedway | Mike Patrick | £5.95 |

The Prediction Series +

1682 7	Prediction Practical Magic	Michael Howard	£2.95
1243 0	Prediction Astrology	Peter West & Jo Logan	£3.95
1784 X	Prediction The Tarot	Madelin Montalban	£2.95
1398 4	Prediction Divination	Jo Logan & Lindsay Hodson	£3.95
1707 6	Prediction Taromancy	Gerald Boak	£2.95
1242 2	Prediction Palmistry	Jo Logan	£2.95
1681 9	Prediction Amulets & Talismans	Jo Logan	£2.95

Music

1521 9	The Book of Beatle Lists	Bill Harry	£2.95
1814 5	The DJ's Handbook	Roy Sheppard	£3.95
1498 0	How to get a Hit Record	Ray Hammond	£2.95
1710 6	So you want to be a Rock & Roll Star	Tom McGuinness	£1.95
1715 7	Top Twenty Book *(Also available in hardback)*	Tony Jasper	£3.95

Occult

| 1711 4 | Lovers Guide to Palmistry | Mary E Anderson | £2.95 |
| 1699 1 | This Haunted Isle | Peter Underwood | £3.95 |

Exchange & Mart Books +

1687 8	Exchange & Mart Guide to buying your secondhand boat	Bill Beavis	£1.75
1623 1	Exchange & Mart Guide to buying your secondhand car	Joss Joselyn	£1.50
1625 8	Exchange & Mart Guide to buying your secondhand caravan	Barry Williams	£1.50
1895 1	Exchange & Mart Guide to Moving Home	Val Redding	£1.75

Health +

1675 4	Power of Holistic Aromatherapy	Christine Stead	£2.95
1609 6	Arthritis	John Rowland	£1.95
1573 1	Barbara Cartland's Book of Health	Barbara Cartland	£1.95
1562 6	Biorhythms at your Fingertips	James Roche	£2.95
1586 3	Fit and Superfit	Laurie Plumridge	£1.95
1569 3	Garlic: Nature's Original Remedy	John Blackwood & Stephen Fulder	£1.95
1442 5	Have Healthy Feet	Lyn Chester	£2.95
1574 X	The Herbal Way to Health	James Hewlett-Parsons	£2.95
1593 6	How to Avoid Cancer	Dr Jan De Winter	£1.95
1676 2	Psoriasis	John Rowland	£2.95
1571 5	Vitamins for Your Health	Len Mervyn	£1.95
1431 X	Have Healthy Teeth and Gums	Mervyn Pichel & Neil Curtis	£2.95
1716 5	Healing Power of Acupuncture	M Knightingale	£2.95